A WALTZ THROUGH FLAMES

Jordan Dugdale

DRAGON MOSS PUBLISHING

A WALTZ THROUGH FLAMES

Jordan Dugdale

For those who fight for their place in the world when all it wants to do is push back. ♥
Your story matters. Your voice matters.

Isles of Míra

Lyvira

VILANTHRIS

Kreznov

Volreya

Spine Mountains

Volendam

Amajin

Wolstadt

Fraheim

Nantielle

Rovania

Wilhaven

Halvdarc

Hestia

Kythera

Daesthara

Shoma

Dalasae

Content Warning

The Whispered Tales series has content not suitable for everyone. It progressively gets darker, but the reader's comfort is extremely important to me. The following content warnings are as followed:

Rats (the rakken are a main presence in WT so if you do not like rats, I highly recommend you do not continue with this series)

Cults (body horror, gore, gruesome sacrificial death)

War (battle horror, death, blood, gore)

PTSD

Dysphoria

Mentions of slavery (very brief)

Child abduction/child death, child abuse

Plague/sickness (rot, death, plague, bugs)

CHARACTERS

The Misfits

- Cassius (Cass-e-us)

- Rooster (Roo-ster)

- Helai (Heh-lie)

- Linda (Lin-duh)

- Intoh (Een-toe)

- Rackjack (Rack-jack)

- Itale (Eh-tall-ee)

Side Characters

- Velius (Vel-ee-us) – Eldrasi, blacksmith of the Firebrand

- Felix, Patrina, Hilde, & Dirk – crew/owners of *The Broken Arrow Inn*

- Drithan (Dr-ith-an) – dwarf of the Stoneheart Rangers

- Obrand (Oh-brand) – head dwarf of the Stoneheart Rangers, nephew of King Stoneheart, dwarf king of the Spine Mountains

Minor Characters

- Golbin (Goal-bin) – Myrlír, owner of the alchemy shop *The Secret Ingredient*

- Tidebeard – head mage/professor of the mage college

- Captain Booker – captain of Volendam's guards

The Ghosts

- Helai

- Massoud (Muh-sood)

- Aryan (Are-yen)

- Zamir (Zah-meer)

- Kílae (Kee-lay)

- Masika (Muh-see-kuh)

- Zahra (Zah-ruh)

- Hosni (Hose-knee)

- Ehsan (Eh-son)

WHAT CAME BEFORE...

The Tidings of Misfits recap

At the beginning of their journey, the vampire Cassius finds himself woken from a tomb he's been imprisoned inside of for the last five years. Fleeing back to his estate, he's only given a short time to collect himself before he discovers a magical gun has been placed inside his arm, and with it, a shadowy woman who urges him north, to Volendam where he may collect other pieces of such magical armory.

His journey takes him through the Spine Mountains, where he is eventually captured by Shoma'kah, slavers of the sands. During his imprisonment, he meets Rooster, a human man with no recollection of his past, Helai, a woman from Shoma, and two drikoty, lizardfolk from Lyvira named Intoh and Linda.

Their journey is forever changed when they fall through a crack in the ground and land inside the mountain, where giant, mutated rats called the rakken intercept the slaver's caravans and mark the five of them with a dark brand. As they fight their way out of the mountain with the help of dwarves they meet along the way, their brand calls to something in Volendam.

After many trials, they find themselves inside the port trading city, where they meet Velius, an eldrasi blacksmith on board a ship called the Firebrand, where he offers them aid. The only price is to infiltrate an exclusive club in the wealthy district and steal a few gems and a mysterious necklace. After meeting Velius, they make their way to the nearest inn, The Broken Arrow, where they're received warmly by the inn workers Felix, Patrina, and Hilde.

Meanwhile, Cassius discovers that the woman in his arm is pulling him towards an abandoned opera house, where something calls him inside. With no weapons to speak of, Cassius refrains from entering just yet, and the ragtag team set out to retrieve what Velius asked for in order to have their weapons made. They end up fighting mermaids in order to grant themselves entry to the exclusive club, where they are able to successfully retrieve the gems and locket for Velius. Upon touching said locket, Rooster has a vision of his past, and of a woman with fiery red hair. He knows it has some tie to his past, so he keeps it for himself, telling Velius it is merely lost.

After retrieving their newly forged weapons from Velius, they make their way into the opera house, where they discover a group of vampires stand in the way of the object Cassius has been sent to retrieve. It's a hard battle but a battle won nonetheless, and as the Misfits move to leave, they're called out to by a strange door. Inside, they discover a ritual being performed by rakken and dyrvak, large woodland creatures that surround a dragon tooth. Their attempts to resurrect the dragon are foiled by the Misfits who stumble back out into the streets of Volendam and discover that the city has been surrounded by an army of dyrvak and they must prepare themselves:

War is upon them.

BRASS RAT

Somewhere off in the distance, the chittering of rats was drowned out by the quiet drum calls of war. The soft patter of droplets echoed off the walls of the sewer, and a lone brass-colored rakken scampered through the shallow water, his heart thundering in his ears.

A rancid smell permeated from the water as it splashed against his fur, but he ignored it; he was used to living in dark, smelly places. The sewers were too dark for any human eye but not him as he turned around the corner and moved deeper beneath the city of Volendam. He needed to move quickly.

His thoughts raced as he traversed the grime-infested sewers. *Must hurry-scamper. Find-sniff him. Quick-quick! Before it is too late. Before he is eaten-sacrificed. Red-haired-one would be angry if he could not seek-sniff Captain-filth.* He paused to lick his wounds—long, thin cuts that wept blood from his paws. He'd inflicted them upon himself just this morning in the faith of his god Rat-King. The god of rakken was not merciful and took great care of making sure his disciples remained loyal. Rackjack had been punishing himself for his god's approval for as long as he could remember.

The kicking of a stone nearby forced him to pause, his ears darting to and fro on his head as he strained to listen.

"You-you!" a voice cried out in the darkness, followed closely by the gnashing of teeth. A rakken slipped from the shadows, its eyes beady and red. Tufts of its dark fur were missing, and it was free of armor as it sniffed the air, pointing an accusatory finger at him. "Seek-scamper to the Great One. We are to be ready." The rakken's voice was hoarse, and the brass rakken realized with glee that the other did not know he wasn't from this city. The longer he remained inconspicuous, the better. It would make his job traversing through the sewers much easier.

"Yes-yes. We will make haste," the brass rat rasped. A glint of purple crested from the other rakken's grasp, and the brass rakken flinched, seething and overcome by want. The other rakken had a piece of draugmin, a magical dragon scale that all rakken craved. If the brass rakken could just get his hands on it... He lashed out at the balding rakken, devoid of mercy, and ignored the screech of protest as he bit down into supple flesh. He no longer cared for the advantage of secrecy. All that mattered was getting his hands on the draugmin.

Blood infected his mouth, sour and thick with rot, but the soft *clang* of something hitting the ground distracted the brass rakken from the foul taste on his tongue. He swept under the balding rakken's retaliations as he scrambled to pick up the draugmin, and the other rakken grabbed at his tail and bit down as hard as he could.

The brass rakken screamed angrily as he ignored the balding rat and slipped the draugmin into his mouth. It was no bigger than a small pebble and went down easily when he swallowed. He shuddered as power coursed through him, as the magical energy flooded his system and unlocked the barriers that would hold him accountable for his magical use. He'd be able to use magic beyond his normal capabilities without fear of a heart attack. Risky, but some things were worth the risk.

He hummed an involuntary noise as he reached out and curled his paw around the other rakken's neck, lifting him in the air with ease. The soft melody of the draugmin sang in his ears as he ignored the quiet struggles of the other rakken, for they were feeble. Soon, sewer rats appeared at the brass rakken's feet.

They were small, insignificant rats, but they came in hordes as the brass rakken reached out to them in whispers, soft commands of magical charge that compelled them to his side. The tiny chirps of their chatter echoed off the walls as they crawled to the balding rakken and bit down on his legs. The balding rakken screeched in pain as the rats pulled flesh from bone, as they crawled up and sank their teeth into the rakken's eyes and pried them out in hunger. Soon enough, they overcame the balding rat, its body disappearing behind a mass of small squirming bodies.

The brass rakken backed up, his head a wave of dizziness as the power of the draugmin took hold of him fully. His body wasn't used to the power the draugmin unlocked, and his head sang with it. He embraced its sweet temptation to let go as he turned tail and scampered down the hall into a small room. The room was filthy; green slime coalesced in cracks in the wall, and several bones dotted the floor, some still marred with gnawed-on flesh. In the corner lay a makeshift bed, born from dirtied rags and straw.

The brass rakken moved to the bed first, sniffing the air to ensure his temporary home had not been compromised. He had only been in the city for a week or two, but it was long enough to feel the weight of being surrounded by enemy rakken. The Mischief of Volendam was quiet in the grand scheme of things, but the brass rakken had no doubt they would cut him down if they knew his intentions were not to aid them in the coming battle.

"You-you," a voice said from behind. The brass rakken stilled, his nose infected with the musk of the intruder as he turned, and though he recognized the other rakken, he remained on guard, allowing his own musk to drench the air and attempt to overpower the other.

"Speak now," the brass rakken commanded.

The other rakken was tall and thin, his fur full and gray. He carried a crude sword in one hand, and his nose was hunched over as it sniffed the air for any signs of danger. "Done what you have asked-sought. Some will swear loyalty-follow."

"Prelk-rat has done a good job. Will be rewarded. This Brass-rat can promise," the brass rakken said, lifting his paw to press against the center of Prelk's forehead. "Cannot stay behind. Must leave-go if those above leave-go. Continue to gather the loyal."

Prelk nodded as the brass rakken lowered his paw. Falling on all fours, Prelk chirped. "Will go-go. Spread the Brass Rat's word. Mischief Roughneck will come to flourish." He was gone before the brass rakken could respond.

A droplet of water hit the back of his head as diluted conversation reached him. He stilled, padding back towards the door and peering down the hall. A small flickering light enticed him to investigate a room further down. Prelk was no longer in sight, and the conversation sounded like it was being held by multiple rakken. As he drew closer, soft chants of worship flowed out of the open doorway, an undertone of deep humming that filled the brass rakken's ears.

Peeking inside, he saw a ritual ensuing. Four rakken stood in a half-circle, covered in hoods, with their paws raised towards the ceiling. A woman's body was strapped to the wall, her entrails spilling out of her stomach and curling at the floor, three diagonal lines carved into her chest. The brass rakken recognized it almost immediately; it was the mark of Gorvayne, one of the dead dragons of the far north who sought resurrection. The brass rakken heard his whispers from time to time, particularly when he was around Sigrun, and had seen the mark carved into some of the buildings above. He'd also seen it branded into the flesh of those he'd been following, a group of misfits.

Edging further into the darkness, the brass rakken did not interrupt the ritual. He would be a fool to. Even with the draugmin coursing through him, he did not care to take on four rats amid worship. He did not know how closely their god was watching, and he had come too far to be killed now.

A whisper caressed his cheek as he slunk further into the shadows, stopping him in his tracks. It was spoken in a language he did not know, but the tones rattled him to his core, filling him with an essence he did not understand. It felt like the effects of draugmin, only ten times stronger, and he shuddered, a soft whimper stitched between chattering teeth. The voice compelled him to join the others, to raise his paws towards the ceiling and give himself utterly and completely to the cause. He was a slave to its drive, and he took several steps forward before his will crashed through, and he paused.

No-no. Sniff and see-go the right way. He steeled himself against the whispering, and soon enough it quieted as the rakkens' chanting ceased to a quiet chattering before fading altogether. The shuffling of feet echoed through the tunnel as the brass rakken pressed himself against the wall, hopeful the sewage would mask his scent as the other rakken fled the room. It was by some stroke of luck that they trailed the other way, and the brass rakken waited long after the sounds of their footsteps faded before he entered the room. A small torch flickered against the wall near the corpse of the woman, who still hung, her hands staked into the wall with pieces of metal. Her fingers and toes had been chewed off, likely eaten by those who'd sacrificed her, and the brass rakken had to refrain from nibbling on the corpse himself. Dark magic spilled off her, making it easier for him to turn away and study the branding iron leaning against the wall. The end was still a cherry red of warmth, and the brass rakken looked back to the corpse, searching until he found the brand, angry and puckered on her thigh.

Excitement forced his heart into a tizzy as he raised the branding iron to the torch, warming it within the flame. As the heat brushed against his face, he thought of nothing other than the path forward. His quest had been marked for him long ago, and he had strayed too long in the darkness. He had found what he was looking for, but to get closer, he had to make some sacrifices. He scorned the god they worshiped, scorned their abandonment of Rat-king, but he needed the brand for what came next.

As the flame flickered in front of him, the brass rakken pulled the branding iron from the fire. Familiar with pain, he welcomed it as he turned it around and brought it down on his flesh with no hesitation. It sank against the skin of his forearm and sizzled as it burned away fur. The heat came first, then the pain, and the brass rakken howled quietly as it surged through him, begging him to pull the iron away. He resisted, knowing he must, and after a few moments, he allowed himself a moment of reprieve. He pulled the iron away and studied the brand. The wound was red and swollen; three diagonal lines marred his flesh. Satisfaction took his breath away as he turned back towards the door, pulling a small silver bead from the folds of his cloak and working it into the fur at his chin.

Coming to find you, Carter-filth.

One

ROOSTER

War drums choked the air with trepidation, and Rooster had never felt so tense.

Only hours had passed since an army had marched against the walls of Volendam, and evidence of the siege had infected the city with chaos. Adrenaline coursed through Rooster as he burst through the door of The Broken Arrow, the tavern where his friends were. Hurrying over to them, he was stopped by Cassius, his eyes carved with a hint of red. The vampire looked as tense as Rooster felt, and Helai paced near the counter, her hair tied up into a high ponytail. She muttered to herself, clutching the eye necklace around her neck, and glanced over when Rooster stepped inside, accompanied by the chill of winter that whispered through the streets outside. Intoh sat at their booth in his human form, and the greka's blond hair was shot up in different directions as he spoke urgently to Linda in drikotyian. Linda was also in their human form, their hulking body taking up most of the left side of the booth, and their eyes lit up when they noticed Rooster.

The inn was otherwise empty, save for the dwarven rangers and staff. Felix and Patrina, the two owners of the establishment, approached the Misfits, their eyes wild with worry.

"We woke to the sounds of war. Who means to siege the city?" Felix asked, his voice hushed. Patrina had her arm tucked through her lover's, her hair covered beneath a bonnet of silk, and Rooster locked eyes with her as she caught her lower lip between her teeth.

"It matters little. You need to leave." It was Cassius who spoke, his expression hard. Helai turned to the dwarves, who spoke in low voices near one of the booths, and Rooster broke away to peer out one of the front windows.

Guards strolled by in droves, coming from the Sails District to heed the guard captain's call, no doubt. The streets were otherwise deserted, with several people who had no means to flee the city holing up in their homes. Lights were dimmed, and the world was silent.

"We have made a friend of the blacksmith up the road." Rooster forced his gaze away from the outside to look at Felix and Patrina, who clung to each other's hands like lifelines. "If you have no way out of the city, he can keep you safe." Velius was more acquaintance than a friend, but Rooster was certain he'd help.

"I do not wish to abandon my home," Felix protested. He spoke several words in a language Rooster did not understand.

Cassius did though. His gaze softened as he replied to Felix in the same tongue, his voice quiet and sympathetic. Gesturing towards the door, Cassius' voice turned urgent, and Felix's shoulders sank. Rooster felt for him; he would not want to flee his home either.

"I know, my love, but I'm sure they'd rather we keep ourselves safe," Patrina whispered, raising Felix's hand to press her lips to the curve of his knuckles.

Rooster nodded in agreement. "Homes can be rebuilt, but lives cannot be reclaimed."

Linda snorted, hitting their chest with a closed fist. "Know this true," they said. "Sometimes run. Okay to run."

Felix stared at Linda for quite some time without saying anything. The war drums still rattled the ground, and Rooster steadied his shaking hands as Felix stepped forward, his brow furrowed in indecision. "This blacksmith of yours. You sure he can take us in?"

"Velius has been nothing but kind to us. I'm certain," Helai said. "Despite my reservations about his intentions, he seems honest."

Felix's eyes flashed in recognition. "I know Velius. He's come in from time to time to enjoy the drinks and company." He pondered silently, his gaze falling on Patrina. Something spoke in his expression; he wasn't fleeing for himself.

A chill ran through the inn, and Rooster suppressed the urge to shudder. The brand on his back burned, ever a reminder that there was more going on than they realized. Rooster still hadn't had any time to process what they'd witnessed in the abandoned opera house just days before, nor what they were going to do about the brands that were anything but normal.

"I will accompany you to the Firebrand. Rooster, you are meeting the guard captain back at the wall, yes?" Cassius' words cut through the air, pulling Rooster from his thoughts, and he nodded. He'd just left Booker's side, and the guard captain had lacked helpful information. The army that appeared beyond Volendam's walls just days ago had not moved. Intoh scurried up, his brow furrowed.

"Must find Tidebeard at the college. Must know his plans. Will take Linda."

Linda seemed hesitant to leave the inn, their eyes straying to Helai, who conversed in hushed tones with the dwarves. Obrand, the leader of King Stoneheart's dwarven rangers, looked particularly distressed, and Rooster sighed. "Yes, I intend to return to the wall. Felix." His gaze went to him as he gestured to the bar. "Do you mind if I fill my flask for the days ahead?" Felix nodded numbly, so Rooster shook some skaels from his pouch and pressed them into Felix's hand. Clapping him on the shoulder, he passed, approaching the bar. His fingers shook, but it wasn't from the anxiety of impending war; it was more likely from the lack of alcohol in his system. He needed to be rightly drunk for the fight ahead.

Pulling the bottle down from the shelf, he poured the whiskey into his flask as Obrand approached. Rooster gestured his flask at him and took a long swig. It burned the whole way down, but the warmth that accompanied the whiskey seeped into his bones as he sighed heavily and turned the lid on his flask.

Obrand eyed the ale solemnly as he pressed his fingers to the counter of the bar. "We've sent Kolin and Jaera to sneak past the dyrvak army and report to our king. If the rakken situation is still under control, I do not doubt my king's aid. We receive a lot of trade and support from Volendam and would hate to see it fall," he said, leaning against the counter.

"The rakken–are they proving to be more trouble?" Rooster thought back to his times with the dwarves. The rakken had been a problem for the dwarves for some time at that point. Giant mutated rats, they sought out draugmin, a fossilized dragon scale the dwarves mined from rock. The rakken used it to channel their magic. Rooster had never seen it used, not that he could remember until he'd fallen through a crack in the earth and had met a mischief of rakken hiding down there. They had infused it into their skin and planted it in their weapons, while the dwarves they'd fought had carved it into their tattoos.

"We have not seen much sign of them, which–" Obrand glanced at the other dwarven rangers before sighing, his hand falling on the nape of his neck. "It's strange, lad. It's as if they have disappeared all over again."

The claim brought a chill to Rooster's spine. If the dwarves weren't seeing any sign of the rakken, then where had they gone? It was horrifying to think they might be working with the dyrvak; Rooster was tempted to confide in Obrand about the rakken they'd seen in the opera house, but something silenced his tongue. Would Obrand believe him? The sight of the dragon's tooth assaulted his mind, and he shook his head, shrugging.

"Strange, indeed." He was tired of dealing with giant rats. If he survived this siege, perhaps he would cross the great sea and never see them again. He could not recall ever crossing their path before stumbling out of Daesthara, the wild forest of the woodland folk in the south a year ago, when the shoma'kah captured him to be sold away.

Helai approached slowly, as did the others. Cassius looked on edge, the muscles in his jaw pulsating as he stood several feet away. A power radiated from him, a subtle energy that Rooster had not noticed until they'd fled the opera house.

"We do not have time to ponder," Cassius said. The tension was thick in the air. Every breath Rooster took brought the reminder that war was on the horizon, and Cassius was right; they could not delay. It did not seem as if the dyrvak army was moving in on the wall, but that did not mean they would remain back indefinitely. Not unless they meant to encircle the city and starve them out, which was a very real possibility.

"I'm going to go seek out the alchemist. If a battle breathes down our neck, I need some supplies," Helai said, wringing her fingers together. Several lines worried her brow, and she spared a glance at the door as shouting rang through the streets outside. "Though I do not think it wise to separate for long."

"I intend to meet Rooster at the wall after I make sure Felix and Patrina are safe," Cassius said, looking about the inn. "Where are Hilde and Dirk?"

"Dirk's family is a few doors down. We sent him home when we heard the war drums. Hilde's gone to the docks to see if her ship has been compromised," Felix said just as Hilde walked through the door.

Hilde's hair was in disarray, and her hands trembled as she drew close. Last time he'd seen the barmaid, she'd been laughing and dancing with some of the sailors to the tune of Patrina's lute. "The city has fallen to madness. My boat is gone." Her face fell as she reached for Patrina's outstretched hands, giving them a gentle squeeze. "I heard a guard say that they have us surrounded and they mean to wait us out. The bay has not been compromised, but I fear it is only a matter of time."

Rooster's face paled. So, he was right. They meant to starve the city. Smart not to risk their army when they didn't have to.

"Will go to college, see if Tidebeard has idea about bay," Intoh said, tugging at Linda's arm. "Come, Linda. Come, come!" Intoh scurried off as Linda grumbled and followed after. The air was frigid as the door opened and shut behind them, and Rooster gestured to Cassius.

"Felix and Patrina are going with Cassius to Velius', where we hope he can keep you all safe from the siege. I encourage you to join them," Rooster told Hilde.

A gentle sadness swept Hilde's face as she looked about the inn. It plagued Rooster with his own sense of mourning, for who knows if the inn would be standing if and when the dyrvak invaded the city. The inn had served a taste of comfort and home for him; he had to hope it would prevail as they would.

"Our safety is more important. You *should* come with us, Hilde," Patrina urged.

"Of course, dear. I go where you go. Who will make sure you both remember to eat?" Hilde's words forced laughter from the group, but the laughter was hollow, stolen by the unease of the coming storm.

"We need a few moments to pack," Felix said.

"Pack lightly. We do not have that much time," Cassius warned as the three of them retreated up the stairs.

Rooster watched them go with a bitter sigh. "I should return to the wall."

"Seek out Velius with me. He is more fond of you," Cassius said, drawing closer. "Then I will return to the wall with you. We are closed in. We have no choice but to meet with Booker and figure out what we are to do."

"More fond of *me*? It wasn't my ass he was staring at last time we visited him," Rooster protested, ignoring Cassius' dark stare. It was fun teasing the vampire. He was so easy to rile up. Still, he couldn't see the difference whether he accompanied them to the Firebrand or went straight to the wall, so he nodded, topping off his flask and then returning to the other side of the counter.

"I will meet you at the southern gate," Helai said, turning on her heel to leave. Her step faltered, and she turned to glance at them once, a peculiar look crossing her face. It looked almost akin to concern. "Don't die," she uttered as Drithan, one of the dwarves, captured her attention.

"Don't plan on it," Rooster said, mainly to himself as Felix, Patrina, and Hilde reappeared at the top of the stairs. All of them carried barely anything, a bag in each of their hands, and Obrand reached out to clasp Rooster's shoulder as he nodded at the remaining rangers.

"We are to go to the guard's captain and see what he means to do. If you are to return to the wall, we'll see you there." Rooster was silent as Obrand nodded grimly and disappeared through the front door with the other rangers.

Felix squared his shoulders as he approached. The torchlight of the room reflected off his face, and he looked older than he was, the threat of war aging him. "We should leave before I change my mind," he said.

Patrina curled her fingers around the neck of her lute as she turned to stare one last time at The Broken Arrow. The inn did not bleed its usual sense of warmth and home, and Rooster was eager to be free of it. His restless state was not soothed, and he did not enjoy the trepidation that sank into the walls of the inn.

"Come," he said, pushing the door open to streets occupied by guards dressed in plate armor bearing the sigil of Volendam. Several of them bore polearms or bows strapped to their backs and none of them spared a glance at the party as they hurried up the street towards the blacksmith's forge.

Rooster's stomach lurched painfully as they stumbled through the Firebrand's portal door and were met with the unsteady sea. Velius' gryphon was absent from its corner, and the opening in the wall where it usually rested showed an angry sea with tall waves and the threat of rain.

"The ocean? Did we just teleport onto a ship?" Felix's questions were drenched with disbelief, and Rooster looked up as he adjusted to the dips of the ship.

"Indeed. Our friend's forge is a unique one." Was Velius a friend? Rooster wasn't sure it was the right term, but if the crew of The Broken Arrow were going to be safe anywhere, it would be on the Firebrand. It was obvious the forge was not sailing anywhere near Volendam.

Behind him, Hilde let out a soft groan, and Cassius caught her as she moved in an unsteady fashion, thrown off balance as the Firebrand tilted to one side.

"Thanks, dear," Hilde said, patting Cassius' arm. "I don't know if I'll ever get my sea legs."

"If Helai can do it, surely you can too," Rooster said. He recalled fighting the mermaids several months ago and how sickly Helai had been. It had taken her a week just to get steady on her feet. Regardless, Cassius pressed Hilde's hand to the crook of his elbow as they reached the opposite door.

"Velius?" Rooster called out, glancing at Felix and Patrina as he pressed his fingers to the wood. The door was cool to the touch and hummed as if it were breathing. The energy that coursed off it filled Rooster with a sense of home, and he shook the dizziness away as he pushed the door open.

He shielded his eyes as the brightness of day threatened to blind him despite being tucked away by dark, angry clouds. The Firebrand was massive, its billowing sails stark white and bearing a gryphon breathing fire as its sigil. Eldrasi sailors garbed in leather armor of golds and greens, with swords at their hips worked in tandem to keep the ship steady, and Velius' voice called down from above.

"Rooster? Cassius? What news of Volendam?"

Blinking, Rooster took a few steps forward and looked up to see the eldrasi blacksmith coming down one of the stairs cradling the entrance to the forge. His hair was half up today, his armor gleaming in a mixture of plate metal and leather. A massive tower shield made for protecting most of the body from attack rested against the ship's railing near the wheel, and his hammer was strapped to his waist.

"The army stands just outside the city walls. We have no idea if their position has changed, but we've heard they mean to encircle the city and starve its people," Cassius said. Rooster recalled being back in Booker's office just after stumbling out of the opera house. The terror that had gripped him when he'd looked out of the slit in the wall and had seen a mass of dyrvak stretching so far that they disappeared into the trees had been unmatched. They were half man, half woodland creatures like that of elk, moose, and deer. Antlers grew out of their heads, and many of them wielded spears and swords. Their language was harsh, and like the rakken, they were almost a myth, not believed by all to exist. Rooster knew how they fought, with careful calculation and brutish strength. He did not know how they could survive their attack.

"We have brought our friends here, hoping you can harbor them," Rooster explained, gesturing to The Broken Arrow crew.

As Velius reached them, he looked past Rooster's shoulder to shout something in Eldrasian. The sailor responded in kind, dropping a cord of rope and stepping forward.

"Dayalas is going to take your friends below decks, where it is safe. I fear a storm is brewing." Dayalas, a young female eldrasi with bark growing jaggedly out of the side of her face and weaving through her dark hair, bowed her head and gestured to Felix, Patrina, and Hilde.

"Come," she said, her voice soft, like a whisper of wind through trees. "We have spare rooms below."

Felix glanced in Rooster's direction, hesitating. "Are you sure you do not wish to stay? No one would blame you if you did. It's not a war you are obliged to fight."

Rooster shook his head. "We will return and see if we can aid the wall in some way." They did not owe Volendam their allegiance; Felix was right about that. A part of Rooster felt compelled to remain on the Firebrand, begging to surround himself with the familiarity of the sea. But no; if he were to stay, he'd never forgive himself.

Hesitation warred in Felix's expression, but his shoulders sagged, and he nodded, reaching for Patrina's hand. "See that you return to us alive–both of you," he said, looking at Rooster before catching Cassius' gaze.

As Dayalas ferried the three of them away, Rooster turned to those who remained. "We should return. We do not know how dire our time is." Rooster's hair whipped about his face as it began to rain, but still, he turned his face upwards, relishing the warmth. Wherever this ship was, it was nowhere near the north, where the chill of winter was biting at their heels.

"Let us step back into my forge," Velius said, gesturing back to where they had come. "The wind does not pair well with a quick conversation." Rooster caught a glimpse of Velius' gryphon flying overhead, its wings outstretched as it screeched, a low guttural sound that reverberated into a deep purr. It disappeared into a wall of rain and clouds as Rooster and Cassius followed Velius back into the heat of the forge. Even though the room looked unused, warmth rolled off the hearth in waves, and Rooster sidled up to it, eager to warm his aching bones before they were to return to the cold.

"Before you leave, I must tell you—war does not only fester in the north. There has been word of unrest brewing in the south. Shoma has been talking about an invasion. Mere whispers right now, but some are saying the sultan there brews a fleet. They cannot cut through the Daesthara Forest, so they mean to take to the seas. They have cut off trade agreements with Hestia."

Cassius inhaled sharply. "They have held trade with Hestia for hundreds of years. My mother did her best trading with Dalasae. What's changed?"

Velius shrugged. "I'm not certain." His brow furrowed in troubling thought. He caught Rooster's gaze, and a hand waved towards his neck. "That necklace...it is the one I asked you to find, is it not?"

Rooster thumbed the silver necklace hanging at his neck. He had nearly forgotten it was there, sitting above the hydra tooth that frequently sat against his chest. The mention of it brought back the memory he'd suffered touching it for the first time when he was at the Silver Moon Club some months ago of a woman with red hair and breathtakingly blue eyes–*Igraine*. A sense of longing plagued him, and he closed his palm over the necklace, shaking his head in denial. "I'm not sure..."

"Please..." Velius lowered his voice, a quiet sadness echoing in his expression. "It belonged to someone very important to me, and I think I can use it to find her."

Hesitating, Rooster looked at Cassius. He paced, his hands clasped behind his back, his gaze far off. Rooster wasn't sure he'd even heard the conversation about the necklace. *The news of war must be really troubling him*, Rooster thought. Pulling the necklace over his head, he offered it to Velius.

"I'm not sure why, but..." The ship rocked violently, and Rooster nearly fell, catching himself at the last minute. Shouting erupted outside, and Velius' attention was diverted to the door leading out to the ship. The rain fell harder through the hole in the wall, beckoning a dreary setting.

Taking the necklace from Rooster, Velius pocketed it quickly. "I apologize but whatever you were going to say has to wait. If I have the means and the men, I will aid Volendam in its defense, but for now, you must go." As they were ushered towards the door, Cassius remained silent. The cold bit at them as they stepped back onto the streets of Volendam.

"Come," Cassius said softly, and as Rooster followed, he couldn't help but wonder if Velius was hiding something from him about his past.

Two

HELAI

Helai shivered against the frigid chill of winter. Snow kissed her
cheeks, and a nervous exhale escaped her as Drithan, the dwarf
who'd followed her out of the inn, reached out and grabbed her arm,
forcing her to stop.

"Helai?" His thick accent rumbled through her, heating her cheeks,
and her gaze slid up to meet his. She hadn't noticed before just how light
his eyes were. Brown but struck with rays of honey-gold. She almost lost
herself in them, if only to be her salvation from the desolate state of the
city. "Are you okay?"

She trembled despite her determination not to, and Drithan reached
out to wipe a snowflake from her cheek. His fingers were hot and rough,
like sandpaper. Still, she found herself leaning in, relishing the heat ra-

diating off his skin. She suppressed another shudder, this time not from the cold.

"I am afraid," she admitted, searching his gaze for answers. "I do not want to die in this city." It was a dark and selfish thought, her desire to abandon Volendam to its fate. She allowed herself to think about it anyway, allowed it to fester for a mere moment before murdering it without mercy. "How do you remain so calm when we stand on the edge of inevitable bloodshed?" She whispered, searching his face for answers. She'd never fought in a battle so large before unless she counted fighting with the dwarves some months ago.

"It's okay to be afraid." He hesitated, working something over in his head as he leaned close, trapping her gaze against his. Helai did not pull away, desperate to feel anything other than the fear pooling in her belly. "I am always afraid before battle," he admitted, his breath caressing her cheek. "Even the bravest are afraid because nothing is certain. No one wants to die. Death can claim anyone on a battlefield. Fear is a tool used to aid you, should you wield it correctly."

Helai blinked away the snowflakes as they fell against her eyelashes, then sniffed, forcing herself to step back. "I have something to give you," she said, shuffling around in her bag. She knew they did not have long as guards rushed past, heading towards the wall. "It's a token and a request."

"Oh?" Drithan said, unable to conceal his curiosity as she pulled out a deck of cards. It was her Sharaha deck. Helai could nearly taste the *lavka* that Massoud, her brother, had stolen for her and Aryan the day he'd pulled the deck from his pocket, sat her down, and showed her each card.

"They were hand painted by a jinn at the request of the owner," Massoud had explained. Helai, no older than seven, had gone through each card and touched the illustration on the back, her eyes wide with glee. "They're supposed to tell you the future, and they are my gift to you."

He'd planted a kiss on her head and had stolen a bit of her *lavka* before disappearing out of the window in the building they'd been hiding in.

"Can you read my future? Does it include more *lavka*?" Aryan had asked.

"Helai?" Drithan pulled Helai from the memory as she pressed the cards to her chest. An embarrassed exhale passed her lips as she lowered the deck, shuffling through them to find the one she was looking for. The cards were faded now, frayed at the edges, but it made Helai love them even more.

"Here. I want you to hold on to this one for me." She stared at the card for a moment before offering it to him. Outlined in gold, a sun and a moon danced around each other in a darkened sky. It must be the moment before sunrise or after sunset when the sun caught a glimpse of the moon. It was one of Helai's favorite cards, and the sun's face was nearly gone from all the times Helai had run her fingers over it.

Drithan took it, staring at it silently for several moments. His own finger etched the illustration, and his mouth parted in awe. "Helai, this is beautiful. I cannot take it."

"I only want you to hold on to it for me while you're fighting. My brother Massoud–" She paused, her expression turning sheepish. "It's silly, but he said the cards are magical. I believe that one will keep you safe."

"Keep me safe? Even more of a reason for you to keep it," Drithan said. He did not let go of the card, however, even as his gaze tore away from it to settle on her. "Are you certain? It appears these cards mean a lot to you."

Helai thought for a moment and then nodded. "I'm certain. Return to me after the siege." *If we survive.* The thought strayed in, made a home in her mind as a softness brushed away the hard lines that frequented Drithan's face.

He nodded, slipping the card into the pocket lining the inside of his cloak. A few moments passed before Drithan grunted, reached into his other pocket, and pulled out a hunting knife.

"What–" Helai started to ask but was startled to silence when Drithan offered the hilt to her. Helai stared up at him with an incredulous nature. "What is this?"

Drithan hummed, looking pleased with himself. "For you. To keep *you* safe."

A warmth swelled in Helai's chest.

"I mean–" Drithan spluttered, his hand moving to the nape of his neck. "I know you've got plenty of daggers of your own, and you know how to fight, but it's my lucky hunting knife. Helped me feed the Stoneheart Rangers for nigh on a century... Killed the great beasts of the Spine Mountain."

Helai couldn't stop the smile from infecting her lips even as Drithan continued to ramble. Reaching out, she placed a hand on his arm, quieting him. "Thank you, Drithan," she said gently. The knife's hilt was made of a beautiful dark oak, where the swirl of grain was etched in an elegant and natural pattern. The blade itself was tucked behind the leather sheath. Taking it from him, she examined the blade; it was very sharp.

Drithan stared at her for a moment. "I've seen you fight, Helai. The dwarves sing songs of the moon, of her beauty and grace but also of her cunning and fierceness." He went quiet for a moment. "You remind me of her. You will survive this battle."

Helai's chest continued to thicken with some foreign emotion. It had been some time since someone had thought to give her something like this or believed in her so fiercely, and Aryan had never been so...caring. The giddiness gripped her with little mercy, pooling in the bottom of her belly.

She stashed the knife in her cloak as the war drums echoed through the streets once more, rattling her resolve. They sounded closer, much closer, and she needed to get to the wall before too long in case something changed and she was needed there.

Drithan seemed to sense her unease because he stepped back, looking down the street. Something inside her begged him not to go, to remain with her and fight by her side where she could watch his flank, but she remained silent. He had an allegiance to his rangers, and she could respect that. She had been the same way with her Ghosts. There were only a few of them: Massoud, Masika, Zamir, Ehsan, Hosni, Kílae, Aryan, and Zahra, but she would have protected them with her life.

Liar. A voice in her head betrayed her, sending a pang of reminder coursing through where her pinky used to be. Zahra died because of Helai, and she'd cut her pinky off in her guilt-consumed grief.

"Need to go find the others. Prepare for the days to come." Drithan gave her an affirming nod, pulling her away from her past, before lowering his head against the snow and moving down the street. She watched him until she could no longer see him before turning to The Secret Ingredient, the alchemist who created various potions and salves for the city.

A crow landed on the sign above, staring at her intently. She halted as it cawed, flapping its wings and demanding her attention. A note was strapped to its leg, and Helai offered her arm to it; it landed on her forearm.

"Thank you," she whispered, scratching the crow under the beak before tugging the note loose. It stared at her with one intelligent eye before taking off, disappearing in the haze of snow.

Huddling closer to the building, Helai unrolled the note, her stomach clinching in shock as familiarity gripped her. This was Zamir's handwriting, one of her Ghosts. It was almost painful seeing his handwriting, and her eyes darted quickly across the letter.

Dearest Helai,

I hope you are well. I have heard whispers in the wind that you are in Volendam. If you find yourself able to travel, I am currently visiting the lovely city of Halvdarc. It would be very good to see you.

  Z

Helai read the letter twice before she processed what it said. Zamir was in Halvdarc? A city in Rovania; it was a good month's journey by horseback to get to the coastal city. What was he doing there? Her mind swam with implications as she rolled the letter back up and slipped it inside her belt. She'd ponder over it when they did not stand on the edge of battle.

The lights were off in The Secret Ingredient, and the building looked to be abandoned, but Helai knocked furiously for several moments before a disgruntled Golbin pried open the door. He hid behind it, keeping away from the glare of daylight, and stared blearily up at Helai.

"Whaddya want?" Golbin's words slurred together as he stood unsteadily on his feet, and Helai realized the small creature was drunk.

"Golbin, we are under siege. Now isn't the time to drink yourself to death," Helai said, brushing past him and out of the cold. She had not realized how fiercely she'd miss the warmth of her homeland until she'd left it to brave the winter months of the northern lands.

"Get out," Golbin protested, swiveling on his heel and falling promptly to the floor. "I do not need your meddling." She ignored him as she moved to his wall of herbs, potions, and other various alchemical items, searching through various bottles that were marked and carefully organized.

"I need to make potions I can use on the wall. I also need more healing herbs and salves. There's an actual army outside your door, and unlike you, I'm trying to do something about it," Helai muttered, running a finger over the engraved word on each drawer. When she was met with silence, she turned, her brow furrowing as Golbin stared at her in defiance.

"You *don't* care, do you?"

Golbin's face devolved in his anger. "We are nestled up against the sea. If they cut us off, it won't be long before we starve," Golbin said bitterly, pushing himself up to his feet and stumbling over to his desk.

"But this city is a trading hub. Does it not have any alliances?" Helai was not familiar with the northern kingdoms or their treaties with their neighbors, but surely if Volendam was taken, the surrounding kingdoms would suffer from the lack of trade?

"The eldrasi of Míradan do not sail from their distant shores for human trifles, and the northern kingdom of Kreznov is busy fighting the vykra of Volreya." Golbin snorted, shaking his head. "No, no. Might as well sit down and drink with me until the starvation takes hold, or the army seeks mercy and breeches the walls to kill us quickly."

Helai flinched at his words, but a small, angry thought cradled the back of her mind, telling her that Golbin was right. She had come here to find the man she considered a brother, but Massoud was not in the city. She could feel that with certainty at her core. The brand on her back burned low, a constant ache that reminded her of the mess she had gotten herself into. She should have fought harder to remain at Massoud's side. Perhaps she would have died with her Ghosts and not among these Misfits she still wasn't sure she could trust.

"No," she said aloud, both to Golbin and herself. "We can't abandon hope."

Golbin snorted. "Hope is for fools."

Helai's anger resurfaced, angry and insistent as she turned on her heel. "You're the fool. Sell me what I need. If you truly believe what you say, they will be destroyed anyway. Might as well let me use them. I will not sit by and let them take me. If I am going to die, it's going to be out there," she said, gesturing to the door. "So, you can either sit here and feel sorry for yourself, or you can help me find what I need." She felt guilty almost immediately. Her courage was unwarranted; she had only interacted with Golbin once. She had no right to judge his decisions.

Still, her words seemed to affect the small creature, whose ears twitched erratically as he moved to the wall. He barely reached the third shelf, but a ladder was placed conveniently against the wall, and he climbed it. It took him several tries as he kept falling off the ladder in his intoxicated state, but he finally found everything he was looking for, having pulled various herbs, salves, and potions from their drawers, and now handed them to her. Each was marked with their name and what they did, and Helai removed her skaels purse and shoved the things Golbin handed her into her bag.

"You truly are the most annoying human I've ever met," Golbin muttered to himself, chirping quietly as he read over the labeled drawers. "I fucking hate humans." Climbing up, he reached into a drawer near the ceiling and pulled out several round bottles filled with a swirling orange liquid.

"Can't say I'm a fan of you either," Helai admitted as Golbin climbed down and returned to her side, offering her the potions. They were warm in color, with flecks of gold floating within.

"Used those shrooms you collected–heated them up and mixed them with pieces from the gullet of a fire salamander from Lyvira. Very explosive, very *expensive*. Use them wisely." Helai handled them with better care as she hesitated, glancing around.

"Do you have a belt I could put these in? I do not think I should have them rolling around in my bag."

Golbin nodded slowly, stifling a hiccup behind his hand. "Have some more things for you as long as you promise to leave me alone after." That piqued her interest, so she agreed, not certain whether she'd be able to keep that promise.

Muttering to himself in a foreign language, Golbin disappeared behind his desk. Helai tapped her foot anxiously as she glanced at the door. He reappeared with a belt with several loops in it for vials in one hand and a leather-bound book that was worn from well-use in the other.

"Last person that helped me died and left these. Don't need it anymore. Here," he said, offering both items to her.

Setting the vials down, she took the belt first. It looked like it could hold ten different potions within the loops, and when she tried it on, it was only slightly too large. She'd work at adjusting it when there was more time. She grabbed the explosive vials carefully and slipped them into their spots before taking the book from Golbin's outstretched hand. It was made from dark leather, and Helai held it hesitantly.

"You've only met me once. Why the gifts?" Gifts were often attached with hidden agendas, ones that were never good. Helai had learned from a young age that whenever Massoud had graced her with treats or trinkets he'd stolen on the streets, it usually meant they were in danger and needed to find a new hole to hide in.

Golbin gestured to his shop. "If we fail to hold back the army, my shop is a plethora of information. It would be a shame to lose it all to those who would either destroy it or use it for unsavory reasons." His ears shifted atop his head as he frowned and snapped his fingers. A burst of gold specks left his hand as a clear glass bottle appeared in his palm, full of a deep-red liquid. He took a quick drink from it and wiped his mouth with the back of his hand. "The book is everything I've learned being an alchemist."

Helai's eyes widened as she opened the book. Each page was chaotic, with notes scribbled in no particular order. Pictures accompanied the text, and each page had a different alchemical mixture to brew for a different effect. The illustrations weren't all that fancy, but Helai pressed it to her chest as if he'd given her a hundred skaels. "Why me though? I've only done one favor for you."

Golbin shrugged. "Right place, right time. Look around; who else will I see before we all die a painful, gruesome death?"

Helai cradled the book. "Thank you."

He waved away her purse when she tried to offer him skaels and turned back towards his desk, nursing the vial he drank from. It looked to be a healing concoction, but he appeared uninjured. What did he need one of them for?

"Pay for it by saving the city. Now fuck off. I have better things to do, like drink to my death."

She didn't argue; the things he'd given her would be invaluable if she survived the siege.

When you survive the siege, she told herself, rushing out of the store.

Three

ROOSTER

A chill rolled down Rooster's spine as a war horn sounded off in the distance, the same sound of the horn blown in the marshes all those many months ago when they'd left the dwarven mountains and made their way to Volendam. A chill threatened his spine at the memory of the dyrvak in the marshlands.

The dyrvak were closing in.

"Won't be long now," Cassius commented. He had only said a handful of things since leaving the Firebrand, but there was a trained calmness etched into his expression—the expression of a knight on the eve of battle. He had spoken once or twice of his knighthood with the White Dawn, and Rooster had fought alongside him long enough to see that knighthood used when he fought. It gave Rooster a small sense of comfort to have Cassius fighting by his side.

Torchlight flickered off the fearful faces of people as they passed, and Rooster could not blame their terror. He felt it too, festering in his belly.

War drums continued to sound through the air, and with it, another pulse of heat shot through Rooster's back, originating from his brand. It had been some months since the rakken had branded them all in the Spine Mountains, but the weight of it never faltered.

They stepped up to the guard's barracks, which were currently overflowing with the town's guards and those who sought to defend their city. Most of them were born in the Hull District, the poor portion of the city; Rooster did not see anyone bearing the clothes of the Sails District among the soldiers.

Cowards, Rooster thought bitterly. The Sails District was full of the wealthy and it did not appear their love for their city outweighed their own desire for survival. The lack of boats in the harbor, when they'd passed, signaled they'd fled the first chance they got, leaving the poor to defend the city.

"Rooster?" Cassius asked.

"Yes?"

"Do you feel it?" Cassius' expression was always hard lines and faint frowns, but this time it was different. A chill rolled off Rooster's shoulders, and he shivered as Cassius' puzzled expression grew tinged with fear. Cassius had never been a man to wear his emotions for all to see, not like Rooster, who cared not to hide them. Something was spooking the vampire.

A current of magic rippled through the air; it tugged at Rooster's chest, sending his heart into a rapid patter. The magic was faint, far off. He wasn't sure it was what Cassius had referenced, but it did not frighten him.

"Worry not, friend. It is merely pre-battle jitters." Rooster clapped Cassius on the back as they approached Booker. The guard's captain sat atop a massive steed covered in plate armor, its tail flicking in anticipation as it stomped the ground with impatient hooves. Cassius wasn't given a chance to respond as Booker addressed them.

"Grivas, take your men to the Sails District. Station yourself at the northern wall. I do not want to face a surprise ambush from behind. Faergus, hold up behind the main gate. Cassius will aid your unit should the gate fall. It looks like they mean to wait us out. They have not made a move to march forward, but we cannot assume such. It would be unwise."

Cassius paused, then nodded. "It would be my honor to defend the front gate." His hand rested on the hilt of his sword as Faergus sized him up, then led Cassius over to his men, who were working hard to reinforce the gate with slats of wood.

Snow began to fall, and Rooster blinked moisture from his eyes as Booker stared down at him.

"Are you any good with a bow?" Booker asked, his gaze distracted as two soldiers fought among themselves several feet away.

"Aye. Was going to go to the local bowyer, but the city went to war," Rooster replied. It was a shame he hadn't made it in time. His crossbow could use a bit of love.

"Good. I'll have you up on the wall. Near the gate in case they have a ram. Raus," Booker said, reaching out and stopping a woman, the woman who had been training the guardsmen the first time Rooster had gone to see Booker. The scar on her face was prominent as Booker filled her in, and she nodded, taking a good long look at Rooster before gesturing with her head.

"I trust you know how to take commands?"

Rooster gave one last glance at Cassius before he followed her up the stairs and onto the wall. "Yes," he said finally.

It was a cold evening, but the chill of early winter was not truly felt until one stood atop the city's walls. Rooster's teeth chattered despite his will not to, and the cold was relentless; even in his armor, it slipped through him like a ghost. The fighting would chase it away soon enough. The boy in him urged him to open his mouth and taste the snow on his tongue, but the man in him refrained. There were dire matters at hand.

Rows of soldiers lined the walls, their bows dangling loosely at their sides. Many of them stood at attention as if the dyrvak army would descend upon them without warning. Rooster could not blame them for their tense stature; he, too, felt the anxious twist of impending war in the air. A way down on Rooster's right stood Stoneheart's Rangers, their crossbows resting atop the wall. Obrand caught Rooster's eye and gave a curt nod before gesturing out to the sea of the enemy before them.

The fog had stretched from the marshlands and now slipped between the trees that dotted the horizon. The open plain in front of the gate was currently occupied by the masses.

Another look at the army took Rooster's breath away.

Dyrvak lined the plain in rows, still as statues. They ranged in size, some no larger than the average dog with little or no antlers to speak of. Others who stood at the front line stood as tall as some of the moose that dwelt within Daesthara. They bore giant eighteen- or twenty-point antlers atop their human-like heads. Moss clung to their faces and hung from their antlers, and several of them pawed the ground as if it would relieve them of their impatience. Some of them looked akin to deer, others like elk; all of them stood tall and stared at the wall silently, unmoving.

"What are they waiting for?" Rooster uttered to himself, clinging tightly to the bow in his grasp.

"Captain Booker thinks they mean to starve us. Cut off our trade and ways out of the city; some are saying those who fled were right to do so."

It was a troubling notion, but the army was not acting as if they meant to wait out the city. They had not set up camp and they weren't moving closer. It was as if they were waiting for something. "I do not imagine it will be good for humanity if this city were to fall." It would bring devastation to the nearby kingdoms if Volendam were to fall to enemy hands. Rooster had little memory of his past, but he knew how trade worked. If there was no port city to bring in traded goods, the neighboring kingdoms would suffer.

"We'll hold the best we can," Rooster told Raus. "There is little other option."

"I–" Raus protested, but whatever she was going to say was silenced as war cries traveled throughout the army beyond the wall. The dyrvak parted as one of their leaders with moss clinging to his antlers walked slowly through the ranks, dragging something behind him. It was a prisoner of some kind, that much Rooster could tell, and whoever it was fought tooth and nail to be freed. It didn't matter; their hands and feet were tied and they were being pulled by their hair.

"Hail Gutvauk! Hail Gutvauk!" the army shouted, pressing their fists to their chests as they raised their weapons in the air. As Gutvauk stepped out from the front ranks of his army, he pulled his squirming prisoner up and displayed him to the wall.

Rooster sucked in a horrified breath when he realized it was Kolin, one of the Stoneheart Rangers. Rooster recalled Obrand saying they had sent Kolin and Jaera out to sneak past the army and flee into the mountains. Jaera was nowhere in sight, but Kolin was heavily injured. He was bruised badly, one eye swollen shut, and the dyrvak that held him laughed, pulling a dagger from a sheath at his chest and cutting Kolin's bindings, dropping Kolin to the ground. Gutvauk was well within shooting range, but no order to shoot had been made. Rooster was thankful; perhaps they merely did not want to harm Kolin.

"Run, little stone," Gutvauk shouted for the wall to hear. His voice was low and rumbling, like rocks rolling down a mountain.

The dwarf spun, looked up at Gutvauk, and promptly spit in his face.

The dyrvak laughed and dropped the dagger as Kolin turned to flee towards the city. Pulling a sword from his side, he decapitated Kolin before he moved out of reach. His head rolled a foot or two away before the rest of his body hit the dirt. Laughter and cries of glee sang through the army as Gutvauk raised his bloody sword.

"You thought more dwarves would come, but we caught him sneaking away. No one come. You are alone. Blood will aid in rising of Whispering Snake. Soak the earth, grant him strength." The dyrvak began to stomp the ground in synchronization, but they still did not move forward. Kolin's blood soaked the ground, the snow melting from the heat rolling off his fresh corpse.

Rooster looked around at the men and women beside him; their expressions were infected with terror. He found the other dwarven rangers some feet down, and Obrand's face was a stone wall of rage. If he didn't say something, some would surely flee. Many of them already looked ready to abandon their post, and Rooster raised his crossbow in the air.

"I know you all are frightened, and I know you have no business listening to me. Never before have I seen a town of such discipline, and never before have I met more unyielding, stubborn people. I see in you all the unwillingness to lay down your weapons and let those horrendous beasts pillage your homes, steal your families, and lay claim to your land. Otherwise," he shouted, gesturing towards the Sails District, "you would have been with the others who fled the city early this morn. Your saga will be sung through the ages. Your courage will be stitched into every blow you deal. If you die upon this city's walls, you best make sure the enemy is dealt the same honor."

Rooster wasn't certain if the words held any real impact on their convictions, but no one bolted, their lips quivering from either fear, determination, or the cold. Looking back, Cassius made eye contact with him, his brow furrowed in unspoken confusion. Rooster did not envy Cassius' position, unable to see anything beyond the wall.

The dyrvak did not make any motions to move, so Rooster glanced at Raus before gesturing to Cassius. "May I have a word with my comrade?"

Raus nodded numbly.

Hurrying down the stairs, his face grim, he stepped up to Cassius. "Kolin is dead." It was not news he wished to bring. Kolin had been nothing but kind to them since they'd met before the battle within the dwarven tunnels. Helai was going to be devastated. Rooster recalled Helai and Kolin fighting alongside each other when they aided the dwarves against the rakken.

Cassius said nothing, but he didn't seem surprised. The snow brought a deceitful sense of quiet, the war drums having stopped, and the men and women around them shifted on their feet nervously. Booker paced upon his horse, halting before Rooster and Cassius.

"So we are truly alone then." Booker's face paled, but he refused to look shaken. His men looked to him for morale, and he raised his sword in the air. Rooster didn't have time to tell him that Kolin hadn't been the only one who'd been sent off to warn the dwarves. Jaera's survival was unlikely, but Rooster clung to that thread of hope.

"Do not despair. The sun will shine upon this city again! If we allow our fear to fester, evil has already won. Straighten your backs, tighten your grips on your hilts, and remember that you fight for your home and your family." Booker's voice rang out, a light in the darkness.

A murmur rolled through the soldiers, but they did as Booker commanded. Though many of them still appeared frightened, there was a renewed resolve that trailed through the air. The snow was beginning to collect on the ground, and Rooster feared a dangerous battle if the ground became slick. The cold would slow them down too–already Rooster's joints stiffened and his movements slowed. He could only hope the same would happen with the enemy.

"Have they begun making camp?" Cassius asked. "If they truly mean to wait us out–"

Rooster shook his head. "They're just standing there. Not certain what they're waiting for."

Cassius' gaze flickered with surprise and concern then. "Interesting."

"They are doing something–" Raus shouted from atop the wall. "I do not know what. It appears to be some form of magic."

Rooster gave Cassius one more quick glance before he rushed up the stairs, halting beside Raus.

A flicker of yellow light illuminated the trees near where the forest met the coast, catching Rooster's wandering eye. The trees swayed, bending against an invisible wind even though those surrounding ones did not shake. A groan echoed through the dampened earth as the snow continued to fall and then a portion of the forest appeared to collapse in on itself.

"What the fuck?" Rooster muttered to himself, shaking snowflakes from his eyes as a wailing sound whistled through the air before loud pops and groans echoed through the forest. The dyrvak army began to chant, a low hum that rattled Rooster to the bone. A shudder rolled through him as the spot where the trees had collapsed reformed, the roots of the trees twisting and binding together until a massive deer formed, a mixture of bark and bones. Its head was nothing more than skeletal remains, a skull with antlers that twisted and curled. Its ribcage hung open, a chasm of nothingness where organs should lay. Moss clung to the ribs, and the deer made no noise. Had they called it forth to break the wall? Rooster swallowed thickly. If that was its purpose, Volendam stood no chance.

The deer did not move towards the wall, however. Instead, it trailed towards the ocean, tearing through trees until it submerged itself in water.

"Shit," Raus said behind him. "Wonder where the fuck it's going?"

Rooster could only imagine. If his suspicions were right, it was going to claim the bay. He opened his mouth to reply, but something rumbled beneath his boot. It was apparent enough that Rooster paused but so subtle he thought he might have imagined it.

"What was that?" Raus asked, murdering any doubts he had. "Captain!" she shouted, turning. "Do you feel–"

Rooster covered his head as part of the wall exploded and collapsed. It was far enough that he was not thrown from his feet, but Volendam fell into chaos as rakken spilled from the rubble in a massive wave, their teeth chattering and their weapons thick with vibrant, purple light.

Volendam was officially under siege.

Four

INTOH

I ntoh's heart pounded like it was going to burst through his chest.

Linda was silent as they made their way towards the docks, but Intoh sensed the adrenaline racing off the krok'ida's body. Linda was always eager for a fight; their people had been bred for it. Intoh could not say the same.

"Smell smoke," Linda said, raising their head to sniff the air. The snow continued to fall, and Intoh shook his head, his nose wrinkled in disgust. He hated the smell of smoke. It reminded him of losing Ekalas, his dearest beloved friend who'd died years ago when they attempted to flee Lyvira.

"Come, Linda. Hurry now," he demanded, pressing his fingers to the krok'ida's side and hurrying down the street. He struggled against the cold, wishing for a deeper coat to keep him warm.

"Don't fret, Inka. This chill is but a passing misery when you taste the first sip of forever." Ekalas' voice enveloped Intoh, and he shivered then. Her voice was as clear as a summer's day, but when he looked around, he saw only Linda.

Snow fell harder as if to mock him as they caught sight of the docks. People scurried to their boats with little in their hands, shouting at each other as trepidation strangled the air. One person barreled into Intoh, knocking him onto his back. He hit the ground hard, pain jarring up his spine. Before he could protest, Linda roared angrily and shoved the man straight over the side of the dock and into the water. No one even glanced their way as Linda helped Intoh up. He reached up to zap the man as he breached the surface spluttering and protesting, but he was distracted by someone calling his name.

"Intoh! We feel a stirring in the water. Something big is coming. If you are here, we could use your help." Tidebeard stood near a cluster of his students, all silent. Some of them stared at the sky, snow hitting their faces and disappearing as it melted against the warmth of their skin. Others stared out at sea, their eyes flickering at any signs of movement.

Intoh nodded quickly. "Will help."

"Should go back. Help other Misfits," Linda argued, tugging Intoh away. The rage that blossomed in Intoh unfurled like a snake, and he reached out and smacked Linda's hand, his brow furrowed in protest.

"Should stay here," he hissed. "Can do more *here.*" Linda had been so...combative lately. It annoyed Intoh greatly, as krok'idas were not usually this way. Back in Lyvira, greka were in charge, and krok'ida were used to build their homes and fight their wars. "Should listen to me; know what's best."

Linda growled, a strange noise to someone who might not know Linda as anything other than a human due to their glamor, but Intoh heard the warning tones in it. Linda meant to challenge him. Back home,

Linda would have been exiled or executed for such disobedience. Grekan leaders would not tolerate such behavior.

"Linda–" Intoh began, but something rumbled in the bowels of his belly, a jarring sensation that caused him to turn and look out at the bay. Something was wrong; a current of magic estranged the air from his lungs as he looked to Tidebeard for answers. Water wove through the mage's fingers like strips of silk, graceful and slender movements that coiled around his arms. Several of the students whispered among themselves in hushed tones. Intoh glanced down at the bay and noticed waves forming. It was as if something very large was rattling the earth, and the fear that sang through him shook him to his core.

"Does anyone else see that?" one of the students said, pointing out at the bay. Something moved through the water, pushing it aside as it came towards the docks. Whatever it was, it was massive, and Intoh swallowed the lump of anxiety in his throat as he looked up to Linda, who was buzzing with excitement.

"Big enemy?" Linda guessed, twirling their war hammer.

"I would say so," Tidebeard agreed. "Gaeva, Tor, to me. We must part the bay." Two of the students stepped up to Tidebeard: a woman with long dark locs and thick bones and a small human boy with mouse-like features, slightly pointed ears, and a limp. Upon closer inspection, Intoh realized the boy was absent of a leg, his prosthetic forged by strong bark and metalwork etched in, allowing him to bend at the knee. It was fascinating. A dark thought festered in the back of Intoh's brain: *find a way to take it. Study it. Figure out how it works.* The thought was quelled as Tidebeard, Gaeva, and Tor raised their hands in unison.

The air thickened with moisture as the mages beckoned the water, drawing it to them. It weaved around them in tendrils as the bay began to move, pulling away to create a ravine in the middle. As Tidebeard and the others parted the water, a monstrous deer burst forth, its skull naught but bone. Water snaked through its skeletal rib cage as it reared up, and spores spat from the void where its organs should lay. One organ did remain: a blackened heart beat unsteadily behind the left side of its ribs. If Intoh could get a clear shot at it...

His heart leapt to his throat as he threw his hands out, helping the other mages control the water as the spores trailed towards the docks in a thick cloud. It was like weaving glass; if he didn't handle the magic with care, it would shatter, and the water would slip through his fingers. A wave moved over the spores, and Intoh sighed with relief. *I do not want to think about what would happen should those spores touch us.*

As the spores dissipated, the deer roared, the noise hollow as it traveled through the cavities of its skull. It pierced the air just as a series of explosions sounded off in the distance, shattering Intoh's concentration. He coughed as the water he directed shifted, and his lungs filled momentarily with liquid. Releasing the magic, he threw up water, his hands shaking as he pressed his palms to his knees.

"Linda–" he rasped, switching to Drikotyian, "Can you fight this creature? Get it to expose its heart somehow?"

Linda nodded, setting their war hammer down gingerly next to Intoh. "Keep my hammer safe," they said, then turned to Tidebeard and spoke to him in broken Vilris. "Keep water away." Linda gestured with their hands, pressing them together and then parting them. Jumping off the dock, Linda met the water head-first, their form disappearing beneath the waves.

Rolling out of the wave, they landed on their feet in the ravine and charged the deer. Intoh watched as the deer landed on its front feet and lashed out to gore Linda with its antlers.

Linda jerked to the right, diving back into one of the walls of water. The deer seemed angered by it, snorting and shaking its head as it reared its head up.

"Drop the walls," Intoh shouted to Tidebeard, his mind a flurry of chaos as an idea formed. "Surround deer in water."

"But your friend," Tidebeard said, a bead of sweat rolling down the side of his face.

"Linda will be fine. Really good swimmer. Have to trust me." The beckon of electricity began in his toes, a faint buzzing that shot up his legs. It begged for release, but no. Linda was in the water. If he electrocuted the water now, Linda would be harmed. Perhaps if he localized the magic to the deer itself, he could stun it long enough for Linda to get to it. He'd never been able to focus his magic on one thing before, but he had to try.

Waves crashed around the deer as the snow overhead fell harder. Cold seeped into Intoh's fingers, and he shuddered against the chill, but he couldn't imagine how cold it was in the water. He worried if it was perhaps too cold for the krok'ida. Seconds passed and there was still no sign of Linda as the deer turned its attention to those on the dock.

Linda, where are you?

Five

CASSIUS

P anic erupted when the wall collapsed and rakken poured through the city. They had been prepared to fight the dyrvak, but the appearance of rakken shattered the resolve of those guarding the front gate, and several men bolted immediately, their fear drenching the air with an unpleasant stench.

"Do not falter!" he shouted among the plethora of bodies pressing against him. "If you do, we are already lost." Their frightened heartbeats cascaded like a wave over Cassius, and the rush of adrenaline sent his bloodlust into a frenzy, vying for control. His knightly training kicked in and the bloodlust subsided slightly; he'd fought in enough battles to swim through the temptation of blood.

"Yes-yes, a Chosen! Sneak-scamper. Hurry-*hurry*. Must take him to the Whispered One." A rakken appeared in front of him, its tooth chipped and its laughter quick and breathless. Its fur was matted with dried blood, and its breath was heavy as it curled in the air. Cassius struggled not to gag as the stench reached him, but he cut down the rakken with ease, falling into a familiar pattern from when he'd fought them in the mountains. Two more appeared in its place the moment the body fell.

He realized of all the beasts and men he'd fought in his long life, he enjoyed fighting the rakken the least. They were too rash, too chaotic, too unpredictable. They fought with little honor, throwing themselves against their enemies with little regard for their own lives. He cut through them like butter, so much so his sword arm began to ache, and his vision tunneled to the next rakken with gnashing teeth and curdling breath.

"Die-die!" One shouted, throwing himself against Cassius. His fur was wet and matted, his breath coming out in quick waves, and Cassius scrambled to grab the back of the rakken's rotten leather armor to pry him away.

He stumbled into a soldier as the rakken raised a dagger, swinging it towards Cassius' side, but the impact of hitting the soldier threw him off guard, and the dagger hit Cassius' armor.

He had no time for apologies as he pulled the rakken free, his sword piercing the rakken through the eye. He turned, but the soldier was already overcome by rakken, his face disappearing beneath their feet.

He lost count of how many rakken he killed. He hadn't even seen a dyrvak yet, which only made the situation dire given how few soldiers remained to hold the line. Many were falling to the persistent stream of rakken, their cries of terror and pain silenced as the giant rats feasted on their flesh.

A soldier grabbed Cassius' arm, his eyes wild with fear. A rakken had amputated his leg at the knee, and Cassius did gag then, the smell of blood overwhelming him.

"Please," the soldier begged.

Cassius didn't get a chance to respond as blood spurted from the soldier's mouth, spraying across the vampire's face. A fleck of blood hit his lips, and Cassius pushed him away, his gaze hardening. His eyes flickered in and out of focus as he wrangled with his bloodlust, but he'd spent nearly a century training to control it. He felt his cheeks sink in, his fangs brush against his bottom lip, and he growled in frustration, curling his fingers over the handle of his shield to ground him. Lucky for him, the blood of the dyrvak and rakken did not call to him, and it helped curb the stench of humanity.

The front gate was a bloodbath. The dyrvak had pushed forward and joined the fight, and while the soldiers of Volendam were holding their ground, it was a losing battle. These dyrvak were massive, their waists where they turned from elk to human resting just above Cassius' head.

A person screamed beside him, and when he turned, they were not staring at the oncoming army as the others did. Rather, they stared at *him* with an open jaw and their eyes rolling in terror.

"Monster," they screamed, pointing. "Vampire!" Scrambling backwards, they hit the back of their fellow soldier, who turned around and yelled at them. Both were cut down by a dyrvak as Cassius forced his illusion to return, his heart thundering in his ears. His cheeks filled back out; his fangs tucked back behind the appearance of mere human canines. It was difficult. He was hungry. His decay demanded to show itself, but he managed, swallowing thickly. The soldiers that had turned at the other's shouting saw nothing but a knight of White Dawn, a foreigner protecting their home alongside them.

He gripped his sword, exhaling slowly, and threw himself back into the fight.

"Cassius," Rooster shouted from above. Cassius looked at Rooster on the stairs; his hair was a wild mess from the snow melting. He was covered in blood and a thick yellow substance, his eyes rich with adrenaline.

"We need to take care of that," he said, pointing at the hole in the wall. It was massive. Dyrvak poured through, thundering over the rubble of the wall, their swords and spears brandished high over their heads as they shouted in war chants. The guardsmen of Volendam defended, but they were being pushed back and slaughtered.

"Can you make it to me?" Cassius shouted back, shoving a rakken away with the bash of his shield. A crackling energy filled the air as a large purple light shot through the snowfall and hit one of the buildings behind Cassius. It exploded into purple flames. He blanched from the heat as it peeled off the canals and threatened to blister his skin. A hiss echoed against his cheeks as he raised his sword and slew another rakken that approached.

Rooster fought his way down the stairs, but Cassius feared the turn of the tide as dyrvak and rakken threatened to overcome the front line of defense. With every enemy he slayed, three more replaced them. The enemies between him and Rooster were far too great.

"Watch out!" Helai's voice called out from behind him. When he turned, she appeared, her eyes trained on the fighting. She held a round vial of swirling orange mist in one hand, and the other clung to an unfamiliar hunting knife.

They locked eyes, and Cassius grabbed the nearest soldier by the arm, dragging him away with him as Helai threw the orb in her hand. He'd seen the danger she wielded when she threw explosives and did not care to be in the range of it again.

The orb hit the ground in the middle of the enemy and exploded. Everything within a fifteen-foot vicinity died, blown apart by the blast. The enemies wounded were picked off by archers with ease, and Rooster finally approached, his eyes wild.

"It's a shit show we've found ourselves in," Rooster said, slinging the bow he carried across his back and unsheathing the sword at his side. The southern gate had fallen, and Cassius grimaced as the brand on his back burned.

"We have no choice but to retreat. We cannot fall here," Cassius said, turning to the soldier he'd saved from Helai's explosive. "Find your captain. Tell him to retreat to the Sails District. This gate is lost."

The soldier complied without question, scrambling off towards Booker as he rode by shouting commands and slaughtering foes from a top his steed. Booker deflected the sword of a massive dyrvak with swirling war paint on its face and chest. It was much larger than the other dyrvak, and its war paint glowed yellow as it opened its mouth. Spores poured from its lips, hitting him in the face. Just before the soldier Cassius had sent reached him, the spores sank into Booker's cheeks, and his screams cascaded over the battlefield as his skin melted from the bone. He was dead in under a minute. Cassius had never seen a dyrvak do something like that, and he stilled, staring as Booker's body ate away at itself.

Cassius turned away. No time to mourn the dead in the heart of battle.

He caught Helai's and Rooster's shocked expressions. "We should fight our way to the docks. It is likely Linda and Intoh require our help. This gate has fallen, and we need to retreat." His training kept his hand and mind steady as they fought their way through the enemy, keeping each other's backs protected.

"Retreat," he called out as they fled down the street. "Retreat to the docks!"

Six

LINDA

L inda's eyes flickered against the adjustment to water, and they twisted the ring on their finger, shedding the illusion on their skin. Their bones cracked, but no pain was felt as they shaped and reformed, their tail shooting out from their tailbone. Their face stretched and elongated, forming their crocodilian snout, and soon they were more lizard than man. It felt good to be in their true form. Their tail oriented them as they shot through the water, and the water carried them towards the deer as the ravine the mages had made began to disappear. Linda didn't sense any lifeforms in the water, and they were thankful for that. The deer would be enough to deal with.

The krok'ida slunk through the water in hopes of finding the right course of attack. They needed to move quickly; they had faith that Intoh would wield what magic he needed to keep himself alive, but Linda wasn't certain they knew what the deer was capable of.

Linda flinched to the side as a cloven foot shot through the water, threatening to come down on their back. Despite the frigid temperatures, Linda was too quick for it to make contact, and Linda used their hidden state to their advantage, latching onto the deer's leg with their teeth. They almost immediately regretted it as the deer's blood pooled into their mouth.

The deer's scream was heard even underwater, and it lashed its foot around, attempting to kick Linda off. The water became a blur of bubbles and kicked up dirt from the bottom, but Linda refused to let go, sinking their teeth in further. The blood that flooded their mouth was sickeningly sweet and thick like sap, and Linda pulled away, veering towards the other leg. If they could get it to rear up again, perhaps its heart would be exposed long enough for Intoh to finish it off.

A haunting melody slipped through the water, etched with the soft scratching of some grotesque sea creature. Several small forms swam just out of sight, cloaked by the murkiness, but Linda recognized them from the last time they'd hunted in the water. Mermaids. Where were they when Linda first entered the water? They could not recall sensing them before, and their ability to remain silent in the water was troublesome.

One shot past Linda's tail, and the krok'ida flicked it away as it screeched. The mermaids zipped in and out of sight, their appearances far more grotesque, their mutations to fish far more along than they'd been before. A vibrant purple glow flickered through the water with the mermaids, and large chunks of something were burrowed into their scales.

Linda lashed around as a mermaid swam by and grabbed it by their teeth. Since the mermaid incident where the mermaids kidnapped Cassius and Felix, Linda's hatred for them had flourished.

The mermaid screeched as it struggled, its blood seeping through Linda's teeth. It tasted rotten and foul as it hit Linda's tongue, but they refused to relent until the mermaid stopped struggling.

Another mermaid lashed out at Linda, dragging a sharp piece of draugmin across their side, and Linda rolled away, attempting to ignore the smart of pain that came from the wound. The pain was different, sharp and so warm it was almost cold. It was accompanied by a fierce burning and a surge of power that urged Linda forward in the water.

Dirt kicked up from the bottom of the bay as the deer stepped forward. Linda dug their claws into the deer's leg and used it to climb. The trek was perilous and tedious, but Linda managed, climbing until they were out of the water and they had made it onto the deer's back. They took a moment to study their wound. It was jagged but shallow, and Linda was convinced it would be healed in no time due to a krok'ida's quick regeneration. Still, a faint, purple glow pulsed at the wound's edge, and as Linda stared at it, it hummed, making them dizzy with an untapped strength. Perhaps they could use whatever strength was granted to them to get the deer to rear up.

The deer moved slowly, as if the water fought against it. If it knew Linda was on its back, it did not react, its attention drawn to the docks where the mages of the college were weaving water as if they were snakes weaving through the chilly breeze. Linda fell forward, using their claws to dig into the deer's back as they inched forward. If they could just find a wound or a place to pierce through the hard, bark-like skin...

"Intoh, now," Linda shouted, piercing the deer's back with their claws and dragging them through the bark-like skin as they slid down.

The deer screamed and reared back, and Linda used that moment to pull away, diving off the back of the deer as Intoh's lightning struck it in the chest. It was jarring, the cold of the water as it hit Linda again, and they braced themself as they kicked off the bottom of the bay, twisting their ring back, transforming them into a human just before they reached the surface. If the mermaids remained, they did not bother Linda again; their silence was worrisome. It made Linda more eager to reach land.

Linda's head breached the water as the deer's body toppled. As lethargy from the cold dug in, their eyes drooped in exhaustion. The deer was dead. Linda couldn't hear the steady pounding of its heartbeat anymore, which was a relief. For the first time in their life, Linda wanted nothing more than to be out of the water. Diving down, they swam to shore.

As Linda reached the docks, they felt the pull of the ocean behind them, like the bay was being disturbed. Tidebeard and several of his students helped Linda onto the docks, and they shivered violently against the cold as one of the students gasped, their eyes trained behind Linda.

"What—" Linda started to say, disrupted by a blast of hot air that hit their back as something burst out of the water. They turned as the deer rose from the water. It was still very much alive as its heart beat once more in its chest, and it roared, the scream high-pitched as it pierced the air.

"Must have just stunned it," Intoh said, his face pinched from shock.

"Formations. We must not let it get any closer," Tidebeard shouted. Both of his hands were raised, and his dark skin contrasted against the snow as he turned to his students. "Form a line. Keep it pressured to stay in the middle of the bay. Maintain your breathing and concentration—do not let your lungs fill with water. We do not have room for error."

"Must go," Intoh said, glancing Linda's way and gesturing to Linda's war hammer on the ground. "Must help."

Linda nodded. They understood. The air was thick with the stench of blood as the horns of the enemy called out through the city. They would keep the approaching enemy from disrupting the mages as they worked on killing the deer, once and for all.

They're coming.

Linda braced against the cold as they reached down and gripped their war hammer tightly.

Let them come.

"Linda!" Cassius' voice carried out through the streets as Linda, against their better judgment, turned their back to the giant corpse of the deer that rose out of the bay. They had to trust Intoh and the other magic wielders were capable of dealing with it as Cassius, Rooster, and Helai ran down the street, followed by a mixture of Volendam's soldiers and the enemy.

It wasn't only dyrvak that thundered down the streets, cutting down everything in their path. Rakken followed in waves, pouring over each other as they ripped through the streets. There would be no reprieve, no time to talk or prepare as Cassius turned to block a sword from cutting into Rooster's back.

"What the fuck is that?" Helai asked as she reached Linda's side.

"Big deer. Killed it once. Didn't work," Linda shouted, raising their war hammer. "Fight with honor!"

Cassius twisted around as Linda met him at his side. The curve of a smile tucked away behind his beard as he sliced through a dyrvak, granting a few archers and Rooster ample time to slip behind him towards the buildings. "By the blood of the dragon!"

Linda wasn't certain what he meant, but Cassius spoke it with such conviction that Linda's belly filled with warmth and exhilaration. Fighting at Cassius' side was always an honor; the vampire fought valiantly, much more honorably than Linda, who tended to swing their hammer with little care where it landed, so long as the battle was won.

They fought side by side so long Linda's arms ached, stiffened by the cold. Where Cassius faltered, Linda was right there to grant him protection, flanking his side so that the enemy could not find a way to slip through. Volendam's soldiers fought as best they could around them, but they were being cut down too quickly.

At one point, Linda turned to see that despite the best effort of the mages, the deer had reached the docks. Several of the mages were dead, eaten away to the bone by some sort of magic. Intoh shot it with lightning bolts, but that only seemed to anger the deer as it reared back.

"Intoh," Linda shouted. "Must go," they said to Cassius.

"Go. I have this," Cassius said, raising his shield to block a rakken's attack.

Linda charged across the street, cutting dyrvak and rakken down with sweeps of *Volroth*. They were used to fighting with cold, hard, brute force, with no emotion to cloud their judgment. They felt a flicker of it now, of a budding seed of emotion in their belly, blossoming into a panic that fueled their rage. They weren't cutting through the enemy fast enough, their desperation making them sloppy.

They didn't see the body of a fallen soldier until they'd tripped over it. They went down hard on their shoulder, the breath taken from their lungs as their hammer remained tight in their grasp.

Get up, they thought, their heartbeat heavy in their ears.

They forced themself to their feet as a small herd of dyrvak galloped around their rising form, their swords raised and their faces stitched with vicious smiles. Linda let out a roar as the dyrvak moved to strike, refusing to despair even though they were horribly outnumbered.

One of the dyrvak howled in pain as they collapsed, and Velius stood before the fallen dyrvak, his face twisted in rage.

"Come on, Linda. *Volroth* hasn't claimed nearly enough lives for you to be done yet," Velius shouted, blocking another dyrvak's attack with his shield.

"Velius?" Linda asked, shocked. They had not expected to see him here but had no time to question it. His armor gleamed, a mixture of plate and leather, and behind him was a large unit of eldrasi soldiers with long poles carved with sharp blades. They pushed up to the docks and lashed out with their magic, cutting down any of the enemies that slipped through to aid the deer at the water's edge. Vines shot from their fingers, lashing out from their line to shield the mages from the deer. The deer crashed into the barrier and the eldrasi held strong, wielding the vines so that they climbed the deer and pulled it down against the bay.

The deer's screams cried out as the vines grew relentlessly against its skin, but Linda was forced to turn away as they lunged at a dyrvak that attempted to stab at Velius while he was distracted.

The fighting resumed full force as Linda fought with Velius effortlessly. He was a skilled soldier with a hammer, his shield nearly the length of him which made him nearly invulnerable to attack. Linda flanked his side, keeping his fighting arm free with the merciless nature of *Volroth* as the dyrvak and rakken spilled into the street, pushing them back towards the cliffside.

The deer had disappeared once more beneath the water of the bay, pulled to the depths by the eldrasi's magic with the help of the force of the mage college. The deer did not reappear again, even as the water from the bay stilled, and Linda flexed their fingers around *Volroth* and prepared for another wave of attack.

Seven

CASSIUS

C assius' breath curled in front of him as rakken and dyrvak alike charged the docks. The snow had stopped falling, but the screams of the dying and dead rang through Cassius' ears as he raised his sword. Linda charged the enemy, pushing aside a dyrvak's sword and slamming their hammer into its stomach. A sickening crunch rippled through the air as blood shot out of the dyrvak's mouth, and arrows flew over Cassius' head as Rooster shouted orders from his balcony.

A unit of rakken approached Cassius, but he'd fought worse and cut them down with ease. There was no time to dwell or think as more replaced the dead. Cassius' arms were heavy from swinging his sword all day and his bloodlust demanded sustenance, but he couldn't think about either now. Not when they were being overwhelmed by enemies.

Something slammed into him, throwing him off balance. His sword flung from his hand, and he hit the ground hard, the cold biting into his entire right side as he met the snow. The movement was just enough to trigger a memory, and suddenly he was a boy no older than seven. The snow was replaced with the cold marble of the courtyard cradled in the middle of his family home in Verenzia, and the pain from falling sang in the joints of his wrists.

"Get up." His father's voice was accompanied by a sharp pain that lashed across his back where the wooden stick his father held made contact. Cassius whimpered, tears threatening the corners of his eyes, but he kept them from falling. The last time his father had seen him cry, he'd been sent to bed without supper.

Shuffling back to his feet, he grabbed his sword where it had fallen. It wasn't fair. The blade was too heavy in his hands, too large for a child as small as him. His brother stood in front of him, slender for his age of twelve, but the sword fit in his grasp. Blood ran down Cassius' cheek from the cut Markus had inflicted on him; their father did not believe in practicing with wooden swords, and Cassius had suffered many wounds from such training.

"Again," Dominic Antonia commanded, and so began their training anew.

A low cry peeled from Cassius' lips as he shot forward, but his intentions were too clear, and Markus parried the sword with ease, knocking Cassius off balance and shoving him to the floor. The impact was more painful than before, and Cassius cried out, using Markus' temporary concern as leverage to barrel forward, tackling him at the knees. He brought Markus down with him, and soon they were tangled against each other, their swords forgotten on the ground as they attempted to achieve the upper hand. Cassius' tiny fist made contact with Markus' eye at the same moment Markus' fingers raked over Cassius' uninjured cheek hard enough to draw blood.

"Enough." Dominic's command willed immediate obedience and Cassius rolled away from Markus before he could be struck again, forcing himself to his feet to stand with his hands clasped behind his back. He did not look his father in the eye; Dominic would command it if that was what he wanted.

Under his lashes, he snuck a glance at his older brother. With a mixture of satisfaction and guilt, he noticed Markus' eye had already begun to bruise and his lower lip was swollen.

"Markus, go and find your mother. Tell her you will be going to bed without dinner, and since you're keen on disappointing both parents today, tell your mother you will be cleaning out the stables tonight." Even looking down, Cassius felt the hard, challenging stare of their father begging Markus to argue.

No such argument came. Just the quick shuffle of feet, the sound of a door opening and shutting, and then silence. The silence drenched the air, thickened like sand, and strangled the resolve from Cassius' small, impatient mind.

Don't look up. Don't look up. Don't look up.

Just as temptation nearly guided him to trouble, Dominic spoke. "Look at me."

Cassius' face shot up. The blood was hot and sticky on his cheeks, but he was too afraid to wipe it away; there was no telling what would anger Dominic Antonia.

"You did well today." The praise came with no warning, and Cassius couldn't help the surprise that flickered across his small features. His father never gave compliments. "You need to learn to loosen your legs and to feign movements so your opponent does not know what you're planning, but you will make a fine soldier someday, Cassius. I have little hope for your brother, but you? You will be my greatest achievement." He reached out, and Cassius suppressed a flinch.

Instead of hitting him, Dominic rested a gentle hand on Cassius' shoulder. It felt almost akin to a hug, and Cassius' heart squeezed painfully. How desperately he longed for the affection of his father.

"If they knock you down, fight as if Khoros' dogs bite at your heels."

Cassius gasped as Linda's voice pulled him from the memory.

"Must get up!" They shouted, standing in front of him as they defended him from the enemy. His head spun in a disoriented state as he struggled to pull himself out of the memory. He hadn't thought about his childhood for a long time. Striking the ground in such a way must have triggered it. His father would have scoffed at such weakness; guilt burned inside Cassius, thick with shame.

Grinding his teeth together, he searched through the mud and snow until he found his sword. Tugging his shield close, he forced himself to his feet, planting them in the ground as he prepared to re-enter the battle.

"Thank you," he said to Linda.

They grunted in response as they brought their hammer down from over their head, slamming it against a rakken that had fallen to the ground.

Cassius didn't know how many he killed as he fell back into the pattern with ease. The memory of training with Markus rattled him, and he suffered a few shallow injuries due to his negligence, but it was nothing compared to the bloodshed surrounding him. He lost count of how many soldiers died. Their blood was overpowering, and their heartbeats heightened in their adrenaline, excitement, and fear. At one point, Helai threw a bomb overhead, the explosion hitting a group of rakken off on Cassius' left. It sent parts of rakken flying, their blood dark as it splattered against the snow and the side of buildings. It was a massacre.

For a time, they held the enemy back with ease. The rakken continued to fight with overwhelming numbers, the dyrvak in strategic but predictable ways. Shadowy hands rose out of the ground as Helai wove darkness through her hands, pulling rakken against the ground so she could kill them quickly and efficiently. Cassius wasn't sure when she'd left the safety of the balcony to join the fighting on the streets. Intoh electrocuted a dyrvak that rushed Cassius, and the smell made Cassius' eyes water.

The air was ripe with death as the sound of metal clashing together rang in Cassius' ears. The dyrvak and rakken blood overpowered the stench of humanity, and he was able to keep his blood cravings under control as he fought his way towards Linda. He had no desire to taste the blood of the enemy.

Linda swung their hammer in a wide sweep. One rakken jumped out of the way at the last minute, its teeth clashing together in rapid succession as it hissed. Drool oozed from its mouth as it shouted at Linda in a harsh tongue, a quick chattering of words that were silenced the moment Cassius cut its head from its shoulders.

"Had it," Linda protested. "Count as mine."

Cassius refrained from the urge to roll his eyes as he ran his sword through a rakken and dodged another's attack. "It does not matter, Linda, so long as the fighting is won."

Linda snorted. "No fun."

Cassius frowned but said nothing. There was nothing fun about war. He'd seen the darker side of battle, of those who'd starved in cities surrounded by the enemy, of friends who'd lay dying on the battlefield, begging for mercy.

A Volendam soldier fell against him, and as Cassius pushed him off, he noticed the man had lost an arm, severed at the elbow, and Cassius' head spun from the amount of blood that soaked the air. His fangs grated against his gums, begging to descend. He swallowed as the enemy forced him to fight against the cliffside as Linda charged into a group of rakken near Velius, their hisses of protest quickly silenced.

The cold remained vigilant as Cassius' fingers threatened to stiffen against the hilt of his sword. He turned, locking eyes with a dyrvak. It wore the skull of a deer over its human-like face. Three jagged lines were painted over its bare chest with dark red paint, and it wielded a flail, its fingers curled around the wooden handle as the massive metal ball covered in spikes hung from its chain.

"Weakness," the dyrvak uttered. Its words curled almost seductively against the cusp of Cassius' ear as the dyrvak stared at him and raised its flail. "Rhavna will rise, and her rage will consume this vile place." The dyrvak charged, and Cassius raised his shield and planted his feet. He did not have time to question who Rhavna was as the flail swung, hitting Cassius' shield. Cassius' arm ached as the shock of the collision rang through his bones, but he grunted and shoved back, pushing the dyrvak away. Up close, Cassius realized it wasn't paint that covered the dyrvak's chest. It was dried blood.

Pain pierced his head so fiercely that white popped into his vision. Quiet whispering scratched at the back of his mind in a low language Cassius didn't recognize. It invaded his mind without mercy and provided just enough hesitation on Cassius' part for the dyrvak to strike.

The black of its eyes filled Cassius' vision as the flail rose.

I do not want to die, he thought, but the flail swung regardless.

Eight

HELAI

Helai exhaled sharply as she turned on her heel and narrowly avoided the rapid slashing of a rakken's blade. She threw her hands up and created a shield of shadow that stopped the dagger from piercing her shoulder and twisted, prying the blade from the rakken's grasp. The shadows crept up her spine like a spider forging its web, and she suppressed the urge to shudder as she tightened her other hand into a fist. A shadow, inky black, formed into fingers that curled around the rakken's throat and squeezed until the rakken went limp.

It went that way, for a time. The enemies had them pinned up against the docks and cliffside, forced to make their final stand in the falling city. Rooster had pushed himself up into the buildings overlooking the street that lined the docks, his calls often followed by a volley of arrows. It was genius really; the rakken could make it through the buildings without too much trouble, perhaps, but the dyrvak would have difficulty climbing the stairs. The archers could fight without fear of being cut down from behind.

As Helai lashed out again with her magic, she inhaled sharply. The shadowy smoke of her magic filled her lungs and she coughed, the corners of her eyes pricked with tears as her chest swelled in panic. *A warning*. Magical backlash took no prisoners and seldom gave more than one warning. She'd seem Intoh toe the edge of it more often than anyone she'd met and knew the muscle in their chest would only take so much abuse before it burst unless granted time to rest.

A rakken crashed into her, the stench from its open mouth wafting over her. She gagged, her lungs squeezing painfully as she was shoved to the ground. Dyrvak ran by, their cries lost in the sounds of battle as they trampled across the road.

"Ah yes. Yes-yes! Man-filth." A black paw pressed down on Helai's wrist as she scrambled, reaching up to use her magic despite her body screaming at her not to. She cried out, her pain echoing against the snow as the rakken stood above her. Its front teeth were bucked and chipped, its shallow breath curling in front of its lips in the cold. Its eyes were hidden behind a hood as it reached down. Purple sores dotted its arm and stained its fur. Wrapping a paw around Helai's throat, it lifted her off her feet with a smile. "Greet-run to your path-walk of the Chosen."

The air cut off from her lungs so quickly that her mind reeled, and she blindly fumbled at her waist for any of her daggers strapped to her sides. The rakken opened its mouth in some sick amusement as it ran a dagger through her waist. The blade burned white hot as it tore through her skin.

Her fingers grazed a hilt, and she did not hold back, burying it into the rakken's side. She pulled it back out, ignoring the shot of blood that hit her fingers, then sank it back into the rat's flesh. And again. And again, until the rakken dropped her, flinching away as it howled in pain. An arrow pierced it through the eye, and Helai welcomed the thrum of pain that jostled her when she hit the ground, her fingers digging into the snow as she looked down at the dagger in her hand. It was the dagger Drithan had given her.

Off in the distance, the low call of a horn sounded, echoing off the buildings. It did not sound the same as the one the dyrvak had used to rally its forces but rather a low rumble that sank into the earth. The fighting did not pause, but Helai's head rose in hope as her fingers went to her side, touching the hilt of the dagger still in her waist. She hissed as pain shot through her abdomen, and she left the blade alone. *Don't want to bleed out before I can find aid*, she thought, dodging underneath the swing of a dyrvak's sword and sliding her dagger across its leg. As it tumbled, she stabbed her blade through its eye, crying out as the movement sent pain coursing through her wound. The squelching sound of the dagger leaving the dyrvak's skull was sickening, and Helai's stomach rolled as she threatened to be overwhelmed, seen as an easy target due to her injury. She raised her blade to defend herself as a sea of rakken moved to disarm her...

The horn call sounded again, this time much louder. The fighting seemed to pause, and Helai's head rang with familiarity. She'd heard that call before.

A sea of purple and silver–Stoneheart's colors–lined the streets of the docks. They poured through the city with grace, their hardy steps thundering across the snow as they moved to offer aid. Obrand, the head of the dwarven rangers, led the charge, his beard braided neatly down his armor to keep it out of the way as he swung an axe, cleaving a rakken's arm in two before beheading it. He shouted to his men in Alkazed as they moved over the estate grounds. The dyrvak were able to hold their ground, stomping the dirty snow beneath their feet as they screamed. For a terrifying moment, Helai did not think their reinforcements would matter. Frantically, she searched for Drithan among the sea of dwarves.

If they were to be overwhelmed, she wanted to stare into the comfort of his honey-brown eyes one last time. The gods mocked her plea for she did not find him in the sea of fighting, so she did what she could while wounded, fighting those who fell upon her with their gnashing teeth or sharp blades.

Dalnor give me strength, she cried out silently, itching with shadowy magic as she thought about her Ghosts. Masika, their assassin, would have had everything under control, her unwavering devotion to Jaleer, Shoma's most worshiped god before Qevayla, granting her with unyielding grace. And Massoud? A master illusionist: no one would have been able to touch him. Little Hosni might have struggled, but he and Ehsan worked together like two lost in the desert desperate for water. Aryan would have had the situation handled with his blades, and Kílae? The only eldrasi in their group would have called upon his earthly magic to his aid. She missed her Ghosts so fiercely at this moment that it gave her the determination to carry on.

For them alone.

A dyrvak rushed past, and Helai was only just able to dodge out of the way as the creature slammed into Cassius, a flail easily the size of a small barrel held in its right hand. Cassius dodged the flail, and Helai's eyes flickered to Velius in terror as he attempted to fight his way to Cassius' side. He was too overwhelmed by rakken, and Cassius' shield shattered as the dryvak pushed Cassius back into an alleyway at the end of the street. Using the shadows, Helai beckoned her magic, using it to slip around and under the enemy attacks. A bead of sweat rolled down her forehead from the magical use coupled with the wound at her side, but she ignored it as she made it to the alleyway.

Helai cried out as the flail swung, slamming into the cliffside and prying rock loose. It fell in droves around Cassius, who rose his arms to cover his head.

The dyrvak used it to swing the flail again, ramming it into Cassius' chest. Helai could hear the bone shatter from where he stood as Cassius' chest caved in. Blood flew from the vampire's mouth as he collapsed, his gaze mingled with shock.

Helai moved forward, but Linda was quicker.

Helai hadn't even seen the krok'ida at first. One moment there was no one behind Helai, and then the next moment Linda was there in their krok'ida form, rising with their war hammer held high.

"*Salsoushi malora,*" Helai uttered into her hand, throwing it out to cause a gust of shadow. It enveloped Linda as they swung their war hammer and disappeared into the alleyway. Helai's brow furrowed as she screamed, the pain from her wound setting in. She did not think anyone of note saw Linda in their krok'ida form, but Helai shrouded them in darkness anyway. Blood shot out of the darkness in all directions, staining the surrounding snow, and the enemy's resolve shattered like glass as Linda walked out of the shadow, the head of the dyrvak in their hand.

Raising it up, Linda shouted, a deep guttural sound that shook Helai's core and rattled her bones. The clanking of metal did not falter as the people of Volendam and the dwarves of the Spine Mountain pushed the enemy back, their fervor renewed. There were so many dwarves that their reinforcements turned the tide of battle, and the fleeing rakken were killed beneath their hammers. The dyrvak's resolve held, and every last one fought until their dying breath.

Helai sagged in relief as the last of the enemy fell, her knees hitting the ground.

The siege of Volendam had been won.

Nine

ROOSTER

hick with the stench of blood and smoke, Rooster traversed down the building into the street, his hands still shaking from battle. Exhaustion shook him to his core, but he would have killed a hundred more rats in order to have a drink.

"Rooster." Helai's voice was quiet as she joined him, her brow threaded with worry. A hand gripped her side, her breath coming out in shallow gasps as red blossomed from a wound in her midsection. The dagger remained inside her, and despite her injuries, Rooster was relieved to see her alive. "Please tell me you are uninjured."

"I am," Rooster confirmed, turning to her. "Intoh should tend to your wound." A gentle feeling urged him to reach out, his fingertips tingling with magic. Perhaps he'd known healing magic before he'd lost his memories, but nervousness stayed his hand. Healing magic was as fickle as fire;

one wrong move and the energy could betray him, overcorrecting the injury or worsening it. He did not want to cause further harm to Helai or have a third arm grow from her side, so he refrained.

Helai shook her head. "Rooster..." Her face was forlorn, her expression ravaged with grief. "I think Cassius–" A sob ripped through her.

Rooster's face paled. All screams from his body for rest were ignored. "Where?" he asked. Anxiety curdled in the pits of his belly as Helai nodded and gestured down the street, towards the end of the docks.

"Just over there, beyond that building."

Velius approached them silently, his face pale. Yellow blood wept from a wound on his head, and he held his hammer loosely in his hand. "Did anyone see Cassius—?" he asked, his eyes flickering to Helai.

"The dyrvak backed him into the alley, just there," Helai said, her hand shaking as she pointed. "I got Intoh, but I think..." she trailed off, her lips pursed as tears danced at the corner of her eyes.

The streets were a desolation of bodies as they rushed towards the alleyway. Somewhere off to Rooster's right, a soft moan echoed, followed quickly by another's sharp plea for mercy. A dying man reached a hand out to Rooster, a sword through his belly. How he was still alive was some cruel miracle, and Helai pulled Rooster on before he could react. Helai locked eyes with him, and they said nothing as they approached the building and turned the corner, into an alleyway nestled up against the cliffside.

Helai inhaled sharply beside him, and as his gaze followed hers, his heart sank.

Intoh wove his hands over Cassius, who was propped up against the wall of a cliff. A massacre of dead rakken and dyrvak surrounded him, pieces of them scattered about as blood stained the snow red. They had not died without a fight, though, as Cassius' armor was tinged dark, and his eyes were glossy. A staggered breath rose in his chest, and Rooster took some relief knowing he was not yet lost.

"No, no-no," Intoh muttered to himself as sweat dripped from his brow. He was in his human form rather than his small, reptilian form, and his cheeks and nose were pink from the cold. "Urge you to stay back. Dying vampire, makes humans look tasty." He held up a halting hand as Helai moved forward, forcing her to stop. A low guttural hiss sounded behind them, and Rooster turned as Linda rose out of the water in their true form, a half-eaten dyrvak beside them. Shaking the water from their scales, they approached, raising their snout and sniffing deeply.

"Smell rotten," they complained, edging nearer. "Always dying."

Velius inhaled sharply beside him. "I saw the dyrvak go after him, but the weight of the enemy was too much." His back straightened. "I left my healer aboard the Firebrand. I'm nearly certain he can be of aid." He rested a hand on Rooster's shoulder before turning on his heel and hurrying away.

Intoh glanced up.

"Need to find dying one. Need their blood. Must speed up his healing."

Rooster's stomach twisted at the thought, but Intoh was right. Better to use the last of a dying man's life to save Cassius'. His thoughts turned to the man they'd just passed.

"Helai has been injured too," Rooster said to Intoh as he retreated towards where the dying man had been lying.

"I'm fine," Helai said to Intoh as Rooster left. "I'd never forgive myself if your heart burst because of me. Use what magic you can on Cassius."

Their voices quieted as Rooster moved out of earshot. Now that the adrenaline from the battle was wearing off, Rooster shivered, the cold hitting him harder than the fight had. Bloodshed never got any easier, even if it did not shock him anymore.

"Sire." The soft voice of the dying man called out to Rooster. He lay in a blanket of snow, tinged red as he bled out on the ground. His breath came out shallow and ragged, and he reached out to Rooster, his expression mingled with desperation and fear. "Please–"

Rooster knelt. If he could get him to his feet…perhaps he could be of use before he passed.

"I can ease your discomfort, but I need you to come with me," Rooster said, his voice gentle. A flicker of guilt tugged at him, but he ignored it, quelled it by the knowledge that Cassius' life was more important to him. The vampire's life could be saved, but this soldier's life was already lost.

The soldier coughed, splattering blood across the ground. He cried out as he attempted to move. "I am sorry, sire. I cannot." The man began to cry. "I cannot feel my legs."

Rooster pursed his lips together and refused his desire to end the man's suffering. Instead, he turned and hurried back to find Linda. "I need your help carrying this man to Cassius," he explained.

Linda nodded, ambling after Rooster as they returned to the man. Linda twisted their ring, shifting into their human form, and the soldier did not react to them as he was lifted off the ground. His tears clung like little crystals of glass to his cheeks, and his eyes had begun to glaze over. He was going to die soon.

They made it back to the others as Intoh pulled away. Cassius looked better than he had when Rooster had left them. He was still unconscious, but his chest was no longer caved in, and his nostrils flared as Linda pulled the man from their shoulder and rested him on the ground next to Cassius.

"Vampire should be able to feed himself. Must get away, might get ravenous," Intoh said, looking at Helai. "Have just enough strength to heal you. Must rest after. Must sleep. Cannot see well." His breath came out in quick bursts, and his hands shook violently as a trail of blue blood dried below his nose, but he turned to Helai and ignored her protests, waving a hand over her blood-soaked shirt. Helai cried out and gritted her teeth as she pulled the blade from her side. It barely had a chance to bleed before Intoh closed it up with magic.

Rooster indulged in Intoh's warning, hurrying away as Cassius' eyes shot open, red on black. He hissed, his fangs extending as he grabbed the dying soldier and pressed his lips to his neck. The man did not struggle and was dead before too long.

Still, he drank until he couldn't anymore, leaning over the soldier's corpse and gagging as if he'd taken in water too quickly after days without it. The blood stayed down, though, and his body healed slowly. Rooster and Helai did not return to his side until his cheeks filled out and his skin went from ashen-grey to brown. His fangs disappeared as his eyes flickered open.

"That was...extraordinarily unpleasant," Cassius said, his breathing shallow. His wound had not yet healed, angry and weeping, and it was still strange to see the rise and fall of the vampire's chest. A dead creature should not have a heartbeat. Still, there was some sort of familiarity to it as Rooster approached, offering him his hand.

"For being a creature of death, you find yourself knocking at her door quite often," Rooster said, lifting Cassius up to sling his arm across his shoulders. Freshly fed, the vampire did not smell of rot and decay, and Rooster was grateful for it, especially with the stench of death surrounding them. The city was a wasteland of corpses, some not yet dead. Some were wounded and merely in need of aid. Among those walking the pathways through the battle was Obrand, approaching with his axe dangling loosely in one hand. Half of his beard had been torn from its braid, and he was covered in the sap-blood of the dyrvak, but he looked uninjured, his eyes clear and happy to see the Misfits.

"I feared our forces would not arrive in time," Obrand said, clasping Rooster's arm roughly and squeezing.

"We did not think the dwarves would come," Rooster said, unable to keep the relief from his voice. "Did Jaera manage to make it through the enemy?"

Obrand shook his head. "The enemy managed to capture and murder her too." Obrand's face darkened at the reminder of his comrades' demise, and Rooster's heart ached for him. Still, it didn't make any sense. He hoisted Cassius higher on his side and cocked his head in confusion.

"So how did you alert the king then if no one got past?"

Obrand tapped his nose knowingly, planting his axe in the ground and leaning against it. "Dwarves aren't known much for their magic, but it runs strong through the Spine Mountain, and we have learned to mine and wield it to our strengths." Reaching up, he pulled his cloak and leather away from his neck, revealing a small rune glowing purple. It was a faint light against his skin, just bright enough to betray its magical nature. Obrand let go of his armor, covering the rune once more.

"All of King Stoneheart's Rangers are branded with the rune. If one of us perishes, the rune alerts us to it. King Stoneheart himself has one, so it likely alerted him to something being amiss." Obrand's expression turned grim. "The city was very nearly lost, lad. The rebuilding–it will take quite some time. The dwarves came at just the right moment. I fear the city would have fallen with the sinking of the sun."

Rooster raised a hand over his brow as he looked up. The sun had begun its descent, and he couldn't help but agree with Obrand. The amount of death and desecration that surrounded him... He didn't know how they'd survived.

By some coincidence or reminder, the brand on his back burned. Perhaps it wasn't some miracle they'd survived after all but a curse holding them hostage. What cruel fate? He shuddered at the thought.

"We are so grateful for your aid," Helai said, her fingers still pressed to her side. It looked as if Intoh had healed it, but circles darkened the underside of her eyes. They would all sleep well tonight, Rooster imagined.

Obrand bowed his head, twirling his axe and swinging it over his shoulder. "After your help in the mountains? Volendam will see more of our aid yet."

Cassius winced against Rooster. "May I suggest we get out of the cold and away from the dead? Perhaps we regroup? Find Velius, see if The Broken Arrow still stands." Cassius' words left a shudder of anxiety rolling through the group, and a fierce hope that the home they'd made in the tavern still held.

"Linda? Intoh?"

Both drikoty nodded silently. The siege was done, and the slow tendrils of relief coursed through Rooster as they fled the docks. Despite the Pyrrhic victory, the city stood. It was more than they could have hoped.

Ten

HELAI

H elai walked through the ruined streets of Volendam, her throat constricting as she came upon the rubble that was The Broken Arrow. Velius had halted when he saw the Misfits approaching, another male eldrasi at his side. Felix, Patrina, and Hilde stood before the Broken Arrow, their expressions stricken with grief. Felix openly wept, held close by Patrina, who stared at the ruined building with a blank stare. Helai did her best not to stare as Velius' wound continued to bleed a yellow sap, not red like humans. It sank down his face, slow as honey, and where it had dried, it had turned an amber hue. It was like that of the dyrvak, which made sense. She recalled the birth home of the eldrasi also being the resting place of the dyrvak, or so the stories told.

"Helai, dear, it's so good to see that you're alright," Hilde whispered, reaching out to take Helai's hands in her own. Hilde's hands, wrinkled and pale, were soft and welcomed as Helai drew forward, the other Misfits not too far behind.

"We hoped that The Broken Arrow had been spared," she said, nodding to Rooster as he approached with a weakened Cassius. Intoh was cradled against Linda's chest, having passed out on their way, and Linda held him gently, his face pressed against the crook of their neck.

"Intoh managed to heal the worst of Cassius' injury, but I imagine he needs rest and to be tended to," Rooster explained.

"Give him to me. I have a spare bed at the Firebrand he can use. Aerve can look over him there." Velius said, looking at the eldrasi and then reaching for Cassius.

"This is not the way to seduce me into your bed, Velius," Cassius groaned, sweat clinging to his brow. The faintest of rot mottled the corners of his lips, and Velius laughed as Rooster slipped Cassius from his shoulders and helped him grab hold of Velius.

"Why ever not? It's really doing it for me–the injured knight. Why, my legs shake at the thought," Velius said, hoisting Cassius up with ease and glancing towards Linda.

"Bring Intoh. There's a room for him too. I know magical exertion when I see it." They disappeared down the street as Helai watched them go, letting loose a sigh. Cassius wasn't unattractive by any means, not with his illusion softening and breathing life into his features, but Helai never understood how someone could overlook the knowledge that he was *dead*. The thought sent waves of disgust rolling through her, but she chased it away when Hilde squeezed her hands and moved to Felix, whose sobs had reduced to shaking shoulders.

"I will be right back," Helai said, gesturing to an alleyway down the street. Rooster nodded in acknowledgment as he turned towards The Broken Arrow crew.

Slipping away, Helai found herself standing before Dalnor's altar in the alley. The shadow god's statue had somehow remained untouched in the siege, and as Helai knelt in front of it, tears fell against her cheeks. They consumed her until she could not breathe, the bite of the cold air piercing her lungs. A hollowness possessed her, numbing her grief; she missed Massoud so much it hurt. *Why did you abandon me?* she thought sullenly as tears froze against her face. *I could use your guidance now more than ever.* She did not know if she spoke of Massoud or Dalnor anymore, and her hand reached up to clasp the eye pendant at her throat.

"Helai?" A voice called out to her from the mouth of the alley, and Helai looked up, her heart pounding. *Dalnor?* She nearly called out for her god but no. She was foolish to think her god would present himself to her twice—*if* that had been him who'd presented her with the mysterious key that had opened the door in the opera house in the first place.

No, it was Drithan who stood at the entrance of the alleyway, wringing his hands together and looking worse for wear. A shallow wound ran across his bicep. Dried blood coated his arm, and his armor was splattered in mud. Still, his appearance was a relief to Helai as she stumbled to her feet.

"Drithan, you're hurt," she said, wiping her tears away. "You should find a healer; they're setting up in the Sails District—"

"Helai," Drithan said again, stopping her in her tracks. She looked down at him then—he was only a few inches shorter than she—and watched the conflicted emotions rage within his expression. Her heart pounded in her throat, and Drithan's shoulders sagged as relief won over his gaze and he pulled her in.

"I thought you were dead," he murmured, his voice quiet as he enveloped her in his arms. She hesitated for a moment before she allowed herself to sink against him, soaking up the warmth that radiated off his skin and feeling the slow and steady beat of his heart. It was strange. Drithan's heart beat so slow compared to hers—comparable to the mountain he hailed from.

"I don't die so easily," she mumbled against him. He reeked of war—death and sweat, but she did not pull away. She did not know what drew her to Drithan, only that he was a light in the darkness and she could not stand to be in the shadows any longer.

"Afraid it got damaged in the fighting," Drithan said, pulling away as he cleared his throat. He pulled her card from his pocket. Helai was devastated to see the card was ripped in the corner, and much of it had been soaked in blood. Still, it had served its purpose and protected Drithan. That was all she could have asked for.

"Your knife killed many rakken. Many dyrvak too," she said, laughing. "Please keep the card. It's protecting you far better than it ever protected me."

Drithan huffed, but after a moment's hesitation, he pocketed the card. "Obrand and the other rangers speak to your innkeeper. They want to help rebuild. We stay here awhile."

"Why?" The question left her before she could stop herself. She recalled Obrand saying they were to stay behind and offer more aid, but she'd been too concerned with the state of The Broken Arrow to ask. The dwarves' homes were in shambles due to the rakken; what were they doing rebuilding other cities before they tended to their own? It would not be a choice she made. If she had the ability to rebuild Shoma, she would selfishly do so.

"Because we know what it is like to be without a home." Sadness struck Helai so fiercely it took her breath away. "It is honor to help these people reclaim theirs. Obrand wants to start with The Broken Arrow as repayment for you aiding us in battle against the rakken."

Warmth flooded through Helai as her chest ached from some unknown emotion. Searching Drithan's gaze for deceit, she found none, and for the first time since she'd met him, she thought about kissing him.

He must have seen the fire in her eye. Like a moth to a flame, he drew forward, his breath tickling her cheek. "Helai..." He uttered her name roughly, his fingers moving to graze hers. As he backed her against the wall, she studied his expression, looking for any signs she should not give in to the adrenaline that coursed through her and begged her to let go of caution. She found no such answers as he leaned in, his fingers moving to rest against the building behind her head. "Can I–"

But she did not want his questions. She did not want to think anymore. She did not want to worry about where Massoud was or the desolate state of the city or if she'd ever be free of the brand on her back. She did not want to think, to hear, to feel...

She moved forward, crashing her lips against his. His beard was coarse as it brushed against her chin, but she pulled him closer, her fingers splaying against the nape of his neck. She pressed against him, raking her teeth against his lower lip. She couldn't get close enough as he pushed her up against the wall, his fingers dancing over her arms and her waist. Heat pooled in her belly, begging for his fingers to slip between her thighs. It had been so long since she'd shared a bed with a lover, and she groaned softly against him as her tongue darted out to run along his lower lip.

The dream shattered as Drithan's hand swept over the wound at her side, still sore despite Intoh having headed it. She flinched, and with it, reality came crashing down. She gazed down at him, her mind a sea of conflicting emotions. Her lust was still a maelstrom in her belly, craving his touch, but her mind was already lost to the idea. *No, no I can't.*

Drithan cleared his throat, his cheeks pink as he stepped away. "Sorry–" he said, his voice rough from their kiss. "I've interrupted. I'll just–I'll go," he continued, gesturing to the statue and trying desperately to pull away from the electricity stitched between them.

Helai stared at him before her eyes were torn away, landing on the shrine. The moment she locked eyes with the raven god, a low hum echoed in the air, but Helai wrote it off as a coincidence. Sometimes, if one were to listen hard enough, it was thought that latent magical energy could be heard, like a whistle of wind through trees.

"You didn't interrupt anything. I just needed a moment away," Helai said softly, sighing. Her lips were swollen from their kiss as tension still clung to the air. She avoided Drithan's gaze.

Drithan lowered his head. "I understand. I also–" He rubbed the nape of his neck. "Ah–*vuk*. Not know where your journey goes, but after we rebuild, I am returning to Kaldrom to continue my apprenticeship with the rhun priests."

A quiet pang collected in her throat, but she swallowed it. *That's good. We have to find Massoud and the other Ghosts. There is no time for distractions.* "That sounds like an honorable cause," she heard herself say, her disappointment still managing to find a way to tighten her throat.

Drithan was quiet for a time. "Aye. We mountain folk don't have magic like humans or drikoty or even the eldrasi, so those of us who can survive the carvings are revered in our culture."

"Survive?"

"Aye. They carve the mark straight into our skin using draugmin." The thought of what that process entailed and the pain the dwarves suffered shuddered through Helai.

"That sounds awful," she admitted.

"It's an honor." Drithan grew defensive, but the way he said it felt almost like he was trying to convince himself as much as her. The wind shifted, and Helai coughed, unable to quell the awkward nature brewing between them.

Drithan took the hint and bowed his head. "I'll leave you to it. I just wanted to make sure you were okay."

She opened her mouth to protest–*no wait; I'll go with you*–but he was already gone, hefting his cloak over his shoulders and whistling as he made his way down the street back to The Broken Arrow. She stood alone in the alleyway, and a shudder rolled through her. She didn't know if it was from the cold or the lingering memory of his touch against her skin, but she steeled herself against whichever it was and stepped back onto the street.

Eleven

CASSIUS

The world was a sea of pain as Cassius woke to a familiar ache in his chest, a familiar urge to go. This urge beckoned him to Halvdarc, just a week's travel from his own estate.

High vampires, blessed by the dragon whose bone marrow sang through their curse, were extremely difficult to kill, though not impossible if they were persistent. It had taken all of Cassius' energy to heal and make it to the room Velius had offered him before unconsciousness had taken him. "Hello, Cassius."

Cassius was startled as he realized he was not alone in the room.

Ahma stood near the window, staring out to sea. No light filtered through, save for the kiss of moonlight that illuminated her face. Her hair was up tonight, a tight bun held together by two, blood-red hairpins. Her kimono was tucked neatly against her slight form, and when she turned to look at him, her fangs villainized her smile. The magical gun that rested inside his arm itched as if it felt Ahma's familiar presence. With it came a stronger pulse. The pulse of the lance he'd gotten from the opera house.

"You didn't think you'd rid yourself of me, did you?"

Gasping, he scrambled against the confines of the blanket Velius had thrown over him. Her eyes narrowed as she sauntered towards him. He did not have the strength to fight despite his desire to, so he watched as she knelt before him and took his hand in hers.

"The next item I need you to seek is a cuirass, the chest piece of the armor set," she said, running her thumb over his hand. "It is in Halvdarc, at the Welker Estate. I think you are familiar with the name?" Raising his hand, she pressed a soft kiss to his palm, her eyes lingering over his as she attempted to gauge his expression.

He took care not to react even though he knew she could hear his heart racing. He'd fed recently enough that it still beat, and it thundered in his ears as he knew what she was asking of him.

Rembrandt Welker was the child the Sanguine Order had commanded he murder, for they believed he was blessed, a child who could grow up one day to be exceptionally powerful. The Sanguine Order, known to many humans as the White Dawn, had charged themselves with the obligation to kill the boy and save Vilanthris from the possibility of his wrath. When Cassius had refused to kill him, the Order had locked him inside a tomb for five years.

"If I refuse?" Cassius asked quietly, tugging his hand away.

She let go, but her smile vanished as she stood. "We *need* the Ebony Fang, Cassius. Without it, the world as we know it *will* fall." Her face flickered as a shadow passed over it, and for the briefest of moments, Cassius thought he saw it shift into a fox, its mouth extended to reveal razor-sharp teeth.

Cassius blinked, and the shadow was gone but so was Ahma. The ache to travel remained, and Cassius groaned. He'd already gotten used to its absence but knew its return could only mean his eventual torture should he ignore it. The last time he'd done that, he'd nearly lost his mind to the desire to travel to Volendam. Its silence had been granted only when he'd found the second piece of the armory, the lance, in the opera house in Volendam.

"Cassius?" The vampire's heart leapt to his throat, but it was Velius' voice that called out for him, not Ahma's. "Can I come in? He pushed open the door. The red of his hair swept over his shoulders as he entered. The side of his face had been cleaned, and he looked at Cassius with mild concern. "How are you feeling?"

Cassius' head pounded, a great and terrible pain that wedged into his temple. He could use a large glass of wine and a pretty neck to bite into, but the burning of his brand accompanied by the itch to go to Halvdarc kept his mind occupied. Still, he eyed Velius with some interest. Eldrasi blood was sickeningly sweet, a delicacy among vampires that they rarely got to indulge in. Cassius had never gotten the pleasure to sample eldrasi blood but didn't imagine he'd enjoy the taste. He'd never been a huge fan of sweets.

"Fine," he grunted, averting his gaze.

Velius saw right through his lie. "Do you enjoy rum? No wine, I'm afraid, but I have my fair share of Vitruesian rum. Those of the sea speak its praises. Say it's the best rum in the south."

"Never heard of it," Cassius said, pushing himself slowly into a seated position. He wasn't a big fan of rum, but he'd take anything to quell the maelstrom of conflicting emotions within him. If he was stronger, he might have even given in to the temptation to pull Velius into bed with him. Alas, the room was unsteady, and the edges of his vision were dark.

Velius seemingly sensed his exhaustion, and he poured each of them a generous amount of rum into goblets. The eldrasi was difficult to discern, his kindness still something Cassius was wary of. He couldn't get a handle on him. His heart was a slow steady beat... As he drew close, he found himself wondering again what the eldrasi's blood tasted like.

"Cassius?" Velius' voice was low as Cassius was tugged out of his bloodlust haze, which was ever present, ever dictating his desires. He looked up slowly, meeting Velius' gaze as he took the goblet offered to him. His fingers brushed the eldrasi's, and his throat twinged, cascading all the way down to his groin.

Velius backed away to sit in the chair across from him, and a part of Cassius was relieved. Had Velius moved closer, he would not have been able to stop himself.

"Sate my curiosity," Velius said, raising the goblet to his lips.

Cassius raised a brow. The rum burned as he tipped the goblet against his lips, but it was a pleasant taste, better than the Hestian rum he'd tried when he'd been human. "Yes?" he asked, attempting to quell his bloodlust with more rum. It failed miserably, and he watched Velius swallow, the vein in his neck distracting as it pulsed in temptation.

"Does it hurt? When someone is bitten by a vampire?"

Rum lodged in his throat, and Cassius coughed, setting the goblet down on the table beside the bed. Shaking his head, he stilled his quivering breathing before answering, "No. Vampires have a numbing agent in their fangs that enters the person's bloodstream when we bite them. Some have admitted to it being pleasurable, but most of the time, it's just relaxing. It is why there are some who willingly offer themselves to vampires," Cassius admitted quietly. "The stress relief is as good as sex."

Velius' brows rose behind his goblet, and he downed the rest of it in one swift, graceful movement as he set it down on the desk and leaned forward, his eyes gleaming. "Eldrasi blood is a delicacy, is it not?"

Cassius shrugged. "So I've heard. I haven't had the chance to indulge."

Velius' eyes darkened. "Would it aid in your recovery? If I could be of aid while also sating my own curiosity..." He left the sentence hanging, and Cassius' mouth dried at the implications. He'd been dancing just out of Velius' reach since they'd met.

"Surely you understand–" Cassius began, and Velius laughed, tucking a strand of hair behind a pointed ear.

"Cassius, I do not wish for you to declare your undying love for me. I know I am beautiful. I know I would not blame you for such a declaration," he said, winking. "I merely am a curious eldrasi and don't like leaving things to the imagination." He waved a hand in dismissal. "Though you *are* injured. I suppose I should leave you to rest."

"Wait." He stopped Velius as he made to leave, speaking before his courage could fail him. Desperation cradled him, eager to feel anything other than the constant ache in his chest urging him to Halvdarc, eager to free himself from the dull burn at the base of his back from his brand. "Okay, but you must come to me. I cannot yet move very much."

Velius complied, trailing over to the edge of the bed. He knelt, his eyes trained on Cassius' as he offered the vampire his hand. A small voice in the back of Cassius' head begged him not to, for what if he lost control and killed Velius? It was always a flicker of fear that stayed his hand, but now that the eldrasi was close, he couldn't pull away.

"Does my wrist suffice, or would you like something bigger?" Velius' voice was husky as he bared his neck to Cassius, but no. The neck was far too intimate.

"Wrist is fine," Cassius said, struggling to keep his voice even. He took Velius' hand in his, admiring the eldrasi's calloused palm. The eldrasi had every right to be arrogant, his work in the forge of master craft. Evidence of it was written all over his fingers, and Cassius' gaze flicked to Velius' as he raised the hand to his mouth and pressed the softest of kisses on his palm.

The quietest of sighs passed Velius' lips as Cassius trailed kisses along Velius' palm and wrist before his bloodlust forced him to move quickly in its impatience. His tongue darted out to wet the skin at Velius' wrist, and he felt his fangs extend, slipping into the eldrasi's flesh.

Velius inhaled sharply, his arm flinching as he resisted the temptation to pull away, and Cassius tightened his grip as he sucked in the first draw of blood. It was thick, filling his mouth rather quickly. He grew dizzy on it as he swallowed and marveled at the taste; it *was* like honey, only there was a hint of something he could not place. It was like a spark at the end, a spice of power that infected the blood with a pleasant hazelnut taste that had Cassius craving more despite being sated more quickly than if he'd drank human blood.

"Oh my." Velius sighed happily, relaxing against the bed. "You weren't kidding. That *is* nice." Cassius was too consumed by the blood to respond. His brush with death had left him eager to dance as far away from it as he could. He shouldn't fear the endless night, but every time he was brought close to the edge, the fear consumed him. Some vampires claimed Drausmírtus ushered vampires to Nelfta's domain when they died. Drausmírtus was Death, after all, but Nelfta was the dragon that gifted the vampires with their undeadly curse. Others claimed vampires merely ceased to exist. Cassius had always been fearful of the latter.

A shudder coursed through him as he forced himself away, completely sated from Velius' blood. His fingers and toes tingled fiercely as the blood rushed to them, offering warmth where there had been only cold. Life returned to his face, chasing away the evidence of death, and for the first time since nearly dying, he felt alive, only more so–like he had before he'd been turned into a vampire. It was an exhilarating feeling, and he licked the rest of the blood from Velius' wrist and raised his head, his face inches from Velius' own. The slightest of movements, and their lips would meet. Cassius' heart thundered in his ears, high from Velius' blood, and his nose flared as his eyes darted to the man's mouth. The consequences be damned.

"Cassius," Velius whispered, only to scramble away as Rooster's voice sounded from the hallway. Both men struggled to regain their composure as a knock came at the door. Helai and Rooster's muffled argument sounded outside as Velius cleared his throat, poured himself some more rum, and then spoke.

"Come in."

Linda squeezed through first in their krok'ida form.

"Linda," Cassius said, still slightly dizzy from the high of Velius' blood. Linda's scales were almost luminescent, vibrant in the torchlight. "You're not cloaked."

"What?" Linda protested, gesturing to Velius. "He know me."

Cassius couldn't argue with the logic. He envied Linda's pride in their true self and their ability to be unapologetic about it around those they trusted. Underneath the beauty of his illusion, he was nothing but a monster. The clarity of it sobered him from his blood-fueled high, and he made brief eye contact with Velius before Helai and Rooster entered the room as well.

"We just wanted to thank you for your hospitality," Rooster said, eyeing Velius, then Cassius. "And see how our favorite vampire was doing. You seem completely healed," he said, his voice thick with relief.

Cassius nodded, thankful for the blanket that covered him in that moment. His cheeks were still heated from Velius' closeness, from his urge to pull the eldrasi into the bed with him, and his mind whirled, attempting to ground itself back into the present.

"Why are you being so...hospitable?" Helai asked, her bluntness directed at Velius. "Not that I am not grateful, but–"

"But not the typical behavior of someone who barely knows you without there being an underlying motive," Velius finished, raising his goblet to his lips. He'd regained his composure far more quickly than Cassius, and he gazed lazily at the other Misfits. "Who says I do not have one?"

Cassius' stomach twisted in immediate distrust, seeking Velius' face for answers. So the eldrasi *was* hiding something. It had always been apparent, but still, the confession from Velius' own mouth somehow made their earlier activity feel wrong, a betrayal to the other Misfits somehow.

Velius laughed, tipping his goblet back and drinking deeply. "Worry not, Misfits! I do not mean to send you all to your deaths."

"Then what *do* you mean to do?" Rooster asked.

Velius sighed heavily. "All in due time. If you must know, I am looking for someone." Sadness and worry tinged Velius' expression, and Cassius studied him quietly. A lover, perhaps? No, he wouldn't have come on to Cassius so hard if there was a lost love out there. "It is why I asked for that locket," he continued, gesturing to the locket now hanging from his neck.

Rooster stilled, his mouth open as if he were desperate to say something but uncertain how to say it. "Do you know who that belonged to?"

Velius nodded. "She's a very powerful eldrasi who—"

Intoh burst through the door, looking infinitely better than when Cassius had last seen him.

"Out of the way. Move out of the way," Intoh demanded, shoving through the others as he approached Cassius' bed. The sparkle had returned to the greka's eyes, and there was no hint of exhaustion as there had been before. Intoh didn't know how to control himself—always using far too much magic.

"Wounds healed exceptionally fast. Fascinating, captivating, interesting; must study further. Could be useful," Intoh muttered to himself as he poked and prodded at Cassius. An irritated side of him threatened to lash out, to push Intoh and his meddlesome nature away, but the beast was quelled by the fact he was happy to be conscious and surrounded by those he might even one day call friends.

"Captain." A muffled voice of an eldrasi sailor sounded through the door, and Velius stood, holding his hands up with a soft smile.

"I will be at the wheel if you have need of me." His gaze scorched Cassius' as they lingered against his, and then he was gone.

"Cassius."

Rooster's voice pulled him from the daze he'd been in since he'd consumed Velius' blood. Looking up, he locked eyes with Rooster, who turned a conflicting gaze from the door Velius had disappeared out of to look at Cassius.

"Glad to see you're okay."

Cassius' mouth twisted, but he gave a firm nod. He wasn't okay. Velius' blood had only silenced the urge to go to Halvdarc and the burn of the brand momentarily, but by all regards, he was alive. It was the only thing he could focus on. He had lived to fight another day. Now he needed to figure out what he was going to do about the Ebony Fang and Ahma. What were her intentions? Sigvald, the vampire from the opera house, told him not to trust her, but why?

Twelve

HELAI

Helai didn't know where they were. After speaking with the Broken Arrow crew, she, Rooster, and Linda had made their way to the Firebrand. Velius was sailing somewhere south, where the heat on her skin was a welcomed relief from Volendam's winter. Her stomach rolled, and her eyes fluttered shut as she pressed her fingers to her stomach, willing her nausea away. She hated boats. She fucking hated them.

Still, she couldn't help but admire the beauty of the ocean. Sea foam washed up against the Firebrand as they sailed smoothly through calm waters. Helai stood at the side of the ship, having just purged her stomach. She hoped staring out at the horizon would curb her seasickness. Eldrasi worked around her, and though a part of her curiosity urged her to speak to them, she left them alone, letting them tend to their work. It was fascinating watching them. Their fingers extended, hardening to bark as they fed cracks in the side of the ship or replaced rotted wet wood with new material. When they spoke, it was quietly, a slow language of ancient Eldrasian. It made little sense to Helai. From what she knew of the eldrasi, those of Míradan had developed a language of their own, a quicker dialect, forsaking the ways of their ancestors. These eldrasi were more human-like in appearance, hinting at their Míradanian roots, but they spoke as if they hailed from the Daesthara Forest, nestled west of her home country Shoma.

"One day, your sea legs will come, and you'll wonder why you ever step foot on land in the first place." Rooster had snuck up behind her, jostling her out of her ogling, and his gaze was far off as he stared out at the endless blue of the sea.

"I don't know about that." Helai shook her head. "I fear I was never meant for the sea."

Rooster's laughter was soft, then a moment of silence settled between them.

"What are you to do now?" Helai asked, breaking the silence. Unease spread through her as conflicting emotions warred in her head and her heart. She knew logically, it would be wise to stay with the Misfits. But there was a tug in her belly, a familiar urge to go south. She wasn't certain if it was to seek out Shoma, to see if Massoud had returned to their home, or if it was something else. It felt almost similar to her urge to seek out Volendam, and that alone worried her. She watched as Linda wandered to the front of the ship and plopped down on their stomach in their krok'ida form. No one on the crew batted an eye at Linda. It made sense. Eldrasi often traded with the drikoty, the lizardfolk of Lyvira, and were probably used to seeing krok'ida.

"I'm not sure," Rooster admitted. "Perhaps we can help Volendam rebuild." He glanced at her. "Do you not agree?"

She hesitated, unsure if Rooster would understand. "I just worry for my family. Massoud—it's not like him to disappear. He would have contacted me by now. I need to go looking for him." The moment the words left her lips, her brand burned so badly it forced her fingers to dig into the railing of the ship, a gasp of surprise leaving her lips. She groaned as Rooster reached out for her.

"The brand? I felt it too just now," he said, his teeth grinding together to mask the pain. "We need to speak with Cassius."

Helai agreed. Perhaps the vampire knew why the brand was causing the strange, familiar urge to travel, only this time it was south.

Cassius' gaze was far off when they found him. Velius sat with him, as he had been for the many days they'd been recovering aboard the ship. His hair was pulled up in a loose bun, and he spoke with enthusiasm while Cassius stared out of the window of the room. The place was thick with a sense of sickness, and Helai felt the bleak nature in the air, but no one else complained. Intoh had perched himself at the desk, a book in hand.

"Ah, I suppose your arrival forces me to resume my duties. You are all welcome to remain here on the Firebrand for as long as you'd like, but I'd urge you to return to Volendam as soon as possible. I am not exactly sailing in the safest waters." He bowed his head and exited the room, leaving the Misfits alone. Helai watched Velius go.

"I saw her again," Cassius said lowly. The room was relatively small, and Helai hovered near the door, not wanting to be anywhere near the vampire. Cassius still gave her the jitters even now, after all they'd been through. A part of her was guilty of her disdain; the other part of her could not help it.

"Who?" Rooster asked, reaching for Velius' forgotten goblet of rum. It must have been empty because Rooster scowled, slipping it back onto the table as Intoh peered up over his book. He was in his human form.

Unlike Linda, he seemed to prefer hiding behind his human face. His hair was a light shaggy mess today, sticking up in random spots as he flipped through the pages of his book. Still, Helai could tell he was listening in on the conversation by the way his gaze kept flickering to Cassius.

"The woman who's urging me to seek out pieces of that armory. It was the reason we all felt drawn to Volendam. She told me the next piece is in Halvdarc."

A shudder rolled through Helai. That was where Zamir was. She didn't like the thought of one of her Ghosts being in the same place as a piece of the armory Cassius sought out. The coincidence seemed too large. "What do we know of this woman?"

Cassius hesitated, then lowered his head. "Her name is Ahma. She is Emperor Aikawa's daughter."

"From Amajin? The vampires of the east?" Helai's tone was sharp but not due to unkindness. Shock rolled through her as her palms began to sweat. Those of the bamboo forests of Amajin were master illusionists; even Massoud, a master of illusion himself, feared the travelers from Amajin. Many who strayed into their bamboo forests never returned. It was rumored that Emperor Aikawa believed keeping his people close was the only way to keep them safe.

"I do not know if they're vampires. Not like you would imagine," Cassius admitted quietly. "They protect their secrets even from my people." Clasping his hands together, he looked at all of them. "I've been thinking about it for a while now." Glancing at the door, he pushed himself into a seated position, kicked off the blankets, and sat over the side of the bed. As he ran his finger along his forearm, a soft moan passed his lips and black blood coalesced from his pores, slowly forming into a gun. It was small, black, and bore the sigil of a many-tailed fox devouring a bat.

Helai eyed it both with curiosity and weariness. Guns weren't a common weapon, newly forged from the heart of Wolstadt, one of the human kingdoms south of Volendam. Still, it was a sleek weapon, and Cassius held it up for the others to study. Intoh's eyes widened.

"That sigil there, on lance from opera house as well?" Intoh asked, pointing to the sigil on the side of the gun. Helai was certain she'd seen that sigil somewhere but could not place its origin.

Cassius nodded.

Intoh sucked in a breath. "Will do more research."

"My estate has an extensive library. I will admit, it has not been touched in a long time, but if we find ourselves going to Halvdarc, Wilhaven is only a short journey from there," Cassius said.

Helai nodded, remembering her letter from Zamir. Since Massoud wasn't in Volendam, perhaps Zamir would know where her brother was.

Looking at Cassius, Rooster shook his head. "If the urge to follow this...armory," he said, gesturing to the gun in Cassius' hand, "is anything like it was before, we don't have the luxury of staying in Volendam. Not while these brands connect us."

"Brands are marks of Gorvayne, yes?" Intoh asked Cassius. "You said there are cults of his in Halvdarc. Perhaps could go there. Figure out about armory, but also find cult. Make them talk. Learn how to remove brand."

The idea was a good one. Helai's teeth dragged across her lower lip as she fiddled with the hilt of one of her daggers. Her stomach rolled as they crested a wave, and she grabbed onto the door frame, frowning softly. The room stank of sea water and rum, which did nothing for her nausea.

"Can we speak of this more when we return to Volendam? The quicker we get to land, the happier I'll be," she said, pressing her fingers to her stomach once more. "I've been sick for a lifetime." Though she doubted this would be the last time she was on a ship.

"This room does not need to smell any fouler," Rooster uttered, straightening. "Cassius, Intoh, are you both well enough to return?"

Cassius nodded as the gun sank back into his arm. "I need to feed soon, but I've recovered." The vampire *did* look better than when Helai had seen him last. His skin was dark and smoothed over by youthful visage, and his hair was rich, dark, and pulled back into his signature half-up bun. His beard had even grown out a bit, thick and short. It left a bad taste in Helai's mouth, realizing that vampires looked the most alive, the most human the more often they preyed on humanity.

"Let us find Linda then," Rooster said.

As they exited the room, Helai exhaled softly.

Clear mind. Clear soul. You'll find Massoud before long.

Thirteen

INTOH

After grabbing Linda from the front of the ship, they returned to Volendam with a quick goodbye from Velius. He seemed distracted, instructing his men in Eldrasian as they sailed near the coast of some foreign city. There was the smell of smoke in the air, and Intoh's nose burned as Velius shuffled them through his forge and back onto the streets of Volendam.

The city looked much the same as it had when they'd left a few days prior. With most of the wealthy gone and many of those who'd been in charge dead, the city was at a bit of a standstill. Some had collected their dead, but most of those who'd died had been left to become a feast for the city's sewer rat population. The stench was nearly unbearable, but everyone ignored Intoh's complaints.

"Misfits!" Obrand called to them from down the street. He was shed of his normal attire, dressed in a simple cotton shirt and pants that cut off at the knee. There were at least a dozen other dwarves with various tools and marble and wood materials.

"The tavern's coming along so nicely, Obrand," Rooster said, astonished. "Dwarves rebuild so quickly." The snow had stopped falling, turning the streets into a mess of mud, and the rubble from the destroyed tavern had been cleared away, transported into carts with impatient horses pawing at the ground.

"Well..." Obrand hefted a hearty sigh, his breath curling in the air in front of him. "We have to stick around, make sure the rakken problem remains under control. With the dyrvak gone, I can't imagine they'll be daft enough to attack the city on their own, but one can never be too careful." He raised a hand to the skeleton of The Broken Arrow. "This was the resting place of the Misfits. Least we can do is help rebuild while we keep an eye on the city, and what better place to start?"

Intoh looked up at the tavern, an empty feeling striking his belly. The structure was nothing but a husk of its former glory, which wasn't even much to speak of before. Someone had set fire to it during the fighting, and it had nearly burnt to the ground. Intoh saw the charred table where they'd all sat, drinking and laughing.

"Hm." Intoh hummed his appreciation. He'd never outwardly expressed it, but he 'd been devastated to find The Broken Arrow lost in the siege. It had become a little solace in his growing quest to find immortality, and now it was gone. It would be nice to see it remade.

"Misfits." The name was to be worn out it seemed, but the annoyance was lost as Felix and Patrina approached. Felix's face was darkened from the cold, his eyes bright with excitement. "You did not tell us you were friends with dwarves."

Helai reached for Patrina, pulling her into a hug with a grin. At one time, Intoh had sensed an aversion between Patrina and Helai, but that seemed to have dissipated.

"And this?" Cassius gestured to the building beside it, where several dwarves dug trenches into the ground. Behind the wreckage, the sea twinkled merrily with no qualms or thoughts of the world's troubles.

"Ah! Felix might have mentioned a want for a bathhouse? Surprise..." Patrina said, wiggling her fingers at the space where the bathhouse was to go.

Cassius inhaled sharply. "When will it be complete?"

"Not for some time. I hear they are electing a new captain for the guard, and it will be a while yet before the lords and ladies of the Sails District return to their homes, so the city will surely be in a disarray. Until we can get more supplies, we're doing what we can," Obrand said, pointing at the supplies that had piled in the street. "A few months, perhaps. It will take a few years for the city to return to normal. Maybe a little quicker for the Sails District. They have the skaels to spare in rebuilding."

Cassius groaned. "The sound of a bath right now sounds divine."

Intoh did not know why it mattered. Humans stank whether they soaked themselves in water or not. Vampires were even worse. Cassius attempted to hide it under layers of lavender and wine, but Intoh was forever plagued with his stench of rot and blood.

"Patience, *ami*. It will come," Felix said, clasping Cassius on the shoulder.

Intoh looked down the street towards the mage college. The Misfits had spoken of leaving soon, so he'd need to inform Tidebeard. Or perhaps he and Linda could remain. The rest of the Misfits would do fine without them, and Intoh wasn't sure he'd utilized the mage college's library enough.

"Before you go–" Rooster had noticed Intoh eyeing the street. "We need to talk as a group."

Intoh sighed. Always at the mercy of others.

Leaving the dwarves to their work and Felix and Patrina to aid where they could, the Misfits strolled through the ruined streets of the city. The dyrvak and rakken armies had left it in shambles, their corpses mingled with those of Volendam. Many of the buildings still stood, but several had been vandalized, marked in blood with three diagonal lines–the brand of Gorvayne, the dragon who sought resurrection. Intoh's brand burned when he looked at it, a quiet whisper itching the back of his head. It was gone before he could try to discern what it said.

"That..." Rooster said, looking at the others, "is precisely why we need to make a decision."

Intoh couldn't agree more. The brand was troublesome, and its insistence distracted him from his studies and goals. He needed it removed so he could focus on finding immortality. "Perhaps stay. Study at college. See if there is anything more to learn from there about dragons."

"We do not know the extent of the curse that has been placed upon us. What if there are consequences for separating? I do not think it is a good idea to part until the brands have been removed," Cassius said, lowering his voice when a couple of Volendam guardsmen strolled by. The wind whistled through the buildings, tousling Intoh's hair. He shivered, scooting closer to Linda.

"Then urge us to delay travel for one day. Do some research and tell Tidebeard I am leaving." He stared at the others as they hesitated. Helai said nothing, staring out at the street as conflicting emotions ran across her face. She looked to bolt any moment, the compulsion to do so flying off her in waves. Intoh sensed her restless nature and could not blame her. Still, something tethered them all together. None of them could flee even if they willed it so.

"If we can find a place to sleep, it shall be so. One more night in the city won't kill us. We need to find transportation anyway. There are many routes we could take," Rooster said, shaking snow out of his hair as some fell from a ruined roof above, disturbed by a fierce gust of wind.

"I do not think we should traverse back through the mountains, not with the threat of dyrvak and rakken," Cassius pointed out.

"We could take the road through Nantielle and Wolstadt. Though..." Helai hesitated. "I do not know if that's a good idea either, considering there seems to be cultists everywhere."

"Plus, I've heard that Volendam and Nantielle are at odds at the moment. Has to do with Nantielle's growing unrest with Kreznov and their disdain with Volendam for remaining neutral," Cassius said, looking towards the docks. A few ships had returned, if tentatively, but the city was still quiet as a ghost, an eerie fog rolling now through.

"Where did you hear that?" Helai asked sharply.

"A party in Fraheim a week or two before I left my estate to come to Volendam. A lord from Nantielle spoke of possible war. Something to do with rumors that the north was joining together under one banner even though that's utter madness. Kreznov and Volreya have been sworn enemies since I was a human." His eyes flashed in a tint of red as he locked eyes with Helai. "Quite a bit of time has passed since then."

"Matters that don't mean that much to us right now. We can't do anything about countries warring with each other, but we *can* do something about whatever the fuck is happening in the shadows," Rooster argued, breaking the tension. "The world will always seek war, but not if it is lost to the return of fucking *dragons*." The last word came out in a hiss as a group of people scurried by, heading towards the docks.

Intoh swallowed thickly. He did not care for the trouble that he'd been dragged into. Dragons and cults were thorns in his foot. What good would immortality do if the world ended?

"Could go by sea. Safest when land is ravaged by giant rats," Intoh suggested, pointing to the large ships that had pulled into the bay. It seemed like the most logical of solutions when it came to travel. No risk for running into rakken, dyrvak, *or* cultists, and it would be quicker than horseback.

The idea seemed to take. "Alright. I'll go to the docks with Cassius and see about finding us a ship that will take us to Halvdarc," Rooster said, waving his hand at Cassius for him to follow.

Helai looked at Linda. "Want to come with me to see if the Flock got compromised? I need to send some letters. After, we can check on The Broken Arrow," Helai said. "See if they need any help."

Linda nodded fervently, then looked to Intoh for approval. Satisfaction coursed through him at Linda's gaze. It appeared they were back to their old self, which pleased Intoh greatly.

He shoved his feelings aside and waved his hand at Linda impatiently. "Go with Helai. Will find you later."

As everyone scurried off in different directions, Intoh's heart thundered in his throat. He didn't know why, but a bad feeling struck him and he found himself looking behind him every few seconds as he hurried off to the mage college.

There was never anyone behind him.

Fourteen

ROOSTER

Rooster found the first person with a ship large enough for them to travel comfortably and approached the ship's captain, a woman with light hair twisted into a loose bun. She spoke quickly in a language that sat thick on the tongue.

"She's from Nantielle, if I had my guess. Could never learn the language," Cassius uttered beside him. Her fingers tapped against the barrel in front of her as her hair, frazzled and dancing around her face, refused to cooperate even as she tried to push it back.

"Excuse me," Rooster said, raising his hand to garner her attention. The woman stopped talking immediately, waving her hand to silence the man beside her as she turned. Her face was pinched, her nose and mouth too small for her face, but she wasn't unattractive by any means. Rooster stumbled for a moment over how impossibly blue her eyes were. They reminded him of someone, of drowning in the sapphires of *her* eyes...

Igraine.

"Yes?" The woman shook him free as he stood at the edge of a flashback, a flicker of deep-red hair teasing the edges of his vision before it vanished and left him feeling uncomfortably empty. His heart cried out in pain, but he knew not what for.

Swallowing thickly, he ignored Cassius' questioning gaze and stepped forward.

"The name's Rooster. My comrades and I are looking for transport."

The woman shook her head, turning away. "Oh no, no. We don't transport. Our ship is for trade. We did not know the city was attacked until we were 'ere. We remained outside of the city until it was safe, but I fear we will 'ave to turn around and go 'ome." Her accent was thick, almost too thick to understand, and Rooster stood silent for a moment, trying to piece it together.

"We will pay, and we will work for our bed," Cassius said, stepping forward. Clearing his throat, he gestured to her ship. "The people of Volendam have suffered greatly. I do not think they can afford your goods, not unless you are generous enough to donate it to them."

"What even happened here?" the woman demanded, looking up at the ruined city.

Rooster was at a loss of what to tell her. The world did not believe in the existence of dyrvak, much less the rakken. Neither race had been seen in hundreds of years, thought to be extinct. Rooster wouldn't have believed it either, if he hadn't seen them with his own eyes.

"Nantielle–does it have positive relations with the dwarves?" Cassius asked, watching the man she'd been talking to take inventory. He worked slowly, eyeing Rooster and Cassius with ill-concealed suspicion as he stared at them behind his clipboard.

The woman nodded her head. "Nantielle 'as decent enough relations with the dwarves."

"Best write to their king. They came to the city's aid, or you can speak to whoever they elect in charge until everyone returns," Rooster said. "Either will be able to explain better than us."

"Ack–" The woman threw up her hands. "As long as I still have a city to trade to, I couldn't care less. Name is Amelia. If you 'ave the skaels, I will take you back to Nantielle with me."

Rooster smiled radiantly, leaning close. "Oh, and what would we have to do for you to take us to Halvdarc?"

Amelia's cheeks flushed as she glanced at Rooster, her eyes betraying her resolve as they flickered to his lips. *Gotcha*. "Oh, Halvdarc? I suppose I could see. My goods could be sold there..."

Rooster nodded, offering her his hand. "Would thirty skaels suffice?" Taking her hand in his, he pressed his lips to her pale knuckles, ignoring the burning guilt in his chest. He could not get the image of Igraine out of his head.

Who the hell is she? Why won't she leave me alone?

Amelia didn't appear to notice as she blushed and then composed herself, straightening her back and nodding. "It seems fair so long as I can put some of your comrades to work." She pointed to her ship, beaming with pride. "The Blue Rose will take you where you need to go."

Rooster had to admit; Amelia's ship was beautiful. Her sails were stained a light blue and billowing gently in the wind. She had no fancy figurehead to speak of, but a painted blue rose decorated the side of the ship, accompanied by *The Blue Rose* in swirling letters. It wasn't the largest of ships but large enough they would be comfortable on their voyage. It should help with Helai's seasickness, at any rate.

"When do you mean to set sail?" Cassius stepped forward, his brow quirked in curiosity. Rooster noticed his hands were shaking. Hunger, perhaps?

"Tomorrow just before dawn," Amelia replied, oblivious to Cassius' bloodlust. It was a dull insistence that scratched the back of Rooster's throat, felt through their connecting brands. He did not envy Cassius' existence.

"We will be here before you leave," Rooster assured her, clasping Cassius' shoulder as he turned. "If you'll excuse us, we have some matters to attend to." He kept his voice light as he added, "My friend here is in dire need of some lunch."

Cassius' eyes flashed in warning, but he said nothing as he bent his head towards Amelia, who waved a distracted hand at them as she turned to speak with the sailor taking inventory. Life was beginning to return to the city even as the dead were being carted away by what guardsmen remained. Rooster took a moment to tilt his head back and let the sun caress his face.

Another memory washed over him, unbidden.

Blinking, he gathered his surroundings. He stood on a beach. Soft white sand slipped between his bare toes as water lapped up onto shore in quiet simplicity. A massive bonfire had been built and people sat around it, drinking and laughing. One of them was the redhead, Igraine.

His feet compelled him forward, nearly crashing him into a small myr- lír that ran by, his large ears flapping as he dodged around Rooster's legs. "Oi, cap'n! Watch it. Gonna give Florence a check if you're not too careful."

Rooster's eyes were torn from Igraine as he took a moment to study the mylír. Florence steadied two mugs of rum in his hands. Mylírs were creatures of the forest realms, created from spores of flowers that grew deep in eldrasi lands. They were small, allergic to the sun, and rich with magical energy. Humanoid in stature, their eyes were round and usually yellow or white, and their teeth were blunted. This one was blind, his eyes covered by a thick band of fabric tied behind his giant ears. It didn't seem to bother him as he tilted his head back.

"Whatcha lookin' at, boss? Rackjack's been looking everywhere for ya. Meetin' him in the crow's nest now if you'd like to join us?"

But Rooster wasn't looking at him anymore, the flash of red hair having snagged his attention. "Igraine?" Her name fled his lips softly, but this memory was strange. He knew Florence could see him; he spoke to Rooster as if he were right there. Igraine didn't look his way though, not even as he shouted her name.

Igraine sat with a hulking man with dark skin and kind eyes and a lanky fellow with several missing teeth and a smoking pipe in his right hand. She laughed at something the large man said and then looked up and caught Rooster's eyes.

Her gaze flashed a painful blue, and Rooster reached out, desperate to feel the soft touch of her hands. Instead, he was met with the small shake of Cassius, his mind ripped out of the memory as he landed back on the docks of Volendam.

Cassius looked at him with fresh concern. "What happened? You looked as if you were dissociating."

A strangled sob etched the hollow of Rooster's cheeks, bitten back by iron will as he clenched his fists at his sides. "Nothing."

"Rooster, I–"

Rooster brushed him away. "You need to go find something to eat, Cassius. You look like shit." The tension that followed thickened as Cassius' gaze burned into the side of Rooster's head, feeding his guilt. He turned to apologize, but when he looked up, the vampire was gone.

Rooster sighed and made his way back to The Broken Arrow. Still shaken by the memory, he tried to quell his anxiety with the promise of ale. Surely some of it had survived the siege.

Fifteen

LINDA

It was strange, seeing Volendam disappear behind them. It had forged a home in their bones, The Broken Arrow a peaceful hearth for Linda's soul. They were sad to see it destroyed, but Linda was thankful the Misfits had remained long enough for Linda to help the dwarves fit some structures for the bath house into place. It spoke to the innate part of them, the part of them that truly loved building things. A memory resurfaced.

Linda's mouth fell open as the heat of the sun bore down against them. They had just laid the last stone on the home they'd been tasked to build, and M'ik had granted Linda a moment's reprieve to simply exist. They lumbered off into the wood to find a clearing to lay in, and did so with ease. The new home their village had relocated to was surrounded by small pockets of clearings, and Linda fell forward into the grass, their exhaustion and delight consuming their waking thought. The grass was soft, so much so that Linda found themself dozing until they felt something press against their nose.

A low hiss escaped them as they opened their eyes to several luminescent butterflies fluttering through the clearing. Many of them were a soft blue with yellow dots lighting their wings, but some of them were a brilliant gold. They contented themselves with resting on Linda's head and nose as Linda settled again, and they watched them fly around curiously. The butterflies were massive, as most things in Lyvira were, but they didn't seem to mean any harm. If anything, their presence filled Linda with a sense of peace, something they hadn't known for a long time. The sunlight bathed them in a soft warmth, and Linda closed their eyes again just as the smell of burning wood infected their nose, accompanied by shouting in the distance...

"Linda?"

Linda opened their eyes. The memory receded, and while they remained drenched in the warmth of the sun, the meadow was gone, replaced with the endless blue of the ocean. Rooster stood at the wheel of The Blue Rose with Amelia, laughing at something she'd said. Helai stood in front of Linda, eyeing them quietly.

"Cassius wants your help carrying some things to the hull if you're able," she said.

Linda nodded silently, pushing past Helai to find Cassius near the stairs. He lifted a pair of boxes with ease, his mouth pressed in a thin line as his gaze found Linda's. "Are you well? I can sense your discomfort," he said as Linda grabbed their own boxes and followed Cassius down the stairs.

Linda didn't know how to respond to him immediately. Looking at their very human hands, their skin crawled. A knot curled in their belly. If anything, they wanted to be in their krok'ida form. It was like a storm raged inside them, like a scream forged inside their lungs. It felt like a stranger sat in their skin.

"Ever feel like..." Linda paused, struggling to find the words as they sat the box down in the hull, away from the swaying hammocks of the crew's quarters. "Not belong?"

Cassius was slow to reply, his back facing them as he bent to set his boxes down. Tension rolled off him in waves, and Linda worried if they had said something wrong. Their Vilris, the universal language of Vilanthris, was a joke at best, and the language barrier frustrated them to no end.

"Many times, my friend. I've not exactly been the warmest to my vampire brethren, and as a result, they've scorned me. And humans? Well..." He scoffed, running a hand over his beard. "The world is not kind to those who are different."

"Can hide," Linda assured, gesturing to the warmth in Cassius' skin, the color in his cheeks.

Cassius nodded in agreement. "Yes, I suppose we can, but it doesn't change who we really are. That can never be taken away from us." He frowned. "No matter how much simpler it would make things."

"Don't mind that," Linda protested, gesturing to themself. "Hate this." Their skin crawled again, like it didn't sit well on their shoulders, and Linda growled under their breath in frustration. The boat swayed, and Linda pressed a hand to one of the boxes to steady themself, their fingers curling to fist. "Didn't choose this."

"Some things aren't a choice," Cassius said darkly. "I did not *choose* to be a vampire. You did not choose this form to hide in. Lucky for you, you're on a team of misfits. If you no longer wish to wear the ring, let it be so." Cassius stepped forward, pressing a hand to Linda's shoulder. "If anyone has anything to say about you being a krok'ida, I will simply liberate their tongue from their mouth."

An unfamiliar warmth of comfort seeped through Linda at the thought. Intoh would have muttered and told Linda they were being ridiculous. It felt strange, a good strange, for someone such as Cassius to care. Still, there were rules to follow and obligations to uphold. They weren't ready to grit their teeth and make the world conform to them.

"Thank," Linda said, reaching up to pat Cassius on the head. "Good sir, good. Must stay. Easier this way."

A flicker of sadness crossed Cassius' face, but it was followed quickly by understanding. He stepped back, heaving a sigh. "I do not think there are many more boxes to carry down."

"Can get rest," Linda told him, already moving towards the stairs.

The days blurred. Amelia moved The Blue Rose quickly to avoid a storm lingering in the distance. Helai seemed to get her sea legs quicker than the time spent on the Firebrand, and Linda followed her around, if simply out of sheer boredom. They couldn't even get in the water, as much as it tempted them.

Intoh spent much of his time in the crow's nest. Linda wasn't well versed in the ways of magic, but Intoh had always been good with the sea and manipulating the air. He had even quieted a small storm once. He stood up there now, his fingers weaving through tendrils of air. How he hadn't given himself a heart attack from all the magic he used surprised Linda. They'd seen those less reckless die from overstimulating their magical muscle.

The next day, however, he sat on the deck of the ship with Rooster before him. Both sat cross-legged across from each other, and Rooster held Intoh's healing necklace loosely in one hand.

"What doing?" Linda asked.

"I asked Intoh to teach me healing magic," Rooster explained. "I think I knew how to do it, you know..." He rolled his hand. "From before."

"Concentration for this magic very important," Intoh said. "Distraction can cause overcorrection, can wound further." Intoh held up his left hand and slowly clenched his fingers into a fist. Linda knew Intoh's joints ached in his left hand from old injuries. "Some hurts cannot heal. Cannot regrow limbs. Cannot take away all pain. Magic only makes process go quicker."

Rooster nodded. "I understand."

Intoh pointed to a small cut on Rooster's leg. "Can practice on that."

"A rakken bit me," Rooster said in explanation, his hand pressed to his leg. A white light seeped between his fingers as he concentrated, and when he pulled his hand away, the mark left was nothing but a scar, shiny and healed.

"Good sir, good," Linda said, impressed. Despite their aversion to magic, Linda could admire the strength it took to wield it. Even Intoh looked impressed, and he was rarely glad to see others succeed.

Linda turned away, leaving them to their lesson as they sought out Helai.

The distant storm caused the seas to roughen, and even Linda's stomach rolled from the waves as they crashed against the sides of the ship with little mercy.

Some of the sailors sang while they worked, pulling at lines and adjusting the sails as a soft, pretty melody slipped from their lips. It was nothing like the shanties pirates sang off the shores of Lyvira, with rowdy lyrics and quick stomping of the feet, and Linda had to admit they preferred the song of the pirates.

"What look at?" Linda asked, trailing up to Helai at the front of the ship. Her hair was down, but the wind tossed it around her face so much that she started pulling it back into a ponytail as Linda approached. She seemed troubled; it rolled off her, but Linda was not well enough versed in human emotions and couldn't guess what might be wrong.

"Oh, just lost in thought, Linda. I got this note before we left. I–" She hesitated, pulling it out of her pocket and showing it to Linda. "It's from one of the Ghosts. He's in Halvdarc, but it doesn't make any sense."

Linda looked down at the letter and the mess of scribbles that meant nothing to them. "Can't read," they said. Helai laughed nervously, shoving the letter back into her pocket.

"Right. Doesn't matter anyway."

"Does matter," Linda said. "Important to you."

Helai shook her head. "Thank you, Linda, but let's drop it."

The ire in her tone tempted Linda to growl, but they did as she asked even if it stung a little. Helai's tone mirrored some of the greka back home, and it paid homage to a time when Linda's shackles had been even tighter.

They reached up, touching the tooth necklace around their neck. The necklaces back home signified ownership: a krok'ida with silver or gold around their neck was never free. Intoh had ripped the gold from Linda's neck the moment he had commanded they follow, and that was perhaps why Linda respected Intoh so much–even if he still shared some of the qualities of the greka that Linda loathed. Sometimes he used that angry tone too.

"I'm sorry, Linda," Helai said, shaking the krok'ida from their thoughts. "I just worry about them. The Ghosts are like family to me. I hate the thought of them being separated."

"We are family," Linda protested quietly, lowering their hand from their necklace to curl over the railing of the ship. Sea spray reached up to brush against their face, and Linda relished it, breathing in the warm, salty air.

"Ah–yes." A troubled expression crossed Helai's face when Linda looked at her, so they nodded in enthusiasm.

"Don't worry! Help find them."

The worry freed itself from Helai as she grinned up at Linda, slipping her arms around Linda's neck. "Thank you, Linda. I'm so lucky you're my friend."

"What this?" Linda asked, raising their hands above their head in confusion. Was Helai trying to choke them? She couldn't possibly; she was way too small.

"It's called a hug. It's a way of showing someone you care about them."

A hug. That comforting feeling from before filled Linda's chest again as they reached down and picked Helai up, pulling her close. She weighed next to nothing compared to some of the things Linda had been tasked to carry in their long life, and after a moment of nervous laughter, Helai leaned into it, returning the hug. Helai smelled of sweat and the lingering stubbornness of vomit, but Linda pulled her closer all the same as Rooster shouted from above.

"What the fuck is that?"

Sixteen

CASSIUS

Rooster's shouting pulled Cassius from his thoughts as he stood at the front of the ship, watching the waves part for the bow of The Blue Rose. Fog had rolled in sometime in the morning, but it was dissipating just enough to reveal the hint of another ship in the distance. Cassius raised a palm over his brow and stilled. It was a longship hailing the sails of those from Volreya. The sight of it was unnerving; what were Vykra–the men and women of Volreya–doing so far south? They were not known to venture far from their god's resting place, which was in the north, where the cold of winter was never-ending.

He'd never had to fight the Vykra before, but he'd heard tales from his brother and sisters in the Order. They fought without honor and with little regard for their own safety. Most of them fought with brutish strength and determination, making them a formidable foe. Many knew that a Vykra ship meant impending doom; they'd already taken half of Kreznov's settlements and forced its people to its western borders. The sight of one of their ships did not mean well.

"We are not going to be able to out-sail that longship if they decide to pursue," Cassius said, turning to Rooster as he stepped up beside him. The wind had halted, the sails billowing softly as if to mock their slow crawl forward. The crew started to scramble across the decks, spurred on by Amelia's commands.

"Then we must be prepared to fight," Rooster said, his gaze far off. "It's a shame that this ship does not have any cannons— Wait, is that the same sigil as our brand?" He pointed, and as Cassius looked, his brand burned in response. Three jagged lines diagonally drawn across a circle marked the sails; it was the same as the markings on the walls in Volendam and the same as the brand on their backs. The sight of it filled Cassius with rage, and he turned, striding up to Amelia and her first mate Ludgara.

"What is our plan?" Cassius asked.

"You are all fighters, *awi*?" When they nodded, Amelia sighed, brushing strands of hair from her face. "We ar' a tradeship, not equipped for battle, but we'll give them all we've got." She turned to Ludgara. "You and Cassius will prepare some of the men to board if it should come to it. Send Baela down to collect whatever weapons can be used. The rest of us will prepare for whatever they throw at us."

Cassius tasted the anticipation, fear, and adrenaline in the air as everyone scrambled in different directions. Many of the crew hoisted the sails, slowing The Blue Rose to a crawl so when the impact happened, it wouldn't be as hard.

Retreating to the sleeping quarters, Cassius retrieved his sword and shield, adrenaline coursing through his veins. He forced his breathing to calm, the quiet pluck of hunger in his throat drowned by the threat of battle.

The boat rocked violently, sending Cassius toppling into the wall as the wood of the ship groaned. Shouts sounded from above, and Cassius righted himself, then hurried back above deck to chaos.

The longship had slipped through the fog, its people staring up at The Blue Rose with solemn expressions. Their faces were covered in the paint of battle. There weren't very many of them, their swords resting at their sides, but Cassius knew longships were deceiving; a standard one could carry fifty men easily hidden below decks.

Cassius looked at Ludgara and the men who'd readied themselves on deck. Many of them carried their weapons with uncertainty, gripping their hilts too tightly or too loosely, and they flinched as Linda walked up, twirling their war hammer in their hands.

"Ready to fight," Linda said, raising their hammer above their head. Intoh was now in the crow's nest above, electricity arcing through his fingers, and as the longship approached, an old man with a long white beard smiled, his teeth black and rotten.

"Lucky for us, they will be forced to board," Cassius said after a quick glance at their longship. "They also have no cannons to speak of." Longships were known for their speed, not their defenses, but Vykra were aggressive fighters and did not need the use of cannons so long as they could get aboard a ship.

A woman prayed beside him as the crew shuffled towards the middle of the ship, preparing for the longship to sail up beside them. Cassius tightened his grip on his sword as the longship slowed. A low chant echoed off the water as an old man on it began to pray, raising his hands above his head. The clouds swirled above, and after a moment, two portals opened, a shroud of purple between the two ships.

"Prepare to be boarded," Ludgara cried, holding the front line with Cassius. Despite the crew not being seasoned fighters, their resolve held as they defended the front line with stubborn courage. Thunder rolled across the surface of the water as lightning danced some miles off, the sea angry with high waves.

Cassius steadied himself as the first Vykra stepped through. Raising his shield, he blocked the Vykra's attack, pushing back against the weight of his sword arm and swinging, catching the Vykra under his raised arm. The Vykra flinched away in pain, only to be decapitated by Ludgara.

Blood splattered across Cassius' chest as more Vykra poured through the portal in droves, shouting in glee. Sheets of rain followed behind their charge as the storm finally arrived, a torrent of wind pulling Cassius' hair around his face.

"Cassius, your left," Ludgara shouted. Cassius raised his shield just quickly enough to block the edge of the blade, but the impact jarred his arm, shooting pain up to his shoulder. Thrusting his head forward, he headbutted the jeering Vykra, breaking her nose on impact.

She flinched back, howling in pain. Her ire burned heavily in her gaze as she spat a mouthful of blood in Cassius' face. He stumbled, his heart bursting in a flurry of panic as a flashback scraped against his mind, crippling him.

"Get up!"

Cassius heaved as an iron-clad gauntlet entered his field of vision, reaching for him. His horse lay dead beside him, run through with a spear, and its blank eyes stared up at Cassius in silent despair. The battle for Fraheim raged around him, an endless noise of steel and the cries of the dying.

Cassius looked up, a sob curling in his throat as he stared into the dead eyes of a fellow vampire. He tried to pull away, but Aleksei, a fellow Sanguine Knight and dear friend, had a tight grip on his arm, holding him in place as the armies slaughtered each other around them. If Cassius did not get up, surely the rain and mud would drown him...choke him until he cried out for death to take mercy upon him.

"Cassius!" The tail end of Cassius' scream pierced the air as Ludgara whipped around, his eyes flashing in urgency. "We need you–" A noise of surprise followed by the spray of blood passed Ludgara's lips as a Vykra ran him through with a sword, its tip of steel protruding from the center of his chest.

Cassius' resolve shattered as his mind shuddered in and out of the past and present, Ludgara's face blurring into Aleksei's, then back again. The man's wordless scream echoed as he collapsed, and Cassius turned and fled as he had all those years ago when Aleksei had fallen. He hadn't thought about his brother-in-arms and dearest friend for quite some time, but the panic consumed him as his vampirism threatened to take advantage of his weakened resolve and feed. His sword dropped to the ground as his fingers curled into his hair, and he fell to his knees, an inhale of air barred by a sob that knotted in his throat.

He was lost.

Seventeen

ROOSTER

The storm raged around them, but Rooster kept his balance with ease as he slashed at Vykra with his sword. He blinked rapidly to keep the water out of his eyes as he cut down another pirate.

"Linda, duck!" Helai shouted from below, pulling a vial from her hip. It glowed a faint purple as she shot forward, throwing it through the portal as Linda dodged to the side and out of the way. Vykra continued to pour through even as the vial exploded behind them. Three were hit, and a sap-like substance contacted their skin, burning through flesh as if it were water. Their screams shattered the air as the wind came to a standstill.

Intoh shouted something from above, his fingers straining as they reached for the sky. Rooster slashed through another Vykra, only to have her replaced with more. Dozens of them stepped onto The Blue Rose and engaged with the crewmen on the front lines, clanking steel. The sorcerer who'd opened the portal stepped through. Standing near its entrance, he shot at a sailor with a bolt of dark-purple energy. He missed as the man twisted behind a Vykra, and the ball exploded over the surface of the Vykra's back with a dark flame.

A Vykra raised his blade against a sailor that had stumbled and fallen, and Rooster moved quickly, lashing his sword out to intercept the Vykra's blade.

The Vykra grinned; the skin around his eyes was snaked with dark red trails as Rooster pushed his blade away and backed up.

"Come and get me, big guy," Rooster said, flexing his grip on the hilt of his sword. The deck of the ship was slick from the earlier rain, but Intoh had since put them all in a bubble of sorts; the rain came in a torrential downpour several feet from the ship but hit some invisible barrier that protected the fighting from the elements.

"Going to collect every little tooth in that pretty head of yours and use them to honor the gods that offer me strength," the Vykra growled, a small axe in his left hand. He came at Rooster with brute strength, and Rooster raised up his sword to catch the axe before it could make contact. He swung his left hand at the Vykra's head in a desperate attempt to disorient him, but the Vykra caught his fist in his palm and pulled him forward. Rooster gritted his teeth as the Vykra squeezed his fist, the pain radiating down his arm.

"Stupid," the Vykra uttered, following that quickly with a string of words in a different language. Up close, the rage in the Vykra's eyes was infectious, a wild maelstrom of blue that heated Rooster's belly and made his own anger fester.

A shadow slipped past, and the Vykra howled in pain and let go, allowing Rooster to stumble away. A deep wound wept from the Vykra's arm, and Rooster locked eyes with Helai as she darted behind him, one of her daggers slick with blood. She'd given him just enough time to recover and retaliate, and he ran his sword straight through the Vykra as dogs made from shadows were born, ascending from the deck and throwing their heads back to howl. They leapt onto crewmen, ripping their throats out with their teeth as Rooster stumbled away.

"Men and women of The Blue Rose," he shouted as the crewmen began to flee, fumbling over each other to get away from the hounds. "There is nowhere to run! Hold your ground if you want to survive."

The crew shouted with renewed vigor and pushed forward, fighting for their lives as the hounds ran the length of the ship. Amelia barked orders to not give up as Rooster fought with his back to the foot of the stairs, striking down any enemy that drew near. He grabbed the railing as he slipped on the slick deck, nearly going over its side. A dark mass flitted through the water, and Rooster stared at it, trying to discern what it was. A shark, perhaps? Or maybe a pod of whales? They would not have gotten so close to the fighting though.

A loud animalistic shout snapped Rooster's gaze around the deck until he spotted Cassius crouching with his head in his hands. Before he could take a step forward though, spines rose out of the water in an arc in Rooster's peripherals, only to disappear into the depths before he could get a closer look. It definitely wasn't whales.

He shook his head and hurried to Cassius' side.

"Cassius," Rooster shouted, stepping in front of the vampire to defend him. "You must get up, mate. Now isn't the time for a breakdown."

A Vykra descended upon Helai several feet in front of Rooster, sliding the blade of an axe across her shoulder before she cut him down with multiple stab wounds to the throat. He collapsed onto her, knocking her over, and Rooster slashed through a shadow hound as it attempted to take advantage of her fall. The dog disappeared into a puff of smoke.

Linda roared, raising their hammer. Somehow, they'd gotten near the sorcerer. They utilized their advantage and swung, striking the sorcerer in the side. It flung him against the mast so hard, a worrisome crack shot up the wood. The portal dissipated in a puff of smoke, same with the hounds, and the remaining Vykra shouted in protest as they pushed forward.

"Liiiinda," Intoh hissed out from above, but the mast remained true and did not break. The sorcerer's breath was labored, but somehow he was still alive as his bones cracked and moved back into place. Dark magic coiled around him like a snake, circling his eyes and mouth and drawing him back to his feet.

Even still, the fighting continued, but it looked to be turning to their favor as they fought off the Vykra. Cassius stood once more, and Rooster turned to flash him a look of concern.

"Are you–" A loud sound pierced the air. Like a cross between a whale and a dolphin, the sound accompanied movement as the ship shook, halting the battle as the world went still. What wind had gotten through Intoh's defenses died, and the hair on Rooster's arms stood straight up as a chill rolled down his back. Something was not right.

He peered over the railing of the ship and saw the dark form swimming towards The Blue Rose once more. It swam too deep for Rooster to discern what it was, but its size was breathtaking. He'd heard of sea monsters hunting the deep sea, but The Blue Rose had remained close to the coast. It seemed strange one would come so close to land.

The ship groaned as it leaned to one side. A colossal, snake-like head breached the water, shooting upwards until it settled nearly thirty feet in the air. As four more heads followed suit, Rooster realized with horror what it was.

"Hydra," he shouted. The beast was enormous, with shimmering blue-lilac scales that dazzled in the droplets of water that poured off it. Large fangs hung from each head's exposed mouth as it hissed, and the storm faded, moving east as sunlight broke through, illuminating the scales of the hydra with brilliant light. Each of its heads moved in a different direction, snapping at the air or sniffing the sails, and its scales flapped lightly in the wind. Its tail curled around the bow of the ship, securing it against its body.

One of the hydra's heads shot forward, grabbing a Vykra and flipping him upwards before swallowing him whole. Using the distraction to their advantage, Linda twisted their ring, shifting back into a krok'ida. They sank their teeth into the sorcerer's uninjured shoulder, using his screams as fuel to bite harder. Blood gushed from the wound and between Linda's teeth as they pinned him against the mast, where Cassius, who seemed to have fully regained his courage, stumbled forward and decapitated him. The head rolled and was stopped by the metal foot of a plated soldier. Ships sailed through the fog, the black flag of a skull with two crossed bones and vampire fangs hailing its mast. The ships had moved so quietly and the fighting had proved too distracting that they hadn't noticed they were getting ambushed until it was too late.

"Oh shi–" Rooster's curse cut short as pain blossomed from his head, and he sank to his knees. He nearly went unconscious as black spots dotted the edge of his vision, but he gritted his teeth and dug his fingernails into his palm as his sword was ripped from his grasp and his hands were forcibly bound. More pirates boarded The Blue Rose as their ship docked beside them, and the hydra made no move to attack. The newcomers moved efficiently, killing the remaining Vykra and capturing the rest of The Blue Rose crew with rope. If any resisted, they were slaughtered. Rooster glanced behind him to see Amelia had also been tied up.

"On your feet," his captor hissed, dragging Rooster to his feet and pushing him towards the middle of the ship. Helai had her hands held out willingly. The air around her electrified with her anger, but Intoh was nowhere to be seen. They had Linda and Cassius bound as well, and they lined everyone up, pushing them to their knees. The hydra retreated as a man stepped onto the ship, his gaze covered by an immaculate black hat. From the way he walked and carried himself, Rooster assumed him to be the captain, his dark skin showcasing his southern heritage. His hair was knotted in locs and hung loose, framing the sides of his face. When he looked up, he grinned, revealing fangs.

He was a vampire.

His eyes were dark red; he wasn't cloaked like Cassius, showing the world his true nature. His nose was upturned like a bat, his ears tapered to points. His fingers were more talon-like than human, and nearly all his teeth were sharpened. He was an apex predator among a ship full of prey. Rooster had heard of vampires adopting the pirate lifestyle, and he held his face up defiantly, glaring at the vampire as he walked the line.

As he reached Rooster, he bent at the waist, still smiling. "Ah, if it isn't da Carter Wingman. Da infamous Captain Delroy Greaves has arrived ta ask ya but one t'ing. Where de fuck is m' skaels?"

Eighteen

HELAI

Helai was tired of being bound and at the mercy of captors. She glared at the woman in front of her, too angry at her situation to be frightened when the woman hissed and revealed the glint of fangs. The captain was a vampire, and it seemed his crew shared his bloodthirsty fate. A crewmember bolted for the side of the ship, but he only made it a few feet before a pirate was at his back, their teeth ripping into his neck.

"You called him Carter?" Helai asked, tilting her head towards Rooster. "Do you know him?"

"Ah, aye. His name be Carter Wingman–he did not tell ya, eh? He be good about de lyin' an' cheatin' hims way out of situation, so don't be offended if he lied t' ya too, girl," Delroy said, laughing bitterly. "Carter, where is me skaels? Ya took it with empty promises, and now I've come to collect."

"I have no idea who you are," Rooster sneered, and Delroy reached out and smacked Rooster across the face. The crack echoed off the ship as everyone remained silent, except for the woman beside Helai who prayed to Lalira, the goddess of mercy. The pirates stood stone still as Delroy drew close to Rooster's face.

"Do not lie ta me boy. Solatso told me ya ran off with da skaels in da dead of night. Are ya calling her a liar?" Delroy asked, gesturing to the hydra behind him. Solatso's main head snaked forward towards Rooster, who stared up at her unyielding. A massive yellow eye drew close to Rooster before Sollazo pulled back, exhaling sharply. Rooster's hair blew back as Solatso shot forward, bumping him with her nose. He toppled over on his back as the woman beside Helai burst into tears. Rooster did not move as Delroy laughed, pressing his fingers to the side of the hydra's head.

"She may 'ave a soft spot for ya, but do not question where her loyalty truly lies." Patting Solatso, he continued to walk the line, halting in front of Cassius to laugh through clenched teeth.

"A fellow night-walker, eh? What are ya doing traveling da seas? Why do ya mask yourself behind da face of prey, hm?" Delroy's questions were met with silence, Cassius' face a hard line. Helai couldn't tell what he was thinking, but the silence only seemed to amuse Delroy, whose laughter deepened. Soon the ship was full of laughter from the pirates, their tones low and haunting. Sollazo curled one of her heads around the mast to rest near Delroy, who pressed a hand to her snout. She exhaled, blowing hot air in their faces, and Helai spoke before she could stop herself.

"If you're going to kill us, do so already."

Delroy clicked his tongue against the roof of his mouth as he stared at Helai. He radiated an intimidation only vampires could pull off, and his cheek pulsated as he worked his jaw, wagging a finger at her. "Ya know da Carter Wingman you travel with? I found him when he was only a little lad off da shores of Lyvira, scared an' alone. Me crew, dey wanted to eat da boy, but he was prepared to fight tooth and nail for hims survival. I saw a spark der, much like da spark I see in *your* eyes, girl." A small hum passed Delroy's lips as his finger trailed along Sollazo's scales.

Waving his hand, he continued, "I didn't let da crew eat him, and he grew ta be one of da most fiercest pirates to ever sail da sea." His gaze fixated on Rooster. "It is why I be giving ya a task, boy. I'm even willin' ta forgive da stolen skaels."

Helai watched Rooster struggling to process the information Delroy was giving. It was a lot for her too. Rooster was a pirate? Where had his memories gone? Why had he traveled with vampires? Her mind was a whirl of questions as Rooster rocked forward until he was sitting upright once more.

"What kind of task would the great Delroy Greaves bestow upon us?"

Delroy's lips split, revealing the gleam of fangs as he stepped forward and rested his hands on Rooster's shoulders. "Dat's my boy." Amelia was silent as she sat beside Rooster, her face pale. Her hands shook, and one of the pirates wove her fingers through Amelia's hair, as if sampling a dessert. The rest of the crew stayed silent, and while she still wept, the woman beside Helai no longer prayed to her god.

"We shall talk in da Captain's quarters, da one the Captain has so graciously loaned to us, hm?" Delroy looked to Amelia, who nodded numbly. "Good. Let us go where we can speak da free tongue."

"Wait. If I am to hear what you have to say, then I ask that my friends come too," Rooster said, gesturing first to Helai and then to Cassius and Linda. Intoh was still nowhere to be seen, but Helai had a feeling he was tucked away behind his invisibility somewhere.

After a moment, Delroy nodded.

A pirate tugged Helai roughly to her feet from behind. His fingers were cold against her neck, and she tried not to gag at the smell of rot and death that permeated off him. She turned to look, and up close the vampire looked nothing like Cassius unless it had been some time since he'd fed, with glowing red eyes and sunken cheeks.

"Eyes forward, meat," the vampire seethed. Helai complied silently as they were led to Amelia's quarters. The room was small, with little more to it than a simple bed and a desk in the corner. A spare coat hung on the wall, as did a map of Vilanthris, and on the desk was a faded photograph of a child hanging off the wheel of a ship with an older man laughing beside her.

Amelia and her father, perhaps? Helai could not tell.

Delroy sat at Amelia's desk, kicking his feet up on the surface as he picked his teeth with a taloned finger. Rooster stood next to Cassius at the window near the back of the ship. His back faced them as he looked out, and Helai stayed near the door. Linda seemed disinterested in anything Delroy had to say, plopping down in the middle of the room. Two pirates remained, standing near the door. Their expressions were unreadable.

"Der is a tree deep within da forest of Lyvira dat has been dormant for da past thousand years. Da rumor is dat a dragon lives in dat tree. Somet'ings waking it up," Delroy said. Helai scoffed, earning the stares of everyone in the room.

Delroy's smile faded, and he looked at her with malcontent. "Do ya think me a liar, girl?"

Helai shook her head, her stomach twisting in disgust. "No. You are not the first person who speaks of lost gods returning." She raised a chin. "How do we know you speak the truth?" Even as she scorned the validity of the pirate's words, the back of her brand mocked her, burning through her shirt.

Delroy's laugh turned bitter. "Aren't ya from da Shoma lands, girl? Ya love to worship da scaly gods." Helai knew he spoke of Qevayla, the dragon of dreams. Her people believed Qevayla once walked the mortal realm as a dragon, only to shed her flesh and ascend to the stars, where she watched over them. Her skeleton still rested in the Za'tifae Desert, housing the holy city of Shok'Alan. Offerings were left on her bones, and to steal them would curse the robber.

"What my people worship does not mean it aligns with my own beliefs nor does it prove their existence now. Again, I ask, what gives us any reason to believe that what you claim bears truth and is a threat?" Helai folded her arms across her chest, uncertain where her lack of fear came from. She knew she was being foolish by provoking Delroy, but she wouldn't be dragged into a fool's errand on the word of a vampire and pirate. Not when her Ghosts were still out there. Not when her brand burned.

"It doesn't matter what ya think, only dat Carter stole me skaels an' now he owes me. Ya were simply in da wrong place at da wrong time." He clapped his hands together as he twisted, placing his feet back on the floor. "I seek somet'ing powerful enough to put a god to sleep. I do not know what kind of artifact bears dat much power, but I will keep in touch."

"And if I say no?" Rooster asked, his eyebrows slanted over a hardened expression. Linda said nothing, their tail flicking back and forth across the rug they sat on. Their tail kept hitting the boot of one of the pirates. He then raised his sword, intending to hit Linda on the back of the head with the pommel. Helai blinked, and Cassius was behind Linda, his fingers curling around the pirate's wrist.

"I would not recommend doing that," he warned, his own fangs bared, and Delroy held up a hand before the pirate could retaliate. The pirate frowned but pulled his hand out of Cassius' grasp, backing out of Linda's tail's range. Cassius remained near Linda, watching the pirate with ill-concealed suspicion.

A gust of wind shot through the room from invisible cracks in the ship, and Helai suppressed the urge to shiver as Delroy's gaze met Rooster's once more. "Ya treasure da Volendam of yours very much, hm? I've been keeping tabs on ya, and last I heard you defended it as if it were your own home. Dat's where you've been hiding an' layin' low. Might pay da city a visit if ya don't go doing what I ask of ya."

The implications turned Helai's mouth to ash. She wanted to scream at him but valued her life enough to know it would be a moot point. She hadn't survived all these years by screaming at those who could easily kill her.

Silence drenched the air, thick as ice. Helai didn't have time to think about doing the errand work of pirates. She needed to find her Ghosts and continue the efforts of freeing her people.

"I guess you leave us with no choice," Rooster said finally, drawing a smile back to Delroy's lips. He stood as the room was drenched in silence.

"I will be in touch, Carter," Delroy said. "We are running out of time. If dat dragon wakes up, da trouble won't just come to me doorstep." Moving past Helai, Delroy opened the door to the main deck. A softer rain fell, small droplets hitting the deck as Helai shivered, wishing for home.

Delroy rubbed his hands together as he moved towards the bridge that had been attached from his ship to The Blue Rose. He glanced at the crew, then to the Misfits. "Ah, but why da long faces, hm? Ya act like I have come with da news of da end of days." He tsked, making eye contact with Rooster. "We'll be in touch."

Delroy waved a hand at them as the pirates released everyone's bonds. Helai's wrists ached as the rope was removed, and she squeezed them as Delroy shouted. "Come on lads; we have da north to hunt!"

Soft cries of relief came from several of the crewmen as the pirates departed. A weight had settled in the air when the vampires had arrived, and it begun to disappear now, leaving the air easier to breathe. Helai glanced at Rooster. She sensed his anger through the brand that somehow connected them. She wanted to approach him, but Amelia stepped forward before she could.

"Are you hurt?" Helai asked, turning her attention to the captain. Amelia appeared uninjured, but a quiet anger of her own sat in her expression. She watched the pirates sail away as Delroy shouted orders in a foreign tongue.

"The only thing wounded is my pride. Crew members died because not one but two enemies snuck up on us." Amelia spat on the ground of the ship as the crew helped each other to their feet. Helai noted only a few of them were wounded. Up in the crow's nest, Intoh reappeared, his head peeking down from the ladder.

"Are they gone?" he asked, scaling down with ease as he came up beside Linda. His hair was a disarray, his eyes wide with fear as Linda grumbled and patted Intoh on the head.

"Bad guys gone," Linda said. They had returned to their human forms, and Cassius was earning the distrustful stare of everyone around him. He opened his mouth to speak, but it was Helai who stepped up, her brow furrowed in ire.

"I know what you all went through was traumatic, but who was at the front line fighting those northmen? Who has traveled with you for a week now? Cassius is not the enemy," she said, scarcely believing herself. Just months ago she wouldn't have been caught dead defending a vampire.

One sailor drew forward, his arm bleeding. "Then why did he flee when we needed him to hold? He ran and because of that, Tommen died. *Ludgara* is dead." A murmur of agreement rang through the crew, and Helai looked back at Cassius, whose mouth was pressed in a thin line.

"Have you ever stood on the blood-soaked land of battle? Have you ever smelled the rot of death and heard the screams of hundreds dying? Have you ever had to raise your blade to end the life of a friend because they begged you to as they bled out on the battlefield? You know nothing of the world," Cassius hissed, pressing forward. Helai stopped him as she raised her hand to his chest, and he did not resist her as he turned away. "Trust me or not. I will remain out of sight until we have arrived in Halvdarc."

"Cassius, wait," Amelia said, but Cassius was gone, a ghost in the wind. Amelia sighed, running a hand through her hair as she turned to her crew. "If you 'ave reservations about Cassius, that's fine. I only ask you leave him alone. Same with Linda," she said, nodding to Linda. "We all saw what you are, and so long as you don't mean to eat any of my crew, you will be treated the same. Is that understood?"

The crew mumbled, but many of them nodded. As Rooster and Linda moved forward to aid the crew in search for damages and pail water from the hull, Helai traveled around, helping Intoh with the wounded. She healed where she could, offering words of encouragement to those shaken by Delroy and his crew. The woman that had been praying beside Helai had not moved from her spot, her hands shaking as they clung to a necklace of silver beads. Helai knelt down next to her, and the woman flinched, ignoring Helai's offered hands.

"They're gone," Helai said gently.

The woman shook her head. "Fucking vampires. They're not known to come so far up north, let alone be serving as pirates. This world is full of evil, dark things, and I don't know how much more I can take." A quiet wail escaped the woman's lips, and on some level, Helai could sympathize. She had faced many nights in the sands, freezing and alone and wondering the point in it all. Her faith in Dalnor, her Ghosts, and her stubborn desire to see a better world had always kept her moving forward.

Helai nodded to the beads in the woman's hands. "You pray to Lalira, yes? Seek out her faith, know that she is watching over you. Do not despair."

The woman's tear-stained face sobered as she met Helai's gaze, her hand finally reaching out to take Helai's. "My faith seeks her out every day, child. My prayers are always met with silence."

Helai squeezed the woman's hand sadly as she stood. "That is when faith is truly tested."

Helai found Rooster tucked between two crates in the hull of the ship. Helai's joints ached from the fight, but thankfully she'd been uninjured this time. Her wound from the siege was still sore from time to time; she didn't need more pains added to it. Exhaustion clung to her with a stubborn quietness as she sat down across from Rooster, who refused to look her in the eye. He hadn't said much since Delroy had left.

"This is the perfect hiding spot, you know. I almost couldn't find you."

Rooster sat with his head pressed against the wall of the ship, perfectly hidden from view as a flask rested loosely in his grasp. He offered it to Helai silently. Taking it, she tentatively took a small sip before handing it back, noting the 'CW' carved into the side. *Carter Wingman; it makes sense now.* The whiskey burned on the way down, but it warmed her belly and cheeks as she gestured to the flask.

"Do you want us to start calling you Carter?" The name felt weird on her tongue, like it didn't match the Rooster she knew at all. In the twenty-four years she'd been alive, her and her Ghosts had taken many names to slip through Shoman city streets undetected, but with Rooster's identity, it felt different.

"No, I mean – I don't know." He set his flask down, and his hands moved to tug at his hair. It had grown out, no longer shaved short, and curled around his ears in small waves. "I've been Rooster as long as I can remember, which truly hasn't been that long at all. I – I need time to think about it."

Helai shrugged, bringing one leg up to wrap her arm around. "Either way, I'll call you whatever you want. It matters little to me what you call yourself, just what kind of person you are." She offered the briefest of smiles. "And considering the kind of things we've all done in our time together, none of us can exactly proclaim a good moral code."

"I don't know what type of person I was before Rooster, but you know the person I am now. I –" Rooster sighed, tapping his head against the wall. He appeared frustrated, and Helai's heart went out to him. Who would she be had the memories of the Ghosts and her home been robbed from her?

"I do not like the idea that someone like Delroy knows more about me than I do. And there's also this name that keeps rattling around in my head–I think it's a name anyway. Igraine. I don't know who she is, but I need to find her. I think she can help me figure out who I was. I don't think I'll feel okay with the name Carter until I do."

Helai nodded in understanding. "Of course. Rooster it is then. I am sure after this is all said and done and we figure out a way to remove these brands, you'll have enough skaels to seek out this Igraine."

Rooster's hands lowered to his face and then he reached for his flask again. "I think Velius knows her. He knows at least more than he's letting on." He went silent as someone came down, whistling a faint tune. The silence was thick between them as whoever it was shuffled around one of the crates and then disappeared back up the stairs.

"That locket I stole from the Silver Moon Club? Velius claimed he could use it to help find someone he knew. And well..." He lowered his voice, leaning close. "When I touched it the first time, I had a flashback I think, and it was of Igraine."

Helai's brow furrowed in alarm. "If Velius knows Igraine, and she's someone from your past, why hasn't he told you anything?"

Rooster shrugged. "Can't tell you."

That news was troublesome. Her earlier suspicions of Velius resurfaced, and she leaned back, staring out of the small round window situated in the wall. Night had fallen, and the pale moon illuminated the sea, casting an eerie glow. Since the attack, Amelia had ordered that they pick up the pace, and Helai's stomach had been suffering for it.

"I intend to pry him for information if we ever see him again," Rooster said with a sigh. "Otherwise, I don't know how to even begin searching for Igraine. Can't even think about it until we get these brands figured out." He went silent for a moment. "And the woman that haunts Cassius—Ahma? I don't trust her. I found him pacing the other night, and the moment I focused on him, I felt it—this strange hunger that twists in my belly."

Helai felt the same hunger too sometimes. It came and went, but its intensity always grew anytime she drew close to Cassius. She hadn't given much thought to it though. The vampire carried many demons, and she wasn't sure she wanted to know what kind. She'd seen him during the fight. He'd felled a man with the swing of his sword, then something had triggered within him. She'd seen some of her Ghosts fight with demons like that, but seeing it on Cassius had sent a chill down her spine.

"We'll talk about all of this later," Helai said nervously. Rooster nodded and eyed her with some hesitation. "What should we do about Delroy?"

"Also a conversation when we can meet as a group." A heaviness settled in the pit of her stomach. "Do you think Delroy will really follow through with his threats should we deny his demands?" she asked quietly. Her hand reached up to grasp her pendant.

"I don't remember what type of person Delroy was, but he didn't look the type to make empty threats." The implications sent silence through the hull for some time as Helai undid her braid, threading her fingers through her hair. She hated the poison of corrupted power. Many men and women wielded it with cold calculation and did not care who it harmed.

After several moments, she nodded. A dark selfish part of her questioned her role in all of this. Delroy had entrusted whatever task he meant for Rooster to fulfill to Rooster and Rooster alone. Felix and Patrina's faces haunted her mind though. She could not abandon them to some terrible fate should Delroy not get what he wanted.

Smiling softly, she pushed herself off the crate. "Good night, Rooster," she said.

Silence met her as she turned away and hurried off to bed.

Nineteen

CASSIUS

A melia was eager to be rid of them the moment they pulled into the port at Halvdarc, Rovania. The rest of the sail down the coast was spent in relative silence with the surviving crew avoiding most of the Misfits as best they could. Cassius kept to himself, seeking solace with the trade goods in the hull for most of the trip. His hunger and restlessness grew with each moment, but a strange calm enveloped him as they drew closer to Halvdarc. His brand was silent, and he was thankful for it. He had enough to worry about.

Ascending the stairs, he greeted the sun and the headache that accompanied it as the crew began to shout. They had arrived.

Rovania was ripe with green hills and lush trees, and the cities of its kingdom did not disappoint. Welker Castle sat high and proud atop a hill surrounded by thick forests, a testament to their wealth, and the waves of the sea crashed up against the side of the cliff it was nestled against. Even from where he stood, Cassius could see the rows upon rows of rose bushes nestled together in various shades of white and red.

"The Welker Estate, if you care to know," Cassius said, stepping up next to Helai at the front of the ship. "As you can imagine, they did not get their wealth through genuine means. They are known by some for their involvement with the shadow market, but they front it through the flower trade. You'll see if they grant us an audience."

Helai frowned. "I cannot imagine them being the pleasant sort."

Cassius shook his head. "Oh no, they're lovely so long as you play their social games. I have only met them once, but I have a feeling we will need to speak with them. If there are cult activities in Halvdarc, they will be the people to ask."

Helai's silence was warranted. Rovania did not see much poverty, their lands flourishing with abundant crops, happy livestock, and a plethora of wineries. Those who went without remained fed through the mild winters, and the kingdom was one of the last that honored bartered trade. Most cities in Rovania still accepted skaels, but it had been a culture shock to Cassius when he'd relocated from Hestia to Rovania in his human years. He still remembered the time his uncle had traded two prized horses for a year's worth of wine.

"I need to get in the castle anyway. One of my Ghosts is in there." Helai's words bled a sense of urgency, felt through the brand, and Cassius studied her quietly. Her troubled nature hadn't gone unnoticed, but Cassius had been too focused on his own worries, he hadn't spent much time checking in on the others. Helai had always felt restless to him, always standing at the edge of a cliff desperate to jump.

"Are you certain?"

Helai nodded. "I got a letter from him just before we left Volendam."

He watched as they sailed through the canal, the coastline of Hestia off in the distance, so far it was but a distant bump that edged the horizon.

He often missed his home. Hestia was known for its grandeur white marble buildings and community bath halls, and Cassius' heart ached at what was lost. He'd buried his home in his heart the moment his father had sent him to go live with his uncle.

"I can feel it through you," Helai said suddenly, pulling Cassius away from lost ghosts. "Whatever your Ahma wants? It's in there." She gestured to the castle.

Cassius' brand pulsed with several waves of emotion, the quiet temptation to follow. Helai was right; whatever it was, the next piece of the Ebony Fang was in that castle. The acknowledgment of it sent a shudder down Cassius' spine more intoxicating than easing his bloodlust had ever granted. He locked eyes with Helai and nodded.

"We will do what we must. I know of an inn near the base of the castle that could grant us an audience with one of their advisers at the very least." It had been some time since he'd ventured to Halvdarc–not since he'd considered killing the Welker child as the Order had asked of him. It was in this city he'd decided to forsake his vows and abandon his task. Seeing it all again threatened his anger, that touch of madness that refused to relent.

"You sure that is wise?" Helai asked.

Cassius nodded, shaking thoughts of the past away. "We have no other choice."

Cassius watched Rooster slip skaels into Amelia's hand as they made port.

"A little extra for the trouble we ran into and the crew you lost," Rooster said, shuffling several more into her waiting palm.

"Do not ask for transport from me again, and we'll 'ave come to an agreement," Amelia said, pocketing the skaels and waving him away in dismissal. "Now go. I 'ope to never see you again." Despite the harsh tone on her tongue, Cassius couldn't blame her. The men and women that pulled goods off her ship were few and far between, and they looked worse for wear. Some even threatened to bolt; Cassius could tell by their wandering eyes and elevated heartbeats.

"Glad to be off ship. Enjoys crow's nest, hated vampires. Would like to find somewhere quiet to read," Intoh said, pushing past Linda as they watched the crew work solemnly. Halvdarc's port wasn't large, nothing compared to Volendam's port, but it *was* the largest in Rovania, being the only way in by boat. Several ships were docked, and the bustle of trade was in full swing as the early morning turned to afternoon.

"Cassius spoke of an inn. He thinks we can get an audience with one of the advisers of the estate," Helai said, pointing to the castle that loomed in the distance. "We might as well scope out where we are to sleep before we venture anywhere else."

Rooster was quiet, uncharacteristically so, but nodded. "Lead the way then."

Brushing past a man selling thick carrots and vibrant cabbages, Cassius led the other Misfits off the docks and into the grassy plains of the city. Halvdarc was built around the forest it dwelt within, and the residents of the city honored the nature that surrounded them by building their homes in ways that did not harm the trees. Those of Rovania tended to be superstitious and weary of their eldrasian neighbors to the south and did not wish to anger some nature god.

Still, something was wrong.

As Cassius traversed the forest, a silence stretched in the air that was not like when he'd been here before. No children played, and the birds were silent. A whisper caressed the back of his head as a shudder of powerful magic accompanied it.

Mother.

Cassius glanced back at the others, but none of them appeared to have uttered anything. He shifted his shoulders as if to shake off the feeling, but it remained, insistent, not too unlike the brush of Ahma's presence.

Mother's coming.

It pulled away then, leaving a hollowness in the small of his mind. If the others had heard it, they did not say, and Cassius remained silent. Best not to give them a cause for concern if there was none. Still, the air tasted of strange magic, of something akin to necromancy, only slightly less so. Cassius couldn't put his finger on it.

The village's center was sat in a large clearing, where the main stores and inns resided. A fountain sat in the middle, made of stone, trails of water shooting up on display.

"Hmm." Cassius' brow furrowed. "Something is strange here. This place is usually bustling with life at this time of day." He pointed to Intoh and Linda. "Drikoty trade is common here; it usually isn't uncommon for one or two of your kind to be walking around either." The silence continued to stretch even here. Several people walked by, but they did so with purpose and did not make eye contact, their faces bent as they hurried quickly to their destinations. Everything *looked* normal, but there was a current of unrest in the air.

"Feel it too," Linda said, their head cocked to the side. "Doesn't feel right."

"Hurry–" Cassius said, pointing to a long building near the road that led up to the castle. "The inn is just there."

"Is it always like this?" Helai asked as they crossed the meadow.

Cassius shook his head. "I haven't been here in over five years, but this place is completely different from the last time I was." A woman locked eyes with him, her gaze turning fearful as she ushered her child into their house and quickly shut the door. "I am eager to see if the Welkers' adviser has answers."

Twenty

INTOH

T he inn they entered, Sapling's Refuge, was very different to The Broken Arrow. It smelled of warm chestnuts and something sweet, almost like honey. Where The Broken Arrow had been bustling with the life, laughter, and conversation of sailors, the inn they stepped into was quiet. No bard played, and while a fire roared in the hearth to keep the hint of chill at bay, the place sent a shiver through Intoh, who held more tightly to the book in his grasp.

The innkeeper was a small woman, slight in stature with dark circles under her eyes despite the fact that the inn only housed a few patrons at the moment, sitting as far from each other as they could. The desire for The Broken Arrow grew stronger the longer they stood here, and Rooster coughed as he trailed up to the counter.

"How much for boarding and food?" he asked, offering a kind smile.

The innkeeper did not return it, her fingers tapping erratically against the bar as she wiped it with a rag.

"Oh, oh yes. Yes, yes. Three skaels a night. Only soups this time of year. It's two skaels per meal." The woman spoke quickly without raising her head to meet Rooster's gaze, and Intoh tugged on Linda's shirt and gestured to the table in the corner. After they nodded, he scurried over, leaving the others to figure out the rooms.

Ekalas appeared at the table as he approached. He was shocked to see her; he hadn't seen the ghost of his old friend since the opera house in Volendam, many months ago. Glancing behind him nervously, he made sure the other Misfits were at the counter and nowhere near hearing distance before he plopped down next to her.

"Hmm." Ekalas' head bobbed as she stared at Intoh with one unblinking eye. "You grow fond of them. Distractions. You remember our mission, hm? Must find way to live forever. Must gain more knowledge."

Intoh stared as Linda pointed at something behind the innkeeper, their brow furrowed defensively. "Am not. Just following to collect sample from fanged one and remove brand. Will resume full attention to mission when free of it."

Ekalas waved her hand over his human body. "Still hide when not necessary. Trading city, know drikoty. Not Intoh I knew. Intoh now grow more into a Misfit." Her words struck him like the blunt edge of a blade. The mission to find the gift of immortality had always been his and Ekalas' dream. To give it up now, after all he'd lost...after all *she'd* lost... would be devastating. She was right. He needed to get back to thinking about what they'd worked so hard to achieve.

"Sorry, my friend. Will get back on track."

Ekalas nodded, her hand reaching out to rest on top of Intoh's. "The answer is somewhere out there. Just have to find it."

He stared at her hand, at the ghostly way it shimmered, just slightly transparent as it rested against his. His thoughts strayed to the conversation the other Misfits had had with Delroy, that vampire captain that took The Blue Rose hostage. The tree they spoke of was well known to the greka as a place of great peril, and going near was rumored to be a death sentence. Intoh had never been anywhere near that part of the forest, but the thought of having to do something with it made Intoh dizzy with fear.

"Do not fret, *inka*," Ekalas whispered. "Sometimes knowledge requires courage and sacrifice."

Intoh blinked as the other Misfits made their way over, and Ekalas was gone, a reminder that she was nothing more than a ghost that haunted Intoh from time to time.

"The innkeeper is going to get in contact with the Welkers' adviser. Said it could take from a better part of the day to a few days to get a response," Rooster said to Intoh as they piled around the table, Cassius with a wineglass, Helai with a bowl of soup for Linda. The few other patrons inside the inn eyed them warily, their hoods up to cover most of their faces, but Intoh ignored them. He was used to the suspicions of others. It made him glad for the ring on his finger.

"Library in city?" Intoh asked.

Cassius nodded slowly, his fingers clasped delicately around the wine he'd brought over. "I believe so. I know the Welker family has an extensive one. Emir Welker craves knowledge as much as you do, Intoh, but I am not certain how much information you will find in the public library."

"Will spend next few days studying. See if answers are there," Intoh said. The thought of being able to spend the next few days reading uninterrupted sent a flurry of joy through him, and it took all of his willpower to keep from getting up and leaving right at that moment.

"I plan on visiting the flock to send some letters out. Is there anything you want me to say to Patrina and Felix? I am going to send a letter to Volendam and see how things are going there," Helai said, pulling a quill and parchment from her bag.

"Missing them already? Or are you inquiring about a certain dwarf?" Rooster teased.

The glare Helai shot in Rooster's direction was sharper than the daggers she wielded, and even Intoh was compelled to flinch away. The emotions of humans were strange; Intoh knew he could never hope to understand, and quite frankly, he didn't want to.

"Tell Miss Hilde that she is missed," Intoh admitted. In the quiet moments when The Broken Arrow had concluded their dinner rush and the Misfits hadn't been trying to figure out the cure to their cursed brand, Intoh had been teaching Hilde how to read. He still remembered the shock that had run through him when Hilde had told him she'd never learned.

"Tell Felix and Patrina that if we ever make our way back, I expect the finest of fish from Dirk," Rooster said. He groaned, leaning back in his seat and patting his belly. "I miss Dirk's cooking terribly."

Intoh's stomach protested in agreement, and Cassius sighed, tipping his glass back and finishing his last bit of wine.

"I cannot wait for the completion of the bathhouse. Traveling again has reminded me why I loathe being on the road." Wrinkling his nose in disgust, Cassius pushed away from the table to return to the innkeeper.

Helai contented herself with writing a letter to The Broken Arrow crew as Linda stared sullenly at their soup. It didn't smell great with some form of questionable meat inside, and eventually, Linda pushed it away.

"Smell bad."

"We'll find someone selling fish at docks later," Intoh promised. His own belly protested, and he couldn't help but fantasize about what kind of fish were caught in Rovania's waters.

What noise had occupied the inn ceased as the door opened. Intoh looked up as two greka entered the inn, and Intoh gulped, grateful to be tucked safely behind the illusion of his ring.

"Oh, we don't–" The innkeeper's gaze trailed around the bar, her eyes flashing in irritation. "We don't serve drikoty here. You might try the inn closer to the docks, where your lot does their trading."

The two greka in question halted at the front door. One was a deep red with three black stripes lining his back, beginning at the tip of his nose and traversing all the way to the tip of his tail. His appearance mirrored a chameleon almost, and he was a fair bit shorter than his comrade, who was taller than Intoh and bulkier in size with three horns, one on his nose and two more on either side of his forehead. He was a light yellow with sandy-orange coloring darkening his arms and legs, and both wielded spears.

"We are looking for a greka named Intoh'gask," the yellow one rasped, his eyes trailing over the patrons of the inn. Intoh sank low in his seat, his heart pounding as he covered his face with his book. Had they been sent here to deliver him back to Lyvira to answer for his crimes? Would they execute him immediately under the will of drikoty law?

"No one by that name here. If you do not leave, I will have to call the guard," the innkeeper warned.

The red one hummed. "If find, tell him want to talk." He quickly switched to Drikotyian, his eyes sweeping the room as the innkeeper sent someone to get the guards. "The voice of Axolli has spoken to us of a prophet, a greka with lightning in his veins. We come to seek him out in peace. We know him to be in Halvdarc as Axolli has led us here. Please, we mean no harm." They shuffled quickly out the door before the guards could get here. Cassius returned to the table with another glass of wine, his expression burning with curiosity.

Intoh shook his head and muttered behind his book. His hands trembled as the others stared at him, his ears ringing from fear. He needed to leave. If there were greka in Halvdarc and they could track him, then that bode ill will for his research. How long had they been following him? His stomach cramped with sickness and fear, and Linda shook him roughly.

"Intoh," they growled. "Who were they?"

"Don't know. Need to leave."

Rooster held his hands up. "Whoa now, let's not be too hasty. They have no way of knowing you are here. You don't look like yourself. Maybe they will just leave."

Intoh shook his head frantically. "Found me here. Know I'm here. Won't leave."

"Why are they after you?" Helai asked.

He knew he should be honest with them, knew they had laid bare their souls to him enough times to warrant a bit of trust. Still, the last person he had trusted had been lost to the cause.

"Must be for taking them," Intoh said, pointing to Linda.

Linda opened their mouth to protest. "Did nothing wrong."

Intoh shut his book, mumbling to himself. He had enough skaels to charter a boat to take him far, far away. Perhaps he would go south. He knew Shoma to be rather welcoming to greka due to their shared love of magic.

"Now, wait... Why not just go and talk to them?" Cassius asked. "If you don't like what they have to say, surely we can handle two greka?"

Intoh was hesitant, his fingers pressed delicately to the cover of his book. He never knew why books brought him such simple comforts, only that they did. The more he learned from whatever was inside, the more he could wield it in his favor. He was a small lizard in a world of giants. Where others had daggers and shields, his words and the electricity at his fingers pushed him to survive. Still, he had seen what Cassius could do with his knightly training, what Helai could wield in the shadows. He'd seen Rooster shoot arrows from impressive distances, knew Linda to kill whatever was in front of them.

"Could meet," he said finally.

"I will go find them," Cassius said, sliding out of his chair. "I desperately need to feed anyway. If the adviser somehow comes early, wait for me. I know him personally." And with that, he was gone. Knowing the Misfits had his back should the worst come to pass comforted him, but Intoh still felt the weight of fear in the pit of his belly.

What if talking with them is a trap?

Twenty-One

ROOSTER

Cassius returned after the second mug of ale, his eyes gleaming with life. For a vampire, he kept himself clean, and Rooster never saw the hint of blood left behind. "We are to meet the greka before dawn in the forest to the north tomorrow. They said you would know where to find them."

Intoh huffed and then nodded, fiddling with the pages in his book. He appeared stricken with anxiety, his hair plastered on his face from sweat.

"It's difficult seeing your past catch up with you, huh?" Rooster couldn't chase the bitterness from his voice even as he drowned his words with ale. Delroy's arrival on The Blue Rose still haunted him at night.

Delroy's words had kicked up fragments of memories in his head. They were more insistent on pushing through his amnesia, and his chest constricted. *Flashes of vampire teeth. Delroy's face swimming into view*

as a cut bled across his open palm. The wrath of the sea crashing over a
dark pirate ship, nearly taking him out to sea. A large hydra bumped him
with one of her heads. A flash of red hair. A myrlír high in the crow's nest,
pointing to something on the horizon.

The memories had assaulted him with little reprieve since Delroy's
arrival. Owing a vampire, a vampire *pirate*, no less, made him sick to his
stomach. He didn't have the slightest idea what he was going to do about
the tree in Lyvira.

The Welker adviser walked in, saving Rooster from spiraling into his
thoughts.

The adviser wore his wealth, and where Rooster admired the class in
which he dressed, he couldn't help but think it was a bit over the top. His
suit coat was long and sweeping, with two tails trailing behind him, and
his hat was round and tall on his head. A small mustache curled at his
upper lip, and he had no beard to speak of. Rooster doubted he could
even grow one, even if his mustache was magnificent. He leaned on a
cane when he walked, the head of it inlaid with the largest ruby Rooster
had ever seen. His skin was dark but not so much that hinted towards
southern Lyvirian roots. No, he looked to be maybe Shoman, and a quick
glance at Helai's discomfort all but confirmed it.

"You are the Misfits?" His accent was thick. *Yes, definitely Shoman.*
His eyes lingered on Helai for a moment before he shifted his attention
to all of them and lowered his head in respect. "Mr. Antonia, it has been
quite some time."

Cassius tilted his head towards the adviser, his mouth pressed in a thin
line. "Indeed." Turning to the others, he gestured to the adviser. "Misfits,
this is Kareem Balil. He is one of the most talented advisers I have ever
had the pleasure of conversation with."

"You are too kind," Kareem said.

Standing, Cassius grabbed a chair from the nearest table and pulled it up. As Kareem sat, he glanced up at Cassius, his tone natural. "I trust that the Order is well."

Cassius stilled as tension thickened the space between them. Rooster still knew little of Cassius' past or the Order he used to serve, but he knew there was trauma there. Something had happened that had forced Cassius to run from his past, much like Rooster found himself doing. Still, Kareem's passing words made Rooster dreadfully curious to know more.

"I have not been with the Order for some time. It is not the same Order that Louelle and her wife envisioned."

Kareem stared at Cassius with a contemplative expression, resting one hand on his cane beside him. "Who are your new friends?"

As Cassius introduced them, Kareem leaned closer, his eyes gleaming with quiet mirth. "And what brings–" He paused, eyeing the group with interest, "the Misfits to Halvdarc, hm? Could it be the plea for aid from the Welker family? They are to pay handsomely for their son's return."

Concern flashed across Cassius' expression.

Rooster frowned, his brow furrowing in confusion. They'd heard no word of a missing boy. "Missing son? Is it a child? How much will our pockets thicken with this task?"

"So many questions, this one." Kareem laughed as he stared at Cassius, gesturing to Rooster. "Ah, Rembrandt is about eight winters old. We have reason to suspect shoma'kah as there was a caravan of them that passed through here not too long ago."

Helai stiffened beside him when Kareem mentioned the slave traders. Slavery was outlawed in Shoma on the surface, but the wealthy still participated in the illegal act behind closed doors under the guise that their servitude is indentured. The shoma'kah were exiled slave traders branded with the slaver's mark, but Mohalis, the grand sultan of Shoma, rarely did anything to punish their actions. "Why did you not force them to leave? You should know better than anyone of their crimes."

Kareem stared at her, his gaze hardening as all of the earlier amusement washed away. "We had no reason to suspect their intentions were unsavory. Halvdarc has laws in place against discrimination even when it is towards someone who has been marked."

Anger simmered off Helai, and Rooster couldn't say he blamed her. He would never forget his time enslaved to them. He had the scars to remember.

"We were wrong, of course," Kareem continued, his eyes flickering to the table as he sighed heavily. "The same day they disappeared, little Rembrandt was gone as well."

"Do you have any idea where they've gone or what they might want with the boy?" Cassius asked quietly.

Kaleem shook his head. "No idea. The boy is quite gifted in the art of healing magic, but his parents have taken great care in keeping that hush-hush for this very reason. They did not want anyone coming after the boy until he was ready to learn how to harness his magic." Kareem raised a hand. "They're offering four hundred and fifty skaels for his safe return."

Rooster blanched at the amount as Intoh slammed his book down on the table in surprise. Only Linda appeared unaffected. They still stared sullenly at their soup, which was probably cold by now.

"It would be foolish to turn from such an offer, but we request one favor in return," Cassius said, staring at his empty glass. "We need a direct audience with Alyse and Emir Welker in their estate upon the same return of their son." He paused there, but Rooster nearly saw the words dancing on the tip of his tongue. Although cults were rumored to be gathering, it was too tempting to inquire about them with Kareem.

"I can arrange the meeting," Kareem agreed. "But only upon the safe return of Rembrandt. The village has been dealing with disappearances as of late. It has people frightened. No one is allowed in the estate unless the lord and lady will it."

"It seems we have come to an agreement then." Rooster reached out to shake Kareem's hand, smiling when he took it.

"Excellent. I will let the Welkers know. I trust you will get it done in efficient time." Staring at Helai, his voice grew thick with a warning. "We both know the shoma'kah move quickly."

Rooster shuddered at the thought. He did not know what lengths the shoma'kah went to when dealing with children, but they did not seem the type to care. He could only imagine what fates Rembrandt would find himself in if they did not make haste.

"We will leave tomorrow. Give Emir and Alyse my love," Cassius said as Kareem stood, straightening his jacket.

"I will." Kareem grinned, tapping his cane against the floor. "Oh, and Cassius? It is good to see that you are doing well. It is a shame that the Order has betrayed your trust. You are a fine knight. Whatever happened, I hope you have made peace with it."

Pain filtered through Cassius' expression before he recovered. "Thank you, Kareem."

Kareem said nothing else, just flashed a brief smile at the others as he left. Rooster watched Cassius wrangle with something, a deep sorrow that bled into the air and sank into the table. Rooster opened his mouth to ask but thought better of it. The vampire would talk on his own terms.

"If we are to be up at dawn..." Rooster said, hitting the table lightly with his fist. "I do not remember the last time I slept properly. I wish to try tonight."

"We should talk about what we are to do," Helai said, unraveling her braid. The lights in the inn flickered low, and the innkeeper looked less than pleased as she went around cleaning the tables. Everyone had retired; the inn was empty.

"We can discuss after the meeting with the grekas," Rooster said, rubbing his head as a headache forged, unforgiving as it settled just behind his eyes.

Closing his book, Intoh pushed away from the table and hopped off his chair. "Going to bed." He tucked the book under his arm, waved for Linda to follow, and then approached the innkeeper, whispering something to her. She nodded and pointed to an opening that led to some stairs, to which he scurried towards and then disappeared upstairs with Linda following closely behind.

"I'm following him," Rooster said, pushing his chair back. The thought of sleep was too tempting to ignore, and Kareem had given him much to think about.

Twenty-Two

LINDA

The first traces of dawn woke Linda from their slumber. The bed they slept on was far too small in their krok'ida form, but Linda refused to sleep in their human form when they were protected behind the doors of privacy. They groaned as they moved, their muscles protesting in anger. Intoh paced in the middle of the room, muttering quietly to something in the corner. Linda rubbed their eyes, but still, nothing was there.

"Who talk to?" Linda asked, their voice rumbling with sleep.

Intoh waved his hand at them, his brow furrowed with worry. He stood in his greka form, his tail flicking behind him erratically, and Linda growled and sat up.

"Who talk to?" they asked again, this time with more force. They grew tired of being pushed around or dismissed when all they wanted was to know what was going on.

"Ekalas," Intoh retorted, his fingers buzzing with electricity. "Shush, Linda. Distracting. Much to discuss."

"No," Linda said, switching to Drikotyian. "It's not fair. Can't just pluck me from Lyvira and expect me to follow you around without question. I believe in your cause, don't believe in you treating me like this." They stood, pointing at Intoh. "Don't silence me too. My voice is important."

Intoh went silent, his throat bobbing as he stared up at Linda with contemplation. He shook, fear flashing through his expression as he glanced at the empty corner again, humming in response to whatever this 'Ekalas' had to say.

"Noted. Sorry." A few chirps left Intoh's lips as the spikes on his spine wiggled. The electricity faded from his fingers as he reached down to twist his ring, calling out his human illusion. "Ekalas was old friend. Died in Lyvira. Still see her sometimes," he admitted, pushing past Linda to grab his book. "Keeps me on path. Fight to find way to live forever. Maybe find way to bring back Ekalas."

Linda had never heard of someone coming back from the dead. Not without powerful magic, or worse...they came back wrong. Still, the hopeful gleam in Intoh's eyes forced Linda to pause. If anyone could accomplish the impossible, it was Intoh.

They nodded. "Live forever. Save Ekalas. Understand now." A part of Linda still did not understand, but despite everything, Linda's respect for Intoh ran deep. Whatever darkness he carried would lead him down a path that could either save him or condemn him. Linda wasn't sure which side he teetered towards, and they supported Intoh's dream for happiness, but they did not wish to follow. They longed to forge their own path.

For the first time, a seed of hope planted itself within Linda. Perhaps their freedom was closer than they thought. Perhaps they would soon be free of feeling like they were no more than Intoh's guard. The shackles of their past, of their guilt from failing their people lessened ever so slightly.

"Come, Linda. Must talk to greka now." Intoh paused. "Be ready to fight."

Linda rumbled in response. They were always ready for a fight.

Ambling through the woods with the Misfits, Linda decided they liked Halvdarc. It hinted at home, minus the heat and the merciless plant life. Linda had yet to see anything that resembled the massive snakes that lived in Lyvira's trees nor the spitting of spiders. They hadn't even *seen* a spider here.

Tugging at their shirt, Linda sighed. Intoh thought it would be a good idea for Linda to hide behind their human form to serve as an element of surprise should the other grekas prove hostile. And even though they did not like it, Linda understood the advantage of hiding.

"It's just like my sneaking," Helai said, noting Linda's uncomfortable nature.

"Want to learn," Linda said. "Your sneak." Despite their aversion to magic, the darkness fascinated Linda. Being able to sneak up on someone and have them suffer the blissful unawareness until it was too late made Linda shiver with glee. Oh yes. They'd very much love learning how to be quiet. They already excelled at it where water was involved, but Linda was determined to learn how to do it on land too.

"One day when we're not running from the threat of being sacrificed," Helai promised.

"What a day that will be." Rooster sighed. "Sure you know where you're going?" he asked Intoh, who then held his hand up and demanded silence. The woods had grown thick, the rising sun unable to filter through the blanket of branches overhead. A small blue butterfly flew in front of Linda almost lazily. As Linda reached a hand out to give it a place to land, Intoh spared a glance in Rooster's direction.

"Can see magical trail through woods. Not far. Can probably hear us coming," Intoh deadpanned. "Greka sense of hearing is *very* good." Just as the butterfly landed on Linda's finger, a spear shot past their left ear and embedded in the tree behind them. Cassius stood inches from where it swung in the trunk, his illusion halfway peeled from his face. It was eerie, seeing human on one side and vampire on the other, and Linda turned as the butterfly, spooked, fluttered away. Watching it leave made them sad, and they weren't sure why. When the sun hit the butterfly's wings, it lit up, drenched in a luminescent yellow-gold.

"Halt." It was the horned greka who spoke, his voice low and gravelly. He spoke in their native tongue, and Intoh gulped, the lens over his eyes blinking slowly. "Come no closer."

Be brave for once. Linda willed the thoughts for Intoh. They could not imagine wearing their fear so plainly on their scales as Intoh often did.

"You wished to speak with me; here I am," Intoh said, his voice quivering despite the tensing of his shoulders. Linda tasted magic in the air as Cassius stepped forward, his hair in disarray, the monster in him tucked safely behind youthful features.

"What are they saying?" Cassius asked, whispering to Linda.

"Not much yet," Linda admitted watching the red greka step out from behind a tree. He had been camouflaged, but his scales were now returning to their normal color from that of the forest surrounding him.

"Sode. Khal." The red one gestured first to Sode, then himself.

Rooster strolled towards them, whistling softly. "Never seen so many greka in one place."

"Come long way," Khal said in broken Vilris, much like Linda.

"Ah, so you speak our tongue?" Helai said, furrowing her brow in suspicion. Her fingers rested upon the hilt of one of her daggers as she glanced at Intoh. "What do you want with our friend?"

"Come to speak to Intoh." Sode eyed them with distrust as Khal forced a physical perimeter by slithering around them quickly to keep them from bolting.

"Friends. Won't go anywhere. Stay with me. Keep me safe," Intoh said sternly.

"Couldn't you have picked a better time to meet? Like say, *after* dawn to give us a chance to catch up on our sleep?" Rooster asked.

"Speak for yourself. I was already awake," Cassius said, clasping his hands behind his back as he studied Khal. "You two are fascinating."

"Not all of us are dead, ClassyAss," Helai muttered, leaning against a tree.

"Please never call me that again," Cassius said, his tone riddled with disgust.

Khal hissed, displaying small razor-sharp teeth. "Silence! Let the prophet speak."

Intoh's eyes flashed in surprise. "Prophet? You do not come to kill?"

Sode laughed, the sound grating against Linda's ears. "No, no. The star goddess Axolli has uttered whispers. One will lead us on right path through dark skies. One day, stars blot out of sky. We come to pledge ourselves to your cause."

Intoh spared a glance at Linda, his eyes tinged with an array of emotion: wonder, confusion, fear, excitement. Linda couldn't help but feel the same; they had heard their home's leader M'ik speak of Axolli, the goddess of stars. Linda wasn't one to pay attention to the praise of gods for Linda was a simple creature, filled with simple aspirations. Speaking to gods felt way above their capabilities. Still, to think Intoh being tied so closely to one as to be a prophet? Linda shrugged.

"Could be right," they said, patting Intoh on the head. "Could be wrong. Don't really know." It was all the advice Linda could offer.

"Pledge yourself to what cause, exactly?" Rooster asked, staring at Intoh. "You have kept something from us, friend."

"No," Intoh protested, shaking his head. "First time heard of this."

"It was Axolli's will only several moons ago. Made haste to find you. Tried Volendam, but darkness festers there. Followed trail south. Intoh'gask," Sode said, lowering his spear and pressing the tip of it into the dirt as he knelt. "My spear is yours."

"As is mine," Khal said, falling into a bow next to Sode. It was strange, seeing two greka bow to another greka. They usually saw each other as equals and did not bow to anyone except for their leaders. It had always been the norm for Linda's kind to bow to a greka. Intoh had never struck Linda as the type to lead. Perhaps they were wrong.

"Rise, I – Please," Intoh said awkwardly.

"This is ridiculous," Cassius said, pressing two fingers to the bridge of his nose. "We have a child to find, and they speak in tongues."

"Our leader dreamed of fire that would burn at the edge of the world. A chosen few have been blessed by the gods to lead us through the flames. Intoh is one of them," Sode said. His words made Linda's brand burn, and they flinched.

"I have own things to worry about. End of world? Fire? Sounds like someone else's problem," Intoh said.

"If the fire burns, it will be everyone's problem," Khal argued.

Intoh hesitated. "This is a lot," he admitted. "If true followers, how do I know I can trust? Need to do more research, know if your words are true."

"Perform magic sleep," Sode suggested. "If true prophet, you will see."

Linda watched Intoh struggle with the information in the same way Rooster had when he'd found out his name was Carter Wingman. The internal conflict forced the world to still, and Linda leaned heavily on their right, giving an old ache in their left leg some reprieve.

"Okay, will take the Sleep Walk," Intoh said. "Need space and silence."

"What is that, Linda?" Helai leaned forward to ask as Sode and Khal moved out of the way, granting Intoh space to sit down upon a nearby log turned on its side and reclaimed by the forest.

"Greka do it," Linda explained, watching Intoh settle down and cross his legs. "Use magic. Walk in dreams. See future sometimes. See past other. Sometimes nothing." Linda's old leader, M'ik, often performed the Sleep Walk, and Linda had liked to watch him when he'd done it. Sometimes nothing had happened, but sometimes whatever he'd seen would manifest itself in front of him, small magical lights and objects that had circled him until he'd woken. Linda hated magic, but watching M'ik Sleep Walk had always brought a sense of comfort.

"Must keep still. Must stay sleeping. Very bad otherwise," Linda warned, backing away. As Intoh closed his eyes, Linda lowered themself to the ground.

"Now we wait."

Twenty-Three

INTOH

I ntoh was never too fond of Sleep Walking. It took the control from his grasp and left him to the mercy of the Dream. He could choose what path he walked, but what the Dream decided to show him was beyond him. He was left to it as he opened his eyes.

He stood upon a tall pillar overlooking Vilanthris. The world below him was split into three areas: the lush forest of Lyvira, the bitter north of Volreya, and the deserted land of Shoma. All three were thriving in their own respected ways, and Intoh knelt to his knees, peering over the edge.

The fire began in the north. Everything was so impossibly white in Volreya, often blanketed by a thick layer of snow. Trees grew there–hardy pines and ones with trunks so black they seemed almost akin to the void, but they all fell beneath the flames as they raged, flickering and blossoming as they poured out of Volreya and shot into the sky, forging the shape of a phoenix dragon, its wings outstretched as it sailed above the form of another massive black dragon slumbering on the ground. It was beautiful in a haunting, destructive way, and Intoh found he could not look away.

A blue serpent dragon ascended from the desert, shaking sand from its scales as it slithered out from its slumber. It bore no wings to speak of, its long, thin body stretching endlessly across the kingdom as it turned a whiskered snout towards the sky. The fire that peeled from its body was magical in nature, spreading with a vibrancy of blue and purple. Shoma stood little chance as the dragon took to the air, fire bursting through its outstretched maw. It did not stop there, spreading the flames until it covered the entire eastern continent. With two-thirds of the world aflame, Intoh was nearly too frightened to look towards his homeland, the forest of Lyvira.

The Sleep Walk did not grant him the mercy of hesitation as his head turned right and landed upon a massive tree in the center of Lyvira. He knew that tree; his heart thundered in fear the moment his gaze affixed upon it. It was the tree Delroy spoke of. Once upon a time at the birth of the eldrasi people, their god had attempted to plant a seed upon the earth that the dragon Mot then claimed as his own. The tree had flourished for only a short time, too short to even birth its children before its presence had been compromised and the dragons had destroyed it. Greka knew to avoid the area. The skeleton of a dragon encircled the dead trunk, and the magic that bled from it was grotesque and caused sickness to most who drew near.

The dragon peeled away from the tree, its scales reforged in a sickly white-pink as massive yellow pus blisters grew from various points of its disjointed body. When it roared, it sounded sick, like its throat was slick with mucus, and Intoh suppressed the urge to shudder as acidic fire burst from its maw and strangled the trees surrounding it. Every step it took sank into the swampy ground, the squelching heard even from the height where Intoh sat, and it carried its sickness through Lyvira until the continent was aflame with green and yellow fire, and the whole world was consumed by flame.

Fire that would burn at the end of the world.

The heat brushed against Intoh's face as each dragon fixed their gaze upon him, their eyes wielding a different emotion. The phoenix dragon bore the coldness of rage, the Shoman dragon that of temptation and power, and the Lyviran dragon of sickness. As they turned their attention to him, as the world burned around him, Intoh closed his eyes.

The fire never touched him.

"Intoh?"

He slowly peeked an eye open. The Misfits surrounded him, their faces drenched in concern, and the cool air of the forest was welcomed as Intoh sagged, his breath coming unsteadily as traces of the dragons' fire still heated his skin. It had been several feet away from burning him.

"What did you see?"

Intoh hissed as he looked down. Burns covered his arms and legs, tendrils of blue, green, and pink flames pulled away by the wind. It looked almost like stars dotted the flames, but the others looked at him as if they did not see them.

After several moments, the flames and the burns faded, and Intoh was given reprieve from the pain. "Saw it. Three dragons, phoenix, and fire. End of world. No, no, no." He bolted from the rock he sat upon, stumbling as he hit the ground. "Whatever cults doing, must stop them. Must not let that future come to pass."

A collective gasp shot through the party as their brands burned so fiercely that Intoh collapsed, his fingers clawing at his side as if he could scratch the brand from his skin.

"Axolli came to us in dreams. Tell us you will lead us to safe dawn. Must walk the path, Intoh'gask, must trust us," Khal said, unmoving as

Intoh writhed. Cassius leaned against the tree, his fist curled so tightly it shook.

"You come to me and talk of end of world. How can I trust?" Intoh uttered as the pain began to fade. His fingers flexed over the brand, and he panted, pushing himself to his feet while glaring at Sode and Khal. "Cannot trust anyone."

Sode lowered his head, his spear planted in front of him. "Will say The Words. Bind with magic. Only way; will do it willingly."

"That is a very serious statement," Cassius said. "Failure to comply in whatever words you bind to yourself will result in your death."

"We intend to honor that code," Khal said, his head raising just enough to make eye contact with Cassius.

Nervously, Linda stepped back.

Intoh's mind whirred. He'd never performed a binding ritual before. The magic was fairly simple to use but could easily be led astray if he did not bind them with the right words. Still, it was the only way he could trust the two greka kneeling before him, and if the world truly was to be threatened, if dragons were attempting to come back to burn it, he needed all the protection he could get.

"Might step back like Linda," he told the others. "Magical backlash likely." Cracking his fingers, he stretched his arms out and stepped forward, laying a hand on each greka's shoulder. A strange feeling settled within him, a wordless echo of comfort; somehow he knew he was doing the right thing.

Exhaling slowly, he forced himself to relax. Casting magic worked the magical muscle near the heart, and he could feel the strain in his chest as the muscle contracted. "Do you swear to speak only the truth in my presence?"

Khal and Sode's gaze caught Intoh's at the same time. "I do," they said in unison.

A surge of magic coursed through Intoh. The power of it took his breath away as his eyes fluttered. He swayed as the world flipped upside down, and he heard Linda growl somewhere to his left.

"Do not interrupt now that he has started. It will only end in his death if you do," Cassius warned.

Steadying his breath, Intoh continued in Drikotyian. "Do you trust me to keep you safe and swear to protect me?"

"I do," they both said again.

Something tugged at his belly, a tether that connected the three of them. He felt the bones in both of his hands break but the pain was absent as his heart thundered in his ears. Had he gone too far? He was at the mercy of the magic now. The brand on his back burned anew, and the Misfits all gasped collectively behind him as it coursed through all of their brands. Would the magic connect them to Sode and Khal as well?

A subtle ringing drowned out all other noise as feeling returned all at once. Tugging his hands away, he whimpered as the pain of his shattered bones struck him, and Helai moved forward, pulling open a flap of her bag.

"Okay," he assured her, trying to reach up and clasp the necklace at his neck. "Can heal myself."

"You have used too much magic already. You need to be more careful. Let me treat and wrap them at least. You can heal them after you have rested," Helai protested, pulling a salve and wrappings from her bag.

"If I may," Rooster said, kneeling down next to Intoh. Rooster swam in and out of focus as Intoh threatened to lose consciousness, but he clung stubbornly to the waking world as he allowed Rooster to touch the necklace. Rooster had approached Intoh on The Blue Rose, eager to learn the art of healing magic himself, so Intoh had taught him the basics. He relented, knowing if he tried to heal his hands now, he would only injure them beyond repair.

His fingers twitched erratically as Rooster's hand slipped over his wounds. Words of magic, naught more than a whisper, were uttered from Rooster's tongue. A soft green glow illuminated against the blue of Intoh's scales, and then the pain faded, replaced by an insistent itching he could not scratch. The warmth that poured through him revitalized his limbs, and his tail, half-grown from when he lost it in the opera house from fighting that vampire woman, grew another few inches.

"Good at this. Should train in healing more," Intoh told Rooster, patting the back of his hand as he flexed his fingers. They were completely healed, and Intoh no longer felt ensnared in the throes of sleepiness.

"Quite a natural indeed," Helai said, impressed. As she tucked her salve back into her bag, a soft breeze trailed through the meadow. Sode and Khal remained kneeling, their spears pressed to the ground.

"Can rise. Can act on own accord," Intoh said.

Linda ambled forward. "Too many," they said. "Need krok'ida."

Intoh understood Linda's logic. With three greka, there would normally be at least one more krok'ida to defend them. Greka were magical creatures, sought after for their blood, and krok'ida kept anything from getting too close.

Intoh patted Linda on the leg. "Have you. All we need." Turning to Sode and Khal, he gestured to Linda. "Linda actually krok'ida. Hide behind magic ring. Keep us safe."

Linda hummed in agreement as Sode and Khal looked at them curiously but said nothing.

"How are we going to have two greka travel with us without any form of illusion?" Cassius asked. "No offense, but the inn in town made it perfectly clear that they are not welcome."

"Can stay hidden. Used to dwelling within forest," Khal said, standing. He was lankier than Intoh, and he gripped his spear with the grace of a seasoned soldier.

"Will remain close. Watch Intoh in case of danger. Otherwise, stay out of sight," Sode agreed. Khal's scales began to shift colors, matching the environment. A whisper echoed through the trees, but when Intoh stilled to listen, it quieted.

"Need to figure out next move. Will return to you when we know," Intoh promised, turning to the Misfits as Rooster drew forward, his fingers reaching for the flask at his hip.

"Dragons, fire, and the end of the world, huh?" he said, leaning his head back to take a sip of whatever was in his flask. "Forgive me, Intoh, but how do we know what you saw is the future?"

"Just one future, not set in stone. What comes to pass if nothing is done," Intoh said, his exhaustion returning to him all at once. The completion of his desires, the path to immortality, seemed further and further away as the threat of the apocalypse loomed. "Sleep Walk would not lie." He longed for the advice of some of his people, but he knew that to be illogical. If he returned home now, they would surely condemn him for his crimes. He could not be the only one who saw the flames in the Sleep Walk though. His mind was a mess of conflicting thoughts. What did Axolli want from him? Would he be doomed to find the cure for death only to see it consuming the world around him?

Intoh swallowed a lump of dread in his throat as Cassius unclenched his fist and peeked through the blanket of trees. "Our focus needs to be on locating the child. Once we have an audience with Alyse and Emir, we can figure out more about what might be going on in Halvdarc and see if the cults can be taken care of. They are the threat if they mean to bring about the return of dragons. We should not let this stray," he said, his tone grave. "This is not a matter to ignore."

Intoh agreed, and a thick silence stretched through the meadow at such implications.

"For now, let us return to the inn. It seems we have much to discuss," Rooster said.

The warmth of the inn was welcomed as they stepped back through. Intoh had twisted his ring just before they'd re-entered town, and the innkeeper paid them no mind as they returned to the table they had been sitting at the night before. Soft music played, but Intoh saw no bard, and the inn was relatively empty, like it had been the previous day.

"Your new friends spoke of you as a prophet. Do the drikoty even view such a thing? I thought their worship was for science and the study of stars," Rooster asked, watching Cassius as he stood. "Can you grab me an ale?" Cassius nodded as he moved towards the innkeeper, and Helai leaned back in her chair and crossed her arms.

Intoh shook his head. "Two gods. Read them on slabs etched into ruins in our homeland. Axolli and Ikotia. Goddess of stars and god of sun. Found tales when first greka explored the old world." Intoh had never been religious, not like the priests of Ashka who obsessed over the study of stars. He'd never been to their temples, but it was rumored those spires were so tall they touched the sky, granting the priests the closest honor to the gods as anywhere else in the world. "Priests in south Lyvira worship the stars."

"Have you ever been to their place of worship?" Helai asked.

Intoh shook his head.

Rooster thumbed his chin, his eyes lighting up when Cassius returned and slid a mug in front of him. "Strange," he said, his fingers curling around the mug. "Why would a group of priests name you their prophet when they've never met you before?"

"Not sure," Intoh said. He really didn't like the implications of being a prophet. It tethered him to something beyond his control, and that made his skin crawl the same way the brand on his side did.

"Regardless of their intentions, it might be good to have them travel with us. We have no idea what we are up against once we locate the child," Cassius said, sipping his wine. "They looked to be worthy opponents with a spear."

"Agreed," Rooster said. "I think we should take a day or two here. Talk to some of the locals and see if they have seen the boy."

"If the locals will even speak with us," Helai said, lowering her voice and leaning close as the innkeeper trailed by. "It has been a bit...strange since we arrived."

Agreement sang through Intoh at that observation. He couldn't quite place what was wrong, only that the magical feeling of the town was strange and had been so the moment they'd arrived. It danced with the taste of necromancy, only not quite so...foul. It was different than any magic he'd witnessed, except perhaps from the cultists in the opera house.

"I feel it too. I think it's likely due to the rumor of cult activity," Cassius whispered.

Rooster nodded. "All we can do is try. They'll talk to us if they want their little lord back," he said with a shrug. "He can't have just vanished. And if the shoma'kah didn't take him, we don't want to be blindly following the wrong lead."

"Want to eat," Linda said, interrupting the conversation as they stared at the innkeeper. "Could be tasty."

"No, Linda," Intoh said. "Tell you time and time again; can't eat people. Not unless they're trying to kill us."

Linda growled under their breath, pushing away from the table. "Find food. Hungry."

"Might have luck again at docks. Will go with you," Intoh said, glancing out the window. The sun was high in the sky, and he couldn't deny the rumbling of hunger that plagued his own stomach. "It is decided

JORDAN DUGDALE

then," Rooster said as Intoh rose. "We'll start looking for answers as to where Rembrandt might have gone."

Intoh nodded.

Twenty-Four

CASSIUS

T he sun glared down on them as they stepped out of the inn. Despite the headache that formed at the base of Cassius' skull, he welcomed the warmth of the sun.

"If the kid was taken by the shoma'kah, they wouldn't have taken him to Fraheim—even if they got past the guards, the city's streets are too busy to remain inconspicuous for long," Cassius said. "My guess is they might have taken him east to Wilhaven or gotten on a boat. If it was the latter, we'll never find him." It would have been a smarter move to charter a boat, giving them a smaller chance of being ambushed on the road, but if the shoma'kah were taking Rembrandt back to Shoma, they would have to travel east.

"I will go to the docks and ask some questions," Rooster said. Something told Cassius he wouldn't find any answers there, but he said nothing. Perhaps his gut was wrong. It had led him astray before.

"I need to feed," he said slowly, glancing around. The city was thriving, so different from when they'd arrived. Halvdarc's streets were so vastly different from Volendam's. Instead of cobblestone streets and canals, moss covered the dirt roads, and trees grew freely within the town. There was no wall to separate the city from the outside roads, and Cassius looked to the rolling hills in the distance. His hunger robbed his chance to admire the green, and Helai chewed on her lip thoughtfully as she nodded.

"And I need to write a few letters. We'll meet back here in a few hours, yeah? When the sun is at its highest?" She gestured to the sun, nestled below the treeline.

Cassius gave a vague nod before he turned away. His hunger would not let him linger.

Searching for someone inconspicuous to feed on was much more difficult in Halvdarc than it had been in Volendam for Halvdarc did not neglect their poor. The farmland was rich and supple with life from the forests of Daesthara, and thus farmers were able to grow food in abundance. Nearly everyone in town was a fisherman, and the sea life surrounding Halvdarc was ripe for fishing.

Even with the strain of trust that seemed to infect the city, Cassius traversed through the buildings and trees with increased desperation. Each person he considered was either too much in the open or accompanied by someone. It angered his bloodlust for it demanded blood and did not care for stealth.

"Get up." A man in noble clothing kicked a boy old enough to be considered a man but young to Cassius. He lay on the ground, covering his head from the wrath of the other man's boots. Cassius tasted alcohol on the older man's breath even from across the road, and he glanced around to make sure they were alone before strolling over.

"Is everything okay here?"

The man glanced over, his face contorted in rage. "Piss off."

The man's face shifted, and Cassius gazed into the hateful expression of his own father, his own memories resurfacing from the many times he'd been at the receiving end of a boot. Cassius remembered one time when Dominic's rage had won against his reason and he'd broken two of Cassius' ribs as a result.

"I would recommend stepping away from the boy," Cassius uttered quietly. He didn't attempt concern or slyness as he approached; ire stitched into his narrowed eyes. No one was around, and Cassius' hunger had his fangs aching to descend.

"It's none of your concern," the man snarled, slurring his words. He stumbled a bit as he reared to kick the boy again, who curled in on himself to prepare for the blow. It never came as Cassius grabbed the man's arm and shoved him back, his voice laced with compulsion magic.

"Come with me." His hunger once more tempted his resolve as the man's face went slack, and he stepped away from the boy.

"What are you–" the boy started, pushing himself up from the ground. "Wait. No."

Cassius ignored him, grabbing the man by the shirt and dragging him behind the building they'd been standing in front of. He barely heard the boy's protests, too consumed by the rage from the witnessed abuse to care. The anger that simmered with him was cold and quiet as he pushed the man up against the wall, his face decaying as his illusion rotted away. The man recoiled despite his compulsion, but Cassius' fangs were at his neck before he could utter a word.

He placed a hand over the man's mouth to stifle his screams. The struggle was short-lived as the liquid in Cassius' fangs dipped into the man's wounds, causing him to go limp. The taste of blood was sweet, and Cassius felt dizzy from the alcohol that soaked it.

"Don't kill him, please." The voice was far off and off to Cassius' right, but the blood singing in his ears flooded his system with new life, and it drowned out the noise. He drew blood into his mouth like he hadn't tasted it in years.

Something grabbed his arm and attempted to yank him away, and he snarled, pulling lips back over fangs as he lashed around, his eyes bloodshot and his mouth bloody. The boy stood before him, trembling from head to toe. One eye was swollen shut and bruised. His heart beat wildly in his chest, and Cassius nearly lost control and sank his teeth into him. What shred of control he had refrained, and he stepped away from the man, who slumped against the wall as blood pooled down his neck.

"Why do you care what happens to him?" Cassius growled, straightening his shirt and pulling his illusion back over himself. The boy did not seem frightened by his undead state; on the contrary, he looked at him curiously, which made Cassius do so in kind.

He was short and lanky, his hair a dirty mess of short, honey-brown curls that frequently got in his eyes, which he cleared with a shake of his head. His eyes were light brown, his facial features slightly pinched and mousy. He carried a nervous energy that radiated off him, and he looked from Cassius to the man, whose breath was unsteady and shallow. A few more seconds and Cassius would have drank too much for the man to recover.

"He's my father," the boy said slowly. "As much as I loathe the man, I do not want his death on my hands."

"It would not have been your death to bear," Cassius said quietly. Still, he understood. He was no stranger to unloving fathers, and he would have been the same as the boy once upon a time. He would have done anything to ensure his father's safety even though he had wished for his death every moment of every day.

The blood had soothed his cravings, but the man's open wound tempted him to taste all the same. Turning his head, he caught the boy's expression, one of terror and something Cassius could not place. The boy's heart heightened at the question, and he wrung his hands together, bouncing from foot to foot. "What is your name?"

The boy answered without hesitation this time even though his lower lip quivered. "Itale."

"Itale." Cassius rolled the name around on his tongue as he gestured to Itale's father. "We do not owe our fathers our allegiance. I learned that the hard way long ago." Despite his words, Itale shook his head, much like Cassius had when he'd been little more than a child. His father's stern and disappointed expression haunted him as he turned away.

"W–wait!" Itale stopped Cassius as he moved to flee the area. His forearm itched, as if Ahma called to him, urging him elsewhere. He grimaced. *Not now.*

"I– You can make people do things, yes? Can you make him forget me?" Itale's eyes widened as if he were trying not to cry, and Cassius stared at him with a sharp expression.

"I do not think it wise," Cassius said.

"Please," Itale begged, dropping to his knees and clasping his hands together. "I do not know how long I can endure him." Something in Itale's eyes tugged a memory from Cassius of a time long before he was a vampire. His older brother had used to stare at him like that, his dirty cheeks stained with tears. He'd even had the same curly hair as Itale's, just darker, and the eyes had been the same–desperate and frightened. Markus had always been soft; it was why their father had turned all of his efforts to Cassius.

A sob threatened to tear from Cassius' lungs as he forced himself away from the memory. He hated thinking about his brother for it always made him sad. He swallowed it, stilling his shaking hands, and turned to Itale's father. He had his hand pressed to the wound at his neck, and he looked at Cassius with nothing but hatred. The look did not faze Cassius as he knelt and caught the man's gaze.

"You will walk to the docks, get on a ship, and leave this place. Your child is gone, and there is nothing left for you here. Now *go*." The magic wove through his words like silk, soft and sweet. Cassius didn't use his compulsion often; he didn't like how it made him feel, but he'd always been good at it.

The man's eyes glazed over as he nodded. "My child is dead. I need to leave and never come back," he mumbled to himself, stumbling to his feet. Cassius caught his arm before he could leave. "Make sure you clean yourself up and hide your neck before you go to the docks."

As the father walked off, Cassius' fingers pressed anxiously on the nape of his neck. "My compulsion magic, while strong, will not last forever. It is likely your father will return one day. If you have family elsewhere, I suggest you seek them out."

Itale sniffed. "All of my family is gone."

Cassius hesitated. He didn't want to get involved, but something sang to him of Itale's situation. Perhaps it was guilt that made him tempted to aid, guilt for not having be there more for his brother when their father had been at his worst.

Pulling his coin purse from his hip, he shuffled twenty skaels from the bag. Offering them to Itale, he said, "Wilhaven is small, but my estate is there. This should be enough to entice someone traveling there to take you along. If you go to the stables, Korvus is the stable master and a good friend of mine. He'll know where there is work to be found and might be able to provide you a place to stay if you are a hard worker."

"I'm not so sure the roads are safe, sire. I heard my father talking about Welkers' son Rembrandt. Somehow slavers got to him. Father said they were heading towards Wilhaven and some other dark, terrible things I dare not repeat."

Stilling, Cassius looked at Itale. "You say the Welkers' boy is in Wilhaven?"

Slowly, Itale nodded. "He made me promise not to tell anyone."

Pulling his hand back, he pocketed the skaels and looked back the way he came. "It seems to be your lucky day, Itale. My companions and I have been charged with finding and bringing home Rembrandt, so it seems we have a need to go to Wilhaven. We can get you there safely."

Itale eyed him wearily. "You don't wish to bring me along just to eat me?"

Offense cut through Cassius, swift and quick. "Why would I go through all of the trouble to free you from your father's hand just to kill you?"

Itale's lips wobbled in thought as he shook his finger at Cassius and turned towards the house they stood behind. "Please, sire, I'll be right back!"

Impatience stuttered through Cassius as Itale ran inside, the door shutting swiftly behind him. He didn't make Cassius wait long, just long enough to grow restless before he ran back outside, several items balanced in his grasp.

"Is that an entire tea set?" Cassius asked, exasperated. This was what the boy treasured?

Itale nodded, his curls bouncing. "I refuse to go anywhere without it. You never know when you might need a good cup of tea." Shoving the set and several vials of loose tea leaves into a backpack he'd grabbed, he exhaled shakily. "I um, never got your name."

Cassius turned, wiping blood from the corner of his mouth. "Cassius."

Twenty-Five

ROOSTER

The docks of Halvdarc bred a different energy than that of Volendam. The grass of the city trailed straight up to the water, which
lapped against large gray rocks. The docks were nestled in a small half-circle, and if Rooster looked out across the massive river, he could see the
hazy borders of Hestia and even Kythera. A fog had settled across the
water in the early morning, and several dock workers tended to their
morning captures.

He moved to step out of the treeline, but something stopped him.
A buzz of energy caressed his back like something was watching him.
Turning, he locked eyes with someone, a person in a mask. No, it wasn't
a mask, he realized. It was a *skull*—a deer skull mask, he thought, with
large swirling horns that curled around the wearer's ears. Whoever they

were, they did not move, half-shrouded behind a tree. It was eerie, and everything within Rooster begged him to flee.

He hissed as his brand burned, a faint whispering caressing his ears. The voice was low and muffled, too quiet to understand the words being said, but it pulled Rooster in, nuzzled against his skin, curled around his bones. The world went on around him like nothing was going on, but he could not move, frozen in place as the masked stranger continued to stare at him. The chanting grew louder, a soft hum that tossed Rooster's mind into a flurry of panic, and then the masked stranger stepped out from behind the tree and walked towards him.

Move, you bastard, he thought desperately, but something held him in place, magic that rooted him to the spot. His brand burned so fiercely he could hardly bear it; it hurt worse than when he'd been branded in the first place, and if he wasn't frozen, he might have collapsed from the pain.

"Do you hear it?" a voice called out, a quiet noise that echoed through the trees. "Do you hear it—whispering, urging, quiet noises? It comes for us, consumes us, and offers us salvation. Come, quietly come. Chosen, we need the blood of the Chosen." As the masked stranger drew near, Rooster realized it was *them* speaking. They bore no distinguishable features; dressed in all black, a hood was drawn over their head so they wore naught but the black cloak and skull, and Rooster frowned, his anger cutting through his fear.

"You are not the first person to speak such tongues. If you want the message to come across, you should really speak plainly." As the words left his lips, the masked stranger halted, their head cocked to the side. His stomach plummeted as the stranger reached into their robes and pulled out a dagger. It was long, the blade curved as it ended on a sharp point.

Rooster offered a weak smile. "I'll scream. I'm awfully good at it. It would be mighty unkind of you to kill a man without giving him a chance to defend himself." His ramblings were met with silence as the masked stranger raised the dagger to strike Rooster in the chest.

"Carter!" Someone barreled into the masked stranger, releasing Rooster from whatever magical prison had been shackling him in place. He caught himself before he fell as he flinched away from the struggle, his brow furrowed in confusion. Had someone just spoken his name? Oh, how he longed for his bow to be on his back or his sword at his hip. He cursed himself for having left them both at the inn.

It was a dwarf who'd tackled the masked stranger, his eyes wild behind a thick flock of orange-brown hair. His beard was full but untamed, and he overpowered the masked stranger with ease. The deer skull was pried from the stranger's face and flung several feet away.

Rooster didn't recognize the man underneath. He was tall and thin with a small beard growing over his chin. His cheeks were peppered with scars, and his skin was light, almost unnaturally so. His eyes were wild with rage as his teeth gnashed together, and he struggled against the dwarf's strength. His dagger had been thrown in the struggle, and Rooster stumbled for it as the cultist managed to grab hold of a rock and smash it against the dwarf's temple. Taking advantage of the attack, he rolled, pressing the dwarf into the ground and wrapping his hands around the dwarf's neck.

"You bear His mark, but you are a deceiver," the cultist hissed, squeezing the dwarf's neck. "Your sacrifice will be honored regardless."

Slipping his fingers around the cool hilt of the dagger, Rooster shuddered at the wrongness that accompanied it. Some form of magic clung to the blade, and he dropped it, unable to stand the way the magic had started to creep up into his arm, but now it settled there.

The dwarf struggled, his legs kicking out from underneath the cultist. Grabbing the same rock off the ground, already slick with the blood of the dwarf, he struck the cultist across the back of the head. It was a miracle none of the dock workers heard the scuffle as the cultist cried out.

The dwarf coughed, scrambling to his feet as he dove for the dagger. Rooster began to call out in warning, but the dwarf grabbed it with ease and was upon the cultist before Rooster could blink, plunging the dagger into his chest. Rooster rushed forward as the dwarf pulled the dagger out, flinging blood, and shoved it back in, not stopping until the cultist's gurgled breathing did.

"Carter–" The dwarf heaved, forcing himself to his feet as he dropped the dagger to the ground. The grass browned where it hit, and Rooster looked at the dwarf in alarm.

"How do you know my name?"

"Been looking for you everywhere. Rackjack," he said, pressing a hand to himself. "Come to find you. Bring you back home."

Rooster looked at Rackjack curiously. The name danced on the edge of familiarity, only to snap cleanly into place. "I had a memory of you," he said. "I spoke with a myrlír who mentioned your name. Are you from my past?" His breath came unevenly as his palms grew sweaty, and Rackjack nodded.

"Yes, first mate. Sailed with you for long time."

Rooster's stomach rolled with nausea, and he pressed his hands to his knees as he bent, trying to catch his breath. The more he learned about his past, the more his body rejected the information, but somehow he knew the dwarf spoke the truth.

"Feeling okay, Carter? Igraine sent me to find you. Said you were gone longer than promised."

Rooster rose, pushing through his anxieties to really study Rackjack. He was tall for a dwarf, and there was a look in his eye that Rooster worried about–an unhinged, 'will kill you in your sleep' look. The clothes he wore were dirty like he hadn't taken care of himself in a long time, and there was a small silver bead tucked into his beard.

"Igraine, you said?" Rooster didn't remember grabbing Rackjack's shirt, but all of a sudden he had him pressed against a tree, his anger pounding in his ears. His brand burned as if it fueled the flames of his rage, and he bent close to Rackjack. "What do you know about Igraine?"

Rackjack clicked his teeth together nervously, his eyes darting to and fro, refusing to meet Rooster's. "Can't say too much. Will hurt Carter. Will hurt him. Has to trust me. Has to come with me. Igraine can speak on her own."

Rooster's eyes narrowed. "How long have you been following me?"

"Since Volendam. Tried to make contact, but got captured by rakken in sewers. Branded me." He slowly offered his arm, and Rooster let go, allowing him to push up his sleeve. Gorvayne's mark burned brightly on his skin.

Swallowing thickly, he turned away, his mind refusing the information Rackjack had just given him. He'd worry about it later. "We need to hide this body."

The moment he and Rackjack moved to grab the body, it sank into the ground, decomposing at great speed. The air around them hummed like magic was at play, and Rooster watched the grass wither and die as the shattered skull of the deer and the dagger remained.

"I cannot just abandon my companions," Rooster said sullenly. As much as he craved to flee, to follow Rackjack to Igraine, he couldn't leave until he knew Rembrandt was safe, until he'd gotten the brand removed from his back. "Come with me. Once we have figured out a way to remove the brands and have dealt with the cultists of this city, I will allow you to take me to this Igraine."

A conflicting emotion ran across Rackjack's expression, as if he wished to argue, but then he nodded as Rooster turned. He was eager to return to the Misfits and get out of the woods. He realized as he hurried back that he'd never had a chance to talk to the dock workers, but he was too shaken now to care. If the others hadn't found any information on Rembrandt, they'd return to the docks together.

Twenty-Six

HELAI

*D*earest Drithan,

There is a saying in Shoman that loosely translates to 'praise the sun's sacrifice and eternal love to whisk away, granting the moon her time.' Your company pleases me greatly, and though I know your obligations require you elsewhere, a part of me wishes we could see each other again. I hope the trials to become a rhun mage aren't too taxing on you. It must be terribly exciting, the thought of becoming someone so important one day.

I just wanted to send a letter even though I do not have much to tell you. We are in Halvdarc, and despite its weary people, it is the loveliest town. I have never seen so much green. The holy city of Shok'Alan is said to have as much green, but I have never been there myself.

We can feel something evil going on here, but we cannot place what it is or why.

Helai paused, her quill poised above the paper as she hesitated. She did not want to say too much for fear of the letter getting into the wrong hands, but it felt good to confide in Drithan. After a moment, she continued.

I know we have only had our fair share of conversations, but I miss you. Something about you was so grounding. ~~You are the sun in the darkness that has been my life as of late. I envy~~

Grinding her teeth, she scratched out the last sentence.

I hope you are taking care of yourself, Drithan. We have plans to maybe return to Volendam after business concludes here. If there is any chance you are there, I will be glad to see you again.

Helai

She sighed, hovering the quill above the paper. She was never any good at telling people her feelings, but somehow letters made it easier. The vulnerability came to her easily when she could write it on paper.

Folding it up, she slipped it into her cloak with the other letters she'd written. One was going to The Broken Arrow, the other to Wolstadt, where she thought Aryan might be. He'd once spoken to her of contacts he had in Graermar, Wolstadt's capital. If they didn't know where he was, no one would. She had to hope, even though seeing him again would only spike her anxiety. She wouldn't even know what to say to him if she saw him again. They hadn't left each other on good terms, and the pain from him breaking her heart was still somewhat fresh. The memory of finding him, neither much older than five, flooded through her. He'd been her rock her whole life until he wasn't. For the first time since kissing Drithan, she allowed herself to think of Aryan and the love they'd lost. Not three years ago she was convinced they would share their lives with one another. She would have done anything to get back to him. Her guilt was relentless, knowing she felt the same longing for another, but Drithan was also out of reach. There was no use pining for either of them when neither love could be in the first place.

She took a deep exhale, clutching the letters in her hand, before step-ping into the flock.

Entering flocks was always a small shock to her. This one had the birds in an open enclosure with wiring to keep them from flying off. There were various birds; pigeons were the cheapest, but the falcons were faster.

"How much for peregrine travel?" she asked, stepping up to the desk. Despite there being hundreds of birds, the place was immaculately clean of feces, and Helai was glad for it. She'd been in some where every inch of surface had been coated in white. It had stunk so badly, she'd left without sending letters off.

The bird master grunted, running a hand over his balding head. "Twenty skaels."

Helai blanched at the price and sighed, looking up. "What about the crows?"

The bird master caught her gaze and called one of the crows down. It stared at her with beady, intelligent eyes. "Five skaels."

Helai nodded, shuffling for her coin purse. "I'll need three." Pigeons were faster, but crows were more intelligent and more likely to find those the letters were addressed to. While the bird master called down two more crows, Helai shuffled fifteen skaels out of her purse and pulled the letters from her cloak. They'd been rolled and each tied with a thin string, easy for the crows to carry.

"Good day," the bird master said, pulling her skaels across the counter and tying the letters to each crow's leg. They took off, exiting through a window the bird master had opened once he'd pocketed the skaels.

Helai waved a hand and exited, turning back to the center of the city where they'd agreed to meet. Her stomach twisted anxiously. She hoped Aryan would respond before she left Halvdarc. If anyone knew where Massoud was, it would be him, but a deeper part of her missed him terribly. It had been Massoud's decision to send him away, and a part of

Helai had never forgiven him for it. She'd never forgiven Aryan either for agreeing to leave.

Still, she thought as she glanced around, pulling out the letter that had come to her before she'd left Volendam. *Perhaps Zamir knows where they are*. He'd requested she find him in Halvdarc, but she hadn't seen him anywhere. The innkeeper hadn't seen him when she'd asked. She could only hope he was in the castle. There weren't many other places to look.

The sooner you find Rembrandt, the sooner you can get inside and look for him. Knowing that a Ghost was likely so close but just out of reach made her restless as she shoved Zamir's letter back into her pocket. She could only hope they found the Welker boy quickly.

"Who's that?" Helai asked as she approached their agreed meeting spot. Cassius stood with a boy who bounced on the balls of his feet, his lower lip trapped between his teeth. A weariness settled within Helai at the sight of him. He *seemed* harmless; he even reminded her a bit of Ehsan, if Ehsan's hair and skin were lighter, but strangers couldn't be trusted, especially now.

"His name is Itale. He said his father told him where the Welker boy went." Cassius caught Helai's eye. "Wilhaven. I told Itale he could accompany us there as a token of gratitude for the information."

Helai nodded as she studied Itale. He was small, not much taller than she, and his eyes were trained on the ground as if he were attempting to hide.

"My name's Helai," she said finally. "Do we know where the others are?" Just as she spoke, Rooster approached. A stranger followed behind him as well, and Helai sighed in exasperated frustration.

"We are being hunted by cultists, and you both seem to think it's wise to add to our party?"

Rooster glanced behind him. "The dwarf can be trusted." Helai watched the dwarf in question. He was...twitchy, his hands rarely remaining still as he grabbed and tugged on strands of his hair. A strange smell surrounded him, not altogether foul but vaguely familiar. She'd smelled it before but could not for the life of her remember where. His eyes were wild, darting around, and parts of his skin were stained with blood.

"Is he okay?" she asked, her voice hushed. "Why is he covered in blood?"

"Saved me from a cultist," Rooster said. "Claims to be my first mate." He hesitated, gazing up at the sky as his hand pressed against the nape of his neck. "I understand if you can't trust him. I'm not sure about him yet either, but can you trust *me*?"

"Of course I do, Rooster," Helai said.

Rooster nodded as if affirming his confidence, then turned to Rackjack. "Show them," he said. The dwarf stepped forward, pulling his sleeve back to reveal his arm. The brand of Gorvayne scarred his flesh, puffy and red. The brand looked newer than theirs, but the sight of it sent a chill down Helai's spine.

"Where did you get that?" Cassius asked, his voice raised in alarm. Itale watched everyone with wide eyes; he looked like a rabbit, ready to bolt at any moment.

"Rackjack got it under Volendam. Rakken got me, branded me," the dwarf, Rackjack, explained, looking to Rooster for encouragement.

"How do we know you did not brand yourself to deceive us?" Helai asked.

"That's part of the 'trust me' request. Please, Helai. If he has any connection to my past, I have to trust it. Otherwise, I'll lose my mind trying to find myself again," Rooster said.

Helai pursed her lips and said nothing. After a moment, she slowly nodded. She *did* trust Rooster, but she'd be sleeping with her blade even closer on the road.

Itale trembled like a leaf in the wind. Helai felt a flicker of pity for him; Cassius should have thought before pulling the boy into their troubles. He looked barely a grown man.

"Itale, how old are you?" she asked.

"T-twenty-one."

Helai flinched inwardly. So young, though not much younger than she was. His fear made him seem younger, but not everyone had survived the streets since they'd been a toddler. A dark thought wormed its way in, a flickering wonder if Cassius had dragged Itale along to maintain his blood supply on the road. It was but a passing thought before guilt chased it away. Cassius was far too responsible with his feeding to think up such an idea.

"Will take you back to Igraine in no time," Rackjack said. "Will help you remember yourself."

"Who is Igraine?" Cassius asked.

Helai remembered Rooster having spoken of an Igraine on The Blue Rose after he'd been told his real name. Another connection to his past. She opened her mouth to intercept when Rooster held up his hand to stop her.

"No, it's okay. I've been seeing an eldrasi woman in what I think are flashbacks?" Rooster sounded uncertain as he spoke, running his hands through his hair. The pain in his eyes was undeniable. Whoever this Igraine was, she was important to him.

Helai understood. Her heart ached every moment she was away from her Ghosts.

"She is your mate," Rackjack said nervously, his eyes darting between Misfits. "Said she would be on Vitruese," he said, shaking his head and tugging on his beard. "Small island, safe place for Carter."

Cassius' eyes flashed. "Velius spoke of Vitruesian rum when I was recovering after the siege."

A storm of conflicting emotions raged across Rooster's face. "My mate? I–" He swallowed thickly. "I had a memory of us once. She told me she loved me."

"Once we find the boy, we return him to his parents, then find a way to deal with the cults here and remove these brands. After, I promise I will help you find this Igraine," Cassius said. "By my honor."

Helai could give no such oath. Once her brand was removed, she had to seek out Massoud. Him having not shown up to Volendam when he'd promised was troublesome. She had her own loved ones to find.

"Thank you," Rooster said quietly. "I think she is the only one who can unlock my memories."

"What going on?" Linda asked, weaving through the trees with Intoh. They came from the direction of Khal and Sode, the other greka, and Intoh looked conflicted.

Rackjack bolted back and hissed, a strange motion from a dwarf, as a bizarre and awful smell rolled off him. Helai's nose crinkled in disgust as she shied away.

"Who they?" Linda gestured to the newcomers. After introductions were made, Itale looked at Linda as if they were the most fascinating creature on the planet, his mouth agape as he cleared his throat and shuffled forward.

Pain shot through Helai's back. As she cried out, it rang through the other Misfits as everyone winced. Even Rackjack snarled, his brand angry and red on his arm. A fresh rage coursed through her, cursing her situation.

"Wait," Itale squeaked. "Do you all bear that sigil? I've seen it before…"

"Where?" Rooster asked, surprised.

Itale's eyes darted over everyone before looking anxiously at the trees. Helai wouldn't blame him if he fled; he had no obligation to aid them in their trifles. Squaring his shoulders, he looked at Rooster. "My father carved it into our living room wall maybe a week ago."

The air stilled as if Mother Nature were holding her breath. A shudder rolled through the party as a weight settled on Helai's shoulders, and the world grew vaguely darker even though no clouds dotted the sky.

He will burn. It was naught more than a whisper against the shell of Helai's ear, gone before she could comprehend that it had happened at all. Reaching up, she touched her hand to her ear and glanced nervously over her shoulder. Again, that terrible feeling gripped her, reminding her that something horribly wrong was happening.

"If we know Rembrandt is in Wilhaven, we should hurry along. I wish to free myself of this place even if it is only temporary," she said.

"I saw the stables on my way to the docks. It will be better than walking to Wilhaven," Rooster said, pointing through the trees.

Helai glanced over her shoulder one last time. Seeing nothing, she sighed. *Get it together*, she thought, hurrying after the others.

Twenty-Seven

LINDA

The stables stank.

Linda frowned as they approached. Somewhere in the barn, a donkey brayed in irritation. The horses looked good enough to be a filling meal, but Linda was certain they'd be reprimanded for attempting such a feast.

"Stay outside," they told Intoh. "Can't buy horse." The one time Intoh and Linda had attempted to buy horses, the horses refused to let Linda ride, seeing right through their illusion.

"Shouldn't split up now. Not with cultists hunting us. Come, come," Intoh hissed quietly.

Linda snorted in irritation as Helai rested a hand on their arm. "Intoh is right, Linda. Especially with Rooster being attacked. We should stick together."

Helai was right, but Linda still didn't like it, their eyes watering as the foul smell wafted through the air. It got worse as they walked into the barn, and a stable-hand approached, his face dirty and his hair drenched in sweat.

"What can I help you with?"

As the others paid for horses, Linda went over to a large cow with horns on both sides of her head. The cow stared at them blankly, and Linda reached out tentatively, wondering if the animal's instincts would kick in and recognize Linda as a predator.

The cow snorted loudly but did not flinch away as Linda's hand grazed the top of the cow's head, and Linda felt themself soften. They did not wish to eat this one. The animal was not intelligent, not in the way Linda and the other Misfits were, but there was a quiet kindness in the cow's eyes that Linda felt drawn to.

"Lookin' to buy Karen?"

Linda turned and shook their head at the stable-hand. "No skaels," they said sadly. "Next time."

"She ain't good for travelers like you anyway," the stablehand said. "Not unless you have a cart that needs pullin' or a field that needs tendin'." Looking at the others, he gestured for them to follow. "I have just the animals for you all."

Rackjack fidgeted restlessly, and Linda watched him, their eyes thick with suspicion. They did not know how it was possible, but the dwarf did not smell like those they'd met in the mountains. He smelled more akin to the rakken they'd fought countless times—sewage water and smoke but the smoke that came with the aftermath of magical use.

The other one, Itale, sidled up next to Linda, his small features pushed together in contemplation. "You are called Linda; is that right?"

Linda nodded. "Linda girl's name. Linda know. Linda don't care. Linda use 'they'." The conversations grew exhausting to explain, and the concept of gender seemed a bit confusing to those dwelling in the East, but Itale seemed interested, not disgusted or confused, and his eyes lit up in quiet glee.

"They, huh? My father would have hated you."

Linda snorted, shaking their head. "A lot do. I eat them."

Alarm crossed Itale's face, but then he laughed, a quiet nervous bubble that burst from his lips as he pushed his fingers through his hair. "I think that's what I call cannibalism."

Linda did not know what that was.

Rackjack sniffed the air, which appeared strange for the dwarf. "Saw it all the time when rakken held me prisoner. Ate their own when they were starving."

"You are strange," Linda said simply. "Am a krok'ida," they told Itale. "Hide behind ring." Holding up their hand, they showed Itale their ring. Intoh would disapprove of Linda being so honest with Itale, but he was so small. If he proved to be their enemy, they would simply eat him. He wouldn't be more than a snack, but he'd go down in one gulp.

Rackjack hummed quietly, staring at Linda with silent fascination. Linda could not tell if he stared at them or their ring.

"Oh? Fascinating," Itale said, tentatively reaching a hand out to brush over Linda's ring. He stopped moments before touching it, letting his hand drop. "You know most drikoty are welcome here, right? You do not have to hide."

Linda's brow furrowed as they reached out to pat Itale on the head. "Have to hide. Element of surprise. Enemies not expect." Halvdarc felt odd, like a predator hiding in wait amongst the trees, just out of sight. If someone meant the Misfits harm, Linda would be ready. Still, the thought of being able to liberate their true form prodded Linda's temptation as the other Misfits returned, each with their own steed.

Helai's horse was brown, a white streak running down her nose. Cassius' was large and completely black, his hooves covered in hair. His steed stood proudly, his head up, where Helai's walked with a relaxed gait.

Trailing behind Rooster was a simple black mule still grazing on the hay in his mouth, his teeth gleaming against his dark lips. Intoh even had a steed, a small mare. It seemed strange, seeing it follow behind him. He'd told Linda once that horses made him nervous.

"We've decided to purchase a cart too since our group seems to be growing," Cassius said, looking at the stable-hand. "It should be out front for us, yes?"

The stable-hand nodded. "Yes, sir. You will find it suitable for your travels. Your horses will be able to pull it, no problem." They followed the stable hand out to the front of the barn. A simple, open cart sat on the road before them. Two wooden pillars were situated on each side, ready to strap the horses in, and the cart itself looked large enough to carry Linda—or perhaps two to three humans.

Linda had a feeling they'd be walking.

The travel through the forest surrounding Halvdarc took two days, and they stopped only to grab Khal and Sode from their camp and then to rest for the night. Cassius stood near the edge of the campfire the following evening, his fingers trailing through the mane of his horse as he spoke to him quietly.

"Can I pet?" Linda asked, approaching.

"Yes. I named him Fírnster. He is quite beautiful, is he not?" Cassius gazed up at him in adoration as he stepped to the side, granting Linda permission to step forward. Linda had to admit, the horse had a certain charm to him. Unlike the cow back at the stables, Fírnster's eyes *did* bear a simple intelligence, sharing that quiet kindness Karen had had. It compelled Linda to reach out their hand despite the horse's nervous neighing and splay their fingers across his neck. Fírnster snorted but held his ground, hitting the dirt with a hoof as he danced in place. His fur was velvety; Linda marveled at the corded muscles that moved under their fingers.

"Like Fírnster," Linda said. "Good, strong horse."

"I am growing quite fond of him," Cassius said, smiling at Fírnster. "I was trained as a cavalry fighter, you know? The ones that fight on horses."

Linda nodded. There were no cavalry fighters in Lyvira, but Linda had heard tales of them before.

"The bond between man and horse, it calls to me even in my undeath. These animals are willing to die for their rider if it is necessary. I admire them greatly." He pressed his knuckle to Fírnster's forehead, right between the eyes. Linda had never seen Cassius treat something so gently before.

"We need to prepare for the worst–that being Rembrandt is dead."

Linda stared at Cassius. "Always chance. Shouldn't worry yet." It would be unwise to think the worst. Linda knew the human child was important in their attempts to remove their brand, but they'd traveled with the Misfits long enough now to know that if it came down to it, Rembrandt's death would not stop them from getting inside the Welkers' castle.

"Yes, I suppose you are right. I do believe it is best to be prepared for all possibilities though." The light of the fire reflected off the vampire's eyes, and Linda bowed their head, stepping away from Fírnster.

"Too many possibilities. Can't think all."

They left Cassius to his contemplation and sat down next to Itale. A small cup with some herbs inside it sat at his side as he raised a jug with a lid over it, pouring hot water into the cup.

"What is that?" Linda asked, eyeing the drink eagerly. "Ale?"

Itale shook his head with a warm grin. "Have you ever had tea before, Linda?"

Linda shook their head. "Never heard of it."

Rackjack leaned forward, his eyes flickering with interest. "Special tea?" he asked, gesturing.

Rummaging through the sack he'd brought with him, Itale produced two more little cups with small handles. "I suppose it's special in its own way." The cups looked delicate, one of them having a small chip at the lip, but Itale handled them with such care that it made Linda want to be careful too as he dropped a couple of bags of herbs inside each cup and then poured hot water over the top. "It has to steep for a few moments, but once it turns a dark brown, I urge you to try it."

Rackjack curled his hands around his cup eagerly, and Linda attempted to mirror him, but their hands were too large, so they settled with holding it by its tiny handle. They did as Itale instructed, though it was difficult. Their curiosity made them impatient, and several times, Itale had to protest as they moved to drink from the cup too early. Finally, after a few painstaking minutes, Itale peered into Linda's cup and nodded, satisfied.

"Okay, now you can try."

Rackjack, ignoring the heat that curled off the top of the liquid, tilted it back and drank it all in one go. Linda took greater care despite their eagerness, slowly raising it to their lips as they ignored the heat that nipped at their skin through the porcelain. Tilting it back, they let the liquid hit their tongue. The taste was bitter and unpleasant.

Coughing, Linda dropped the cup into the grass. "Do not like."

Itale frowned, scrambling for the cup and picking it up delicately. Soft laughter danced on his tongue, however, and he shook his head. "It's not for everyone, but you could always try it with a spot of honey; it takes the bitterness away."

Linda eyed him wearily. They weren't certain they believed him.

"When does it make you dream while awake?" Rackjack asked, peering into his empty cup. "Would like to watch the world change."

"Oh...oh!" Itale shook his head, shaking his hands in front of him. "It isn't that kind of tea, I'm afraid. I apologize if I led you astray."

Disappointment ran across Rackjack's expression as Helai drew forward eagerly. "If you're offering tea, I'd love some," she said.

Sode eyed the tea with interest as he leaned against his staff. "Would like some too, if offer."

Itale seemed elated at the idea of others wanting tea and got busy steeping two more cups. "This tea, I had it imported from Nantielle. I'm from there originally, but Father–" His back straightened and a pained expression crossed his face. "Well...Father's business brought us here."

"Do you miss home?" Helai asked, taking the cup from Itale's offered hand and blowing gently on the tea to cool it.

Itale nodded, sighing wistfully. "Terribly so. I remember sneaking away to visit the baker down the street from our estate. She'd let me help her sometimes. It felt good, having somewhere to put all my emotions." He coughed, his cheeks reddening. Helai had once told Linda that some people's cheeks reddened when they were embarrassed, but Linda wasn't sure what Itale had to be embarrassed about.

"Sounds wonderful," Helai said, raising her cup slowly to her lips. "Perhaps you should open your own bakery in Wilhaven?"

Itale's eyes widened in wonder. "You think so? I bet they've already got one." But his expression turned thoughtful.

"We must stop. My stomach protests at the thought of pastries," Rooster said, patting his stomach. After that terrible rabbit stew disaster for supper, a cream-filled pastry sounds delicious."

Something rustled the brush near the edge of the camp, and everyone tensed.

"Just a rabbit," Cassius assured as a small gray rabbit slipped through the brush, took one look at them all, and immediately disappeared. A sigh passed through Helai, her shoulders sagging.

"Just a rabbit," she repeated as Linda reached over to pat her on the top of her head.

Just a rabbit, perhaps, but the rest of the evening was tense as if they all waited for something to jump out at them from the bushes. They took turns staying up to watch. The sun touched the horizon before too long, and it was Cassius who roused Linda from their sleep.

"Come, Linda," he said quietly, offering them his hand. "I am eager to be back on the road."

Twenty-Eight

ROOSTER

"**S**o...this is Wilhaven?"

It had taken them a better part of a week to travel by cart and horseback from Halvdarc to Wilhaven. Luckily for them, the plains of Rovania were relatively flat, with only a hill dotting the horizon on occasion.

Rooster had spent much of the trip questioning Rackjack about his past. Still, no matter how much the dwarf told him stories of his times as Carter Wingman, Rooster could not seem to push past the mental block in his head. Not like Delroy had, and even then, those fragmented memories were merely flickers of images and a maelstrom of emotions.

"Igraine will be able to help," Rackjack said firmly. The more he said it, the more Rooster began to believe him.

Wilhaven wasn't much to speak of, nothing more than a simple farming town with wineries as far as the eye could see. Rooster saw touches of Hestia's and Kythera's influences in Wilhaven's architecture with marble-accented walls and grapes carved into the wooden sides of the buildings. The roads were little more than dirt paths through the town, but unlike Volendam where the constant rain and water made the roads wet and muddy, the dirt here was dry. The horses tossed up dust as they strolled into town. There was no wall and no guards to speak of, and Rooster eyed Cassius with an eyebrow raised.

"Seems like a relaxed place to settle down. How did–eh, someone like you manage to remain undetected?"

"I wasn't undetected by some," Cassius admitted. "A deal was made."

"A deal?" Helai asked, unable to hide her shock. "What kind of deal?"

"The kind where I offer my protection, and in exchange, I remain...well, fed."

Helai's horrified expression was almost comical as Rooster leaned forward to pat Jet on the side of the neck. The mule had kept a steady pace alongside the cart for some time and was well due for rest.

"Would you rather I take what I need by force?" Cassius asked. "I did not ask for this curse and do not wish to starve myself. Middle grounds have been met."

"He's right, Helai," Rooster said. Helai's reservations towards vampirism were justified, but it was obvious Cassius suffered for it enough on his own. "There are worse stories about vampires taking what they want by force."

"You have been known to do that," Helai pointed out.

Cassius nodded slowly. "No one is free of doing what is necessary. You grew up on the streets, no? You cannot tell me you have been spared from doing what you had to in order to survive."

Helai went silent, her jaw pulsing as she worked over something in her head.

"Oh, quit picking on ClassyAss. At least he has an excuse for his actions. You love Linda, and Linda has admitted to eating people for *fun*," Rooster said, jutting his thumb in Linda's direction.

"It true," Linda agreed. "Only if annoying."

"I suppose you are right," Helai agreed, if not a bit begrudgingly.

"Sometimes will eat. Very hungry now," Rackjack said from the back of the cart. His eyes were wide with want as he stared at Helai. His expression hungered, and Helai coughed, scooting closer to Intoh, who scowled and moved further away.

"Please keep him away from me," Helai protested.

"We will search for food when we get into town," Rooster promised. His own stomach protested loudly at the notion. After having next to nothing on the road, the prospect of a warm meal in an inn was all too tempting.

Cassius nodded. "While you do that, I will ask around and see if anyone has seen Rembrandt. There are only a few guards in this town, but the community here is a strong one. They will know if slavers came through here."

Quiet rage simmered in Rooster's belly. Slavery at its root was an evil, vile practice, almost nonexistent in the present world, but to sell kids? His fingers clenched against the leather of Jet's reins at the satisfying thought of making the shoma'kah bleed should they find them.

"My estate is just up there should we need a place to rest," Cassius said, gesturing to the hillside. A massive estate sat on a hill. Vines had overcome its gray stone, and it looked to be genuinely abandoned, a tension surrounding it in silent warning. The path that led up to the gate was winding, and Rooster raised an eyebrow.

"Looks welcoming." His sarcasm earned him a glare from Cassius, though he did not disagree.

"I might take you up on that offer," Itale said, looking up at the estate with poorly concealed curiosity as he hefted his backpack over a shoulder and hopped off the back of the cart. "I am not used to traveling just as we did."

"The house is in a bit of disarray," Cassius warned. "I have not been able to tend to it in some time."

Itale waved his hand in dismissal. "I will just clean it if I must." Rooster watched him go as Rackjack also hopped down from the cart, edging up to the side of Jet.

"Very hungry. Must eat."

"Yes, okay. Cassius, is there an inn in this town?"

"Just down the road and to the right. We get a lot of travelers on their way to Fraheim. They will not blink at the sight of a dwarf either. Occasionally, we see them traveling through here."

Rooster's stomach twisted in uncertain anxiety as the party prepared to split off. There were more people out and about than in Halvdarc, and even with Khal and Sode with them, no one seemed to blink an eye at the drikoty.

"Linda be krok'ida?" Linda asked, pressing their fingers to their ring.

"Halvdarc does many dealings with drikoty. Wilhaven is less so, but they are a welcoming sort. I do not see why they would give you any trouble should you wish to be in your true form." Cassius' gaze flashed. "I will make sure no one takes issue with it."

"As will I," Rooster interjected darkly. Linda's growing distress at hiding behind their ring's illusion had become more apparent, and Rooster could not blame them for their discomfort.

The assurance seemed good enough for Linda as they twisted the ring on their finger, and their krok'ida form flourished. The relaxed nature of Linda was far more apparent in their krok'ida form, their shoulders sagging as their maw parted in explicit joy.

"Feel better," they said, shaking their scales out. Intoh frowned but said nothing, speaking quietly to Khal and Sode from the back of the cart as Cassius turned Fírnster towards the road leading to his estate.

"I think I will follow Itale. There are things I need to attend to there to prepare for guests," he said, flicking Fírnster's reins. "And then I intend to find some food. It has been too long." His gaunt cheeks and reddened irises signified such.

Rooster nodded. "Then we will get some food at the inn and find you at your home." He turned to look at the rest of the party, gesturing to Rackjack. "Are you all accompanying us?"

They all agreed and separated from Cassius, who kicked the sides of Fírnster and took off up the hill. Helai and Intoh remained in the cart with Khal and Sode while Linda followed as they moved into town.

Rooster pulled up beside the cart on Jet, staring at Rackjack. The dwarf was quiet, too quiet, and Rooster still wasn't certain of his allegiance. He had reason to trust him, having apparently known him from his past, and that instinctual familiarity kept him from looking too far into the dwarf, but something did not seem right.

"Carter Wingman–what kind of man was he?" He was almost afraid to ask, almost afraid of his answer.

But Rackjack did not hesitate. "As told before: good man. Strong leader. Carter just wanted to help and welcome, no matter who you are."

The words brought a sense of relief. Rooster was not blind to his indifference towards crime, but he had to believe he only did them for the sake of necessity or good. After a moment, he nodded and stayed silent, his head swimming with questions he desired to have answered.

"Cannot say much more," Rackjack said nervously, glancing sidelong at Rooster. "Might hurt your head if reveal too much."

"Why is that?"

Rackjack murmured under his breath, his teeth clicking together in quick succession. "Do not know for certain. Think memory loss is caused by curse."

"Who would have cursed me with amnesia?" Rooster asked. It did not ease his anxieties, thinking there might be enemies out there he had made and did not know about. *Let them come*, he thought sullenly. *They cannot be worse than cultists and rakken*.

"Maybe a god?" Rackjack suggested as they dodged around a cart leaving town. Cassius was right; other than the barest of stares, no one batted an eye at the drikoty. Wilhaven was bustling with life, so unlike Halvdarc. A farmer pulled a longhorn through town, much like the one they'd seen in the stables back in Halvdarc. The cow's quiet resistance was almost comical as it fought against its companion. Children chased each other through the main road, a long ribbon flowing in the wind behind them, and Rooster laughed at Rackjack's words with a shake of his head.

"The gods do not care for human trifles, Rackjack. For what purpose would it serve to rob me of my mind?" He went silent for a moment. "Unless it was simply to be cruel. In which case, I say this to the gods." He raised his hand, flashing the sky his middle finger as Rackjack shook his head and looked warily up at the sky.

"No, no Carter. No sense in tempting them."

Rooster laughed. "I jest, Rackjack. The gods aren't likely to be listening anyway."

Rackjack ran his hands through his hair, visibly calming. "Can't be so sure. Must always be careful."

"He's right. The wrath of the gods isn't to be dismissed, Rooster," Helai said, her hand pressing against the side of the cart as they hit a bump in the road.

Rooster hummed in acknowledgment but said nothing. He didn't have the heart to tell them that he didn't believe in the mercy of the gods and he certainly didn't believe in their wrath. If gods existed, they simply *were*.

As they approached the inn, the sun peaked high in the sky and Rooster's stomach rumbled without mercy. A simple sign that read *The Longhorn* atop the horns of a wooden cow swung gently in the wind.

The inn itself wasn't large by any means. It stood about as large as The Broken Arrow had been. Hay bales decorated the front, and it was lined with hooks to tie up the horses. There wasn't another horse in sight, and Rooster was glad for it. Perhaps then it wouldn't be busy, and they would be left to their own conversation without fear of eavesdropping.

Rooster slid down from Jet's back, attempting to and barely succeeding at keeping his footing as the numbness from sitting in a saddle all morning took hold.

After gathering his bearings, he helped lead the horses pulling the cart over to the side of the inn, where there were more hooks to tie them to. Leaving Helai to tie them, he led Jet to his own.

Linda reached up as a small gold butterfly landed on their finger, its small wings opening and closing as it took a break. It was quite the unusual sight, and Rooster watched as Linda stared at it curiously.

"Butterflies seem to follow you wherever you go," he told them, rolling his shoulders and hissing as a shoulder cracked painfully. He hated traveling by land. His joints ached, and he was ready for some ale to soothe his pain.

"Really like them," Linda said softly, staring intently at the butterfly. Even as it took off, fluttering about their head, Linda stood still as stone until it disappeared around the corner of the inn.

"Ready?" Helai asked.

Rooster nodded. "More than."

The inn was warm, a welcome relief from the biting cold that had settled outside. Winter was arriving in Rovania, and Rooster was not looking forward to the travel back to Halvdarc if it kept getting colder.

His earlier suspicions were correct; the inn was nearly empty, with only two farmers situated in a corner of the room talking quietly among themselves. The innkeeper, a large woman with a kind smile, waved them in.

"G'mornin'!" she called out. "Sit wherever y'd like. I'll be right with ya."

They sat at a table on the opposite side of the room from the two farmers. Khal and Sode sat on either side of Intoh, facing the door, and the chair Linda sat in groaned in protest as the full force of their weight strained the wood. Rooster couldn't stop the laughter from slipping from his lips at the sight.

"The bartender might have seen Rembrandt come through." Helai leaned forward to whisper, her gaze flickering to the bartender. "It will be worth asking anyway."

Rooster nodded, his eyes flitting up to the innkeeper as she bustled over. A thin sheen of sweat graced her hairline, but her eyes were clear and friendly as she offered a wide smile, one hand pressed to her hip.

"Quite th' group. I 'ave some raw fish in the back imported from Halvdarc jus' this mornin' for the drikoty folk if they want 'em," she said, gesturing to Linda, Khal, and Sode. "Th' name's Ulga. Food 'f th' day is beef stew with some fresh carrots an' potatoes. If wine ain't your thing, our ale's good."

"I'll take an ale," Rooster said. "The stew sounds good as well."

Helai and Rackjack mirrored his order, and the drikoty all ordered raw fish, save for Intoh, who ordered his cooked.

"Do we need rooms for the night as well?" Ulga asked.

Rooster shook his head. "Our friend's estate is just on the hill near town. We'll be staying there."

"Ah, yes, 'f course. Food should be out before too long."

"A question before you go?" Rooster raised a hand to stop her, and she halted, her eyebrow perked in curiosity.

"Have you seen a young boy come through here? He would have been with a group of Shoman. Please, your information is invaluable," Rooster said, shaking some skaels out of his bag and offering them to her. "We believe he is being carted by shoma'kah, if you're familiar with the term."

Ulga's eyes darkened at the name, and she glanced over at the farmers before drawing closer, waving away Rooster's offered skaels. "My information can't be bribed when I give it freely. I 'ave 'eard of the slavers in the south, but I'm afraid I 'aven't seen anyone like that 'ere. Not lately." Lowering her voice, she leaned closer. "There are talks 'f folks going missing up north. An abandoned winery. Anyone that goes to investigate doesn't come back." She shrugged, straightening. "Might be worth checkin' out." She tapped the table with her knuckles. "I'll come back with your food an' ale."

Once she hurried off, Helai leaned across the table, her brow furrowed in distress. "An abandoned winery? Why would the shoma'kah take Rembrandt there?"

Rooster didn't know, and if they spent the time to check it out, there was a chance that the shoma'kah could slip further away with Rembrandt. It was risky, and Rooster wasn't certain which route was the right one to take. "Unless there is something happening there that the people of Wilhaven do not know about, I don't know," Rooster admitted, pressing his fingers to the bridge of his nose. A headache was forming, a merciless one that pinched at his eyes, and he sighed.

"No one saw shoma'kah come through here. Winery is best," Intoh said, his eyes gleaming. "Want to kill shoma'kah anyway. Hope Amir is with them." His voice darkened as Rooster looked at him with alarm. The greka was never one to express his emotions even in his human form, but he displayed a hint of cold rage at the mention of the man who'd kidnapped them nearly a year ago. Rooster had to admit the death of the shoma'kah would please him greatly as well. His joints ached in reminder of the fighting rings they'd been forced to participate in.

Ulga returned alongside the cook with their food and drink, and Rooster's stomach grumbled in anticipation as the soup's scent wafted over. His mouth watered as he stared at the bowl eagerly. He took a long draw from his ale. Ulga was right; it was divine.

"I nearly forgot," Ulga said, sending her cook away. "My neighbor *did* speak 'f th' unsavory sort passin' through maybe a week's past. 'M not sure it was your missin' kid, but they did 'ead north where people 'ave been goin' missin'."

"Thank you, Ulga," Rooster said, wiping his mouth with the back of his hand. The party took a moment to silently dig in. The fish the greka had gotten laid on a bed of rice and greens, a lemon aroma settling around the table, but Rooster's eyes were on his soup as he gave in to his hunger and cupped the bowl. It was nothing like The Broken Arrow's food, but it still beat the rabbit they'd been eating on the road.

Rackjack finished his soup and bread in under a minute. Slamming his bowl down, he groaned. "Not enough. Want more." The amount of food Rackjack ate was admirable but oftentimes troublesome too. Rooster glanced over.

"Do you have any skaels?" he asked between bites. The longer he ate, the more convinced he was that the cook of this establishment could give Dirk a run for his skaels. The bread was certainly fresher. When dipped in the soup, Rooster couldn't get enough of it. Gods, *he* might go back for seconds.

Rackjack shook his head. "You always handled my coin."

Rooster laughed bitterly. Of course he had. "We'll get seconds."

"I'm not usually a fan of beef, but this soup is decent. It lacks the spices that Dirk puts in it though," Helai said, eating slowly. "I miss The Broken Arrow."

"As do I," Rooster agreed. The inn was lively enough, but it didn't come close to the homeyness or charm of The Broken Arrow. "Have we made our heading? Based on Ulga's information, I think it would be a good idea to check out the abandoned winery. Sounds like Rembrandt might be there."

"Think we should," Linda said around their fish. They had not cared to remove the bones, and the sound of bones breaking against their teeth echoed across the table. The two farmers that sat in the corner got up and left, waving their goodbyes to Ulga as she cleaned mugs at the counter. It felt too quiet when they left, and Rooster nodded, pushing his empty bowl away and shifting in his seat.

"Then that's what we'll do. My gut is telling me we are right about this. We'll finish up here and get Cassius' opinion on it, yes?" The others nodded, and Rooster's stomach twisted unpleasantly. While he was certain the shoma'kah had taken Rembrandt north, there was unease that came with it. What if they were wrong? An audience with the Welkers was dependent on locating the child. They couldn't fail.

Rackjack tugged on Rooster's sleeve, pointing to his empty bowl.

Raising a hand, he flagged Ulga's attention.

"Can we get two more?"

Twenty-Nine

CASSIUS

"**Y**ou weren't kidding," Itale said, glancing up as Cassius entered the estate. "The state of this place is..." He trailed off, running his finger along the surface of a table situated to the right of his sitting room, which was off the main entrance. The plush velvet of the carpet runner silenced Cassius' step as he moved forward.

"The estate has been left unattended for quite some time. I was drawn away before I could attend to it myself," Cassius said, staring solemnly at the entrance hall. His uncle had loathed Hestian decorum and had wanted no traces of it in his design when he'd had the estate built. Cassius had injected some himself after his uncle's passing, and marble statues stared unseeing at him from their spots, untouched by time.

"You are a knight, yes? Is that what called you away?" Itale asked, gesturing to the suit of armor sitting behind glass as Cassius moved to the sitting room. Light filtered in between the peek of curtains, highlighting the dust that clung to the air, and Cassius whisked over to brush them open, bathing the room in light. His eyes rebelled, a headache appearing suddenly, but he retaliated by relishing the warmth that graced his face, his heart squeezing painfully as he recalled his imprisonment in his tomb.

"In a way," was all he said in reply to Itale, his fingers falling to clasp comfortably behind his back. "Itale–" He turned to find the boy brushing his fingers delicately against the glass case. Cassius refused to look at the armor, his exile from the Order too fresh a wound. "You said your father was carving a sigil into the wall. What did you say he did for work?"

Itale's shoulders tensed, his heart rate frantic against his ribs. It cradled Cassius' ears in temptation, but he ignored it, searching Itale's expression for answers. "I – He – He's an art collector, but he sells them as often as he collects them. He bought something from Volendam, something that interested Emir Welker, so we traveled to Halvdarc to sell it to him, only Father decided to remain after Emir purchased the item."

Cassius' own anxiety spiked as he drew forward. Itale coughed nervously and took a step back. "Sire? Is everything alright?"

"When did he obtain the item from Volendam?" he asked.

Itale's eyes darted around, searching for an escape, and his hands shook. "I – Maybe one moon before you arrived."

Cassius stilled. That would have been around the time they'd exited the opera house, and soon after, the city was sieged. The wealthy hadn't remained in the city when it was attacked, which left their estates ripe for the picking. If Itale's father had obtained something from the city a month ago, it hadn't been purchased from the wealthy and it certainly hadn't been from anyone in the Hull District. This only left assumptions that Itale's father was dealing in the shadow market, in which case...whatever Emir had bought off him wasn't good. No items sold through the shadow market were good in nature; they were usually cursed or dark items. The implications did not sit easily with Cassius as he gave Itale some space, turning to stare into the empty fireplace.

"Cassius?" Itale seemed hesitant. "I – My father was not a good man. I've known that my entire life. He changed after my mom died." He went silent, so long that Cassius turned to see him staring at his hands as he twisted them anxiously. "I was born a girl, you see, knew almost immediately something wasn't right. Mother had always protected me, even after I visited our village's...erm, I don't know the Vilris word for it. Ah, sort of like a *changer*—she helped me look more like how I saw myself." He gestured to himself. "I take a potion, and it helps my body change. But then my mom died..." He inhaled shakily. "Father changed," he said again. "His drinking made him bolder in his disdain."

Cassius moved forward and Itale flinched, the fear in his eyes calming when the vampire's hand rested gently upon his shoulder. "Your father was a fool. The world does not care about such things. He will drown in his own self-loathing." Cassius scoffed. "You are free from that burden, and you do not have to worry about such judgement from the company I keep."

Itale's gaze filled with emotion, and he cleared his throat awkwardly. "Anyway, I don't hope to defend him, but I believe he's entered something he cannot get out of. The item he sold to Emir. I never got a chance to see it, but I know it wasn't a painting or sculpture."

"All the more reason to find Rembrandt and get access to the Welkers' estate," Cassius said, giving Itale space. "If you still wish to speak with the stable owner here, I can take you to him."

"I –" Itale's hesitated. His gaze had hardened; he was warring with something. It sat deep in his eyes. "I would like to help you find Rembrandt if I may. My father knew where Rembrandt went–" He shuddered. "Said they were to 'bleed him' for his magic. I do not think I can live comfortably until I know the little lord is returned safely home."

The rage that swept through Cassius was swift. He'd heard rumors of blood farms, dark aspects of the shadow market that harvested human blood to make magically enhanced potions, but he'd never imagined a child being sent to one.

"Do you mean to say that they're taking Rembrandt to a blood farm? Why didn't you mention any of this before?"

Itale flinched as if the anger in Cassius' words had struck him. "I don't know where he is, or what exactly Father meant by 'bleed him'. I can only imagine something terrible is happening to him." Tears pricked the corner of Itale's eyes. "Forgive me. I did not think it was important."

Cassius' nostrils flared, but he forced himself to calm. "Every detail, down to what your father was wearing on the day Rembrandt was taken, could be of importance. Is there anything else you have not told us?"

Itale shook his head. "I promise. That's all I know."

Cassius sighed. "Are you familiar with combat? Can you fight? We cannot focus on protecting you when we need to find Rembrandt."

"I cannot," Itale admitted. "But I'm good at staying out of sight and would not feel right staying behind while you all save the boy. Please."

Itale's quiet pleas were interrupted as the other Misfits filtered into the house, their quiet conversations causing Cassius to turn.

"We believe Rembrandt has been taken north," Rooster said as he strolled in. "The innkeeper said there is a winery up north where folks have been disappearing. It would be worth it to check it out."

"Then we should make haste," Cassius muttered, drawing forward. Glancing back at Itale, his face gave way to sympathy. He understood Itale's conflicting emotions, but he couldn't worry about the boy when there was a great possibility they would be walking into combat.

"I am sorry, Itale, but you should remain. I cannot in good conscience let you come along."

Itale's disappointment was apparent, but after a moment he conceded, lowering himself into a chair. "You're right, of course. It was silly. Please, all I ask is that you return quickly. I am eager to know nothing terrible has happened to Rembrandt."

Cassius nodded. He could do that.

The change was sudden. The horses pawed at the ground nervously as they urged them forward, the sun fading as rain-stricken clouds cloaked its rays. The woods they traveled through went from thriving green trees to angry dead ones, their thin branches reaching towards the sky as if desperate for relief from their agony.

"Sourapfel Winery used to be fruitful in its success," Cassius said, confusion threading his brow. He'd gotten some of his best wine from that winery. To hear it had fallen into a state of disarray was news to him. "I do not know what happened to this place." The brand on his back burned a dull ache. He patted Fírnster's neck as the horse snorted, shaking his head as they rode forward. The road was slick from recent rain, and occasionally, flecks of mud hit the bottom of his legs. He would do anything to be tucked inside his estate, his bath hall full of steam.

"Must have pissed off the local witch," Rooster called back from ahead as Jet navigated the muddy roads with sure feet. Cassius refrained from rolling his eyes.

"Witches don't come this far north. They stick to the edges of Daesthara, where the magic in the earth is stronger." Cassius steered clear of witches if he could help it. They practiced the same magic as those who dwelt within Daesthara Forest, and that magic was ancient and difficult to control. Cassius was never certain what made the magic so different than that used by the common mage, but eldrasian magic at a base was more chaotic and wild.

Rooster waved his hand in dismissal, and they pulled the horses to a stop as the wood opened up to fields of dead vines attached to trellises, their grapes shriveled and puckered.

"We should leave the animals here," Rooster said, swinging a leg off Jet.

"You two stay with them," Intoh said to Khal and Sode. "Need to make sure they stay alive."

"Came to protect you, not them." Khal shook his head. "Must stay with you. It is the will of Axolli."

"I will stay. You keep Intoh safe," Sode told Khal. The other greka looked hesitant to split up, but after a moment, he nodded, eyeing the horses with some suspicion. Perhaps it would have been wise to bring Itale along if just for him to remain with the horses, so they could have Sode fighting with them. *Too late, now.*

The air was still and silent. No birds sang to each other nor did the wind sift through the tree branches in a quiet caress. It was as if the vineyard was caught in a standstill, where time no longer existed. It had Cassius on edge as Fírnster pranced to the side and nickered nervously.

"Something is not right here, but I cannot place it." A current of energy coursed through Cassius as he spoke. It touched his innate magical nature and beckoned it with a touch of power, but a sense of dread raised the hairs on the back of his neck all the same. As they drew closer, the smell of blood scratched at the back of his throat. A faint pattering of heartbeats was a symphony of sound, coming from the massive, abandoned barn on the other side of the field.

"What is our plan? We should not go in blindly. That did not work out for us when we went into the opera house," Cassius said, turning to the others. Khal had drawn close to Intoh, and his frill was up in alarm.

"I imagine if anyone is here, they're in that barn," Helai said. The wood on the barn was rotting, and the structure was falling apart, held together by age and will. It stood tall against the sky, a menacing web that beckoned the Misfits to walk into its trap.

"Rackjack, can you fight?" Cassius asked, turning to the dwarf.

Rackjack fiddled with something on his arm, a piece of metal that rested on top of his skin. Veins of purple magic ran along the silver, and Rackjack pointed his arm away from everyone as he squeezed his palm. Flame shot out of the metal tube, and Cassius flinched away from the warmth.

"Can fight," Rackjack confirmed, unclenching his fist. The fire stopped, and Rooster stepped forward, amazement written across his face.

"What is that?"

"Used draugmin, made it myself," Rackjack said, his chest swelling with pride. The contraption *was* clever, with its sleek design. Cassius wouldn't have been able to guess what it did either, which made for a dangerous weapon.

"Rooster and I will go first. Linda, you can take up the back just in case anything is waiting to ambush us."

Linda had turned away from the group, their head lifted to watch a group of small blue butterflies fluttering around their head. The sight would have been whimsical had the surrounding landscape not been so desolate nor their time dire.

"Linda?"

Linda turned at Cassius' call. "What?"

"Did you hear anything I just said?"

Linda's expression was hard to discern in their krok'ida form, but it appeared almost sheepish as they waved their hand around their head, forcing the butterflies away. "No."

"This is serious," Cassius said, exasperated. A headache was forming, and any ebb of patience Cassius had was long gone.

"Explain again," Linda said. "Be more interesting."

Cassius opened his mouth to retort, but Rooster stepped in, holding his hands up.

"Let's just go investigate. Linda, you're going to watch our backs. Think you can do that?" After Linda nodded, they set out, leaving Sode behind to tend to the horses.

"I'm going to go around," Helai said, gesturing to the back of the barn. "Just in case we need eyes elsewhere." She strayed from the group, slipping through the trellises of dead vines as she stared up at the barn in quiet contemplation. The vineyard appeared abandoned at first glance, but Cassius could see the ground was kicked up as if there had been recent foot traffic. It all led towards the barn, and he glanced over at Rooster and nodded to it. "If that is where we truly are to investigate, we should tread carefully."

Rooster nodded solemnly, no backhanded retort to be heard as his hand rested on the hilt of his sword.

"Don't feel good," Linda rumbled, ambling behind Cassius as Intoh climbed onto their shoulder. He used his staff to keep his balance, and he stared at the barn with ill-concealed fear in his expression.

"Do not know what is in there, but magic very angry here. Why all things are dead."

Cassius couldn't deny Intoh's words as the air thickened. The ground grew soggier as they drew closer to the barn. Cassius glanced down as his boot sank into the earth. The stench of rotting flesh festered just beyond line of sight, and Cassius wrinkled his nose in disgust. The air was ripe with death.

"Can smell it too," Rackjack whispered, his voice hoarse.

"The boy is surely in there if he is here at all. Are we certain we are ready to face whatever might be inside?" He was ashamed to admit it, but fear stitched itself in his lungs and stole a bit of his courage. He ground his teeth in frustration; he'd seen far too many battles to fear whatever was beyond that door.

Rooster nodded. "I don't think we have a choice."

Cassius sighed as Khal stood in front of Linda, his spear stretched out in front of him.

So be it.

Reaching a hand out, he paused a few inches from the barn door as something compelled him to stop.

"What is it?" Rooster asked in a hushed tone as Cassius shuddered, refusing to pull away despite the skin on his hand crawling in repulsion.

"It feels like necromancy, only it's *wrong*. I know what necromancy feels like. The energy that curses this land is sick." It was the only way he could describe it. Sickness plagued the air. His lungs rattled with each breath he took. He'd never felt magic like this before in his life.

Steeling himself, he flashed Rooster and the others a warning look before grabbing the door and prying it open.

A brush of cold air pressed against him as the barn's interior was bathed in warm light. He tasted the illness in the air as several people coughed, and he looked on in horror as rows of people lined the barn, chained to the wall. Wounds, open and angry, leaked blood into waiting buckets. Off in the distance, someone whimpered, only to be followed closely by the wet laughter of someone cloaked in darkness.

"What is this place?" Rooster uttered in hushed horror. The wood surrounding the barn was rotted and falling away. The ground was covered in a thin layer of hay. Cassius sensed musk and the sharp tang of copper in the air, and he knelt next to one of the people, reaching out to press his fingers to their chains.

"Why are you here?" he asked the woman. In his heart, he knew this to be one of the blood farms he'd heard of, but his mind rebelled, unable to comprehend how something like it could exist. The woman's hair had all fallen out, save for a few clumps that clung stubbornly to her head, and she bore exhaustion in her expression. Cassius was certain she was not long for this world. Several sores dotted her arms, open and weeping a thick, yellow sap. Cassius was sure not to touch her as he drew close.

"Saelic farm is what I hear them call it. Our blood is harvested for the shadow market," the woman rasped, her hands trembling as she reached out. "Please..." But her blood was tainted with something Cassius couldn't identify. It smelled almost sour. Despite the hunger that clawed at the back of his throat, he felt no compulsion to drink.

Glancing up at Rooster, he frowned. "Remember that man rambling on the streets of Volendam?" The memory of the man grabbing Rooster's arm in sick desperation flickered to the forefront of his mind as Rooster nodded. "We may have found what's flooding the market. Someone is using human blood to enhance the magic." The thought was troubling, and he ignored the woman's quiet pleas for mercy as he stood.

"See this in part of Lyvira. Don't go near. Never allowed. Never wanted to," Intoh said, shuddering. "Big tree. Causes sickness like this if you stray too close. Saw it in my Sleep Walk. Tree Delroy spoke of. Should go."

"The boy could be here," Rooster said, moving further into the barn. "We should free these people and burn the place."

Cassius drew near, lowering his voice. "We do not know if these people carry a sickness that will spread. We should just have Rackjack burn it."

The look Rooster gave him was sharp. "If that is the case–"

A voice cut him off in the darkness, quiet and quick. "Oh, Dahlia. Look! We have found new fruit ripe for the meal. I count...five, no six! But oh, the sixth one is dead. That will not do. No, no, no. Mother Sickness will not have him. The one next to him though...yes, yes. Mother Sickness really wants him." Cassius looked at Rooster in alarm as Intoh squeaked behind him.

"Will just tell humans their son is dead. Want to leave," Intoh whispered, his fingers buzzing with small snaps of electricity. Khal's spear was pointed at the other end of the barn, and Rackjack had his arm raised, his own weapon at the ready.

Cassius almost agreed; something was clearly wrong. That compulsion, though, was stifled by pure, blind rage at the thought of the land being sullied by such wrongness.

"Stop speaking and reveal yourself," Cassius demanded, unsheathing his sword. Several of the sick looked over at his words, curling in on themselves and whimpering in pain and fear. Several minutes passed and then a woman finally materialized, peeling away from the darkness to shed light on her identity.

"Gods," Rooster whispered beside Cassius.

The woman was rotting, her fingers darkened by sickness. Pus secreted from bulbous yellow pores that dotted her arms and neck, and when she smiled, her skin cracked and flaked, dead skin clinging lightly to her cheeks. She bounded forward, her breath rattling in her chest as she coughed. "Do not speak to me, *pest*. The gods have chosen me for the Reckoning. You will do well to throw yourself at my feet and beg for my gift."

"Don't want gift," Linda roared. "Smell sick."

The woman laughed, and as she did so, long, skinny bugs with many legs slunk out of her mouth, skittering across her right cheek and disappearing behind the cusp of her ear. "Oh, but that is the gift, don't you see? Mother Sickness will purge the true corruption from your heart and welcome you home." She kicked one of the buckets, spilling it over. Blood seeped into the earth as one girl with dirty-blonde hair and dark circles under her eyes cried out and scooted away, clinging to her chains.

"This is madness," Cassius said, gripping his sword tighter.

"Madness?" the woman asked gleefully, clapping her hands together. "Oh, Dahlia! The dead one calls this madness!"

Another breath, heavy and drenched in shuddering pulls, sounded from the rafters overhead. Cassius looked up as another girl swung down from the ceiling and landed off to the first woman's right. This one was far larger than the rotting woman beside her, her muscles bulging so tightly in her skin that her veins popped. Her eyes glowed yellow in the dim light of the barn. She looked more monster than man, as if she had been on the cusp of transformation and then stopped at the last second. Her face was identical to the others, but while her twin's heart still beat a steady rhythm in her chest, this one's did not. She did not look nor feel like any vampire Cassius had ever met, and he couldn't feel any necromancy at work.

"Back up, back up, *back up*," the second twin heaved, moving erratically through the center of the room as she shooed the ones sitting around buckets. "Morrigan," Dahlia rasped, pointing to a dirty-faced child near the front. "His blood sours and thickens with Mother's Kiss." Dahlia's teeth chattered in quick succession as she lashed out at the boy, but Cassius moved to stop her.

"I command you to halt." The words fled Cassius' lips before he could help himself. He didn't look like Rembrandt, but the boy looked barely older than ten winters. He'd never admit it out loud, but he housed a soft spot for children.

Laughter escaped both sisters' lips as Dahlia pulled away from the trembling boy and turned to Cassius. Morrigan gestured to him, her eyes flashing as she twisted her head to the side in unnatural angles.

"You seek to command my sister as if you hold power here, dead-walker?" Morrigan whispered, drawing closer. She stopped as Cassius raised his sword in warning, her mouth pressed thinly in anger. Black oozed from the corners of her eyes, and she coughed again, black blood seeping from between her lips.

A noise shuffled in the rafters above, and Dahlia turned, grabbing onto the wood beam of one of the stalls and disappearing into a flurry of shadows. Intoh shot a trail of lightning after her, but it missed and hit the ceiling. Several pieces of rotting wood fell to the floor.

"Rooster–" Cassius said quietly.

"Yes, I agree," Rooster murmured from beside him. Cassius' skin crawled, like hundreds of tiny bugs were rolling over his arms and legs, but he ignored it as he raised his sword to strike.

Thirty

HELAI

Pressing low to the ground, Helai trailed behind the barn. Fear caught a lump in her throat as she felt the grass with her fingers. They sank into the soil as cold seeped into her skin, and she jerked her hand away, her brow furrowed. The tips of her fingers tingled as if she had lost feeling in them, and she stared at the ground suspiciously as she rose to her feet.

Shielding her eyes with her palm, she looked up at the looming barn. The others had gone inside, and it was quiet enough for her to hear the quiet scuttle of someone or something moving quickly through the rafters. A large open window sat above, but it was too dark inside for Helai to see anything from where she stood.

She'd have to climb.

It would be a good vantage point if she could find a way up. There were several old barrels, likely used to store wine, piled up against the side of the barn. She eyed them as she tied her hair back in a high ponytail. Resting her hands on her hips, she gauged the climb. It was a stretch, but she thought she could make it. *Damn you for never teaching me how to shade step, Massoud.* She recalled all the times he had used the shadows to traverse through and sneak up on her. It was infuriating, his laughter echoing in her ears from the memory, but it had come in handy for him on missions.

After rubbing her hands together, she pulled herself up onto one of the crates, trying not to groan in disgust as her fingers grazed over some mold that had collected on the corner of the wood. Reaching up, she clasped her eye necklace, steadying herself. The world felt strange. The air was thick with unease, and as Helai raised herself off the ground, a few centipedes crawled along the soggy grass as they failed to reach her ankles.

The climb was steady, and Helai found herself at the top of the stack of barrels in no time, a small sweat slicking her brow. There was a minor commotion from inside, and then Linda roared, shaking crows from nearby trees. Rotting algae grew on the side of the barn, pulsating with some sap-like secretion, and Helai eyed it wearily before peering up at the window. If she jumped, she could make it. Probably.

Tightening the sheaths at her waist, she bent her knees, took a deep breath, and jumped. The impact rattled her to her core as her fingers found perch on the windowsill, and the *thump* she made when she slammed against the wood echoed in her ears in warning. She was a thief of Dalnor; how ashamed her god would be, knowing how loud she was being.

Hanging from the edge of the opening, she held her breath, hoping no one had heard. Cassius' muffled voice sounded through, followed by the wet noise of someone coughing. It didn't appear that anyone had heard

Helai, so she pulled herself up and rolled into the lofted space above the barn.

A putrid smell hit her first, her eyes watering as she curled in on herself to make sure she wouldn't be seen. There was no light in the loft, the corners forging ghosts where there were none. Dust collected over old hay bales, long forgotten, and Helai thought she smelled mold. Apprehension etched into her skin as she peered over the edge.

Her stomach plummeted in horror as she was greeted with the sight of a barn full of sick people, all of them connected to some sort of tubing that pulled blood from their veins. Some of them were dying, and there were enough women and children to make Helai's chest ache with rage.

The other Misfits stood at the center of the room in front of what looked to be a very sick woman, her long dark hair matted and greasy. Sick, weeping wounds covered her arms, and she walked with a slight limp as she moved towards Cassius, who had his sword out. Her skin crawled; was there someone watching her? She was familiar with the deception of shadows, and a quick glance behind her revealed nothing. Who sat in wait just beyond her reach? She shuddered at the thought and stared into the darkness so long her eyes ached.

A shuffle of movement flickered in her peripherals, followed by a quick giggle, and Helai shot forward, prying a dagger from its sheath. She lashed out in the darkness, but someone caught her wrist, attempting to tug her into the shadow.

"Shhh, quiet little mouse. Quiet, quiet. *Shhh*." The woman's ragged breath curled in the air before her as she giggled, and Helai gagged, nearly vomiting. The stench was overwhelming as she attempted to pry her wrist free, but whoever ensnared her was deceptively strong.

"Dahlia will grant you freedom. I will. I will." The woman, Dahlia, spoke through a thick layer of mucus, her voice drenched in illness.

Helai managed to pull away then, tugging Dahlia into the light of the barn, and Helai's terror blossomed at the gruesome sight before her. The woman's tongue was black and flaking, the dead skin leaving a white trail down the inside of her mouth like someone had scratched her there. She half crawled, half walked, her hair framing her face in clumps.

"What happened to you?" Helai breathed in disgust as a commotion broke out below her. Rooster shouted as electricity hit the ceiling of the barn, rotting wood falling and hitting the ground below. Somewhere, a child began to cry, her coughs drowning out the pounding of fear that pulsated in Helai's ears.

Dahlia's head twitched to the side as if she contemplated Helai's words. "Mother Sickness came to claim us. Came to claim our home, our precious pear trees." Giggles burst from her lips as she reached into a sack at her side, producing a rotting pear infested with maggots. It took all of Helai's will to keep herself from throwing up as the maggots wiggled, fighting against Dahlia's grasp.

"Sister Morrigan made a deal, and Mother Sickness set us free."

Helai stumbled away, risking a quick glance behind her to see if she'd survive jumping from the loft. No, she would surely break an ankle by jumping from such a height. Khal and Intoh fought side by side, their backs pressed to the door. Rooster flanked Cassius as they fought the other woman—Helai presumed it to be Morrigan. Dahlia's twin cast her arms out and pointed her fingers to the ground.

"Oh, she's coming! She's coming, she is!" Glee slipped from Dahlia's lips as Helai ducked, dodging her attempts to push her off the ledge. Dahlia slipped herself though, and her laughter carried through the barn as she fell, the crunch of breaking bones sounding as Dahlia hit the ground. She stood as if it did not affect her, her hand slipping into her sister's.

Scrambling, Helai pried a glass orb from her belt. She studied it closely in the shadows of the loft. A swirling gray was imprisoned within the glass, and Helai peeked over the edge and dropped it.

The glass shattered as it hit the ground, and the barn began to fill with smoke as the grotesque twins started to chant a dark tone, the howling wind dying outside. Linda's bloodstained maw was the last thing that disappeared as the smoke curled up, and the barn fell prey to chaos. Helai steadied her breathing as she pressed her fingers to the wood, feeling her way forward. She recalled pillars lining the left side of the barn. If she could reach them, she could climb down.

Nearly slipping on some hay, she teetered at the edge before righting herself. Gripping a pillar, she lowered herself to the bottom level. A low growl sounded in the fog over the soft cries of those who were chained in the barn, and Helai went quickly to work on freeing them. The twins called something to them, and the barn darkened as the clouds outside grew black and swollen with rain.

"Shhh," Helai whispered softly, finding a boy in the back with a long cut on his arm. He seemed to have lost a lot of blood, and his eyes fluttered weakly as he cried out and attempted to scramble away.

"No, please," he whimpered. "Mama? I want my mama." His cheeks were dirty and bright with fever, his eyes wide. He was young, too young to see such horrors, but then again, Helai had been much younger when she'd been forced to survive the streets of her home. If Massoud hadn't found her, she wouldn't have lived past five. Her heart ached in sympathy as she reached out for the boy in front of her.

"If you can trust me, I can get you out of here." She lowered her voice. "I need you to hide behind these hay bales. Do you know how to be brave?" Tears collected at the corners of the boy's eyes as he shook his head.

The barn groaned as something landed in the loft above her. The boy cried out in fear. Helai tugged her eye necklace over her head and held it out to him. "See this? My people say it can keep you safe from all evil so long as you're wearing it. Can you wear it for me?"

After a moment, the boy reached out and tentatively took it.

"What's your name?" She asked as the boy slipped the necklace over his head.

A sniff. "Rembrandt."

Cassius shouted as a high-pitched screech filled the air, and Helai's heart rose to her throat. She'd found the boy they'd been looking for. He was skinny, too skinny, his ribs jutting against his dark skin, and his blond hair was filthy, as if it hadn't been washed in weeks.

"It's nice to meet you, Rembrandt. My name is Helai. Can you hide behind those barrels until I come and find you?"

Rembrandt shook his head and frantically pointed into the smoke. "Fire! Fire!"

Helai cursed and turned. The boy was right. Rackjack stepped through the smoke, the weapon on his arm breathing fire as it shot out and blossomed when it hit the wood of the barn. With how dry the barn was, it spread quickly, and the gleam of flames chased away the smoke she'd caused earlier. The other Misfits fled the barn, followed closely by Morrigan and Dahlia. Whatever stood above her screeched and stumbled out of the barn the way Helai had come in, and Helai looked at Rembrandt.

"Come here. I'll get you somewhere safe." Collecting the boy in her arms, she silently cursed at how light he was as she stood. She had never been great with children, but something about the boy made her protective of him. She swallowed a lump of regret in her throat as she passed several begging for her aid, still chained. Their demise was all but sealed as the fire raged around them.

"Close your eyes, *sabi*," Helai whispered into Rembrandt's cheek as she darted around the heat of the flames and out of the barn.

Thirty-One

LINDA

Linda threw themself through the wall of the barn as it went up in flames, the sounds of those being burned alive ringing in their ears. Scorched wood crashed around them as they landed on the ground, grunting in pain. A jarring pain shot up their right arm, but they were safe from the flames. Gripping their war hammer tightly, they forced themself to their feet.

Good, they thought, relieved to see the other Misfits fleeing the barn. It was short-lived when Dahlia and Morrigan followed through the wreckage. Both uninjured, they held hands, the grass dying beneath their feet with each step they took. Dahlia giggled, her laughter echoing throughout the field as Morrigan held out her other hand and dropped a rotting pear to the ground. It sank into the soil as if it were quicksand. Black rot oozed from the grass, coagulating into some grotesque form, small cords of inky black fingers protruding through the grass.

"Sing a little song...before it all goes wrong," Morrigan sang, her voice high and grating. Linda nearly covered their ears as a rotting creature, small with long disjointed limbs and sharp claws, pried itself upward. "Hear our words of dread...for soon you'll all be dead." The last word was uttered with a deep conviction as Dahlia launched forward, her fists raised to bring them down on Cassius. He raised his shield in time just as the field fell into chaos.

Linda raised their hammer to deflect an attack from whatever disgusting, rotting thing appeared in front of them. Its claws caught against the hilt of *Volroth*. The sound of claws meeting metal was piercing, and Linda growled as they shoved forward with all their strength, pushing the creature back. It smelled sickeningly sweet, like mint, and it infected Linda's nose as the creature screeched. It moved on disjointed legs as it attempted to claw through Linda's defenses, and it was deceptively strong as Linda planted their feet to adjust, their muscles straining against the weight. Morrigan remained near the burning barn as a swarm of bugs flew from the trees, encircling her until she was barely visible. Rain began to fall as a massive vulture screeched overhead, landing on a tree nearby to wait patiently for its meal.

Several more of the rotting creatures pried themselves from the earth, reaching for Linda. A surge of electricity struck one, and it shrank away, yowling angrily. At first, Linda thought it might have been the will of nature, but then Intoh appeared, his fingers coursed with lightning.

"Going to try something," he said, slipping underneath Linda's arm. He was being far more courageous than Linda had ever seen him, and he reached out, snapping two fingers together in the creature's face.

A clap of thunder ricocheted over the field, and everyone flinched against the noise. Linda was the first to recover, the ringing fading in their ears as the creature in front of them still flailed around in pain, stunned by the sudden noise.

Bringing the hammer over the top of their head, Linda unleashed a roar and brought it down upon the creature. It collapsed in a mess of rotting slime, only for its absence to be filled with three more. Their heads shook in a speed that Linda could not follow, and behind them, Rackjack raced across the field, his flame weapon lighting swarms of bugs on fire through the rain.

It did not matter where Linda looked; the rotting corpses surrounded them, their eyes endless pools of voids that drew ever closer.

The world darkened as they pressed in on Linda, clawing, suffocating, preventing them from raising *Volroth*. Linda had only felt such a presence once before, when they'd swum too deep off the coast of their homeland. Linda was able to hold their breath for a long time, but they'd sunk and sunk and sunk until the pressure had built up in their head and their lungs had screamed for mercy.

Daylight broke through the rain, bathing Linda in a warm glow. The plague creature reared back, burned by the light, and Linda lunged out without hesitation, biting down on the creature nearest them.

It burst into flames.

Linda flinched away in surprise as the creature squealed in agony, crashing into another one near it and setting it ablaze as well. At first, Linda thought it might be Rackjack saving them from the creature's wrath, but no, he was on the other side of the field, still dealing with the swarms of bugs.

The flames licked at the creature's skin, burning away rotting flesh until there was nothing left, not even bone. The sun disappeared behind some clouds, giving Linda no time to react as more creatures descended upon them.

"Could sense magic," Intoh said, shocked. He threw his hand out, blinding a creature with lightning as Linda swung *Volroth* around, slamming it against the creature's side and breaking its ribs. "How did you do magic?"

"Don't know," Linda shouted, bringing *Volroth* down on another creature. "It just happen!" They were granted a momentary reprieve from the fighting as the last of the creatures were killed. How *had* they wielded magic? Linda had never heard of a krok'ida using magic before.

Unhinged laughter echoed off to Linda's right, and Linda turned just as Dahlia rolled away from Cassius and landed in front of Linda, her head tilted as she grinned up at both of them. Drool fell from her lips, dripping down to hit the ground and brown the grass, and Linda growled, flexing their fingers around *Volroth*.

"Tasty little reptile. The marrow of your bones will be a feast. Yes, yes!" Round bones jutted out of her knuckles as she rose up to her full height. She was grotesque and misshapen, her back hunched over as fresh wounds wept on her arms. Maggots wiggled in her smile, her teeth rotten and black.

"How many times? Not taste good," Linda yelled, stepping to the side to flank Cassius. His hair had been torn from his ribbon. He drew his shield up, protecting his left side.

"We need to get to her sister. Her magic is strong," Cassius said as Morrigan raised her hand, and a sickly green ball coalesced at her hand and she flung it at Rackjack, who dodged out of the way at the last moment. Dahlia moved quickly as she lunged forward, slamming her fist against Cassius' shield. A ring sang out across the field as Cassius shoved her back, and Linda raised *Volroth*, bringing it down in a vertical arc. Dahlia rolled out of the way before it could make contact, and *Volroth* hit the ground, sinking into the earth.

Reaching out to where the hammer's handle met the head, Dahlia tugged and ripped *Volroth* from their grasp. Linda cried out in despair as Dahlia's laughter mocked them as she threw it away.

Rage squeezed Linda's lungs. The importance of their war hammer was unmatched, a personification of Linda's freedom. Losing it made Linda's brand burn, made them sick with anger, made them want to rip Dahlia apart with their teeth.

"Little reptile mad?" Dahlia's laughter fueled the fire that burned inside Linda, and despite Intoh's and Cassius' protests, Linda shot forward, reaching out to strangle Dahlia where she stood. The rage pulsed through Linda like a disease, whittling away their senses, and although Dahlia reached up to protect herself from Linda's wrath, the woman was no match for Linda's brute strength. Linda shoved her to the ground, their hands around her throat.

"Dahlia," a voice cried.

Linda was pried from Dahlia, then dragged down into the earth by rotten hands that reached out of the ground. Cassius moved forward to try and cut away at the hands, but the vulture squawked as it took flight from its perch on the tree and dove towards his head, forcing him back.

Lying on their back, Linda tried to pry the hands away, only for several more to burst from the ground and trap them where they lay, imprisoning them beside the rotting corpses that surrounded them.

Linda's throat rattled in frustration. They were so tired of being chained.

Thirty-Two

ROOSTER

The heat from the barn licked at his back as he fled the burning building, air hissing between clenched teeth. Sode approached, his spear clung tightly in his grasp as Rooster's lungs burned, desperate for clean air.

"Itale came, said there are those who worked with his father in the village. Believe they are cultists, like ones you all have spoke of. Came to warn," Sode said, gesturing behind him. Itale stood behind a tree, trembling as he stared out at the burning barn with fear in his eyes.

"Get back, both of you. This place is evil. It –" His words were lost as vultures flew around the side of the barn, their wings thick with wilting feathers and open wounds. They screeched as green phlegm shot out of their beaks. When it hit the ground, it sizzled, the grass browning and dying.

Rooster moved towards the treeline with Sode in toe, reaching Itale's side. "Do either of you know where the animals are? Are they safe? Jet has my bow."

Gesturing to the dead trees behind them, Itale paled. "Back there, but–"

"Rooster! Sode!" Helai broke through the front of the barn, her hand pressed against the back of a child's head as she carried him away from the flames. Screams of those burning alive inside haunted Rooster's ears as she approached. "Itale? Where did you—? Never mind; can you take him and find somewhere safe to hide?" Her gaze flickered to Rooster, and she mouthed a name: *Rembrandt.*

Relief flooded through him. With the location of the boy, they were one step closer to figuring out how to remove their brands. "Is he okay? He looks like he's lost a lot of blood," Rooster asked, seeing the cut on Rembrandt's arm.

"He *has* lost a lot of blood, and he's sick with something. I'm going to go with Itale and see if I can heal him or at least stop the bleeding until Intoh can look him over." Her eyes flickered to the field, where Morrigan and Dahlia moved towards Linda and Cassius. "I'll return if I can."

"He's our top priority," Rooster said, pointing to the boy. "Keep him safe. Sode, I know your priority is to protect Intoh, but I need you to protect Rembrandt. If he dies, Intoh remains in grave danger."

Sode nodded, retreating with Itale and Helai. Rushing forward, Rooster grabbed Intoh, pulling him out of the way of a vulture's phlegm that then landed in front of them.

"Thanks," Intoh said, shuddering. "Would have been unpleasant."

"You don't say," Rooster muttered. "I need to find Jet." Rain had begun to fall, and the sound of fighting filled the air, but he raised his fingers to his lips and whistled for the ass anyway, hoping the mule would hear. Jet had proved his intelligence on the journey to the winery; he hoped Jet's courage outweighed his fear.

A moment or two later, he heard it, the braying of a mule. It was music to Rooster's ears.

"Do you hear that beautiful noise, Intoh?" Rooster asked, whistling again.

A burst of electricity cascaded from Intoh's fingers and hit one of the vultures in the chest. It squawked in pain as it fell from the sky, and when it slammed into the ground, it shattered several trellises and did not get up again. "Not beautiful," Intoh said to Rooster. "Very unpleasant."

Rooster ignored him as Jet came running through the trees, his eyes rolling with terror. His nose flared as he brayed, and Rooster ran his hand over the side of Jet's neck as he grabbed his bow and quiver. "You're such a good boy, Jet," Rooster cooed, letting the mule nibble on his fingers. "Now run, get away before you're hurt." Slapping Jet on the ass, he turned just as he came face to face with a vulture, its eyes bloodshot and crawling with maggots.

"Shit," Rooster muttered just as Jet brayed again from behind him and shoved him out of the way. Knocked to the side, he stumbled away as the vulture shot phlegm at Jet. The mule cried out as the acid ate away at his fur, and Rooster drew forward, horrified as Intoh brought the vulture down.

"No." His denial fell on deaf ears as Jet collapsed, falling to his side as the acidic phlegm went to work. Rooster lowered himself to Jet, cradling his head in his hands. The shock was a low noise in his ears, deafening him to the fighting going on around him. It was just a mule, he wanted to tell himself. But as Jet looked up at him, his eyes full of pain and understanding, Rooster couldn't stop his heart from shattering, a sob rattling his lungs.

Jet took one last shuddering breath and then died.

A dam broke inside Rooster, a rage that sang poems in his blood as he gently lowered Jet, half-eaten by acid, to the ground. He was sick with anger as he stood. He did not know where it came from, only that it came, and with it, the burn of his brand and reckless abandon.

Pulling the sword from the ground where he'd tossed it, he locked eyes with Morrigan as she laughed maniacally. She flung herself towards Cassius, her path leaving behind a trail of rot in the soil. Cassius held her off as Linda choked Dahlia in the dirt, but both twins were holding their own with little trouble.

A wordless snarl left Rooster's lips as he attacked Morrigan from behind, bringing his sword down to pierce her in the back. She was quick though, curling in on herself and rolling away. Landing on her knees, she stared at Rooster as she pulled a rotten pear from a bag at her side, her smile black and rotten.

"Silly, stupid," she cried. "Your bones will be a feast for Mother Sickness, your skin a witness to her gift." She bit down on the pear. Maggots swam through the fruit as bugs fled to her feet, crawling over her toes and ankles.

"My bones don't taste very good," Rooster said, swinging his sword. He missed as she chucked the pear at him, the distraction granting her just enough time to push forward, her stench making Rooster's eyes water.

"Rooster, look out," Cassius cried. He was at his side in a moment, but it was too late. Morrigan's lips pulled back as she smiled and raked her long fingernails against the side of his neck at the same time a dagger slid across his waist, peeling open his stomach. The pain was unimaginable. *Where did you get that?* he thought, eyeing the wicked blade.

In his mind's eye, he watched Dahlia and Morrigan, younger and healthier, read under a flourishing pear tree. The scene shifted to Dahlia lying beneath a rotted tree, a cultist in a dragon skull mask pinning her to the ground. Morrigan begged for her sister's salvation, but the memory washed away, blackened by rot and darkness.

Pulled out of the memory, he was aware of the rain hitting his face. How had he gotten on the ground? He didn't know, but Morrigan's face no longer swam in his vision as it blurred, slanted sideways. Cassius replaced her, his pupils blown, his nostrils flared. His fangs were descended, and for one horrifying moment, Rooster thought he might meet his end at the hand of the vampire's bloodlust, but Cassius held his composure as he pressed a hand to the wound at Rooster's belly. He cried out, but his whimpering was muffled by the roar in his ears.

"We need to move you," Cassius said, but his voice was far off, his face darting in and out of focus as Rooster's adrenaline took hold. Cassius scooped him into his arms, and for the moment, the fight seemed to be done.

Thirty-Three

CASSIUS

"Helai," Cassius called out, darting towards the woods where the horses had been left. Jet lay dead on the ground some feet away, half of his corpse rotted from acid, but the fighting looked to be over. Vultures feasted on what corpses there were, and Morrigan and Dahlia had disappeared the moment Morrigan had wounded Rooster, sinking into the ground as the grass rotted as nothing was left of them but a small cloud of bugs, which dissipated soon after. Where they might have gone was a cause of great concern, but Cassius had no time to dwell on it as Rooster's breathing grew shallow. The shadow hands had released Linda the moment the twins had disappeared, and they ambled to their feet, grumbling in Drikotyian as they retrieved *Volroth*.

"I watched them. They just sank into the ground," Helai said, her hair plastered to her dirt-stained cheeks. Hysteria etched her laughter as she stumbled to Cassius, and he was relieved to see her unharmed. "Those women just disappeared into the dirt –" She halted, her eyes widening. "What happened to Rooster?"

Cassius' lips pursed. "One of the women stabbed him. I can smell the sickness that infects him. He needs something until we can get him back to the estate."

Helai nodded, glancing behind her as the drikoty minus Sode approached. Intoh looked exhausted, his eyes at half-mast. As he attempted to climb up to Linda's shoulders, Linda shied away, their mouth parted in protest.

"No, not carry anymore."

Intoh hissed and rubbed the back of his head. "Not very nice. Will remember this."

Cassius hefted Rooster in his arms. The sickness in his blood was helping him combat his bloodlust, but his fangs still raked the inside of his mouth, begging to divulge. "Linda? I'm so sorry, but we lost Jet. Do you think you can pull Rooster in the cart while the rest of us walk or double up on horses?"

"Rooster is hurt?" Linda asked, tilting their head to the side and sniffing the air. "Will get cart. Wait." As they ambled off, Khal held up his spear, his gaze attentive as Helai approached Rooster with a salve.

"The wound doesn't look to be too deep nor does it appear to have hit any vital organs. Still, I worry about infection." She locked eyes with Cassius as Linda approached with Itale and a boy resting in the cart behind them.

"Itale, what–" Cassius asked.

"I will explain on our way back. I heard Rooster is injured," Itale said, his eyes flashing with worry. The rain had subsided. The air was now thick with moisture as Cassius laid Rooster gently in the cart.

"That's Rembrandt," Helai explained, noting Cassius' curious glance towards the child. "He's sick also, but I think rest will cure his ailment. I did what I could to help his body fight whatever plagues him."

Cassius nodded. For once, Cassius felt the shift of luck on their side as he mounted Fírnster. Rackjack was silent while he climbed into the cart, remaining near Rooster as they made their way back to Wilhaven.

As they burst through the door, Rooster's shallow breathing filled the halls of his home. Rooster had woken at some point on the trip home, and Rackjack had held him down as he'd screamed out in agony. Cassius carried him now, and he glanced at Linda in desperation.

"Please take him," Cassius said, his voice hoarse from the blood that tempted him, aching in his throat.

"Don't tell me I stink now," Rooster said, his voice a whisper of its normal tone. Khal and Sode spread throughout the house, their spears raised as they sought out the threat of enemies. Cassius didn't sense any heartbeats, but for all he knew, a vampire could have taken up residence in his home, as it had been deserted for quite some time.

Linda hoisted Rooster into their arms and he groaned, his face slick with sweat. Cassius wasn't certain where to go as Rackjack tugged at his beard in distress beside him, his eyes trained on Rooster. Gesturing, he had Linda carry Rooster to the living room to the right of the main stairs, where he hoped to light a fire.

The room was as he'd left it. Large red velvet curtains covered the windows, preventing any light from coming in, and two black couches mirrored each other in front of a large mahogany fireplace. His plate armor was encased in glass to the left of it.

"Learned new magic. Watch," Intoh said, swirling his finger in an upwards pattern. "*Reisa*," he uttered. Small droplets of water collected near the ceiling, and all the dust rose from the surfaces of the room and were pulled into the orbs, where it disappeared. The room was left spotless, and Intoh looked more than pleased with himself.

"Put him there," Cassius said, gesturing to one of the couches. "Intoh, can you do that for the rest of the estate? I will offer you a vial of my blood in exchange so long as you promise not to do anything weird to it."

Intoh's eyes widened as he nodded three times in quick succession. "First I need to look at Rooster."

"Must do what you can. Has to survive," Rackjack said, his fingers curling tightly against the back of the couch. "Can't die. Just found him again. Red-haired-one would be very, very angry."

The fight at the winery must have left Intoh's magical muscle sore, his fingers massaging his chest, but still he walked forward.

A sheen of sweat dotted Rooster's brow as he muttered, "Igraine," in his unconscious state. Rackjack watched on without blinking, his brow furrowed in a silent threatening nature. It rolled off the dwarf in waves while Helai eyed him warily as Intoh took Rooster's hand in between his own.

He swayed to the side and purged his stomach.

"Intoh," Helai said, her voice alarmed.

"Very sick," Intoh rasped, his throat raw from his recent vomiting. He curled his fingers tightly around Rooster's to keep himself steady. "Going to make me very sick to heal him."

"Don't, then," Helai said. "Rooster's strong, and the medicine I have should be enough for him to heal on his own. You shouldn't exert yourself to speed along the process.

"No," Intoh protested, slapping her hand away. "Can do it."

His tail had finally grown back, and he slapped it against the ground. A soft light bled between his palm and Rooster's. Rooster moaned as black ooze began to seep from his pores.

"Need...bucket..." Intoh gasped, pulling the ooze into a glob that swirled in the air with nowhere to go. "Magic keep slipping. Hard to pull."

Helai pushed herself to her feet and disappeared as a ball of ooze circled over Intoh's head. Cassius was a safe distance away, near the window, and the ooze still made the room feel thick, like Rooster was sick with a plague. It made Cassius' own palms slick with sweat, his breath rattling in his lungs.

"Can help," Rackjack offered from behind the couch.

Finally, Helai returned. "I suppose I shouldn't have been surprised that the vampire doesn't have anything in his kitchen except copious amounts of wine, but I *finally* found a bowl." Setting it down next to Intoh, she backed away as he and Rackjack lured the ooze into the bowl.

"It is a shame those terrible women managed to get away." Helai shuddered. "I am saddened we weren't able to save the people in the barn, but I am glad they cannot continue their horrible practice."

"For now," Cassius muttered darkly. He loathed to think how many people would suffer, should those women decide to return and continue their dark practice.

As soon as the ooze was safely tucked away, Intoh turned to Rackjack. "Your magic is strange. Feel like chewing on lightning."

Rackjack clicked his teeth together as he tugged at his beard. "Not sure what mean. All dwarf magic strange."

Cassius frowned. He'd never noticed how quickly Rackjack's heartbeat was until now. It was way quicker than any dwarf he'd met.

Intoh stared at Rackjack for another minute before turning back to the bowl. "Bury it," Intoh said, waving his hand at Helai. "Don't let it touch your hands."

"But–"

Intoh looked up sharply. "Only way to get rid of it. Will only kill grass for a little while. Yard already dead." He turned to look at Cassius. "You won't notice."

After getting a nod from Cassius, Helai conceded, taking the bowl in her hands and disappearing out the front door.

"We might have to stay here for a few days," Intoh said.

"So long as we keep a watchful eye," Cassius said, glancing towards the window. Itale had filled him in on the cultists in town, and their sudden appearance in Wilhaven made him nervous. He did not want to bring their wrath down upon the people of the town if he could help it.

"Is he going to be okay?" A meek voice sounded behind him, and Cassius turned to see the wide eyes of the boy staring up at him. Rembrandt had slept most of their journey back to the estate, save for the time Intoh had woken him to heal him, and he hadn't gotten a chance to speak with him yet. Dark circles stained the skin underneath Rembrandt's eyes, and he still looked pale, but Intoh said he would recover.

"Perhaps you can show him the gardens?" Helai said, nudging her head towards Rooster. "This isn't the place for a child."

Cassius was so accustomed to the sight of blood that he'd forgotten the child probably did not care to see it. A tension formed; despite his love for them, he never knew how to act around children. He would never harm a child, but it did not save him from his hesitation.

"Come, Rembrandt," he said after a moment. "Perhaps there are some flowers to see out back." Pushing Rembrandt light on the back, he led the child out of the sitting room.

"I'm coming with you. I also do not fair well at the sight of blood," Itale said, trembling. He was white as a sheet, and his heart was quick as a rabbit's. Cassius smelled the sweat gleaming off his fingers as he pushed through the kitchen.

"How are you doing?" Cassius asked, helping Rembrandt down the steps that led to the gardens. The back of the estate grounds was massive, with a large, enclosed greenhouse taking up much of the right side of the lawn. Hedges swirled at the center surrounding a horse fountain, and Rembrandt gasped as he looked up at the rearing statue.

"I'm tired," he said to Cassius, only to be distracted by the fountain. "My mama has horses just like this one." In the short time they'd been away from the blood farm, warmth had returned to Rembrandt's cheeks. Though Cassius still sensed a lingering sickness in him, Rembrandt's eyes were brimming with life.

"Did you see all of those people when we came into town?" Rembrandt asked, peering into the murky water of the fountain. A chill clung to the air, but Cassius barely felt it as he drew forward, staring down at his own reflection. The bared hints of decay mottled the corners of his eyes and lips, but his hunger remained sated...for now.

"I thought you were sleeping."

Rembrandt's smile was sheepish. "Sometimes I pretended. I thought you guys were bad men." He frowned.

Cassius' heart thumped painfully in his chest. "There is a festival going on," he explained, drawing his finger through the water. It rippled, and Rembrandt coughed, his shoulders shaking.

"I wanna go."

Cassius shook his head. If cultists were in town, it was too dangerous. Still, he'd have to go at some point to feed before they left. "Maybe later."

Rembrandt's lower lip spilled out into a pout, quickly replaced by fear. "Ghosts," he cried, dipping behind Cassius to hide.

Cassius' mouth dropped in shock as he looked to where Rembrandt gestured. Itale stood in front of the stables as several ghostly apparitions rose out of the ground. They were naught more than steeds, horses that kicked the ground and pushed their noses in Itale's waiting hands, eager for his affection. Itale did not seem afraid, and Cassius looked down at Rembrandt and shook his head.

"They will not hurt you." Reaching out, he took Rembrandt's hand. If only Dmitry could see him now, offending the Order further by interacting with the child he'd refused to kill. Each time he looked down at Rembrandt's face, he was more sure of his decision. How could one child be of harm to an ancient vampiric order?

"Did you call out to these?" Cassius asked Itale, gesturing to the spectral horses. "I did not know you're a necromancer."

"Nor I," Itale admitted, his voice breathless as he stared up at the horses with a simple fondness. "I've always been able to see ghosts and felt a connection with the dead, but this is the first time I've been able to conjure them out of nowhere. I – I think it was an accident." He waved to Rembrandt. "Come here."

Rembrandt shook his head, his lower lip trembling in fear as one of the ghost horses snorted and lowered its head.

"It's okay, Rembrandt. Ghosts cannot harm you," Cassius said quietly, reaching out and letting one of the horses nibble at his fingers. The horse wasn't solid, its teeth sinking through Cassius' skin. A shiver crawled up his palm, but he smiled despite it. He remembered these horses, famed ones of his uncle's, and it made his heart flicker with joy seeing them again.

Slowly, Rembrandt reached a hand out. His laughter soon rang through the stables as another horse nudged his palm with the velvety tip of its nose. Cassius allowed the barest hint of a smile to tempt his lips despite the sudden twist of anxiety in his belly.

"Itale, your necromancy changes things."

"What do you mean?" Itale frowned, brushing curls out of his eyes.

Cassius glanced at Rembrandt, but he was busy cooing and talking to the horses, his curiosity keeping him distracted. Still, Cassius turned away and lowered his voice. "Wild necromancy can be dangerous to its wielder. If you don't learn how to control it or leave it dormant for too long, it will begin drawing from within." He raised his brows, hoping Itale knew what he hinted at. Wild necromancers rarely lived past thirty winters. It was an unstable type of magic; it was never meant to be wielded by anyone other than a vampire.

Understanding flickered across Itale's face. "Oh dear..." He trailed off, his shoulders sagging. One of the horses reared up, its eyes rolling in fear, and Rembrandt screamed, stumbling backwards and falling roughly on his back.

Cassius reached out a hand to try to calm the horse, but when he lashed out with his own necromancy, he brushed up against Itale's. It was a maelstrom of raw necromantic power. The force of it surprised him; he'd never felt necromancy this powerful before.

"Itale," he said sharply. "Pretend you are building a wall in your mind. Cut off the flow of magic." Magic was strange. Brushing up against Itale's felt physical almost, like he'd reached out and taken Itale's hand.

Itale's eyes rolled into the back of his head. His magic overpowered Cassius', shoving him back as the horse shifted from a vibrant blue spectral to one of shadow, mutated in the darkness to grow sharp teeth and red eyes. A ghost could not harm the living, but a shade? Shades were ghosts fed by strong emotional magic, and they could slip into the living world if they became strong enough.

A high-pitched screech pierced the air as the horse reared back again, its body solidifying to sharp leathery skin pulled taut over bone. The air thickened with the trepidation the presence of ghosts often brought, and Cassius' gaze flickered to Rembrandt. He screamed again, tears streaming down his face as he backed away.

The horse moved on disjointed legs, and Cassius murmured his apologies as he punched Itale in the face.

The moment Itale went unconscious, the shades dissipated, their angry wails rattling in Cassius' chest. He immediately went to Rembrandt, who clung to a pillar of wood as if it would grant him protection.

"You are unharmed?" he asked, looking over Rembrandt. He was relieved to find the boy had sustained no new injuries, but Rembrandt was rattled. He shook, flinging himself into Cassius' arms. It was strange. Cassius wasn't accustomed to the innocence of children. The ones of Wilhaven spoke of him as a monster and contented themselves with throwing rocks through his windows or whispering dark rumors of him in their friends' ears. Rembrandt was too warm, as if he held a small fever, and Cassius allowed himself a moment, a flicker of one, to hug Rembrandt and pretend that everything was normal. Once, a very long time ago, when he'd been nothing more than a human man, he'd allowed himself the desire to have a family. That hope had been shattered so long ago; he'd nearly forgotten it.

"Rembrandt, if you promise to be brave, I'll take you into town to see our baker. They make the best pies you've ever tasted. Can you go and check in on Rooster, see if he's doing okay?"

Rembrandt pulled away, nodding solemnly.

"Good," Cassius said, studying him for a moment before straightening. "Run along now."

As Rembrandt hurried up the stairs to the estate, Cassius knelt next to Itale. He came to slowly, a soft exhale of pain fleeing his lips as his eyes fluttered.

"Wh–what happened?"

Cassius clicked his tongue against the roof of his mouth. His morality wouldn't allow him to leave Itale to a gruesome fate such as wild necromancy...but he cared even less for the feeling of responsibility for the boy. Still, the strings of guilt tugged at Cassius' belly.

"I know you spoke of remaining here in Wilhaven after ensuring Rembrandt's safe return, but what about traveling with us for a time? I can teach you how to control your necromancy."

Itale pushed himself up, his fingers rubbing his temples. "I – Your friends like to get into the worst of trouble. I'm not certain I'm suited for the life you all live."

Cassius couldn't blame him. Not after what they'd seen at the blood farm and in Volendam. "As is your right to choose, but as I mentioned earlier, a necromancer with no handle on his magic lives a fleeting life." Cassius stood, offering a hand. "Come with us for a time. Learn to wield the undead. If you are adamant about starting anew here, I will give you the estate as a matter of good graces so long as I have the right to return here one day."

Itale stared up at him, silent. He was still for so long, Cassius wondered if he'd offended him somehow. The breeze was subtle as it sifted through Cassius' hair, and finally Itale reached up to take Cassius' hand, allowing him to pull him to his feet.

"That is something I can agree to."

Cassius nodded. "Good. Now that that is settled, I have promised Rembrandt a journey into town if you care to join."

"I would love to."

Thirty-Four

INTOH

A sneeze left Intoh, and he grumbled in frustration as he moved through the estate. Rooster was resting comfortably in the sitting room, watched over by Helai and Rackjack, and it had left Intoh with the task of cleaning up where he could. His magical exertion was starting to make his chest tight, but luckily it did not take much to remove the dust. Still, it was probably the hundredth time he'd sneezed as he'd whisked it away, the action causing his nose to twitch in irritation. The room he was in had to be a guest room, far fancier than anything he'd seen but still no less *Cassius*. A bed with dark sheets was made, and curiosity got the better of him as he passed the sitting desk near one of the windows. He glanced behind him to make sure he was alone. Khal and Sode stood at the door, ever watchful for the threat of danger, so Intoh pulled the middle drawer open.

A letter sat, partially curled with age. Intoh's gaze darted over it, but the letter was written in a different language, one Intoh could not read. It was signed by someone named Dominic Antonia. Cassius' father, perhaps?

Shutting the drawer, Intoh turned to leave, but a low humming forced him to pause, his head cocking to the side to listen. It came from down the hall, and Intoh slipped past the other greka towards the noise. Once he found the room, he opened the door to a massive bedroom with a large canopy bed nestled in the middle. Tall floor-to-ceiling windows decorated the opposite wall, and the doorway across the room hinted at a private bathroom.

The humming grew louder, a small vibration in Intoh's throat, and he pushed through his fear and scurried into the room even though it was the only one free of dirt.

"Careful," Khal warned from behind him in Drikotyian. "Do not know what that is, but feels wrong."

"Will be careful," Intoh said, waving him away. While he was grateful for their protection, he couldn't help his annoyance. Linda never questioned him like Khal and Sode did at times.

Nearing the bed, he noticed whatever was making the noise seemed to be coming from underneath, and he swallowed thickly. His mind screamed at him to run, but a quiet urging beckoned him forward. He was at war with himself, but the latter won as he bent at the waist and pulled up the bed skirt.

A small squeak left his lips as his eyes landed on a large mark carved into the floor underneath the bed. Three squiggly lines in a diagonal pattern, identical to the brand on his back. He released the skirt and stumbled backwards as a whooshing noise slipped past his ear and rattled the glass on the window. Sode drew forward, his hand reaching out to catch Intoh before he fell.

The humming stopped.

A sense of disquiet settled in its place, and Intoh pushed Sode away as he fled the room. There was no way he was going to stay a moment longer. Not when there was the dragon sigil carved into the floor.

After assuring Khal and Sode he was fine, he left them at the door to the sitting room, where he approached Helai as she dabbed a wet washcloth to Rooster's forehead while murmuring quietly in Shoman. Rackjack remained as well, standing behind the couch and hovering over Rooster, his face twitching in distress.

Helai looked up as Intoh approached, her face falling to relief. "He seems to be recovering, but I'm sure the next few nights will tell us." Her face was pinched with worry as Cassius entered the room.

"Linda, Itale, and I are taking Rembrandt into town."

Intoh's heart thundered in his ears as he stumbled away from Cassius, pointing an accusatory finger at him. "Saw mark of Gorvayne under your bed. Why?" He had lowered his guard around the vampire from their time spent together, but his walls threatened to rise again as Cassius narrowed his eyes.

"What?"

"Cleaning rooms, heard humming. Went to investigate, and it came from your room. Sigil is under bed."

Helai rose quickly to her feet, brushing her hair from her face. "Why would it be there? We're the only ones that have been inside this house for some time. Isn't that what you said, Cassius?"

Cassius' gaze flickered to Helai as he turned abruptly on his heel.

"Where are you going?" Intoh asked angrily.

"To see it for myself," the vampire said.

"I'm coming with you," Helai said firmly.

"We'll be right back," Cassius told Linda, who was knelt down as they let Rembrandt study their tooth necklace. He seemed uncertain of Linda at first, but Linda was being surprisingly gentle as Intoh pushed past and followed Cassius and Helai up the stairs. Khal and Sode silently stepped up behind Intoh, now his constant shadow.

Suspicion coursed through him, a monstrous beast that claimed all the trust he'd built for Cassius. It was the vampire that had been called to Volendam, to the opera house that had the dragon tooth inside. What if Cassius had been planning to get them here all this time?

As they moved down the hall, Intoh couldn't help the thoughts that festered under the guise of his suspicion. The humming had stopped, but the anxiety grew in his chest the closer they got to the door of Cassius' bedroom.

The room was cold when they entered, colder than when Intoh had left it. It was dark and foreboding when he stepped inside, and the tension in the air was so thick his lungs constricted.

"Where was it?" Cassius asked, pacing about the room.

"Under the bed," Intoh said.

Helai remained near the door, stone silent as Cassius strode over to the bed and bent down. Lifting the skirt up, he went still. Intoh struggled not to hyper-focus on how loudly his heart sounded in his ears as Cassius raised his head, his eyes flashing in ire.

"There is nothing."

Disbelief crossed Intoh's face as his gaze darted quickly to Helai, then back to Cassius. "Impossible. Was just there. Was humming. Big mark underneath bed." He scurried over, lifting the skirt of the bed himself.

There was no mark. The floor was smooth, with no sign that there had been anything scratched into the wood at all.

"No, no, no." He shook his head, backing away from the bed. "Does not make sense. Was certain I saw it."

Cassius was quiet and contemplative as he pointed at the series of windows that lined the outer wall. "I was stabbed, just there, with a stake before I left to travel to Volendam. A lover—" his jaw pulsed. "Makes me wonder if that sigil was under the bed all that time ago and I just never knew."

Intoh suppressed a shudder at the thought.

"Cassius does have a brand, just like the rest of us," Helai said slowly. "Luring us here doesn't exactly make the most sense."

Helai was right, but the whole situation still made Intoh's scales crawl. "Do not want to stay in here any longer. Sorry I doubted you." He brushed past Helai and exited the room, eager to be freed of the strangeness that had taken hold of the bedroom.

He brushed past Linda, Itale, and Rembrandt without saying anything, and pulled himself into a large, overstuffed chair. Rooster was still sleeping a bit fitfully, muttering something in his sleep, and Rackjack stood over him, his stare unblinking. Helai did not return immediately, even as Cassius collected the others at the door and they left, leaving the house relatively silent.

"Should be reading. Finding way to live longer." Ekalas came into view, her tone disapproving. On some level, Intoh agreed. He was already eight. If he wasted too much time, it'd be too late.

"Have to help Misfits," he said. "Remove brand."

"You care for them," Ekalas accused. "Have you forgotten me?" Her tail flicked in agitation, and Intoh's heart squeezed painfully.

"No," he cried. "How could I have forgotten?"

Ekalas' eyes were sad. "If you don't carry through with our purpose, my death will have meant nothing."

Intoh flinched as if she had struck him. "Not fair," he whispered. "Doing my best."

"Sometimes talk to myself too. Helps me think," Rackjack said, interrupting the conversation. Intoh turned to Rackjack, who was watching him from behind the couch. Intoh's mouth parted as he sucked in several quick breaths.

"Must try better than best. Best not good enough. Best won't get you where you need to go," Ekalas urged, leaning closer. "Must not trust–" She disappeared as Helai reappeared, a bottle of wine in her hand, but Intoh got up and shot past her, ignoring her questions.

Only when he rounded the corner did he allow his fists to unclench and his fingers to shake. His right hip twinged in pain; it was going to rain soon. The old ache of his joint reminded him that his life was moving forward. If he didn't do something to halt it, then Ekalas was right.

Her death would have been for nothing.

Thirty-Five

LINDA

Linda's belly was warm and full of food. Rembrandt kept close to Cassius, a purple dragon plush that Cassius had bought for him at a shop in town hanging from his grasp. Itale spoke through bites of pastry from the baker, and despite the threat of cultists, there seemed to be no sign of them as they made their way back to the estate.

"What name?" Linda asked Rembrandt, gesturing to the dragon doll.

"Gloop," Rembrandt said happily, holding the dragon out in front of him. "Gloop the Brave!"

Linda narrowed their eyes at him. Gloop wasn't a very good name.

"Cassius told me it would keep me safe from bad guys," Rembrandt continued. "He said it would help me be brave when I'm scared."

"Yes," Cassius said. "So do not lose him."

Rembrandt shook his head, pulling Gloop close. "I won't. I promise."

The trail that led up to Cassius' estate was long and winding, and at one point, Rembrandt stopped, a small frown stretching across his face. "Carry me?" he asked Cassius, who shook his head.

"It is not far now."

Rembrandt's lower lip jutted out, and Linda shrugged. "I carry you?" After all, they were used to carrying Intoh. Rembrandt didn't look all that much bigger than Intoh.

Excited, Rembrandt held open his arms, allowing Linda to pick him up and wrangle him around their shoulders. He didn't seem too frightened of Linda even in their krok'ida form. Squealing with laughter, Rembrandt gripped the sides of Linda's head as Linda held him up by pressing their hands against his legs. Gloop, the dragon, rested between the back of Linda's head and Rembrandt's stomach, and it wasn't long before Renbrandt's cheek fell against the top of Linda's head.

"Keep him," Linda said to Cassius. "Care for him."

Cassius shook his head. "We cannot keep him, Linda. Our travels are no place for children."

Linda *hmphed* in frustration, tilting their chin away from Cassius to hide their disappointment. Cassius was right; deep down, Linda knew that. Still, they'd grown quite fond of little Rembrandt. It would be terribly sad when they had to say goodbye to him.

As they slipped through the gate of Cassius' estate, a shudder rolled down Linda's back, like they were being watched. Itale and Cassius had moved ahead. They were talking animatedly about something, but their voices were warped, as if Linda were in a bubble. A soft whisper cradled Linda's ear, a crescendo of words spoken but nothing Linda recognized. It was a language that made them feel unmade, nothing more than the goo they had been pulled from the day they'd been born.

Looking up, a rage swept through Linda as their eyes fell upon a man standing in front of the estate, his face half covered by a mask. The mask was made from the skull of a deer; antlers curled upwards as his mouth was left free. An unsettling smile stretched widely across his face, and he wore all black. He was unnaturally tall, his joints distorted as he seemed to blink in and out of existence.

The Whispering Lords will rise.

Linda was frozen in place, their hands curled tightly around Rembrandt's ankles to keep him from falling. They attempted to move. *Just one foot*, they thought, but Linda was stuck in place. It wasn't fear that bound them to the front yard, but rather something else entirely.

Phoenix Mother will wake them and set us free.

The voice spoke almost as if it were in Linda's head, a deep caress that followed a piercing pain as it shot through Linda's temples. They growled, their gaze locked with that of the masked stranger, but when they blinked, he disappeared. Freed from their invisible shackles, they stumbled forward, catching their balance as Rembrandt cried out and teetered, threatening to fall. He gripped the sides of their head so tightly it hurt, and Linda groaned.

"Too tight," they complained, reaching up to grab at Rembrandt's arms. "Let go. Set you down." Rembrandt, after some hesitation, let go of Linda's head, and Linda lowered him to the ground with Gloop cuddled tightly in his arms.

"I saw it too," Rembrandt whispered, causing Linda to still. They thought he'd fallen asleep.

"You did?" Linda asked, looking cautiously to where the masked stranger had stood.

"Uh huh." Rembrandt's eyes widened with fright. He shivered, but Linda knew it wasn't from the cold. "Linda, I'm scared. They looked like some of the bad men."

"Grip Gloop tight," Linda said, patting Rembrandt on the head. "Cassius keep safe."

"That's right," Rembrandt exclaimed, his eyes brightening. "Cassius is a knight, isn't he?"

Linda nodded even though they weren't sure. Cassius had spoken at times of his past as a knight, but he didn't speak much about his Order. Linda wasn't too familiar with knight orders. There were some knights that touched the southern borders of Lyvira but none within drikoty culture.

"Let's go. Check on Rooster." Linda paused, then booped Rembrandt softly with their nose. "Will be okay. Nothing to fear. Misfits with you."

"Thank you, Linda," Rembrandt said, wrapping his arms around Linda's leg. *That's right, like a hug.* "You're nicer than anyone I've met in the whole entire world."

As Rembrandt pulled away and ran up the stairs to the front door of the estate, Linda stood for but a moment and allowed the foreign warmth to spread through their chest. It was a good feeling, one that had begun the moment Rembrandt's words had left his lips, and Linda rumbled in joy before following Rembrandt inside.

Two days passed with little improvement to Rooster's wounds. Helai, Rackjack, and Intoh lived in the sitting room where Rooster recovered, their constant care required as Rooster's fever kept spiking before falling back to manageable levels. Linda felt the tension in the air at the stress and worry over Rooster's health, but they attempted to keep Rembrandt distracted as the days passed.

One evening, Linda found themself keeping Intoh and Rackjack company while Helai got some much-needed rest. The fire roared in the fireplace, and everyone sat in relative silence as Rooster muttered in his sleep.

"Linda, need to ask, haven't been able to figure out how you used magic at winery," Intoh whispered, drawing Linda from their thoughts.

The warmth of the fire made them drowsy, but they pulled their gaze from the flames and settled on Intoh, who watched them from his spot on a tall velvet chair. "How did you do it?"

Linda shrugged, recalling the soft light that had bathed them just before their bite had set the creatures aflame. It had just happened; Linda wasn't even certain it had been magical in nature. They'd never heard of krok'ida being able to set things on fire with their teeth.

"Does your god talk to you?" It was Rackjack who asked, shuffling closer as his curiosity in their conversation snagged his attention. He settled on the couch next to Linda, eyeing them expectantly, and Linda shook their head.

"No god. Just Linda. Never heard god." Krok'ida were less connected with Ikotia, the god they worshiped. Unlike greka, whose connection to Axolli was seen more frequently among those devoted to her, krok'ida merely claimed lives in Ikotia's honor, his sun warming their backs and keeping them invigorated during battle.

"Could be your god. Think cultists chose the Misfits because they are Chosen. Intoh, you said you are prophet of Axolli?" Rackjack asked, glancing at Intoh as he nodded. "Think gods are preparing for big war. They do not want the dragons to wake."

"Don't like that," Linda said, shaking their head. "Too much gods." The will of gods was above Linda, who only wanted to sunbathe and fight in exciting battles. They cared little for the will of gods.

"If the case, must do more research. Maybe Sleep Walk again," Intoh muttered to himself. Linda fought sleep as Rackjack hummed, drumming his fingers against the table.

"Is Rackjack talking of gods again?" Rooster rasped, his eyes slitted. "Gods, I'll talk of gods with you if you get me a glass of water. I don't think my throat has been so dry."

Linda's heart squeezed with relief at Rooster's wakefulness. "Glad you're awake," they told him, their throat rumbling in content.

"Go get Helai," Intoh said, shuffling down from the chair and scurrying out of the room. Rackjack left to get Rooster a glass of water, but was quick to return, helping him take a small sip from the glass. Rackjack did not seem the gentle type. Linda had seen him fight, but he defied stereotypes when it came to Rooster. Linda felt the admiration roll off Rackjack when he was near the human.

Helai returned with Intoh at her heels, her hair in disarray and her eyes heavy with sleep. "Oh, by Dalnor's grace," she breathed, kneeling next to Rooster. "It's so good that you're awake. How are you feeling?"

"Like shit," Rooster said, grunting in pain as he attempted to shift on the couch. "But better than I was. "Give me a day or two more, and I'll be good to travel."

"I'll be the judge of that," Helai murmured, glancing at Linda. "Go," she said gently. "You are tired. I'll take over from here. Go find rest."

Linda complied, ambling out of the room. Sleep could not come quickly enough.

Thirty-Six

HELAI

They set out a few days later at dawn, and the return to Halvdarc was done quickly and without trouble. The road was quiet, as it had been on the way to Wilhaven, and Rembrandt was a pleasant child, if not very quiet. He spooked often and kept close to Cassius of all people when he was frightened. They had better luck hunting and even managed to kill a deer for food on the third night. It was a relief with Rooster's returning appetite, that they did not have to worry about hungry bellies.

The tension returned the moment they arrived in Halvdarc, and Helai found herself looking over her shoulder more than once or twice as they entered. The village was as silent as when they had left it, and Helai still wasn't certain why. The unease forced her to turn to Rembrandt as they both sat in the cart.

"Do you enjoy living here, Rembrandt?" she asked, forcing a smile.

Rembrandt nodded, clinging to Gloop. "Mama said one day she'd teach me how to sail a boat." Rembrandt sighed, his lower lip wobbling. "I love watching the boats come into the docks from my bedroom." He stilled, looking sadly at his dragon. "I haven't seen many boats lately."

"That's strange. Doesn't a lot of trade happen here?" Rooster cut in, his brows furrowed in suspicion. Intoh peeked his head over his book and nodded.

"Know drikoty trade here. Seen Halvdarc's sigil in port cities of Lyvira."

"They do quite a bit," Cassius interjected from atop his steed. "It is strange if the trading has indeed cut back. That is likely to be the city's livelihood."

The party fell to silence after that as they approached the front gate of the estate. Nestled on the cliffside, it was a sight to behold up close, with rows and rows of rose bushes lining the estate and gardens in beautiful, vibrant shades of red. The vast size of the estate left a sour taste in Helai's mouth. If a fraction of its wealth went to the people, would there be those suffering at the feet of its home? Cassius had said they were different, that the city did not suffer, but her experience here as of late contradicted that claim. She looked at Rembrandt, whose cheeks were once more round and rosy, the sickness from his time at the winery growing more absent by the day. A beautiful child that would one day surely grow to mirror his parents' greed. It filled Helai with a terrible rage.

"Little Rembrandt!" The guards at the gate had moved to block their path, but once they saw the blond of Rembrandt's hair pop up from the cart, their demeanor shifted from annoyance to explicit joy.

"Open the gate," one of the guards shouted. "The little lord has come home!"

As the gate swung open, Rembrandt climbed down from the cart after Cassius stepped off the seat and helped him.

"Kral! Jordy! These nice people saved me from the bad men! And look, look at what Cassius got me!" As he held Gloop up, Kral's and Jordy's eyes widened in exaggerated delight.

"Looks like a mighty fine protector, little lord. Come along. Your parents will be relieved to know that you are alright." Kral looked up, gesturing to the cart. "Leave the cart and horses. We'll have someone escort them to the stables. The lord and lady of the house will want to speak with you post haste."

As everyone shuffled forward, Jordy grunted. "Quite the party you have. You mercenaries?"

"We are Misfits," Linda said, puffing their chest out proudly.

"What Linda means is that we are a mercenary group called The Misfits," Rooster said, glancing at Linda as he steadied himself, gripping the side of the cart. He'd all but healed from the illness that had plagued him, but his wounds had yet to heal, and dark circles covered the skin beneath his eyes. "We heard of Rembrandt's disappearance and wanted to help."

Jordy stared at them, working over whether to believe them, and Helai swallowed her annoyance before it could cross her face. She loathed guards and their ability to make anything sound suspicious.

"I'm sure. An' these?" he asked, gesturing to Linda and the three greka. "We usually see the drikoty folk near the docks, where the tradin' happens. What are you doing, traveling with them?" Jordy's question set everyone on edge.

"Be nice to my friends, Jordy!" Rembrandt cried, reaching up to tug on Jordy's fingers. "They saved my life. If you don't stop, I'm going to tell Mama, and she'll send you away like she did my reading tutor." His little face scrunched up in anger, and through the repulsion of such behavior, Helai smiled.

Jordy spluttered, straightening his back. "'Course. Deep apologies, little lord. Let us go find your parents."

Helai glanced at the others, sighed, and then moved to follow.

Into the belly of the beast of greed.

"Rembrandt? Rembrandt!" A woman stood too suddenly as they entered the dining room. Her knee hit the table, and the cup of tea she'd been drinking rattled on its saucer, but she was already pushing away and darting around the table.

"Mommy!" Rembrandt clutched tightly to his dragon doll as he ran into his mother's arms. Alyse Welker was a slight woman, an inch or so shorter than Helai, and her hair was thin and wispy as it danced around her face in soft curls. Her dress billowed around her as she fell to her knees and wept, pulling Rembrandt into her arms.

"Oh, my sweet baby. Are you okay?" As she pulled away, her fingers ghosted over her son's cheeks, through his hair, down his arms. He winced as her fingers pressed into the crook of his elbow where they'd been bleeding him. She frowned, straightened his arm, and stilled.

"Jordy, go find Emir. Tell him his son is home. I believe he is in the gardens," Alyse said, reaching over to the wall and pulling on a string. Somewhere off in the distance, the tinkling of a bell sounded.

Jordy bowed and retreated out of the room as Khal and Sode shuffled to the other side of the table, their eyes trained on the windows. The room was large; a long table decorated the middle. A fireplace nestled behind where Alyse had been sitting. There was no fire going now, and a woman bustled into the room dressed in a simple black dress, her hair tucked neatly into a bun.

"Ma'am?" she asked gently, her eyes widening as they landed on Rembrandt.

"Rembrandt has gone through an ordeal. Can you please go up to his room and prepare a bath? I will come up with him as soon as his father has celebrated his return."

"Of course, ma'am." She paused, smiling down at Rembrandt. "It's good to see you home, m'lord."

Rembrandt tugged on his mother's arm, gesturing to Helai and the others. "Mommy, these are my friends. They saved me."

"They did, huh?" Alyse finally glanced up to take in the Misfits, her eyes widening as she took them all in. "Quite the...crew you have. I did not know dwarves traveled out of their mountains."

Rackjack twitched nervously, pulling his hand away from a plate of pastries. His cheeks bulged, and he eyed Rooster sheepishly as he shuffled closer, half-hidden behind Rooster's frame.

Rooster stepped forward, offering Alyse his hand as a man burst through the door, his gaze wild as it searched the room.

It landed on Rembrandt, and his lips peeled back in a wide smile. "Son, oh, it's such a delight to know you have been returned to us safely. Come here." As Rembrandt darted into his father's arms, Helai realized with startling clarity that the head of the house, Emir Welker, was from Shoma. Helai's eyes flickered to Rembrandt, watching as Emir peppered his son with kisses.

"Who are these?" Emir asked, gesturing to the Misfits as Rembrandt squealed with laughter.

"Was just about to introduce us to your wife, sire," Rooster said. After the introductions were made, Emir studied them silently for several moments before he kissed the top of Rembrandt's head and set him down.

"I'm going to take Rembrandt up to his room," Alyse said, slipping her hand around Rembrandt's and pulling him towards one of the doors. "Find me when you're done," she said, and then her and Rembrandt were gone.

"What happened? I want every last detail," Emir said, his voice sharpening. All the joy and relief was absent on his face; all that was left was pure, unadulterated rage. It rippled through the room, and Helai shivered as it caressed her, prying at old anger that sat endlessly in her belly.

How is he doing that? Her thought crossed her mind as Emir's eyes met hers and she frowned. The anger intensified when their eyes locked, and Helai wondered if foul magic might be at play. "I do not know how long you have been away from the sands," she said. "I'm sure you are familiar with the shoma'kah?"

Recognition flickered across his face as his fingers went up to scratch his beard, his eyes dark and foreboding. He waved for them to continue.

"We believe they took your son and sold him to..." Rooster paused, gazing sidelong at Cassius as he hesitated. Helai understood; no parent would want to hear of the horrors that had taken place at that abandoned winery.

Still, Cassius urged him to continue, so Rooster stepped forward, his expression thick with sympathy. "Cultists north of Wilhaven. We found him at a blood farm. One of the victims also called it a saelic farm. They were harvesting blood for its magical properties and in turn, infecting the victims with some sort of disease."

"He is lucky to be alive," Cassius said, his hands clasped tightly behind his back. "I do believe he will carry the scars of that ordeal for the rest of his life."

Emir bristled. "He is unharmed though?"

Cassius shrugged. "He will live, but I would keep a close eye on him. We're not sure what exactly happened to him during the time he was taken."

"Thank you for saving him," Emir said thickly. "We would have been lost without him. He is our light."

Helai winced as a sudden urge coursed through her, spurred on through her brand. It was like it had been in their time in Volendam, only much stronger. It sank into Helai, making her skin crawl.

"I am sure you are wanting your payment of skaels." Emir seemed oblivious to their discomfort, and slowly, the urge faded, replaced by a desperate relief. "And perhaps a ball, fit for the honor of you all rescuing our sons from slavers." Emir heaved a sigh. "The people would benefit from the distraction. There have been rumors of cult activity in the recent months."

"Oh, that is not –" Rooster paused. "You are aware of the cultist activity then?"

Emir nodded slowly. "We have some of our best guards working to weed them out. We hope to return the city to a state of normalcy by the next full moon." Clasping his hands together and resting them in front of his mouth, Emir gave an affirming nod. "Which happens to be soon. Will you agree to a ball in your name, then?"

The Misfits all looked at each other. Helai wasn't the type to attend balls, much less those held in her honor, but the longer they were welcome to stay here, the longer she could look for Zamir without arousing suspicion.

"I don't see why not," Rooster finally said. When no one argued him, Cassius stepped forward.

"Your hospitality is most welcome," Cassius said.

"Of course, Sir Antonia. You've always been welcome here, and I'm sure all your friends would desire a bath and some clean clothes." Emir's eyes flickered to the drikoty. "We even have some drikotyian fruits imported from B'kota for our western friends."

Emir turned to exit the room before pausing at the door. His gaze flickered to the Misfits. "You are welcome to roam, but the west wing is off-limits, I'm afraid. The library is on the second floor should you want to make use of it, and the gardens are still lovely at this time of year."

As Emir pulled his hand from the door frame, the sleeve of his shirt hiked up just enough for Helai to notice a small tattoo of a phoenix on the inside of his wrist. It pulsed with some sort of red energy, curling through the black ink like it was alive. When Helai blinked, Emir had covered it, a smile forged on his lips.

"Until we meet again."

Helai felt odd. Despite her disdain for the wealth of the place, there was a certain energy within the walls. It fought against her innate shadow magic, like its hackles were raised, but she couldn't see anything that appeared off.

Still, Helai couldn't shake the feeling that they'd stepped into the center of a spider's nest, and if they weren't careful, they were surely to get ensnared.

Thirty-Seven

LINDA

As soon as Linda entered their room, they shuffled over to the fireplace roaring with flames. The room was not large but larger than the one they'd shared with Intoh at The Broken Arrow. Seated on the floor in front of the fireplace was a massive pelt of an ice bear of the north. Ice bears were enormous with shaggy white fur and feet easily the size of Linda's head in their human form. The pelt would easily accommodate either form Linda decided to be in.

Linda collapsed on top of it, relishing the warmth of the fire coupled with the softness of the rug. It had been some time since Linda had felt the comfort of merely existing, and it was nice to see humans who welcomed Linda in their true form. Perhaps Cassius was right. They were a Misfit now. If they wanted to stay in their true form, then damn the consequences.

"Linda?" The door creaked open slowly as Rembrandt's voice carried through the room. Linda turned as he snuck in, his fingers still gripping Gloop as he looked at Linda sheepishly.

"Hello, Rembrandt," Linda said, their heart swelling with joy. They had grown very fond of the little human, his curiosity and strength after all he'd been through something to be admired.

"Can I sit with you for a while? I had a nightmare..." Rembrandt's cheeks were freshly stained with tears, and he trembled, looking about the room as if he waited for something to leap out at him. "When I was in the barn, those women were not very nice, and they spoke to things...things I couldn't see."

Linda sat up, patting the bear rug next to them. Rembrandt ran over, sat down next to Linda, and rested his head against their leg. He didn't fear Linda at all, something Linda wasn't accustomed to, and as the fire crackled in the fireplace, Linda watched Rembrandt fiddle with his dragon.

"Gloop keep safe," Linda said.

"I actually wanted to give Gloop back to Cassius," Rembrandt said. "Do you think he'd be mad?"

Linda cocked their head to the side, confused. "Why?"

Rembrandt stared at Gloop, running his fingers along the doll's snout. "He seems sad and scared. Maybe Gloop will make him feel better like he makes me feel better. Plus, you guys are gonna leave soon. He can keep Cassius safe on the road." He looked up at Linda with his wide blue eyes; a cord was struck within them.

"Think he'd like," Linda said, nodding. Cassius was a difficult man to gauge, especially for Linda, who rarely understood human emotions. Linda could spend forever trying to figure him out, but they knew he'd taken quite a liking to Rembrandt. Surely he wouldn't turn the boy's wishes down.

"Are you ever afraid, Linda?" Rembrandt asked suddenly. He stared at them, a peculiar look upon his face, and Linda met his expression sharply.

No, they wanted to say. *A krok'ida does not know fear.* That would make Linda a liar though. A shudder threatened them, a shudder that brought on the pain of remembering. They'd been afraid when their village had been attacked, when the dark things had come out of the shadows and washed their home with flames, when the cries of dying drikoty had filled their ears... So much fear had festered in their belly then that they had sat before the ruined village for a very long time to atone for it.

"Yes, sometimes," Linda admitted, looking at the fire. They did not like the taste of fear; it stole away their courage, froze them in place.

"I saw you at the barn," Rembrandt said, holding Gloop out in front of him. "You didn't seem very scared then."

"Had to protect," Linda said simply. "Friends in danger. Must be brave." If they weren't brave for their friends, then how could they possibly protect them? It was a thought they couldn't even consider. "You're friend too," Linda said. "Keep you safe."

Rembrandt's smile turned radiant. "Will you go find Cassius with me?" he asked, pushing himself to his feet. "Sometimes he scares me."

Linda looked sadly at the warm fire and thought of how comfortable the rug felt beneath them, but they nodded. They could admit the vampire was quite intimidating when he wanted to be. "Not too scary. He next door. Will show you."

Rembrandt bounced on his feet as Linda rose, fighting against their aching joints. They had served in many wars and had come out of them with too many aches and pains. The one in Linda's knee protested as Linda stretched, and then they led Rembrandt out of the room.

"I did not expect to see you again so soon, little lord," Cassius said, pulling the door to his room open. His hair was down, freed from the ribbon that usually tied it back, and his eyes were thick with exhaustion. He had a glass of wine in his hand, and Linda's mouth dried. They craved the taste of ale.

"I brought you something," Rembrandt said in a sing-song voice as he brushed past Cassius. The room given to the vampire was similar to that of his estate, and Linda rumbled with laughter at how over-the-top it was. Decorated in red velvet, the bed was massive, tucked away under dark sheets. There were even several decanters of wine and a bathtub in the corner, which was currently full of hot water.

"Interrupt?" Linda asked, gesturing to the bath.

"Oh, it would not be the first time," Cassius said, sighing. "It is fine. Plenty of time to rid myself of the stink of horse." Setting his glass down, he moved to a chair as Rembrandt followed him, looking to Linda for courage.

After an encouraging nod from Linda, Rembrandt offered Gloop to Cassius. "I want you to have this."

Cassius' smile was small, and he looked at Linda for an explanation. "I do not understand. What could I possibly want with a dragon doll?"

Rembrandt's courage stuttered as his face fell. "Oh, well..." He trailed off.

It cut Linda deep, seeing Rembrandt so wounded by Cassius' reaction. They glared at Cassius as they patted Rembrandt on the head. "Remember, Rembrandt," they said. "Be brave."

Rembrandt puffed out his chest and furrowed his brow. It was almost humorous, and Linda held back laughter as Rembrandt shoved Gloop into Cassius' lap.

"He protected me while I was scared, just like you said. I want you to keep him. I know you'll leave soon, and I have my mama and papa to protect me, but you'll be out on the road like when those bad men took me. Gloop will keep you safe." Rembrandt spoke quickly, and Cassius stared at the doll for a long time before he answered.

"You know, Rembrandt, when I was training to be a knight, they taught me how to protect myself," Cassius said, but he gripped the dragon tightly and pulled it close. "They did not, however, teach me how brave little boys can be even when they are frightened." Holding up Gloop, he nodded. "He will not leave my side, and when I am frightened, I will remember you, and I will be brave."

Rembrandt's grin widened. "I wanna be a knight just like you one day," he said, turning to look at Linda. "And maybe I can be big and strong just like you, Linda. I wanna be able to fight with a war hammer one day."

"Hammer is best," Linda admitted. Fighting with anything else now felt like a disservice, and the reminder left them craving combat, if only to have the satisfaction of caving one's head in with their hammer.

"If that is all, I wish to bathe now. Perhaps if your parents allow it, I will find you tomorrow and can show you some fighting techniques my own father taught me long ago," Cassius said, waving his hand towards the door. "But now you must go off to bed. It is late, even for little lords such as yourself."

Rembrandt nodded, hurrying to the door. "I hope tomorrow comes quickly," he exclaimed, prying the door open and disappearing down the hall. The silence that accompanied his absence was stifling, and Linda spared a glance at Cassius as he moved over to the tub, his gaze far off.

"Are you okay?" Linda asked.

Cassius' head raised. There was a darkness in his expression, a silent contemplation that Linda didn't understand. A gentle urge coursed through Linda, as it had in the dining room when they'd arrived, and Linda recognized it immediately. It was the same urge they'd felt leading them to Volendam, the same aching to *go*. Linda loathed the feeling, like something scurried under their skin, leaving them in a perpetual restless state.

"Something feels...off about this place. I cannot quite place it," Cassius admitted, running his fingers over the surface of the bathwater. Steam still rolled off it, drifting into the air, and Linda sensed it too–the feeling he described. It was a quiet hunger, a waiting anger that settled into the bones of the estate.

Something crept in the shadows.

Prowling.

Watching.

"Feel it too," Linda said. It didn't feel at all like the pull that had dragged them all to Volendam, then here. It felt strange, like a brush of magic that tugged at the essence of who they were. No, there was something familiar about it, almost like when they'd stepped into the ritual room in the opera house where the rakken and dyrvak had been praying around the dragon tooth.

"We must simply remain on guard," Cassius said softly. He stood as a soldier did, his back straight, his movements rigid. Linda noticed he got that way sometimes, as if he were trying to prove something to himself. Linda wasn't sure about the vampire, nor his past, but they knew what it felt like to hold oneself to impossible standards. Still, despite Linda's desire to comfort their friend, they could not seem to find the right words to say.

Instead, they lowered their head and moved towards the door. "Good night, Cassius," they rumbled.

They heard no reply as they shut the door behind them and ambled back to their room.

Thirty-Eight

HELAI

Helai stepped out of her room the next morning, closing the door behind her. Her skin crawled, as it always did when she was surrounded by extreme wealth. She'd spent the last few days searching for Zamir, the Ghost who had sent her that letter, but if he was here, he remained hidden, frustratingly so. The hallway bustled with life, and the estate's servants whisked through with dusters and trays full of food. The ball being held in the Misfits' honor wasn't set for a week, but preparations had begun early. A sweet smell wafted through the estate as Helai hurried down the hall, dodging servants to seek out Cassius' room. There was something off, a feeling she could not place. Perhaps Cassius would know something about it; perhaps he felt the same electrifying current in the air.

Eyes hit the back of her neck, standing its hairs on end. She glanced behind her, only to see nothing, but it was enough of a distraction to send her barreling into someone, the tray of puffy sweets they carried flying. Air freed itself from her lungs as she stumbled, only to be caught by the person she'd run into.

"I'm sorry. I should have–" Her words died on her tongue as she looked up into dark eyes, and familiarity struck her so hard, she got dizzy.

"Zamir?" she asked softly. The hallway slanted as Zamir kept hold of her arms, staring at her in concern. Her relief was swift. *Finally*. His hair was shorter than when she'd seen him last. He was the first Ghost to have entered their ranks when Helai, Massoud, and Aryan had formed the group, and the last time she'd seen Zamir had been the meeting before they'd assaulted Mohalis' palace. They hadn't even gotten inside before the mission to assassinate the grand sultan deteriorated with the death of Zahra and they were all forced to scatter to remain out of the clutches of Mohalis' guards. Capture would have meant certain death.

"Helai? Is that really you?" Zamir's voice was as soft-spoken as she'd always remembered it being, and he tugged her away to get a better look. His eyes were honey-soaked and large, sitting slightly too close to his nose. His brow, usually free of worry, was furrowed now, and there was no signature smirk in sight. Helai could scarcely believe he was real and that he stood in front of her now.

"Yes, but what –" She waved her hand, gesturing at him. "You are dressed as a servant." She glanced around, scooting closer and lowering her voice. "Are you on a mission? Did Massoud send you here?"

Zamir glanced over Helai's shoulder as servants moved around them. One or two looked their way, and Zamir offered Helai a friendly smile and bowed.

"My apologies for running into you, my lady, but I must get back to work." He leaned close as he moved to step past her, his breath tickling her ear. "Meet me in the gardens tonight. I'll explain then. It's not safe to talk here."

Helai nodded silently and watched him bend to shuffle the ruined desserts off the floor and back onto the tray he'd been carrying before hurrying off down the hall. Only after he rounded a corner did Helai snap out of her trance. It was surreal, finally seeing Zamir after craving her Ghosts for so long. She almost forgot where she was heading.

Cassius, right.

She padded down the hall, careful to avoid running into any other servants as she halted in front of Cassius' door. After a shaky exhale, she composed herself and knocked.

Something crashed against the wall behind the door, jarring the servants surrounding Helai, and she glanced their way before pushing her way in without knocking again. She was met with the sight of Cassius and Linda circling each other, both drenched in rage.

"What–?" Her question was cut short as Linda lunged forward, reaching for Cassius. The brand on Helai's back screamed, urging her to join the conflict, to get them to stop fighting...even if it meant killing them. The thoughts were dark, but she thought them anyway as they festered, sickening her mind. She curled her fingers against the knob of the door as she gritted her teeth together and forced herself forward.

"Stop!" Her command fell on deaf ears as Linda missed Cassius altogether, his dodge too quick to follow. Grabbing Linda from behind, Cassius attempted to pin their arms to their sides, but Linda headbutted him and threw him with such force against the wall that the room shook again, dust falling from the ceiling. Soft laughter echoed from the balcony.

"Fight for the Phoenix Mother. She may pray for your rebirth if you do." The voice was quiet, a trickling sound that echoed in Helai's ears in a soft caress, and it was spoken behind the billowing curtains of the open balcony.

Helai blinked, and the anger dissipated. Cassius sat with his back pressed against the wall, his head in one hand as he groaned. Linda stood in the middle of the room, shaking their head in confusion. "What happened?" they asked.

The anger drained out of Helai, ending at a final pinprick of pain at the bottom of her back before disappearing entirely. Dizziness remained as fear thundered mercilessly in Helai's belly. Linda's question rattled in her head, fueling her own confusion.

"I don't know," Helai admitted. "This place is strange."

"Clearly," Cassius muttered, forcing himself to his feet and patting down his shirt of wrinkles. The tension ebbed out of the room as suddenly as it had appeared, and Helai felt the creep of exhaustion. When was the last time she'd been awarded a decent night's sleep?

"You just tried to kill me," Cassius accused, glaring at Linda.

"You try me," Linda protested, offense dancing across their expression as they ambled over to a tooth that had been knocked from their necklace and plucked it off the ground. "Just defend."

Cassius snorted, running his hands through his hair, which had been pried from the ribbon he kept it tied with.

Helai glanced through the door. While the hall seemed suddenly empty of servants, she took no chances and shut the door, lowering her voice. "Regardless, I do not know where Intoh and Rooster are, but I finally ran into my old friend. I'm not sure what he's doing here, but I'm to meet him in the gardens tonight. Perhaps he'll have answers."

Cassius narrowed his eyes. "An old friend? One of those Ghosts of Light you speak of?"

Helai nodded.

"We go with," Linda said.

Helai hesitated. It would be good for the other Misfits to be in on the conversation, but it would not be wise for them to all go and arouse suspicion. Shaking her head, she crossed her arms across her chest. "It wouldn't be a good idea. Someone might see if we all go. I'll meet him and then we'll meet to discuss. Make sure the others know."

Neither Linda nor Cassius seemed too happy with it, but it was Cassius who agreed first. "That is logical, I suppose. It is strange you've found one of your Ghosts here, of all places."

"We are accustomed to figuring out how to survive. Something must have led him here," Helai said simply. In all honesty, she did not know why Zamir was in Halvdarc. It would make more sense for him to blend in in Verenzia or Alavae, where Shoma's trade was frequent. His sudden appearance had filled her with a sense of relief, confusion, and dread.

"I just hope he has an explanation for whatever..." She waved her hand at the wall that Cassius had been thrown into. "That was."

"Me too," Cassius said, giving Linda a lingering look before his lips pursed, and he lowered his head. "I am sorry, Linda."

Linda growled lightly, their mouth open just enough to show their teeth, sharp and gleaming in the torchlight. All the anger was washed away though, and Linda shook their head. "No, sorry too."

"Did either of you hear something speak about a 'Phoenix Mother'?" Helai's voice was hushed, but even uttering the name sent a shudder of cold energy through the room as if saying it would cause something to materialize. A soft breath hit the back of her neck, and her fingers went to press at the nape, willing it away. *Don't turn around.* The compulsion to do so was overwhelming, but fear rooted her in place as the room filled with tension once more. *Don't look behind you. They're watching.*

"Let us not speak of it," Cassius uttered quietly, eyeing the room with poorly concealed concern and suspicion. "Let us see what your Ghost has to say about the place. Linda and I will find Rooster and Intoh and see if they've been able to snoop around the estate for some answers. I know Intoh was keen to see the library."

Helai nodded, exhaling shakily as the tension ebbed away. Whatever presence had been in the room was gone, and Helai turned, racing towards the door. The sooner she was free of the room, the better.

Glancing at Cassius and Linda, her weariness came crashing down on her shoulders. "Just–don't try to kill each other again."

Thirty-Nine

INTOH

A s soon as the morning started, Intoh found himself in the library
with Sode and Khal. It was fascinating what one human could
collect for his own personal enjoyment and curiosity. The library was
immense; it could give the one Intoh had studied at in Volendam a run
for its skaels. Bookshelves lined up the room, filled to the brim with titles
of anything Intoh could possibly imagine. A giant globe sat in the middle
of the room, enclosed in an ornate wooden structure that held it up a foot
or two from the ground. Large cathedral-style windows drew sunlight
in on the opposite side of the room to where he was, and between them
were several artifacts, some of which called to Intoh's attention.

"Feel something strange here. Will go investigate," Sode said quietly,
slipping through the rows of bookshelves that lined either side of the
room. How vast the library truly was, he did not know. Every time

he thought to go exploring, a title or interesting artifact whisked his attention away.

Khal hummed softly beside him, moving towards the window to look at the grounds below. Khal and Sode went everywhere with Intoh now, and while he appreciated their loyalty and protection, a part of him missed the comfort of isolation.

"Khal–" As Khal turned, Intoh looked up, noting the illustration painted on the ceiling. It was beautiful, breathtakingly so, a radiance of sunlight bathing a phoenix with her wings outstretched. "Can you search for any books on extending life?"

Khal lowered his head and scurried off, his tail weaving around a table leg nestled near the globe before he disappeared behind a bookshelf, granting Intoh a momentary reprieve from greka company. He relished in it as he approached the windows, studying the artifacts settled inside glass cases before them. One was a long and wicked stake, its hilt decorated with the finest silver Intoh had ever seen, and it came in abundance in Lyvira. The stake was made from wood Intoh didn't recognize and looked to be dipped in something, its point dusted with black. Dried blood flecked the grain, and Intoh drew closer as a faint whispering caressed him, pulling him towards it.

Movement in his peripherals forced him to pause, shaking him from his trance, but when he looked over, he saw nothing. He must have imagined the movement, even though unease coursed through him. The library was strangling him with a sense of someone standing just out of sight, and Intoh looked around nervously, clawing at his throat. When had it gotten so difficult to breathe?

"Just Sode and Khal," he muttered to himself, moving to the next artifact. "Stop being so paranoid." The self-chastising didn't work, and Intoh hunched his shoulders as he struggled to keep fear from bubbling up from his stomach and settling in his throat. The library was alive with light, and yet Intoh could not trust the thickness that seemed to settle in its dark corners.

The middle glass box housed a small purple-like velvet pillow, its edges embellished in gold. A lamp was nestled in its center, its sides worn with age. It was unable to be cleaned or polished for if anyone rubbed it, surely there'd be a jinn inside. It was the only possible explanation as to why it was tucked behind glass, preserved and protected as it was.

Intoh recalled Helai being distressed over one she'd possessed when they'd been taken by the shoma'kah, and Intoh wondered if this was the same one. He wasn't certain how common jinn lamps were. Perhaps if *he* took it, he could ask the jinn to grant his wish to live forever or better yet: wish for Ekalas' return.

He reached out, but his hand recoiled as dark magic brushed up against his fingertips, prying flesh from bone. He hissed in anger and pain as he pulled his hand away, stumbling back and away from the lamp's pedestal. He backed into a chair and fell over it, hitting the ground hard.

Sode and Khal came running, slinking through the bookshelves with grace and ease. Both looked around for danger, and when they found none, they approached Intoh, who moaned softly and looked down at his wounded hand to assess his injuries.

"Stupid, stupid," he muttered, frowning at the bones that poked out the tips of his fingers. Whatever magic that protected the lamp was dark, dark enough to sink through his own innate protective magic.

"Let me," Khal rumbled, reaching out to clasp Intoh's wrist. Intoh allowed it, if only to reserve his own magic. His fingers tingled as Khal's magic wormed its way up to his fingertips, reforging scales anew.

"Don't go near," Intoh said, gesturing to the lamp. "Heavily protected." Strange that he hadn't sensed the magic surrounding it. He slowly rose to his feet as Sode and Khal retreated to grant him space.

"Did not find what you asked. Need more time to look," Khal said. With Intoh's nod of approval, he ventured off again. Sode remained close, and his tail twitched as he cocked his head, listening.

Intoh's thoughts strayed to the artifacts in the glass cases. The lamp had to hold a great deal of power if it were so heavily protected. Just like the tree in Lyvira...perhaps there was a book on such artifacts, one that could tell him of something that would grant him his deepest wish.

"Stay here," Intoh said, moving towards the bookshelves opposite where Khal had disappeared to. The familiar smell of books soothed his anxious thoughts, and he trailed his fingers over the spines until he found what he was looking for: *Artifacts Lost to Time*. It was a thick book, and unlike in the library at the college in Volendam, where the books were ravaged by dust, these ones were kept clean, cared for in their most pristine condition. He wasn't certain Emir would even *have* a book on immortality, but he had to start somewhere. Perhaps the answer was in some lost artifact. This book would be as good a place as any to start.

Flipping through the first few pages, he found nothing. But then a word caught Intoh's attention, and he paused, his finger resting above the page.

A tome of godly power resides in the heart of Osgol the Sick Tree of Ka'lek. It is speculated that this tome keeps an ancient beast from waking, doomed to eternal slumber. However, whoever reads the text inscribed within the tome is said to be gifted with their every desire if the wielder is willing to perform a great sacrifice.

He ran his finger over the page as he continued to read. It was jarring, realizing that the one thing he'd been chasing all these years might have been in his home country all along. Anxiety twisted his belly at the thought of it being at the Tree of Osgol though. The knowledge simultaneously disgusted and excited him, and he closed the tome. Tucking it under his arm, he rose to his feet. Surely Emir wouldn't notice it gone.

A flicker of movement behind him forced him to pause. When he glanced over his shoulder, he *thought* he saw a dark shadow slip behind a bookshelf. It shuffled out of his view, and the bit of courage he'd mustered to investigate died the longer he stood rooted in place.

"Run, Inka. Run away," Ekalas whispered in his ear.

"Did you find what you were looking for?" Sode's voice carried over to Intoh, pulling him from his paralyzing fear, and he took the terror from his thoughts and turned, nodding profusely.

"Found it. Must leave. Must find Helai. Tell her lamp is in library."

As they found Khal and shuffled out, Intoh couldn't shake the feeling they were being watched.

A flicker of movement behind him forced him to pause. When he glanced over his shoulder, he thought he saw a dark shadow slip behind a bookshelf. It shuffled out of his view, and the bit of courage he'd mustered to investigate died the longer he stood rooted in place.

"Wait, Takai. Run away." Ekiala whispered in his ear.

"Did you find what you were looking for?" Soek's voice carried over to Imoh, pulling him from his pathway-ong fear, and he took the error from his thoughts and turned, nodding profusely.

"Found it. What leave. Must find Hotai. Tell her lamp is in library."

As they found Kital and shuffled out, Imoh couldn't shake the feeling they were being watched.

Forty

CASSIUS

The morning sun drenched the balcony Cassius sat upon, nursing his glass of wine. Someone might judge him for partaking so early in the morning, but Cassius had found long ago that wine curbed the blood cravings to a manageable level. The estate grounds were beautiful, comparable to his own estate in the height of his care, and he watched a stablehand lead a couple horses to the stables as his door opened and the thunderous beat of Linda's heart sounded from behind him.

"Hello, Linda," he greeted, looking over to see them offering a tooth from their open palm.

"Knocked it out," they said, opening their mouth. "Sorry for fighting."

"Oh, Linda," Cassius said, waving them away. "I don't need one of your teeth."

"Make tooth necklace," Linda protested. "Show you're strong."

"Tell you what," Cassius said, standing up and brushing past Linda to the crystal decanter that sat next to his abandoned bath. "I bet Rembrandt would adore having one of your teeth as a way to remember you." He stilled as he poured the wine into his glass. "Have you seen him since he gave me Gloop?"

He turned to see Linda shaking their head. "No."

"Hmm." That worried Cassius. It was likely Rembrandt was merely preoccupied with his parents or healing from the ordeal he'd just suffered. His lack of presence shouldn't have worried Cassius. Still, he couldn't shake the strange feeling that something was lying in wait. He stared at Linda, guilt twisting in his belly. He didn't know what provoked him to attack Linda. He'd been sitting peacefully in his room when the air had grown thick with the heat of rage. It had overcome him suddenly, and it had filled him so fully he'd blacked out. It was so unlike anything he'd ever felt, an anger that washed away all other emotion. Perhaps it would be nice to get out of the room. "Want to go find the little lord with me?"

Linda nodded, so Cassius tipped the glass of wine back and drank until it was empty. It wasn't the best wine he'd had, but anything to take the edge off.

The hallways were bustling with maids and servants preparing for the ball. Decorations were being hung, and different flower arrangements were nestled on side tables. The servants weaved around Cassius and Linda as they made their way to the hallway overlooking the grand entrance room. Many of the servants seemed content working here, laughing with the others as they dusted the walls. Someone had set up a giant statue of a dragon in the center of the entrance room, its horns curling around the sides of its head like a ram.

Alyse stood at the door, directing men and women carrying massive bouquets of red flowers. The floral notes of roses hit Cassius as he approached Rembrandt's mother, who smiled brightly at his approach.

"Cassius, Linda. I trust you both have settled in?"

A pulse coursed through Cassius, piercing him so strongly he blinked, attempting to reign in composure so Alyse would not notice. His hand shook as Ahma's pull settled in his blood, the soft sigh of her impatience echoing in his ear. He sensed the next piece of the Ebony Fang somewhere close by. He was still uncertain whether he wanted to find it, but he felt chained to Ahma's desire for it. It pulsed in his arm where the gun and lance rested beneath his skin. Perhaps it was Ahma's impatience that caused his unease, and it made him feel restless. He loathed the feeling, which only made him determined to find the piece so that it would quiet.

"Cassius?" Alyse stared at Cassius curiously, pulling him from his thoughts. "Linda said you are looking for Rembrandt? I believe he is playing in the gardens this morning, but he has some studies later he needs to catch up on, so I'm not sure he should be bothered today."

"A shame," Cassius said. "I hoped to make sure he was readjusting well after all that happened to him."

"He is home now," Alyse said gently. "It will take time, but he is safe. We intend to keep a close eye."

"How did he ever evade your sight in the first place?" Cassius said before he could help himself. Alyse's eyes flashed in anger, and Cassius was quick to regret his question. "I apologize. I did not mean to sound so harsh–"

"You will do well to remember you are a guest of my house, Sir Antonia." Her chastising wounded him more than he'd like to admit, the ghost of his father's stern lectures echoing in Alyse's words. Cassius recalled Dominic Antonia saying something almost identical to Cassius when he was but thirteen winters old.

"You're right. My apologies, my lady."

"Linda want food," Linda said, easing the tension.

Alyse brightened, pushing the wrinkles from her dress as she nodded and gestured to one of the maids. "I will have some food sent up to your rooms."

"Thank you," Linda said, their jaw parting in excitement.

"My lady? Kareem was telling us you and your husband are avid collectors," Cassius said. "I am somewhat of a collector myself and would love to see what you have obtained over the years."

Alyse nodded. "Oh? Yes, that would be quite lovely. We'll go and find Emir now! I am certain he'll be honored to show you our collection room." Cassius lowered his head in concealed glee. If he could just *see* where the cuirass was, he could retrieve it when the ball was taking place and the Welkers were busy entertaining guests.

"After you then," Cassius said, gesturing with his hand. Linda followed along as Alyse led them to a door situated between two staircases leading up to the second floor. It appeared to be an office, grandeur even in Cassius' tastes. It looked similar to his uncle's old office back at his own estate, only twice the size and with swirling vines and grapes carved into the wood of the desk. Bookshelves were made into the wall behind it. A painting of Emir with Alyse and Rembrandt sat above the fireplace on the opposite side, where several chairs were situated atop a rug made from the pelt of a northern ice bear.

"Cassius, Linda, what a pleasant surprise." Emir sat at his desk, his hair in a state of disarray as he swept his hands through it. A splattering of papers covered his desk, and he set one down, sighing. "You have caught me at a peculiar time, I'm afraid."

"Anything we can help with?" Cassius asked. Even though he'd never been an official lord, even with his uncle holding a small claim in Wilhaven, he knew of the obligations and tasks they were expected to uphold. He did not envy the task.

"Ah, not exactly. Nothing you should trouble yourself with," Emir said, shuffling the papers into a pile. Cassius glimpsed Alavae's sigil on one of the wax seals before it was tucked away, which left him wondering... What did Hestia want with Rovania? They did not tend to do much dealings, save for the occasional wine trades, but the papers didn't look like trade agreements nor would they have been a cause for Emir's concern if so. Emir set them aside before Cassius could glimpse anything more.

"Emir, darling, Cassius and Linda are interested in seeing the collection room if you have a spare moment."

"Oh, yes. Of course." Emir's eyes lit up as he stood, adjusting his jacket. Emir was tall and slender, his skin a bit darker than Helai's but his accent just as thick. Most of Shoma's wealthy remained in Shoma, so it had been strange learning Halvdarc's lord was not of Rovanian descent. Perhaps it was the prosperous land and trade port that had drawn Emir to Halvdarc, securing his place among the wealth with his marriage to Alyse.

"It's this way, over here," Emir said, pointing to a side room in his office. The door was nearly hidden, tucked against the wall in a way that Cassius would not have known it was there had he not been looking for it.

As they slipped through—Linda with a bit of difficulty due to their size—Cassius marveled at the room. It opened up to a large square room with various glass cabinets and armor stands. Small magical orbs darted about the room, filling the space with a warm light, and Emir stepped to the side, stopping Linda at the door.

"Ah...I mean no offense, Linda, but I think it would be better for you to remain here. The value of this room far exceeds what you would be able to pay should anything break," he said, his smile apologetic.

Linda didn't seem offended as they nodded, looking about the room with mild interest. Cassius knew they were eager to find Rembrandt, but his attention was tugged away from his friend as he descended upon all that Emir and Alyse had collected.

Rows of artifacts lined the walls and the center of the room. Various weapons of war nestled against the wall, settled above glass cabinets that held various tomes and vials of unknown liquids.

Intoh would love it in here, Cassius thought. A shudder rolled through his forearm, beckoning him forward. Tasting Ahma's impatience, he complied to her demand, drawing forward until he stood in front of a cuirass hanging on an armor stand. It was beautifully ornate and definitely vampiric in nature, the front of it bearing the sigil of a dragon flying towards the rays of the sun. It was the sigil of the Sanguine Order. *What does Ahma want with something like this?* It hadn't been clear with the gun and the lance Ahma had had him seek earlier that what she sought might belong to a vampire of his Order, and Cassius' head spun at the implications.

"You have good taste, my friend," Emir said. "That belonged to Sir Khoros Drakos. I trust you are familiar with him? He was a knight of the White Dawn."

Cassius' eyes flashed in surprise and alarm. Dmitry, head of the Sanguine Order, had always spoken highly of Khoros, a vampire legend in his own right. He'd singlehandedly led many cavalry charges through the wars across time, so much ingrained in history that some humans, his father included, had worshiped him as a god of war. He'd been killed in battle long before Cassius' time, but Khoros' portrait and accomplishments were all over Dragon Keep. His leadership and bravery had been something Cassius had always admired.

The question beckoned once more: what did Ahma want with Khoros' arsenal?

Cassius swallowed thickly and forced a smile as he sought Emir's gaze. "Do you believe the stories then? That he led a cavalry charge so great and so victorious that the gods granted him with the godship himself–a god of war?"

Emir's lips split to reveal the pearly shine of teeth. They were almost eerie in the glow of light, but Cassius had become preoccupied with the shallow cut on Emir's palm. His vampirism demanded he feed soon, and the wound tempted him.

"The gods are good to the devout," Emir said, pulling Cassius out of his bloodlust. "If your cause is just and in line with their vision, then I do believe they grant mercy."

Not exactly the question he asked, and it was a struggle not to scoff at the notion. Cassius hid behind a feigned interest, moving to gaze at the sword beside the cuirass.

"That one is a sword that belonged to Zhalzor if you've ever heard of him. Massive krok'ida," Emir said.

"Know him. Be like him," Linda said from the door. Alyse had disappeared, and Linda marveled at the blade. Cassius couldn't blame them; the sword was beautiful. The sword's hilt was inlaid with several teeth. It wasn't smooth nor metal forged like a traditional sword but rather made from the enamel of some giant beast if Cassius had to guess. There had been many strange creatures that had walked the old world and saw the birth of Vilanthris.

"Very beautiful," Cassius commented, distracted by the pull back towards the cuirass. Ahma was insistent, her will urging him to reach out and grab it, to kill the Welkers and flee the estate.

Nothing matters but the cuirass.

Her words etched desperation into the hollow of his bones, and he refrained from quivering despite the taste of power that coursed through him like a heartbeat where the gun and lance rested beneath his skin.

He turned instead, gracing Emir with a smile. "Thank you for sharing your collection with me. It makes mine at home look quite small." It didn't exist; Cassius had never been one for collecting expensive trinkets.

He was never home long enough to appreciate such things. No, his tastes were in wine and other simple delicacies.

"I have been collecting for a very long time. Took me forever to get this piece," Emir said, gesturing to a large tooth anchored to metal seats in the center of the room. The tooth seemed to pulse with innate magic, and as Cassius' gaze flickered over to it, the brand on his back burned so badly, he flinched. From across the room, Linda did the same, their leg twitching in pain.

Emir said nothing, but Cassius felt his gaze burn into the side of his head. "Dragons have been lost for a very long time. Though we know of some of their burial sights, like Qevayla, in my homeland of Shoma, or even of Bulgash in Lyvira, it is quite tricky to get your hands on any of their skeletal structures. This one cost me a fortune."

"Where did it come from?" Cassius asked, though he suspected he already knew the answer. It looked the same as the tooth that the cultists had been chanting around inside the opera house.

"A collector brought it to me, says it came from Volendam."

How Cassius had missed the tooth on entry was lost to him for its size was vast. It took up most of the center of the room and still had dried blood on it from where it had inevitably torn through flesh and bone.

"I'm afraid there are matters I must attend to. If you wish to return, another day might suit better," Emir said, holding his hand out to the door.

Cassius reluctantly followed him out behind Linda, and his eyes caught sight of the cuirass one last time before Emir shut and locked the door. He slipped the key into the top drawer of his desk, and Cassius tucked that information away. If he was going to sneak into the office during the ball, he'd need to move quickly.

"Get food now?" Linda pondered. "Go see Rembrandt?"

"Yes, yes," Cassius said, composing himself. Emir had returned to his seat behind the desk, his attention drawn back to whatever Hestia needed from Rovania. That news still troubled Cassius; if there was unrest in the south, then that was a cause of great concern. "Come, Linda. Alyse said Rembrandt is busy today, but there is food waiting for you up in your room."

As he followed Linda, Ahma's whisper caressed his ear.

Soon.

Forty-One

HELAI

T he gardens at night were proving to be more comforting than
Cassius' room had been, and Helai allowed her shoulders to relax
as she rubbed her hands together. Somehow the rose bushes surrounding
the garden had not succumbed to the cold yet, and they bloomed with
lush vibrance. Helai couldn't help but admire their beauty and perse-
verance. There hadn't been any snow in Halvdarc yet, but the cold was
creeping in, and Helai wished for the warmth of her home.

One day I'll see it again.

Helai swallowed. Homesickness festered without mercy, and it was
only the sight of Zamir's approaching face that kept her from losing
herself to it. It was such a welcomed sight to see him that the moment he
drew close, she tugged him into a hug. He smelled like the kitchen, honey

glaze and some sort of smoked meat, but he returned the hug almost immediately, the softest of sighs tickling the top of her head.

"It is so incredibly nice to see you," Helai said in Shoman. "I was told to meet Massoud in Volendam, but when I arrived, he wasn't there. That was *after* escaping capture by shoma'kah." Pulling away, she sought out answers in Zamir's eyes and found a spark of recognition.

"Massoud is in Alavae."

Helai's throat constricted. "Alavae? What is Massoud doing in Hestia?" Her mind was lost to a torrent of thoughts at once. She felt both dizzy and warm, and her urge to flee was so strong that Zamir's eyes furrowed in concern as she attempted to pull away. "Why didn't he meet me?"

Zamir didn't answer immediately as he stepped back, slowly pulling away from Helai as his gaze trained to the garden behind her. Shutting his eyes, he exhaled slowly, and Helai's heart plummeted.

"Hestia and Shoma have declared war, Helai."

Helai blinked. The world had been at surface-level peace for as long as Helai could remember. Each country faced its own issues, and tensions had been high from time to time, but Helai had been certain that Shoma and Hestia had been on good terms.

"What changed?" Helai asked breathlessly. This conversation wasn't going at all like she'd thought it would. If countries were going to war, it was only going to make the task of freeing Shoma from Mohalis that much more difficult.

Zamir lowered his voice as he led Helai further into the shadows of the tall brush that lined the garden so they had no hope of being seen. "Mohalis declared it by demanding it is the will of Qevayla." Zamir spat on the ground. "The Dragon of Dreams continues to poison the sultan's mind. It is the only reason I can think that would cause such recklessness."

"It should not come as a surprise," Helai said sullenly, clasping her hands together in worry. "So what does the war have to do with Massoud?"

"He was forced to illusion as a soldier. Last I heard, he was in Alavae feeding Hestia intel."

Helai blanched at the news. "He is betraying his own people?"

Zamir's eyes darkened. "You know as well as I, Helai, that Shoma's soldiers would, without hesitation, murder us in the streets. He is betraying no one." He spoke with conviction as sickness grappled Helai, and she groaned.

"Oh, this is not good."

Zamir shook his head. "I have been sent here to steal something Emir Welker bought not too long ago that could aid in the coming conflict. A lamp."

Helai's head shot up. *Oh no.* "A lamp? How?" Jinn lamps were uncommon, usually gifted to sultans or rich bloodlines to protect the families. Jinns were honored in Shoma culture; to give a jinn's lamp to one not dwelling within the sands, even if the caretaker was of Shoman descent, was dishonorable by nature.

"Shoma'kah sold it to him. Not sure how they managed to get their hands on one though." Zamir sighed, running a hand through his hair. Helai smelled the threat of rain in the air; they didn't have long if they wished to remain dry.

"Zamir, we have to get that lamp," Helai uttered, reaching out to take his hands in hers. "I'm not certain it is the same, but that lamp..." She hesitated but no. Zamir would not judge her. "I plucked the lamp off someone as I was fleeing Dalasae." Ignoring the alarm in his expression, she squeezed his hands. "I thought it could turn the tide of that failed assassination attempt. I thought I could get somewhere safe, and Zahra..." She trailed off as her voice shook. The spot where her pinky used to be ached in reminder.

"What happened to Zahra wasn't your fault," Zamir said gently.

"I should have…"

"Should have what, Helai? We knew what we were getting into when we joined the Ghosts. You cannot burden yourself with that guilt, nor do you have to continue down this war path of…" Zamir paused, his tongue clicking against the roof of his mouth. "Many of us have moved on. You are young. You would do well to live your life; stop letting Mohalis rob it from you."

Helai frowned. "You speak as if the Ghosts are lost."

Zamir remained silent, his shoulders sagging in defeat. "I believe the lamp is inside Emir's library. I'll attempt to get inside."

"My, eh, friend Intoh might be able to help us. He's spent the better part of the day inside the library," Helai said, more a thought to herself than to Zamir.

"There is something strange going on here, Helai. The city whispers of a coming darkness, of things crawling out of the shadows, of someone called the Phoenix Mother." Zamir's words forced Helai to still, his urgency thick in the air as a raindrop hit her cheek.

"Did you say Phoenix Mother?" Helai asked, her eyes wide as she looked up at the estate behind her. The home looked dark and menacing at night, like the shadows would leap out at her at any moment. "Zamir, there's no time to explain anything, but I think there are those who mean to resurrect the lost dragons. Remember the stories?"

Zamir laughed breathlessly, pulling away. "Just stories, Helai! They're meant to scare people into order. Dragons aren't going to come back, and they're not going to purge the world in fire. You're starting to sound like Moha–"

"Don't," Helai warned. "I'm not anything like him."

Mohalis had always spoken of such Comings, and Helai had always scoffed at the notion. After what had happened in the opera house though… She shuddered to even think of the possibility.

"The ball is in a few days. Let me try and gather some more information. We'll meet again in two days." The rain began to fall harder, a symphony of white noise that made Helai crave a fire and a warm cup of tea. Helai blinked through the droplets as she nodded in agreement and turned away.

"Oh, and Helai?" Glancing over her shoulder at Zamir, she was met with a radiant smile. "I would love to meet your new friends."

Forty-Two

ROOSTER

"Rooster?" Helai's head stuck through the door of his room as the sun danced below the horizon, granting the moon her time in the sky. The past several hours had been filled with a sense of deceitful calm. He'd had the delicacy of having the windows open during the day, the wind of early winter chilling the room. Coupled with the roar of the fire, he was left lethargic and at peace. His wound from Wilhaven was healing slowly, but his strength returned a little more each day.

"Hm?" Rooster raised his head from his view of the fire. Rackjack sat on the sofa to Rooster's right, his beard covered in the crumbs of the biscuits he nibbled on. Rackjack never let Rooster out of his sight now; a part of Rooster was uncomfortable with the constant company. Rackjack was quiet and exuded a nervous energy, constantly moving.

Rooster had never seen a dwarf so...*twitchy*. Still, there was something familiar about him, a feeling he could not place. The others looked at Rackjack with suspicion and sometimes disdain, but Rooster only felt a protective nature when he was near the dwarf, like an old friend had come home and needed to be kept safe from the judgment of his new ones.

"Can I come in?" Helai asked. "Well–we need to have a meeting. Shall I go and get the others, or would you rather meet elsewhere?"

"Have them come here. The fire is warm, and I do not wish to move." The heat of the fire pulled at his conscious state, lulling him into the space between wakefulness and sleep. If the urgency in Helai's voice hadn't been so alarming, he might have drifted off.

"Don't go anywhere," Helai said and then she was gone.

"Didn't plan on it," Rooster said to himself, pushing up into a more seated position. The fire cast a glow in the room as Rackjack paused from eating, his head cocked as he looked up at the ceiling.

"Hear that?" he asked, his voice hushed. "Something in the walls."

Rooster listened, but save for Rackjack's rapid breathing, Rooster heard nothing. "Perhaps you hear the logs shifting in the fire," Rooster suggested, shrugging his shoulders.

Rackjack's brow furrowed. "No–"

"You all have an uncanny ability to interrupt me as I'm enjoying my bath," Cassius said, opening the door to Rooster's room. His hair was soaked, and he wore nothing except for a long black silk robe. His bare feet padded silently through the room.

"Shhh, ClassyAss, I wouldn't have pulled you away from your precious 'me' time if it wasn't important," Helai said, waving her hand in dismissal. "Besides, you practically *live* in that bath. If you didn't want interruption, we'd never see you."

"Precisely," Cassius muttered.

Helai took a seat next to Rooster, tucking her feet underneath her as she did. Ignoring Cassius, she said, "Intoh and Linda are on their way. I've got my friend coming too."

Cassius remained standing, his fingers pressed neatly against the mantle of the fireplace. "Your Ghost friend, I presume?"

Helai nodded. "As I said this morning, he spoke of some concerning things." Tension rolled off Helai, and Rooster sighed, raising his hands to clasp them behind his head at the nape of his neck. 'Concerning things' did not surprise him, but he'd be lying if he said he wasn't growing tired of hearing them all the time. Did they not deserve good news every once in a while? It dredged up the news Delroy had brought about his past and the danger of a dragon waking from some distant tree. He hadn't thought of in some time. He couldn't avoid it forever.

Linda and Intoh stumbled in not too long after, Linda with an ice bear rug thrown around their neck. The head of the bear clung to Linda's left shoulder, and Intoh flexed his fingers as he pulled himself up into a velveted chair. He was free of a book, which looked strange, and he was also free of Khal's and Sode's company, which was even stranger. The two greka were rarely seen anywhere but at Intoh's side as of late.

"Where are your bodyguards, Intoh?" Rooster asked.

"Told them to stay behind. Would be with Misfits. Didn't need their protection," Intoh explained.

"I did not wake Itale either. I figured I could inform him of the contents of tonight's meeting come morning," Cassius said. "Now that we are just waiting–" He was interrupted by the door opening. A short Shoman man walked through, his movements quick as he shut the door behind him, and his gaze found Helai.

"Good. I am the last to arrive, as is tradition."

Helai laughed and then went around the room and introduced everyone. "This is Zamir. He's the Ghost's scout. You ask this man to climb something, he can do so with ease."

"Ah," Zamir said, shrugging. "Dalnor's grace helps with it, no?" And with his words, he disappeared in a flurry of shadows, only to reappear on the other side of the room. Black smoke coiled off him as he curled his hand, beckoning it into his palm. An easy smile graced his features, and Helai grinned as she got up and moved to Zamir, pressing a hand to his shoulder.

"He likes to show off," she said. "But he's good at what he does."

"Teach me how?" Linda asked, impressed.

Zamir laughed. "It is a gift from my god, I'm afraid. Only if his will allows it and even then, it is not an easy feat."

Linda's face fell, and Helai patted their arm sympathetically before her face grew solemn. "Tell them what you told me."

Zamir's silence was deafening before he filled them in on the war between the two countries. When he finished, the room was drenched in thick silence, and Rooster frowned as Cassius stepped forward, shocked.

"That cannot be. Hestia and Shoma have had the longest-standing peace of any two countries in the world. Their trade agreements alone are worth more in skaels than the entirety of the dwarf capital."

Rooster was not familiar with the politics of all the countries, but he did know at the end of it, war was never a good thing. Especially if what Cassius said was true, and their peace agreements had been as old as the countries themselves.

"Do we think it correlates with everything that has been going on? The siege at Volendam could not have been a coincidence. Not if there is war brewing in the south," Rooster said, leaning forward to turn and stare at Zamir and Helai.

"The head sultan of Shoma dwells within the skull of Qevayla, the Dragon of Dreams. I fear–" Helai hesitated, locking eyes with Zamir. "I do not think those that attacked Volendam are the only ones hearing whispers in the dark."

Zamir held his hands up, a confused question crossing his face. "Wait, wait, wait. Volendam was attacked? When?"

"About a month ago," Cassius answered, his gaze torn away from the flickering flame in the fireplace as he pushed away from the mantle. Rooster could not discern his expression, but it was a solemn one as he went to sit beside Rackjack, who muttered quietly under his breath. "The city won but only just. We left it in ruin."

"That is...not good." Zamir frowned. "If Volendam was attacked, that is a direct declaration of war upon humanity."

"How so?" Rooster asked, staring at Zamir. He didn't seem much older than Rooster himself, if he was nearing thirty winters at all, but stress seemed to have aged his face, already causing a lingering wrinkle or two to form on his forehead and around his eyes.

"Volendam is a central hub for trade. Nantielle and Wolstadt do not have the ports for it, and Halvdarc is tricky to get to, especially if your ship is too large. No, no, if Volendam falls, human cities will suffer greatly. Kythera and Hestia are too concerned with their own livelihoods and tensions between them to worry about other struggling kingdoms." He began to pace, his fingers drawn to his chin.

"Regardless, it is concerning that these attacks seem to be happening all at once. They have to be connected somehow," Cassius said.

"Could be dragons," Intoh piped in, staring at the ground in contemplation. "Trying to bring one back in Volendam. Sultan lives in dragon skull. Could be connected."

"You all speak as if we stand upon the precipice of the end times," Zamir said, his gaze flickering to each of them before landing on Helai.

"I know it is hard to believe, but Zamir –" Helai's hand reached out to grab his. "I need you to trust me. What's happening is not some isolated thing. The world's roots are changing; dragons or no, something terrible is happening."

After a moment, Zamir nodded, squeezing Helai's hand. "You have never led us astray, *ibibi*. I trust you." Straightening, he ran his hand over his face as if it would wash away the stress. "It is dire then that I find the lamp Emir bought and return to Hestia. Massoud will be relieved to know you are okay."

A peculiar expression crossed Helai's face, one that made Rooster nervous. It was that of someone desperate to dart, to flee. He knew Helai treasured her Ghosts above all else, and the mention of Massoud would tempt her.

"If you are going to Hestia, I'm going with you," Helai said.

Tension filled the room. They'd all been traveling together for so long, it felt strange, the prospect of them splitting up.

"Though I cannot leave until what we have come here to do is done," Helai continued, pressing her hand to the back of the couch. "We have been connected somehow and must find a way to relieve us of the mark."

"Mark?" Zamir questioned.

Helai turned, gesturing to her lower back. "Branded; it connects us somehow."

Zamir reached forward and lifted Helai's shirt just enough to see the brand marring her back. He whistled lightly through his teeth, his brow furrowed in confusion.

"I have seen this before. It has been marked in various places around the estate. Nothing too large or noticeable, but you know me, Helai. Nothing passes beneath my wandering eyes."

The implications of his words were not lost to Rooster. The last time they'd seen the mark of Gorvayne on buildings, the city had been besieged. If there were buildings being marked in Halvdarc, it could only mean some ill fate.

"We will have you show us," Cassius said. "Perhaps it is also wise to inform the lord and lady of the house."

Intoh nodded. "Yes. Yes, yes. Believe it is imperative to know where they are located and what is marked."

Zamir glanced about the room and stepped closer, lowering his voice. "I do not know if Emir and Alyse Welker are to be trusted, if you want my honest opinion. I have been here for weeks observing them, trying to find a way I can..." He eyed Helai, his grin wicked. "*Obtain* one of their prized artifacts, and they have been meeting with the most unsavory of people."

"Who are they?" Rooster asked. He'd had an uneasy feeling forming in the pit of his stomach as if the shadows in the corners of the room curled in on them. Waiting. Listening.

His brand burned.

Hissing, the others flinched too. The brand on Rackjack's arm burned red and angry as he picked at the skin surrounding it with merciless fervor, his gaze drenched in rage. He picked until blood secreted from his arm, and Cassius' nose flared up beside him.

"It would be wise to stop," Cassius said, grabbing Rackjack's wrist and pulling it away from his arm.

"I have never seen their faces. They have done a fantastic job at keeping their identities hidden, but I know they have all met here for some purpose. What that purpose is, I do not know," Zamir said, his gaze finally tearing away from Rackjack to stare at Rooster. "I believe they are using this masquerade as a front."

"I have seen Emir's collection room. He had a dragon tooth inside," Cassius said, his voice grave. A shudder coursed through the room, and Rooster shifted in his seat, his heart pounding. A dragon tooth? It felt almost like the opera house all over again.

"We must remain on guard," Cassius continued. "We cannot leave until we've gotten what we've come here for." Cassius' words rang true. Since arriving at Halvdarc, the brand hadn't let them forget the shared burden of whatever ailed Cassius. His search for the Ebony Fang was a venture that Rooster did not know if he could trust or understand, but it was difficult to dissect it when all he could feel was the urge to claim it.

"Also use masquerade?" Linda suggested. "Sneak around."

Helai shook her finger at Linda, her expression thoughtful. "That's not a bad idea, Linda. If they mean to use the masquerade as a front, then we should do the same."

Linda nodded. "Just like Club."

It felt so long ago, their heist at the Silver Moon Club. How small their troubles had been then, when there had been no talks of war nor the resurrection of dead dragons. Rooster sighed. Had he known then, he might have taken more advantage of the bar.

"After everything is said and done, we should also take care in making sure we have not brought little Rembrandt into any sort of danger," Cassius said. The implications caused nausea to plague Rooster's belly; surely the Welkers would not cause harm to their own child?

"Of course," Helai agreed. She paced, her movements a distraction from the conversation. Footsteps sounded outside the room, followed by the soft murmur of conversation, and everyone quieted, listening with bated breath.

Silence remained long after the footsteps faded.

"The lamp I need to obtain is in the library, I believe," Zamir said, his voice hushed. He glanced nervously at the door, and though Rooster strained to hear, no more footsteps found their way past his door.

"Saw it there." Intoh nodded. "Saw lamp in case. Tucked away be-hind some horrible magic. Will have to accompany. Believe I can break it." Intoh flexed his fingers, one hand gripping his opposite wrist, and Rooster finally stood himself, ignoring the small bout of dizziness that caused him to sway.

"Perhaps–" Helai hesitated, then turned to Zamir. "How dire is it that you return with this lamp? The wish–we could have these brands removed with jinn magic."

Zamir's eyes flashed, and he kicked his head back. "They're counting on me to return with the lamp, Helai. Though..." He sighed, pressing his palms to his eyes before catching Helai's gaze. "I do think Massoud would rather you use it. If it was yours originally, and it will free you from whatever curse is shackled to you, then use it."

Rooster's stomach plummeted in anxiety at the thought. He wasn't familiar with jinn magic. "Is it safe?"

Helai looked over, nodding slowly. "If the wish is worded right, we should not invoke the wrath of the jinn inside. It grants us its wish, and it will be freed of the ancient magic that traps it inside the lamp." She flashed Zamir a smile. "We'll try what we can to remove the brands otherwise, but it's an option. Thank you."

Zamir said nothing as he flashed Helai a tight-lipped smile.

"Cassius, you have...something to collect as well, yes?" Rooster stuttered slightly over his words, uncertain whether the Ebony Fang should be knowledge shared with others. Zamir and Rackjack didn't seem to notice, and Cassius studied Rooster for a moment before giving the briefest of nods.

"Yes. What I need is inside Emir's office. I believe I should go alone. It would be too risky if anyone came with me due to its location."

"Are you sure that is a good idea?" Helai asked. "What if you are caught?"

"I am more resourceful than you think, Helai," Cassius said, an amused expression crossing his face.

Rooster cut in as Helai moved, her mouth opened in protest. "I think that's fine. If we're all absent from a ball that's being held in our honor, it'll arouse suspicion. Linda, Rackjack, and I will remain with the other greka and Itale. If anything, we can make it our goal to distract Emir and Alyse so they don't think anything is astray."

Rackjack nodded silently in agreement as Linda moved closer, their tail trailing behind them on the carpet.

"Think that good," Linda said, parting their maw to reveal a row of very sharp teeth. "Will be human. Don't cause scene. Take war hammer. Just in case."

"Ah, I don't know if that will go well with your attire, Linda," Cassius said, holding up a hand. "You are a formidable foe all your own. Leaving your hammer in the room will cause less suspicion."

"Have good point," Linda said after some thought.

"Then it is settled. Let us keep our heads down until the ball. Next time we should include the others if they are to be a part of the group," Rooster said, moving to a small decanter near the balcony. Somehow, someone had known to fill the decanter with rum instead of wine, his favorite.

As the group murmured in agreement, Rooster poured himself a glass, trying to curb the shaking in his hands. The rum sloshed in his cup as he raised it to his lips. He relished in the burn as it slipped down his throat and warmed his belly, where it settled. He had a few more days before the ball to wrap his mind around everything going on: Rackjack's sudden appearance and what that had to do with his past, what Emir and Alyse were up to, and if they truly were in danger.

"If we have come to a decision, I would like to retire," Cassius said. Rooster could tell the vampire was eager to leave, so he waved him away.

"Go, Cassius. Enjoy your bath. May it be uninterrupted this time."

Everyone filtered out, leaving Rooster alone with Rackjack, who, despite his constant movement, was uncharacteristically still.

"What do you think of it all?" Rooster asked, gripping his glass and moving back to the couch. The warmth of the fire was all too comforting, and he stared at the flames for a moment before catching Rackjack's expression.

"Think there is something going on," Rackjack said, fiddling with his fingers. "Must be careful; don't trust Emir. Gives me wrong feelings."

"Ah, yes. I never trust anyone with this many skaels," Rooster sighed, leaning back against the couch. The couch wasn't even comfortable by any means, but Rooster sank into it anyway, his eyes growing heavy from the flames and the drink in his hand.

"Will keep up and watch," Rackjack said softly. "Can go sleep if you want."

"I think I might," Rooster said, downing the rest of his drink and setting the empty glass on the table beside him. "But don't stay up for my safety. I don't believe we're in any immediate danger."

Rackjack shook his head and said nothing.

As Rooster slipped into bed for the evening, he couldn't help but feel comforted by Rackjack's ever-watchful eye. He slipped easily into dreams of a woman with red hair dancing around a fire, a myrlír and rakken sharing a drink, and the ever-roaring laughter of people just out of sight. It was a welcomed relief from the nightmares that had plagued Rooster as of late.

Forty-Three

ROOSTER

Rooster tugged at the collar of his tuxedo, already wishing for the night to be done. A sigh fled his lips as he grabbed his mask from the vanity he'd gotten ready in front of. The Welkers had outdone themselves on the masquerade masks. Rooster's was white with blue sapphires rimming the edges of the eye openings, and rooster feathers adorned the edges on either side. Slipping it on, he took one last look at himself in the mirror before exiting his room, nearly bumping into Cassius.

The vampire cleaned up well when he was freshly fed. Rooster had learned never to ask where or how Cassius managed to keep up with his blood cravings. For some reason, it had never bothered Rooster. Perhaps that had been due to the fact he'd grown up on a ship of vampires.

The thought of Delroy threatened to sour his mood, so he turned his attention to Cassius as he gestured down the hall.

"I am sure the others are expecting us," the vampire said. Dressed in deep-red velvet, Cassius' mask was black embellished with rubies that gleamed in the torchlight. He wore black gloves and had a black pocket square folded immaculately in his chest pocket.

"Where are they?" Rooster asked quietly, allowing Cassius to step in front of him as they sidestepped a few servants walking down the hall with last-minute trays of food.

"Helai was to be in the main entryway. I'm not certain where Linda and Intoh are. Itale told me he would meet us at the ball," Cassius uttered under his breath. "Where's Rackjack?"

"Wanted to scout ahead as well," Rooster said. The dwarf had left the room just minutes before Rooster had, muttering about making sure the ball was safe before Rooster arrived. Rackjack had grown increasingly stressed and suspicious of the estate the longer they'd stayed here. It was almost a relief to finally be at the night of the ball, where they could get it over and done with and leave this place.

"Do we trust the jinn's powers?" Rooster met Cassius' confused expression. "The lamp. Do we trust it to do what is asked of it?" Rooster knew next to nothing about jinn but thought them to be nothing more than evil, trickster spirits bent on doing the ill will of their wielder.

Cassius shrugged. "Questions for Helai, I imagine. They belong to her culture."

They fell into silence after that. It left Rooster with his thoughts, a dangerous venture that was thankfully cut short once they reached the main entryway. The halls were fairly empty due to the ball, and Rooster had never been so glad to see another Misfit when they rounded the corner.

Helai stood near an ice sculpture of a dragon. It was massive, twisting around a central pillar with its mouth open as it roared towards the ceiling. Helai was dressed in a slim-fitting dark blue dress with small white teardrop diamonds embellishing the lining. It left her shoulders free, and her mask was nothing fancy–a simple black with dark-blue feathers at the eyes. He could tell by the frown that graced her features that she was not happy. Her hand wiped away invisible dirt at her hip, and she stood uncomfortably in heels.

"Ack," she said, muttering something in Shoman before switching back. "The quicker we get through the night, the better. I hate this dress."

"We just need to get this lamp of yours and the armor piece Cassius has come for and then we can leave," Rooster said, looking around. There was no sight of Intoh and Linda yet. "Tell me of this jinn of yours. I am not familiar with them."

Helai gave him a pointed look. "Much to the contrary belief, jinn are respected in my culture. A spirit of the elements, they exist alongside us as any spirit would. Where we excel in physical strength and the ability to outwit, they are stronger than us with magic as they *are* magic in its purest form. Those who figure out how to trap them in lamps are foolish, but the jinn can then barter for their freedom by granting a wish." Helai paused. "Even if we can't remove the brand with it, figuring out a way to release the jinn is the right thing to do."

"There are plenty of things we can wish upon, I'm sure," Cassius said.

Rooster was inclined to agree. A part of him longed to use the jinn for his own selfish desire to have his memories returned to him. He felt his memories dance just past reach, the edges of his mind's eye desperate to bring them into the clear picture. It was frustrating beyond belief.

Helai noticed his silence and pursed her lips. "We will find a way to return your memories one way or another."

Rooster shrugged, forcing a smile. "Of course. It's a relief, really. Now I can be whoever the hells I want." He attempted to keep the bitterness from his tone, but it slipped through regardless. 'Carter Wingman' was his name, but he didn't feel like it belonged to him. It was nothing more than a ghost of the man who refused to quit haunting him.

"Not sure about these. Too confining," Intoh complained, walking down the stairs. His tuxedo had tails that flapped behind him when he walked, and Linda followed behind in their human form, their tuxedo matching Rooster's in style. The only difference was the ice bear rug they'd had adjusted, now a cloak they wore over their shoulders.

"Gotta play the part, Intoh," Rooster said. "Where are your two shadows?"

Intoh gestured vaguely. "Somewhere. Told them to stay close but out of sight."

Rooster glanced about. Khal was excellent at camouflage and could easily be tucked away in plain sight, but Rooster didn't think Sode was the same. Still, the greka were constantly surprising them.

"Emir has door to cellar heavily guarded," Rackjack said, approaching. For the first time, his beard was tamed, pushed into place by various oils. The silver jewel hanging in it gleamed, and he tucked himself next to Rooster, staring at the group with glee. "Think they go there for shadow market auctions."

"That would be our next best chance at finding something to remove these brands if we aren't to use the lamp," Helai said, her eyes trailing over the arrival of guests. The main entrance hall had quickly filled with people, their identities hidden behind masks and fans. It made Rooster feel oddly at home—a man with no past among those with their identities safely hidden.

"We might as well make our way to the ballroom and do a bit of scouting ourselves," Rooster said, watching a woman trail a feather wand over the bare shoulders of another woman she was with. One laughed at something the other said, and Rooster quickly looked away when they both made eye contact with him.

"Indeed. I will not lie, this is going to be a pleasant night for me. Something about parties..." Cassius sighed happily, offering Helai his arm. "The last time I was at a party, I went home with a good share of men and women, and it was *divine*." He stilled as Helai took his arm, if not after a bit of hesitation. Her and Cassius' friendship had blossomed over their time forced together. She no longer looked at him with blind disgust.

"The Misfits have arrived." Their name rang through the ballroom as Rooster and the others stepped through, the butler's voice casting out across the room. String instruments resumed their soft melody in the corner, and on the opposite side was a table full of food nestled against the massive floor-to-ceiling windows. People danced at the center, a flurry of movement as men and women twirled around their partners. Everyone was masked, and while some of them were simple in design, like those of the Misfits, there were many who bore the likeness of a dragon. Horns swirled up past the sides of their heads, their entire faces covered behind what looked to be bone.

Rooster suppressed a shudder and locked eyes with Cassius, who gave him the briefest of nods. *We need to be careful.*

Rackjack went rigid beside Rooster and took off without explanation, pushing through the crowd towards Itale, who stood near the food with a plate full of pastries. Something in Rackjack's movement betrayed his distress, but Rooster couldn't begin to guess what had spooked the dwarf.

"Sense magic," Intoh said. "See leaders?"

"I do not," Cassius said. Rooster tore his eyes away from Rackjack and Itale to scour the room, but Emir and Alyse Welker were nowhere to be found.

Stopping one of the workers carrying a tray of drinks, Rooster smiled. "We mean to thank the lord and lady of the house for such a wondrous ball. Do you know where we might find them, Miss...?"

"Elyse." Elyse was middle-aged, her accent hinting towards Wolstadt-ian roots, and her eyes darted towards the door before flickering back to meet Rooster's. Unlike the guests, all of the servants were unmasked. "The mister and missus were trying to find the little lord, sire. They should be arriving at any moment."

"Cassius." Rooster turned as Itale approached the vampire, his fingers twisted in an anxious knot as he darted close. Dressed in all black, Itale's mask bore small pink flowers sewn into the fabric.

"I tried to tell Rackjack to stay, but he said he...he said he smelled something? He went to the kitchens to investigate. I haven't seen him since." Itale bowed his head and quivered, flinching when Cassius went to rest his hand on the boy's shoulder. Rooster didn't know what demons haunted Itale, but he felt a kinship with him, a darkness of abuse that was difficult to heal from.

"It's okay, Itale. You need not be afraid." Cassius' voice was soft, but despite the music that played, Rooster heard him perfectly clear. It wrapped around him like silk, and suddenly *he* wasn't afraid. Neither was Itale, who looked up at Cassius with bright eyes as he gestured to a door at the other end of the room.

"That's where Rackjack went."

"Hmm, can't trust him. New to us, don't know if he has good in-tentions. Should keep close eye," Intoh said, watching the spot where Rackjack had disappeared.

Despite Rackjack's obvious connection to Rooster's past, he couldn't blame Intoh for his suspicions. The dwarf was strange, and his sudden disappearance did make his gut twist in anxiety.

"Those of us remaining behind can keep an eye out for him. I'll ask what he's up to when he returns," Rooster promised.

"Speaking of, I do not know how much longer I can wait," Cassius muttered, glancing towards the door. "I can feel her urging me to the next piece of the Ebony Fang."

"We mustn't go yet," Helai uttered, her eyes trained on a masked woman who stared at her with a wolfish grin. "Else we might cause suspicion with so many eyes on us."

"Can go eat?" Linda wondered, staring eagerly at the tables of food. A soft breeze trailed through several open doors that led to balconies overlooking the gardens, and it brushed against Rooster's face. He nodded to Linda.

"Go with Intoh. See if you can hear anything of interest and don't go too far." He didn't like the idea of straying too far. He didn't even like the idea of most of them sneaking away to steal the artifacts they needed to steal. Something was off, like they stood on the edge of some great evil. His brand didn't burn, the absence of its pain odd now that he'd been living with it for months.

"I'll go with them too. If—if it's alright?" Itale asked, glancing nervously up at Cassius. "I think they're serving tea, my favorite, if I read correctly. Tea to calm the nerves sounds agreeable."

Cassius nodded, and Linda, Intoh, and Itale hurried away.

"Dance?" Helai inquired, glancing at Cassius. "I hear ClassyAss has quite the talent for it."

Cassius was stoic as ever, but there was a vague twitch of annoyance in his left eye at the nickname, but he nodded. "I'm quite certain all we can do is wait and speak with the Welkers when they arrive."

"I'll try to talk to some of the guests. Perhaps someone knows if there will be a shadow market auction tonight," Rooster said. With their agreement, he slipped away into the crowd.

Forty-Four

CASSIUS

It had been so long–too long–since he'd been to a party quite like this. The music was intoxicating, almost to the point where Cassius grew dizzy from the energy of it all. Bodies mingled closely on the dance floor, skirts pooling at his feet as people danced around him and Helai. It was strange. Halvdarc traded with drikoty and eldrasi frequently enough to warrant their appearance, but he didn't see either tonight. In fact, he did not hear anything other than that of humans, save for those in his company.

"Cassius?" Helai's voice shattered through the cascading symphony of heartbeats. Cassius looked down at her, his fingers curled against hers as they circled the dance floor. "Do you hear that?" The room was too full of people to hear anything other than the steady roar of hearts and the pleasantries of conversation, but he *felt* it–a low hum in the soles of his feet.

"Is that coming from below us?" he asked.

"If I may have this dance?" a voice cut in. When Cassius looked up, he met the eyes of Zamir glittering behind a white mask. He had shed his servant clothes and had somehow managed to find himself a tuxedo, and he blended in with the guests as he gestured to Helai.

"Oh, he is a good dancer too? We are lucky Massoud isn't here," Zamir said, his voice pleasant.

Helai snorted. "Cassius would not be able to handle Massoud," she said, her lip twitching in amusement.

"He is quite the handful," Zamir agreed, taking Helai's hand as Cassius stepped away. "I will only steal her for a moment." Watching Zamir whisk Helai away, Cassius made his way through the crowd. A bad feeling had settled at his back, raising the hair on the nape of his neck. He glanced over his shoulder and made eye contact with a woman in a dragon mask standing among the dancing guests. She stared, and even when Cassius caught her eye, she did not look away. His gaze shifted and fell upon another, standing and staring.

Fingers grazed his elbow, and he jumped, his fangs descending slightly as he lashed around to whoever had touched him. Ahma stood, her mask covering half of her face and depicting a white fox with red painted at the ears and along the mouth. Her eyes were glittering pools of amusement as she ran a red-painted nail along Cassius' arm. "For a knight, you are quite skittish. Like a little fawn," she purred, splaying her fingers across his bicep. "Dance with me, little fawn?"

His feet moved as if on their own accord, leading Ahma to the dance floor. She wore a sweeping black dress with long sleeves. A fox, deep red, decorated her dress, its tail wrapped around her waist as its head came to rest at her bosom. Flashing her fangs, she grinned as she tucked herself securely against Cassius, and they began to dance.

"You have been in Halvdarc for quite some time and have not yet come to possess the cuirass. I thought you would have learned your lesson in Volendam," she said, her voice subtle and seductive as she glanced up at him from under her eyelashes.

"The Aikawa family, they are vampires, no? Why ask a vampire of the west for aid?" Cassius pressed his fingers to the small of her back, drawing her closer so he could lower his voice. He'd meant to sneak away soon, to go after the cuirass under the cover of the ball, but with Ahma here, he was desperate for answers.

Ahma hummed, reaching up to brush Cassius' cheek with the back of her hand. "If I am honest with you, will you stop denying your destiny?"

He searched her expression for malice, not knowing whether or not agreeing to her terms would prove wise. It seemed as if the ball had come to a standstill. They danced but everyone around them danced in slowed movements, as if time was stopping.

Finally, he nodded, and Ahma flashed him a toothy grin.

"The Aikawa family has long been blessed by the fox spirit Kísae. Our gift of eternal life comes from that blessing, not vampirism."

Her words sent a wave of shock through Cassius. "How?" Kísae was a many-tailed fox god, a god of trickery and illusion.

Her head lolled to the side, her face thoughtful. "You needn't know all of the fine details, only that our family was wrongfully cursed, and I lost my beloved because of it. His return could aid in the coming storm."

Cassius' eyes darkened in understanding. "You are Khoros Drakos' lover? You are spoken of in legends, but no one was ever able to figure out who you truly were."

Ahma nodded, her gaze consumed by grief. "It is why I ask you to help me bring him back. Doing so will secure our aid in the east. Cassius—" She pulled her mask free, allowing it to slip from her fingers and hit the floor, and yet...it made no sound. Her breath tickled his lips as her gaze darted from his mouth up to his eyes.

"What will be required of me?" Cassius asked, his tone hardening. Something didn't add up. If she meant to bring back her lover, why was she looking at him as if she wanted to tear his clothes off? "If I find these pieces for you, will that be the end of my obligation?"

A flash of darkness soured her expression. "Evil has made a home here. If we do not cut it out at the root and quickly, it will be too late." Instead of answering his questions, her lips pressed gently against his. A quiet noise cradled the back of his throat as he drew her in, drunk on the power that radiated from her body. Pain bled from her kiss, and when Cassius pulled away, his heart thundered in his ears, his chest, and his groin. Her power made him sick with want and repulsion, and he shook his head, his mind dizzy with conflicting thoughts.

"No. I was a pawn to my father when I was just a boy. I was a pawn to the Sanguine Order too. And now? Now you want me to be a pawn in whatever scheme or plan for vengeance you may have. If you seek to restore whatever beloved you lost, seek it on your own terms. I will have no part in it." His lips pulled back over his fangs as he growled, his eyes darkening as he wrapped his fingers around her neck. "You had no right to put that gun in my arm, no right to free me from my tomb. I do not trouble myself with deceit. I will no longer play your wicked games."

Rage filled her expression. "Then you will suffer me," she hissed. He blinked, and she was gone, the world righted once more. Guests danced around him as if they'd never slowed at all, and Cassius pressed a hand to his head as a dizzy spell overcame him.

A simmer of anger flourished through him. *Drain them all dry*, it whispered. *Kill them. Drink them. Monster. Monster. MONSTER.* Another growl passed his lips as he abandoned the dance floor, ignoring the protests of guests around him as he hit their shoulders or stepped on their skirts. Fleeing the room, he tucked himself away in a hallway, leaning against the wall and shoving his face in his hands. A quiet buzz roared in his ears, and despite his hunger, his heart beat heavily in his chest.

"Sire, are you alright?" A gentle voice called out in the darkness, but Cassius was already lost. The monster had taken hold and wrangled him, and he reached out quickly. The person did not even have the time to scream before Cassius shoved him against the wall so roughly, his shoulders slumped. The music from the ball was just loud enough to mask the deed as Cassius sank his fangs into the man's neck. The relief of the blood hitting his tongue softened his distress, and slowly his mind quieted, tucked safely behind the high of life humanity gave him. He drank until the blood would not come, and he pulled away, blood dripping from his chin and hitting the floor. He sucked in a breath before the world crashed down upon him, and the weight of his despair pressed in on him from all sides.

He was doomed to be a puppet, his puppeteer constantly changing faces. His struggle against the strings that tied him to their hands only forged stronger bonds, and he wept, sliding down the wall next to the corpse of the man he'd just killed. He feared it was Itale at first. The frame and hair were the same, but as he ripped the man's mask away, it was no one he recognized. His shoulders shook, and he cried for the lost boy who'd only ever wanted to be loved.

Forty-Five

CASSIUS

No one else approached Cassius, and he was grateful for it. The corpse of the young boy was not easy to dispose of when there was an estate brimming with guests, but he managed, slipping it into an empty room where it would not be discovered until Cassius was long gone. It was foolish; *he* was foolish. The consequences of his carelessness would one day catch up with him. He knew it to be true. How he'd managed to avoid the ever-watchful eye of the Inquisition, of Blodrägr, those who hunted vampires, was lost to him. Still, it never stopped him from continuing down this path. The door clicked shut as he retreated from where he stuffed the body.

A whisper etched its way down the hall, beckoning him. He thought it was Ahma at first, manifesting once more to torture him, but no. Someone stood in the door frame of the room down the hall, shrouded in shadow. Danger soaked the air, and Cassius inhaled sharply, his brow furrowed in ire. Whoever stood at the end of the hall wore nothing but a cloak, their mask half obscured by the door frame. What half showed was beautiful and ornate, a deer skull with a three point antler.

"Do you require something?" Cassius asked, his voice too loud as it echoed down the hall. Something was wrong. The longer he looked, the longer the hallway grew, stretching endlessly as the masked stranger stood and stared, ever silent.

Cassius swallowed thickly. He didn't often get frightened, not anymore, not after all he'd seen, but the magic that drenched the place was *wrong*, a heaviness that pressed against his shoulders. It was almost invasive, the way it picked and pried at his skin as a lover might, and Cassius shied away from the sensation.

Turning, he was eager to return to the ball and relieve himself of the strangeness, but he did not like having his back to the masked stranger, so he found himself glancing over his shoulder.

The stranger was closer and stood in the middle of the hallway, still as a statue. The moment Cassius looked upon him, the mask cocked to the side as the stranger strode forward, flinging something so hard against the wall, it shattered, fragmented pieces flying everywhere.

It only took Cassius a moment to realize what it was as the stranger flung another, the noise of it breaking crashing down the hall.

They were skulls, and they were too small to be adult humans.

They were the skulls of children.

Cassius reached for his sword, only to remember it was up in the room and that he wasn't in his armor either. He cursed, stumbling backwards as the cultist moved faster, approaching far too quickly.

"Your fear delights me, Chosen. How quaint for the hunter to be hunted?" The cultist's voice rasped, just feet from Cassius now.

Rage festered inside Cassius at being trapped. It coiled in his belly, a serpent eager to strike, and Cassius let his illusion drop as his vampirism came forth at full force. He hissed, lips slipping back from teeth as fangs descended, and the stranger laughed, a hollow noise that grated over Cassius' ears. The sound only fueled the forest fire of anger inside Cassius.

"Her resurrection is an inevitability. You feed her with your rage. Run, little knight. You always run, do you not?" The cultist moved forward at a speed too quickly for even Cassius to follow and then he was being shoved back against the door that led into the ballroom.

The stranger's laughter followed as he landed on his back, his illusion tucked neatly back into place against his will. He exhaled sharply as he hit the floor, and then groaned, curling on his side. The ball went on, as if no strangeness had occurred, and Cassius forced himself to his feet, ignoring the curious or concerned eyes of those around him.

He wondered, not for the first time, what was happening. No one else acted strangely, and conversation went on as normal around him. He wanted to scream, to shake the woman nearest to him as she laughed behind fingers pressed to her mouth. It lodged in his throat, an endless wail that settled just out of reach. Emir and Alyse were still nowhere to be seen, and Cassius hadn't yet seen Rembrandt since the day they'd arrived. A horrible thought shuddered through him of the child skulls that cultist had shattered against the wall.

No.

He felt it in his bones though. A sense of wrongness so fierce, so perverse, that he felt lost against its persistence.

"Sire? Dance with me?" It was a lovely woman who spoke, her dark curls pinned up in glittering sapphires. Her eyes matched, hidden behind a black lace mask, and Cassius took a moment to drink her features in before he shook his head and waved her away. The panic had settled, the ball falling upon his ears in a sense of normalcy, but he needed to find the others. His eyes sought them out, but he saw only an endless sea of guests.

"I cannot. You're lovely. I am certain you will not find a lack of potential dance partners," he said, desperate for the curl of Itale's hair or the blue of Helai's dress or even the bulk of Linda.

"Please," the woman purred. "I insist." She lowered herself into a curtsy, and Cassius' mouth dried as her blood called out to him. An old ache in his groin twinged as well, and Cassius sighed, scanning the room once more for the other Misfits. His desires won as he spotted none of them, and he took the woman's outstretched hand with a smile.

"You won me over."

"What can I say?" the woman said, smiling brightly. A dimple cratered one of her cheeks, and Cassius' heart fluttered, a memory of a girl from his childhood tugging at the back of his head. This woman reminded him of a girl he'd chased when he'd been sixteen winters, when the thrill of the company of boys hadn't sang poems in his chest quite yet. He'd never forgotten her, even when his father had sent him away not long after. The dimple in her cheek, that's what it was. Hers was in the same cheek as this woman's had been, and his head swam with vertigo as he led her onto the dance floor, his hand coming to rest on her hip.

"I'm told I can be quite convincing," she continued, falling into place as the music began anew. He twirled her around the dance floor, his movements graceful and fluid, like a soldier on a battlefield. He loved dancing; it was its own battle, in a way, and his partner was exceptional at it, her eyes trained lazily on his behind her mask. Something about her eyes chased the anxieties away. He no longer thought of the stranger in the hallway nor of Ahma and what consequence might come from refusing her. Wait...he needed to find the Misfits...

"Do I have the pleasure of knowing your name?" he asked.

The woman's smile curled deviously, and for a moment she hid her face against the curve of his shoulder. "It would take away the mystery if I told you. Perhaps you must earn it."

Cassius' grin turned wolfish as the girl pulled away. This felt like it had before, when he'd been a young man who'd just gone to live with his uncle. His uncle had harbored a great dislike towards Cassius' father, one he'd extended to Cassius himself, but it hadn't stopped him from taking Cassius to parties the lords and ladies had frequently held. It had been Cassius' only reprieve from knightly training. Everything had changed the night he'd been turned, though the parties had always remained the same. The only difference had been the company changed, and Cassius had become privy to the amount of vampires that lived in secret among humanity.

"Cassius?"

The woman drew him from his past, like plucking a ghost from haunting its halls, and he slowed, dancing in a small circle versus the large loop they'd been making just before. "My apologies. I–" But the words died in his throat. "Wait – I didn't tell you my name."

As soon as he realized, the cellist's bow slipped, sending an unpleasant note throughout the room and then the atmosphere shifted. The room darkened as the music warped, a dark melody that sounded almost as if it were being played through water. Cassius attempted to pull away from the woman, but her grip was like iron, and her smile curled unnaturally high as she tilted her head.

"Are you afraid to die, Cassius?" The other guests pressed around him on all sides, and he was lost to the panic, his heart thunderous in his throat. He stuttered back and forth from the memories of battle, of being overwhelmed by bodies, of nearly suffocating beneath the weight of his dead comrades to the present, to the weight of guests pushing against him, their laughter trickling in his ears.

"Get away," he snarled, tugging with all of his might. It was no use. He was doomed to suffocate beneath them, the dark music melodic as the woman's eyes locked him in place. Surely he would drown in them.

Darkness overwhelmed him as he was shoved to the floor. Darkness, laughter, and nothing more.

Forty-Six

LINDA

Linda had never been to something quite so fancy, had never heard of a ball before. It was exhilarating, the sway of bodies and the soft music coming from objects people held in the corner. It reminded them of the Silver Moon Club in Volendam.

Their desire to dance was smothered by the desire for ale. A woman approached, carrying a tray of glasses, and she offered one to Linda. "Drink?" she asked behind an easy smile.

Linda took one gingerly, raising the glass to their lips and drinking. Their tongue was shocked with a prickling sensation, and Linda growled, dropping the glass and backing away in disgust. "Do not like."

"It's bubbling wine, Linda! It comes from Nantielle. It's quite good," Itale protested as several nearby guests scooted out of the way of the shattered glass and whispered behind shocked fingers. The woman that had offered Linda the drink murmured quietly as her fingers curled towards the ground, and the shattered glass disappeared in a swirl of magic.

"My apologies. If it is simple wine you prefer, I can go and grab you a glass?"

Linda shook their head and turned away, Intoh and Itale at their heels.

"Where do you think Sir Cassius has gone?" Itale asked. "I think I sense strange magic here, but I cannot pinpoint where it is coming from."

Linda wasn't very good at sensing magic, having no magical bone in their body. They could not sense the magic Itale spoke of, but it did feel like something was wrong. Linda's innate sense to danger was screaming, begging them to fight whatever threat presented itself. The problem was: Linda did not see any threats.

A door opened off to Linda's right, and Cassius stumbled through and fell, landing on his back. It took a moment for him to regain his composure as he rose and straightened his jacket. He appeared shaken, but Linda was unable to grab his attention as he disappeared into the crowd of people dancing.

"Went that way," Linda told Itale, pointing to where Cassius had disappeared. "Acting strange."

"Excuse me, sire–" A young masked man approached, his light curls slicked back. "Care to dance? My dancing partner ditched me, and I'm afraid my friends are being quite judgmental," His eyes, dark underneath his mask, batted at Itale, who coughed as his cheeks heated in embarrassment.

"I don't– I'm afraid–" He cursed under his breath. "I apologize. Can we start over?" Itale giggled nervously, flashing Linda his 'help me' eyes. Linda had seen Intoh give those eyes to them many times.

Linda snickered softly and shook their head, walking away as the young man took Itale's hand and swept him into the crowd. They danced around Rooster and a red-headed woman, who was laughing at something Rooster said. Linda watched them for a moment before Intoh tugged on Linda's arm.

"See Helai, going to her. Stay out of trouble." He was gone before Linda could say anything on the matter. The aroma of food drew them away from the dancing couples, and Linda looked at the man behind the table.

"Any raw fish?" Linda asked.

"Raw...fish you said?" the servant asked, eyeing Linda nervously. "No sire, I'm afraid not." He gestured to a plate of something soaked in butter and some sort of green herb. "Might I recommend some Snaeot?" The sight of it made Linda's stomach turn.

Disappointed, Linda shook their head and backed up right into a group of people, all with drinks in their hands. Several stumbled, spilling their drinks on the people beside them, and their angry exclamations caused Linda to flee even though their instincts to fight burned in their belly.

Fresh air. They needed fresh air. It wafted through the room from the open doors that led to the balconies overlooking the gardens, and Linda shuffled out, ignoring the quiet conversations of couples surrounding them. The breeze felt nice against their skin, and it was the first time since Intoh had plucked them out of their ruined city that Linda was truly alone.

The full moon bathed the balcony in a soft glow, and Linda sat down on a stone bench, allowing one ankle to tuck behind the other. It was nice to just simply sit for a change. It gave them a taste of home, when life was little more than sitting, building, floating, and fighting. As they were tempted to fall away into a daydream, a low hum echoed in Linda's throat. They settled, their fingers clasping together over their belly.

"You are one of the six, yes?"

A voice forced Linda's eyes to open. Their irritation at being interrupted caused them to scowl. "No," they said. "Go away."

The man that stood to the left of the open door was sheathed in shadow, his mask of a deer skull. Its antlers stopped in several points, and his smile was wicked, the only thing drenched in the moon's light. "Phoenix Mother beckons you home, Lindrz'kt."

He raised the hilt of a dagger, aiming for Linda's temple. Linda reached up and caught the man's wrist before it could make contact. They roared, startling the other guests on the balcony, who hurried inside as Linda twisted the man's arm, a resounding pop shattering the peaceful quiet as they dislocated the man's shoulder.

The man did not cry out in pain. His silence was jarring, and Linda did not see his other hand move until a dark dust-like substance was thrown into their face. Linda coughed, lifting the man up off the ground in their rage as their sight flickered in and out of focus. They threw him over the edge of the balcony and did not react to the sound of him hitting the ground below nor the screams of those walking in the gardens who'd witnessed it.

Have to find others, Linda thought, stumbling back towards the door. Two more masked strangers met them there, and Linda lashed out. They evaded Linda's every attempt to attack, so Linda barreled through them.

"Rooster," they shouted, spotting him through the crowd. "Rooster." They pushed through people to get to him, and the redhead he danced with protested angrily as Linda grabbed Rooster's shoulder and pulled him away. Everything inside Linda screamed of danger, and after facing those masked strangers on the balcony, everyone appeared as a threat to them.

"What's going on?" All irritation melted off Rooster's face when he caught onto Linda's distress, and his own eyes flickered around the room, trying to seek out whatever had caused Linda's fear. It festered in their belly and preyed on their rationalization, and Linda pointed to the balconies.

"Bad men there. We must leave." People continued to dance and twirl around Linda, and each of them looked like an enemy beckoning combat, their intentions tucked away behind their masks. "Find the others."

"Yes, alright. Sorry, love," Rooster said, glancing at the redhead. "Dancing with you was quite lovely, but alas! I must go and find my companions." Linda was far too impatient to await the redhead's response, dragging Rooster through the crowd until they stood on the edge of the dance floor. The music had changed, grating on Linda as they struggled to remain calm. Their instincts begged for them to flee.

Flee.

Run.

Go, go, GO, LINDA.

A small growl passed their lips. "Do not see."

The sounds of the ball pressed in around them, and Linda's anger grew as it became overwhelming. It was as if they were back in the midst of their homeland, the forest on fire around them, only this time their enemies were hidden, cloaked behind the masks of their allies. A compulsion washed over Linda, a desire to rip through the guests of the ball until no one stood but them, bathed in their blood. It filled Linda suddenly and without mercy, and only when Rooster pressed a gentle hand to their shoulder were they liberated from the darkness of rage.

"I just saw Cassius disappear down the hallway. Just there I think," Rooster said, gesturing to a door that led out towards the kitchen. "It wasn't too long ago. Perhaps we should start there?"

"But saw here," Linda said, gesturing to the crowd of dancers. Something strange was happening as Rooster's brow threaded in confusion.

"I just saw him. Perhaps he aims to sneak away? He's after that piece of the armory." Rooster laid a hand on Linda's arm. "We should go look. If there are cultists here, we should find a way to warn the others."

Linda nodded, still disoriented by the strength of emotion that had just passed through them. It came and went suddenly as of late, a constant occurrence since being branded. Linda had always wielded their anger like a tool, a weapon in the heart of battle, but it felt like the roles had been switched, and they were the ones being used.

They attempted to will it away as they followed Rooster to the other side of the room, ignoring the quiet protests as they pushed through guests to get there. The door swung shut behind them as they entered the hall, and Rooster pointed to the other end, where someone stood with their back facing them.

"That look like Cassius to you?" Rooster asked, his voice hushed with uncertainty.

Linda studied the form for a moment, then nodded. "Has red ribbon," they said, pointing to the ribbon that tied the person's hair back. Cassius didn't go anywhere without it. The form was broad enough to be Cassius, his height right, and Linda was convinced if it wasn't him, then someone had made themself look like him.

"Cassius," Rooster called out, louder than before. "Have you seen the others?"

Cassius did not turn, his face hidden from view. An unbidden chill rolled down Linda's spine; something didn't feel right. The longer Linda stared down the hall at Cassius, the more convinced Linda was that it wasn't him after all.

"Wait," Linda told Rooster, pressing a hand to his shoulder. "I don't think–"

Linda's words were lost as pain blossomed over the back of their head, knocking them into the wall. A dark form shoved a bag over Rooster's face, and they attempted to reorient themself as another drew close, shoving a bag over Linda's head as well. They fought valiantly against their kidnapper, but it was of moot point; whoever had hold of them was stronger.

Forty-Seven

INTOH

The sounds from the ball faded behind Intoh as he followed Helai and Zamir towards the library. What people walked the halls did not pay them any mind, and none of them looked on in suspicion, but Intoh's heart pounded regardless. He had demanded Khal and Sode remain at the ball and keep an eye on the other Misfits. Five in the library would be too many, and he'd kept himself safe from harm for this long.

"Don't go near when we go inside," Intoh said as they made their way up to the library. "Very strong, very bad magic."

Helai and Zamir made eye contact and they both nodded.

Pushing open the door, they entered. The library was sheathed in darkness, save for the full moon's light, but the moment Intoh shuffled in, fire lit up in the sconces on the walls. The library was eerie, more so than the last time Intoh had been here, and he threw a glance over his shoulder as he dodged around the tables and settled before the lamp.

"It *is* the same one," Helai said from Intoh's right.

"How you managed to get your hands on a lamp at all surprises me, Helai," Zamir whispered. "Many don't travel with them unless they're confident they cannot be stolen."

"Steal it for yourself," Ekalas whispered in Intoh's ear. *"Rub it before they can take it from you. Wish for forever."*

Forever isn't the same without you, Intoh thought miserably, but the thought grew in the back of his head all the same. He found himself wondering if the jinn could bring back those long since dead. "Why do you not wish for your own resurrection, *inka*?" he muttered quietly.

"What did you say?" Helai asked in a hushed tone. Her fingers curled over the back of a chair, and she glanced down the long halls between bookshelves with a concerned expression.

"Nothing, nothing," Intoh said, waving away her question. "Must give me time. Do you know how to read? Go, go. Need silence."

Helai's expression turned to shock as he glanced up at her. "Of course I know how to read."

Zamir shrugged with a shake of laughter. "Are you sure, dear Helai? Massoud wasn't the best of teachers."

As they hurried off, Intoh heard Helai utter, "You've read my letters. I wouldn't be able to write them if I couldn't read."

Intoh shook his hands, ignoring the phantom ache from the last time he'd tried to touch the lamp. That reminder was enough for him to take greater care, and he stood several feet away as he reached out with his magic, prodding the darkness that surrounded the lamp. It immediately lashed out, coiled like a snake. Intoh's will was strong, and he fought against its attacks with an iron grip. It did not catch him by surprise this time, and his magic danced around it as it searched for a weak point where he could shatter it.

Intoh... A voice called out to him in the darkness, tempting his will away. It caressed against him like a trail of wind through subtle air, beckoning him to relax. He fought against it until a headache formed in his temple, his gaze unblinking as he saw nothing but the lamp in front of him.

A loose scale in the dark magic presented itself to him, and Intoh did not hesitate, lashing out against the soft flesh of the beast with his magic.

Something crashed where Helai and Zamir had disappeared, the sound of a flurry of books thrown to the floor followed by the quiet grunt of pain. It was enough to cause Intoh's concentration to waver, but lucky for him, he'd already sent a current of magic through the trap. It fizzled and died as the door to the box holding the lamp snapped open. He bound forward and grabbed the lamp, only to cower when Zamir shot out from between bookshelves, his eyes wild with fear.

"Go, we must hide."

"Where is Helai?" Intoh asked, gripping the lamp delicately. He took great care in making sure he didn't rub its sides as he followed Zamir through the shelves on the other side of the library.

Zamir did not turn. "Something took her. The *darkness* took her."

Darkness clung to all sides, and Intoh's fear raced through his mind as they both clung to the end of a bookshelf, tucked out of sight from anyone that might be in the middle of the library. A faint screeching pressed against him, so high in pitch it was nearly lost, and Intoh trembled as he heard dark laughter from the middle of the room.

"Come on out. If you think you can hide, you are mistaken."

Intoh locked eyes with Zamir as footsteps echoed through the library, edging ever closer. "Take lamp," he whispered, tossing it to Zamir. "Get out. Will distract, can go invisible."

Zamir caught the lamp and instantly disappeared into a trail of shadows leading out of the room. Intoh went invisible as he scurried away from the approaching figure and rounded a bookshelf. He wished for

Linda and their protection, cursing himself for having told Sode and Khal to remain behind. He flinched away as a hand shot through one of the bookshelves, reaching for him. They missed, and he tumbled, pain smarting up his arms as his elbows slammed against the floor. Lightning shot from his fingers, sending several books flying off the shelves, and Emir came around the corner, unmasked and his face lit up in concern.

"Is there someone there?" he asked, his tone hushed. "Please, I think there's something in here with me."

Intoh hesitated. His gut screamed at him to remain hidden; the other Misfits had voiced their concerns over the lord of the house, but Emir had been gracious enough to open up his home and library to him. If there was something dark and evil laying in wait in the darkness, two people fighting against it was better than one. If it came down to it, Intoh could always throw Emir to the darkness to get away.

"Here," he whispered, willing away his invisibility. It washed from his skin, and he shivered, suddenly bare to whatever it was that was hunting him. "Do not know what is happening. Fear there is darkness laying in wait."

Emir drew forward. "I think the ball brought some unsavory people to it. Come. I know of a secret way out. If we're being followed, they will not be able to find us." He gestured to a suit of armor tucked between two bookshelves against the wall. Emir ran his fingers alongside it, muttering quietly in Shoman. Intoh watched on nervously, ignoring his instincts as they screamed at him to flee, to fight, to do *something* other than stand here as the darkness encroached and closed in on him from all sides.

Soft footsteps drew near, inching along the other side of the bookshelf, and Intoh peeked through the books.

A masked figure knelt to meet his gaze.

He flung himself back in terror, but the world went dark as a bag was shoved over his head.

Forty-Eight

HELAI

W hen the darkness took her, it was like when Massoud took her with him when he shade stepped. Zamir had never been any good at bringing anyone along with him, so she'd only ever gone with Massoud, but she'd always hated it.

The void pulled at her skin and whispered against her arms and then she found herself sitting in a small dirt room filled with nothing but wine barrels and the other Misfits. Her wrists and ankles were bound by rope, and she sat pressed up against the wall, her head pounding angrily inside her skull.

She groaned, whimpering softly as she blinked away the stars in her eyes. Her headache was merciless, and coupled with the burning of her brand, it almost made her lose consciousness. She fought against it as

Rooster rustled and attempted to push himself up in a standing position, using the wall for leverage.

"Are we all here?" Helai asked, looking about the room. Everyone except Intoh was present. Rackjack, Zamir, Itale, and the other greka were also absent, and Linda was back in their krok'ida form, their tail slapping angrily against the floor as they struggled against their bindings.

"This rope must be magical in nature. I cannot break it," Cassius said, seated against two barrels. He was looking particularly gaunt, his eyes red with anger.

"Where are we?" Helai's voice sounded slightly muffled, like she spoke through glass, and her right ear rang sharply, forcing her to suck in a painful breath. Whatever had attacked her in the library had not been gentle and had caught her by surprise. She would not be so careless next time.

"The air is stale. I believe we are in the cellar or underground some-where," Rooster muttered, his muscles flexing as he fought against his rope. After a moment, he relaxed, sighing in frustration. "Linda and I were in the hall when we were attacked. I'd say it was a masked stranger, but that doesn't narrow it down at all."

"I was in the ballroom," Cassius muttered, glaring up at the ceiling.

Helai wiggled her wrists behind her back. She cursed the dress she was in, wishing for her armor and blades, and took a moment to steady her breathing as she studied the room. A wine cellar, perhaps. Rows of barrels lined half of the room, and a foul stench permeated the air. It was so faint, it was almost lost to her, but occasionally, she'd get a whiff of it, and her nose would wrinkle in disgust.

A swirl of darkness collected in the corner, so quickly that Helai blinked, and it was gone. Intoh sat in its place, his face pressed to the floor as he lay on his side with his wrists and ankles also bound. He came to, wiggling and cursing in Drikotyian, his brow furrowed. He stilled when he noticed them, his expression panicked. Unlike Linda, he remained in his human form, his hair damp with sweat as it laid plastered against his face.

"Emir not good. Emir betrayed–" Intoh heaved, his words falling into a blur of his native tongue as he rolled on the ground. His words were clear enough to send a shiver of horror rolling through Helai; they'd been right all along. Their hosts were not as they seemed.

"Misfits." A door on the other side of the room opened and closed, and Rackjack peeked his head around the side of a wine barrel, his beard vibrant against the dim lighting. All suspicions of Rackjack washed away to relief as he hurried over, stopping at Rooster first.

"Think you can get them undone?" Rooster asked, turning to give Rackjack a better look. The dwarf's fingers moved deftly along the rope and then he tugged it into his mouth, gnawing on it with his teeth. The sight of it would have been comical had they not been in the situation they were in, and Rackjack muttered under his breath in frustration as he attempted to find a weaker spot in the rope.

"Okay, I cannot be the only one who's finding that a little...weird," Cassius said, nodding his head to Rackjack. "There is more to you than meets the eye, is there not? Like why your heart beats very quickly for a dwarf. I demand you explain yourself."

Rackjack hissed, flinching behind Rooster as he shook his head. "No-no. Cannot. Will not. Not safe. Will not like it."

"Cassius is right, Rackjack. If you mean to have us trust you, then trust us with whatever you hide," Rooster said, stepping away. "If I am truly your captain, I demand you tell us."

Rackjack trembled, his eyes darting over to each of them as he plucked at his beard. After a moment, he conceded. "Fine. Fine–fine. Will show. Promise not to scream?" Reaching up, he pulled the small silver bead out of the braid in his beard, and the shift was immediate. Just as Intoh and Linda shifted between human and drikoty, Rackjack's features shifted as well.

Helai's mouth dried as a brass-colored rakken appeared before them. He wasn't tall like some of the ones they'd fought in the dwarf tunnels or in Volendam, but he was still taller than he'd been in his dwarf form, and his paws and fur were littered with scars. Some were still fresh and weeping, and his eyes were red and beady. He stood on two feet, his back hunched as he breathed quickly, the unsteady rise and fall of his chest present as he looked between them. His paw went to tug at his whiskers, and he eyed them all nervously, his mouth parted in bated breath.

Everyone flinched away, unable to defend themselves as they were still trapped within their bindings. Helai's heart beat mercilessly against her chest, but she refused to move too much, fearing she'd accidentally roll over and bare her back to him. Seeing him filled her head with horrible, accusatory thoughts as she turned to Rooster, her brow furrowed in rage. Rage was better than fear, which was all she'd felt in the last few minutes.

"You knew, didn't you?"

Rooster flinched as if she'd struck him. "Of course not."

"Will not harm-hurt," Rackjack said, gnawing on the fur at his paw anxiously. "Had to come find Carter-filth and bring him back-back to Igraine-filth. She will speak of my honor-innocence." Now that he was bare to them, his dialect sounded similar to the rakken that had spoken in the Spine Mountain. How he'd managed to hide it all this time would have been impressive had Helai not been so frightened of him in this moment.

"I will not go anywhere with him," Helai said through gritted teeth, her anger white-hot and all consuming. She was back in those caverns, watching the rakken rip apart the other slaves. In her mind's eye, she saw Ayla's corpse and how the rakken had chewed through her lower half. She recalled the fear and disgust as the rakken had crawled out of the tunnels, pouring over each other until they'd been nothing more than a wiggling mess of bodies. She shuddered at the memory of it.

"Rakken," Cassius said, his brow furrowed. He didn't look disgusted, as Helai did, but he did eye Rackjack with a sense of hesitation. "Can you remove these ropes or not?" Helai glared at Cassius as Rackjack nodded quickly, looking up at Rooster.

"Must free Carter-filth first."

After a moment, Rooster nodded, and with his permission, Rackjack scampered over to him, grabbing the rope that bound his arms, and biting into them with his teeth. Now that he was rakken, they cut like butter, freeing Rooster's hands from behind his back. Rackjack did the same to Rooster's ankles, and soon enough, he was free, his hands rubbing his wrists.

"Can get your weapons, yes-yes. Will prove my honor-innocence. Saw them take small human through tunnel-path," Rackjack said, gesturing to a tunnel that led further underground. The darkness seemed almost unnatural, its inky blackness so black that no matter how hard Helai strained, she could not pierce it.

"You mean Rembrandt?" Cassius asked suddenly, his voice thick with alarm.

Rackjack nodded again. "Yes-yes. He was sleeping. Will go-go." He hissed, dissipating in a burst of purple shadows shaped in the form of rats crawling all over one another. His absence did not ease the tension in the air, and Rooster pulled out a hidden dagger from inside his boot and knelt next to Linda.

"No one is to harm him," Rooster said, sawing at Linda's bindings with his blade. "Not until we know more."

"Don't be ridiculous," Helai protested, her anger formulating as nausea in her belly. "Since when do we spare the lives of those...*things*?" She spat the last word as if it were poison. Vampires and drikoty were one thing, but rakken? She could not begin to imagine a scenario where she could trust Rackjack.

"Think about it, Helai." Rooster turned to her as he freed Linda, who rolled their shoulders as soon as the rope fell away. "How long has he traveled with us? How many opportunities did he have to murder us in our sleep? He was with us at that winery and could have left us for dead several times. He did none of those things. Yes, he's rakken." Rooster shuddered in disgust. "But things are never that simple. You would have said the same thing about Cassius once upon a time, hm?" He pointed his dagger at her as she opened her mouth to retort. "I won't argue. He's the only connection I have to my past that can grant me answers. He's under my protection. I will not hesitate to protect him." His warning ran loud and clear, and Helai's anger boiled inside her. She couldn't believe this was happening.

"Do not trust him," Intoh said, rolling onto his back. "Do not–"

Rackjack reappeared, still in his rakken form as he held a pile of weapons in his hand. "Your war hammer very heavy," he said to Linda, struggling to hold all of their things.

"Kill many," Linda said. "Keep it strong."

Rackjack dropped the hammer and other weapons at his feet, twitching as he rubbed his paws over his face, his whiskers bobbing nervously. He would not look Helai in the eye.

Good, she thought. *I can't believe we're just going to ignore our time with the dwarves or the horror that was brought down upon us in Volendam.*

Cassius stood as Rooster freed him, eyeing the room wearily as he rubbed his wrists. "I do not know why, I only just fed, but already I feel the pangs of hunger. We should get out of here."

"Really rakken?" Linda asked Rackjack, eyeing him curiously. "Killed many rats. Better stay away."

A foul smell filled the room, originating from Rackjack as he shook his head. Rooster stepped up next to him, looking around at the other Misfits as Cassius knelt to help Helai and Intoh out of their bindings. "No one is to harm him. Understand?"

"We heard you the first time," Helai said, watching Rackjack darkly. The only reason she did not defy Rooster's request was because he was right; Rackjack had been traveling with them for weeks. If he meant any of them harm, surely he would have done it already.

A collective hiss of pain coursed through them as their brands burned, more painful than it had ever been. It almost felt like when the brand had originally been carved into her flesh—the branding iron pressed against her skin. She cried out as the pain blinded her and then it stopped suddenly, followed by laughter to her right.

"It should not surprise me that you found a way to free yourselves. Though a rakken? The most surprising part, I will admit." Emir tsked, his tongue clicking against the roof of his mouth as he pulled himself out of the shadows. "Too bad it will not matter. Once we sacrifice the child, Vilanthris will only know fire." A round black mask with three white lines running diagonally across it covered his face, but his voice was unmistakable.

Helai's rage was sickening as she bent low to the ground and grabbed one of her daggers where Rackjack had dropped it. She was quick as she sprinted towards Emir, but he was quicker, reaching out to grab her wrist before she could shove her dagger into his chest. His grip was like steel, and Helai didn't see his knee draw up until she was bent over, gasping for air.

Emir slipped through the tunnel before anyone could attack him. Intoh's lightning hit the wall beside the tunnel he'd disappeared into, and the others scrambled to grab their weapons, the tension from Rackjack's reveal mostly forgotten.

"Wait, wait, wait," Cassius said, blocking the entrance to the tunnel. "We need to figure out what we're going into. It is obvious he is leading us to a trap, and we are not exactly dressed for the occasion."

"This door is locked," Intoh said, rattling the door at the other end of the room.

"Let us be weary and on guard moving forward," Rooster said, glancing at each of them. "We have no idea what we're up against."

"You are starting to sound like me; where is the one with sarcastic retorts when I point out the obvious?" Cassius asked grimly.

Rooster was right though, and Helai straightened, ignoring the pain in her stomach from where Emir had retaliated against her. The fear in the air was tangible, a heavy weight that blanketed the Misfits as Cassius stood before them, his sword and shield raised in defense. Rooster stood behind him, his own sword raised, and Intoh took up the space beside Helai with Rackjack and Linda at the rear. Linda growled as Rackjack moved too close, and Helai turned, shaking her head.

"I will follow behind. Go on." She stepped out of the way as Rackjack muttered something in a quick harsh language and took his place next to Intoh, who spared the rakken only a quick side-glance.

"Ready?" Cassius asked.

After a murmur of agreement, Cassius pushed forward, allowing the darkness to swallow him. It was too dark to see anything, and Helai ran her hand over the wall, jumping when she grazed some iron bars. Were there cells down here, and if so, why? A low moan sounded off somewhere in the darkness, and Helai continued forward, swallowing her fear. She did not like being blind with Rackjack and the threat of cultists surrounding her and gripped her daggers more tightly as they moved forward. A soft draft carried through the tunnel, accompanied by stale air and something foul, and Helai murmured her apologies when she stepped too close to Linda, who growled a warning.

"I hear something up ahead," Cassius said in a hushed tone. "Be ready for whatever it is." Helai strained to listen. A few voices spoke, too quiet for Helai to discern any true message.

"Are we sure they have Rembrandt?" Helai asked. "What if this is a trap?"

"Undoubtedly," Rooster said from up ahead. "But what choice do we have?"

They walked for a few more minutes before light shone ahead of them, gracing them once more with the relief of sight. Helai saw the opening to a room between Rooster's and Cassius' broad frames, and she swallowed the urge to flee.

Courage, Helai, she thought to herself, squaring her shoulders and adjusting her grip on her daggers. *Courage for Rembrandt.*

"Undoubtedly," Rooster said from up ahead, "but what choice do we have?"

They walked for a few more minutes before light shone ahead of them, gracing them once more with the relief of sight. Held saw the opening to a room betwixt Rooster's and Cassius' broad frames, and she shoved the urge to flee.

Courage. Please, she thought to herself, squaring her shoulders and adjusting her grip on her dagger. Courage for Rembrandt.

Forty-Nine

HELAI

They stepped into a small circular room. Emir was nowhere to be found, but cultists stood against the walls between torches, their unmoving forms unnerving. One tilted their head up towards the ceiling as if to listen as the others turned to look at the Misfits.

Everything moved quickly then. The cultists rushed towards them, and the Misfits split apart, granting each of them room to fight. Cassius raised his shield, the high-pitched scrape of the cultist's dagger dragging over the surface. It sent chills through Helai as she whispered into her palm, then threw her hand out towards shadows dancing at one edge of the room.

A shadowy hand lashed out from where Helai beckoned it, grabbing a cultist and tugging him into the darkness. His cry was swiftly cut short as Helai's magic ripped him apart, and she raised her dagger to catch the blade of another cultist as he approached. Stronger than her, his blow threw her backwards, and the gleam of the cultist's smile was bright against his face as he moved forward.

Fire blossomed from Helai's right where Rackjack shot forward, his teeth gnashing angrily. Purple flames encased the cultist as heat licked the air, and the cultist thrashed as he screamed, burning alive. After a few moments, he collapsed, and Helai rolled away, a snarl etched into her tongue.

"Stay away from me," Helai hissed, throwing out her hand and uttering quickly under her breath. A dusting of darkness sprang over a cultist's eyes, and Helai quickly stabbed her in the chest to bring her down. Cassius fought valiantly in front of her, cutting down cultists even as more replaced them.

"No," Linda shouted, barreling into a group of cultists as they knocked Intoh out. Sidestepping Linda's charge, they used some sort of barrier-like magic to slam into the krok'ida, sending Linda to the ground. They were on Linda like ants to food, and struck them hard on the forehead. Linda stopped moving.

Someone grabbed Helai from behind, and she threw her head back. Pain split across Helai's skull as her head met the hard bone of a mask, and the cultist laughed as they ripped the dagger from her grasp. In front of her, Cassius had somehow lost his shield, and though he cut down three more cultists, they managed to overpower him, their shadow magic transporting him. His disappearance sent a flurry of panic through Helai, and she threw her leg back, hoping to get the cultist to let go of her. His grip on her only tightened and then darkness took her.

Helai woke in a large circular room, more significant than the one they'd just come from. Her wrists and ankles were tied, and she hung from a wall. Torchlight flickered against the faces of masked cultists, and the other Misfits and Rackjack were also chained to the wall except for Linda, who was chained to the floor. An uncloaked Cassius knelt forcibly against the floor before a small round basin. His chains were of silver steel, his arms forced behind his back, and Emir stood before him still as stone.

Helai exhaled softly, trying to remain calm. She couldn't prevent a whimper from leaving her lips as she looked to her right to see an unconscious Rembrandt strung up against a wooden pole, much like they used in Shoma to string up those who defied the sultan. She'd seen Zahra's body strewn up on a pillar similar to that just before they'd fled Shoma.

Helai's arms ached like she'd been hanging from the wall for quite some time. It appeared she was the first to waken, and after testing the strength of the chains she was bound with, she relaxed. Struggling would only tire her more quickly, and she needed all the strength she had if she was going to get out of this.

"Alyse, dear, one of them is awake. Send for the others." Helai's face shot up as Emir spoke with his wife, gesturing to a far-off door. They both wore masks, this time bearing the white paint of a phoenix.

Alyse nodded, disappearing through the door with one last look at her son. Helai's heart plummeted to her stomach when she realized the Welkers must have put Rembrandt on that pillar. They were in no hurry to cut him down at the very least.

What have we done?

Helai groaned as pain coursed through her back from her brand. When Alyse returned, she was followed by at least a dozen more cultists, their masks resembling deer and dragon skulls. Several of them carried something covered by cloth on their shoulders, but the nearer it got, the more Helai's brand burned. She gritted her teeth as they set it down in the middle of the room just feet from where Cassius knelt.

"What are you doing?" Helai found her courage to speak, and it reverberated around the room. Her question was met with silence as the cultists pulled the fabric off what they'd been carrying.

Helai's breath caught in her throat. It was a dragon tooth, similar to those that still hung from Qevayla's skeleton in Shoma, only smaller. It hummed with energy that pulled at Helai's skin and made the hair on her arms stand on end. She shuddered as Intoh groaned and woke next to her.

"What happened?" he asked, then stilled. "Not good. Linda, wake up. Linda." But Linda did not wake, their soft snores heard even from where Helai hung.

"It appears that we've walked right into a trap," Helai said bitterly as a cultist walked along the walls, testing the chains. When she got to Helai, a quiet laugh left her lips.

"You are honored by the gods to be a Chosen, and yet you scorn their gift. How pitiful," the cultist said, her voice twisted with disgust. A dark thought festered in Helai as anger shuddered through her brand, not entirely her own. How she desired to slip one of her daggers in the cultist's belly and twist, to feel the warmth of blood stain her fingers as the cultist's eyes drained of life. How elated she'd feel to know the world was rid of such evil. The notion sent a wave of dizziness through her, and the cultist laughed again.

"Your rage is *divine*," the cultist purred. "Our Phoenix Mother will take great pleasure in devouring it."

Helai tugged at her chains, her lips peeled back over her teeth in a wordless snarl. It was of a moot point for the chains held strong, and the cultist's glee continued as she moved on to test Intoh's, then Rooster's chains.

"The time is finally here," Emir said, his hand reaching out to tug back Cassius' head, revealing his neck. "How long have we endured the quiet of her whispers? How long have we waited for the Chosen to make their way to our doorstep? We sent Nadia out to collect the vampire, and he evaded her, but how lucky are we to have him collect himself?"

The cultists remained silent as they formed a circle around the tooth in the center. Rackjack thrashed about, gnashing his teeth in frustration. "No-no! Can't let them sniff-seek path to resurrection. Very bad-bad. Must find a way to escape-gnaw," he cried.

Emir continued as if Rackjack hadn't spoken at all. "The other sacrifices will serve as a warning to the false gods who will look on and see the rebirth of a true god."

Cassius woke as Emir's words rang through the room. He fought against his chains, but a pained cry left his lips as his skin burned, peeling away to bone. Helai had never seen silver hurt Cassius, not like it was hurting him now, and after a moment he stopped, his fangs on display as his eyes, dark and bloodshot, flickered up to Emir, who still tugged his head back.

"Shh," Emir cooed, producing a stake from his cloak. "For the first time in your life, your deeds will urge on a greater purpose."

"Wait! Wait!" Rooster called out, his hair wild and untamed as it fell in his face. "Have any of you stopped to consider that whatever you're trying to bring back might be dead for a reason?" The usual easygoing nature of Rooster was gone, replaced with quiet unbridled rage.

"Daddy?" The soft voice of Rembrandt caused Helai's head to turn, horrified as Rembrandt pulled at his ropes in confusion. "Daddy? What's going on? Mommy? Mom–" Rembrandt's cries grew panicked. "I wanna go home. I'm scared. Please–" A sob rose like bile in Helai's throat. She swallowed it as Alyse walked up to comfort her son, and Rembrandt flinched from her reaching grasp, tears streaming down his face. "Please don't hurt Cassius and the others, Daddy. Please. You promised."

"Shhh, darling. It's alright," Alyse cooed. "Daddy is helping us go to a better place."

Rembrandt shuddered, his chest heaving, and shook his head. "I don't wanna go to a better place. I wanna stay here."

Helai tore her gaze away, unable to watch any longer. Intoh muttered incoherently in Drikotyian beside her, and Rooster's gaze stayed threaded with rage.

Clear mind, clear soul, Helai thought, looking about the room. There seemed to be no other exits save for the door at the other end.

"If you resurrect whatever this is," Cassius said, looking right at Emir. "Your life is forfeit. Your son's life is forfeit. Are you willing to make that sacrifice?"

Emir remained silent, his expression smooth as stone. The stake he held was bone white and jagged, secreting some sort of sap at its tip. "Seek comfort with your god, Cassius," he said, bringing the stake down straight through Cassius' heart.

Fifty

ROOSTER

Helai cried out as Cassius slumped over, and Rooster no longer felt Cassius' presence through the brand that connected them. It was as if all warmth was being sapped from the room as Emir pulled the stake out of Cassius' chest.

Rooster had never seen a vampire die, not that he could remember. Some spoke of them turning to dust and bone, the magic keeping their life suspended in eternity ceasing to exist. That did not happen to Cassius. There was so much blood that it poured out of his corpse in droves, caught by a bowl that Emir used to collect it.

"Dad—Daddy, please." Rembrandt was crying as the other masked cultists stepped forward, surrounding the dragon's tooth. His mother still stood at Rembrandt's altar, but she did not react or move when her son's cries echoed throughout the room. Horror coursed through

Rooster as Emir walked up to the tooth, bowl in hand, and dipped his fingers into Cassius' blood. Running his fingers over the enamel, he pulled away as Gorvayne's sigil was left in dark, black blood that dripped from the tooth and stained the ground beneath it.

"Fools," Rooster hissed from the wall. "Gorvayne will kill us all. Don't you understand?"

Emir did not turn as he addressed Rooster with a bitter laugh. "We are not calling to Gorvayne. It is his general, Rhavna, the Phoenix Mother, whom we pay homage to. She will be the one to grant us salvation. With the vampire's blood, we will use Gorvayne's sigil to resurrect Rhavna anew." Emir's smile grew wide. "Only the blood of a dragon can call our Phoenix Mother home."

A shudder rolled through the room as the cultists clasped their hands together and began to chant. Magic curled around Rooster. It was as if he was being torn apart, only nothing happened. The pain was excruciating. Heat swam through his blood as he gritted his teeth. To his right, Linda roared, struggling against the chains that bound them, but their trials were cut short as a deep cracking sound echoed across the room.

The cultists did not stop, even as the dragon's tooth began to weep blood. The mark of Gorvayne had dried on top of the enamel, but red lines secreted from it as it started to grow into a skull, as fresh skin grew into scales. The head of the dragon was forged first–glittering dark scales that formed around the swirl of two large horns atop her head. Her snout was short and thick with black tinging the end, and when she opened her mouth to breathe new air, her teeth were easily as long as Rooster.

One eye opened to study the room, an eye of brilliant yellow-orange. There was fire in her gaze, an anger that swept across the room and pierced Rooster, so hard he nearly forgot the pain in his lungs.

"Rhavna has risen!" Emir cried, dropping to his knees as he bowed before her. The rest of her had been made, a dragon in her full glory. Her tail plumed out at the end as if it were feathered like a phoenix, and her wings, also feathered, bore one long claw, similar to that of a bat. If Rooster wasn't so focused on her anger, he might have taken the time to admire just how magnificent of a creature she was–a cross between a dragon and a phoenix. *Phoenix Mother*.

Rembrandt screamed as Rhavna raised her head and roared, the sound shaking the room. Several of the cultists stopped chanting, their resolve teetering now that there was an actual dragon standing before them.

"No!" Emir shouted as two of them bolted, but Rhavna did not let them leave. Lashing out, she had one between her teeth before Rooster blinked. The man's screams were quickly stifled as the dragon closed her mouth and swallowed him whole. The other cultist was caught between her teeth. His screams were cut short as she bit down, killing him. Blood shot down her chin, seeping to the floor as she devoured his corpse.

Emir did not flinch away or move, his forehead pressed to the ground in worship. The air was ripe with magic as Rooster struggled against his chains to no avail. He locked eyes with Helai and then with Rackjack as sadness gripped him.

He was going to die without ever knowing who he truly was.

Carter Wingman–a nameless man with no identity to take with him to the Beyond.

Screams of terror tore Rooster's expression from Rackjack to Rembrandt as his mother approached him, wielding a dagger.

"Mommy," Rembrandt cried, tears streaming down his face. "Mommy, please." Rembrandt's wrists were raw and bleeding as he tore against the rope that tied him to the altar. It was difficult to watch, but Rooster could not look away. A sob lumped in his throat, and he swallowed it even as tears fell against his cheeks.

Rhavna turned from Emir to fix amber-hued eyes on Alyse and Rembrandt. The other cultists remained strong, still as statues where they stood as Rhavna stepped towards the altar.

"Phoenix Mother, we know of your story. We know you demand the blood of children, that you lead them first into the light of the beyond, where it is safe. This babe of my womb, I offer him to you. Take him to salvation as you did for your own womb-sons all those years ago."

Laughter echoed deep within Rhavna. It shook the walls and caused the torches on the walls to waver. She snaked her head forward to sniff Alyse, who raised her hands in offering. Rembrandt screamed until his voice was hoarse, his chest heaving.

"How can you? He's your son," Helai screamed, but it did not matter. Alyse ignored her as she stared at Rhavna. The phoenix dragon reared back onto her hind legs as several feathers from her wings burst into brilliant flames. Fire doused in vibrant, cosmic colors shot out of her mouth, and Alyse's courage buckled as she was washed in their heat, her dying screams mingling with Rembrandt's as both were burned alive.

It didn't take long for them to die; the dragon's fire burned hotter than any other flame Rooster had ever felt before. As the heat of it spread throughout the room, Rooster shut his eyes. If this was to be his end, then so be it.

Fifty-One

CASSIUS

Cassius woke to darkness.

No, he thought as he pushed himself to a seated position. *I died.* The realization should have scared him, as the thought of death once had, but he felt nothing. No fear, no curiosity, no relief. He didn't feel at all; he had to look down to make sure his hands were still there. They were, but they felt light, like there was no weight to them, like he could just float away if he didn't find something to grab onto. His bloodlust was absent for the first time since becoming a vampire, and the relief from its reprieve was unmatched.

Standing, he looked upon a hellish landscape ravaged by flames. It choked the air with heat and smoke, and Cassius' eyes watered as he rose to his feet. The Ebony Fang was silent as well; it no longer called out to him, even as his blood sang with life. No, all was silent for but a moment before a voice called out to him, a voice he did not recognize.

"Cassius." The voice was androgynous, a soft caress against his cheek. It was a warm summer's day, a final drift to sleep after a long day of fighting. It was the sharp edge of a knife, a plague sickness healed by a bathing light.

Was that what death sounded like?

A head snaked out of the darkness, a massive dragon's head with its skull exposed. As it padded closer, or perhaps Cassius' eyes merely adjusted, the dragon in its entirety was exposed. Its rib cage was pulled away from the flesh of its stomach, but no organs rested inside. It was hollow, the husk of the beast it used to be as it snaked over Cassius. Parts of its legs were naught but bone, and where its eyes used to be, there was nothing but void space.

"Drausmírtus?" Cassius guessed, surprised by his own voice. How could he speak if he was dead?

The dragon nodded, their breath hot on Cassius' face as they lowered their head. An empty eye socket stopped in front of him. Cassius did not know what he'd expected to see when he met the goddess of death, but the creature standing before him wasn't what he'd imagined.

"To what lengths would you go to for absolution?" Their voice was soft, like trickling water over rocks. It pulled Cassius under as if it meant to drown him, cradling him like he was a child. Once, when he'd been young, he'd nearly drowned at the beach by his family estate. His father had been the one to pull him out as he'd spluttered and gasped for air. There had been a moment, though, when the sea had attempted to claim him, and he felt that same calm darkness of peace.

That memory shattered into a million pieces of glass, breaking against the dragon's side, floating away into the void. Cassius swallowed thickly as shadowy hands rose from the ground, crying out for Drausmírtus, who ignored them, their gaze fixed purely on Cassius.

"Anything," Cassius whispered.

Drausmírtus lowered their head in amusement. A low growl left their lips. "And what lengths would you go for power?"

Cassius shuddered then, the question rubbing against him seductively. A moan lodged itself between his teeth, and he shook, his fingers curling into fists. Power was all he'd ever wanted. Power was his liberator, a way to break the chains he'd been shackled with by his father, his maker, his Order.

Power would set him free.

"Anything," Cassius said again, this time with more conviction. Shifting, he moved to rest on his knees, bending over to kneel before the dragon. Since becoming a vampire, he'd refused to worship the goddess of death as so many other vampires did; he'd feared Death's wrath and being chained to something so powerful as a god. If the dragon could give him the power he needed to free himself though, he'd gladly devote himself to them.

His answer seemed to please Drausmírtus as they stood, their bones creaking like wind passing through the woods. They said nothing else as large black chains shot out of the ground and snaked up and around Cassius' arms. A flicker of regret shot through him; he'd been foolish to think that trading shackles for another under the guise of freedom would be a worthy exchange. It was too late, though, as the chains forced him lower, pressing his forehead to the ground.

"We will grant you your wish, Cassius Antonia, but know this. I will spare you this passing only once. The next time I come to claim you, your soul will be mine."

In his mind's eye, he stood upon a hill overlooking a wasteland. Various colors dazzled the sky as if the stars reached out to kiss the ground. An army of the dead stood before him in breathtaking numbers. With bated breath, they waited, watching Cassius with a silence that could not be achieved in the waking world.

A feeling surged through him, an aching of great power. He cried out as pain, white-hot and breathtaking, coursed through him, ripping the skin at his back. Two wings, leathery and dragon-scaled, shot out between his shoulder blades and curled around him, cradling him in his transformation. His blood was aflame, burning through him as if it was washing away who he was to replace him anew. He was unmade and reforged. His fangs extended as the chains tugged him up. His fingers sharpened to talons, and his wings spread wide. He was naked before Drausmírtus, who breathed hot, vibrantly colored breath against his quivering form.

"Rise again, Cassius Antonia."

He hadn't felt pain like this since Vera had turned him. The act of dying and being reborn was not an easy road. The dragon's blood that coursed through him was not made to be bound to mortal flesh, but the vampiric curse demanded it, and only the strongest survived. Cassius felt himself being tested again as Drausmírtus' breath washed over him. A soft, cowardly part of him begged to let go. He couldn't though. He did not want to die.

When Drausmírtus stopped, they pulled away, their head snaking above him. He panted as the chains slowly retreated into the ground, but he found himself strong enough to stand without their aid. His newly forged wings twitched in anticipation as a horse rose from the front, snorting and pawing the dirt with his hoof.

"Fírnster," Cassius breathed, shuddering under the weight of his transformation. It felt like a snake slithered through his veins, breathing new life into his vampiric curse. His horse's nose flared as great leathery black wings shot out of his back, an undead pegasus in his own right. His eyes glowed red as he circled Cassius, shoving his nose against the back of his arm.

"A gift. I plucked him from your world and granted him a rebirth," Drausmírtus said.

Cassius ran his fingers through Fírnster's mane, cooing softly as the horse nickered, pleased by his companion's touch.

"Both of you will whisper change into the wind, now go," Drausmírtus uttered, reaching a talon out to press it to Cassius' forehead. The dragon disappeared back into the void of darkness as Cassius' stomach plummeted, and he was transported.

He blinked as another dragon appeared before him, a dragon of red and gold with feathered wings and eyes burning with hatred and rage. He no longer stood in the void of death but rather the room he'd been sacrificed in.

That is not a dragon. Not really, he realized, studying the creature before him. *More like a phoenix.* Fírnster was gone but Cassius felt his presence, waiting in a pocket space nearby to be summoned whenever Cassius might need him.

His friends were still chained to the walls, and the altar Rembrandt had been strapped to was no more, a pile of ash. Cassius knew in his heart the boy was dead.

"Cassius," Rooster called out, his voice thick with surprise.

"No," Emir shouted, raising his head in shock and anger. "It cannot be." All of the other cultists were dead, the room awash with blood and flame, and the dragon before him opened her maw, spittle flying in all directions as she roared.

"Stop," Cassius said, feeling Drausmírtus' power still flowing through him. His voice was not his own but rather an anchor that kept Drausmírtus tethered to this world. Their voice seeped through his, a soft but ancient tone that made him sick with raw power. "Blasphemous is your nature, a stain on my kind. Gorvayne may have made you, Rhavna, but here you will be unmade." Through him, Drausmírtus raised his hand towards Rhavna, her chest and feathered wings lit with purple-red flames. His hand came to rest atop Emir's head as if he were forgiving him of his sins.

Before Rhavna could purge them all with fire, magic shot from his fingers, a dusting of vibrant starlight. Cassius had never seen such magic wielded before, not without the direst of repercussions. It blossomed over his hands and trailed through Emir's eyes, burning flesh from bone. He screamed, clawing at his face, but it mattered little. He was dead before he hit the ground, and the magic did not stop there as Drausmírtus lifted Cassius' hand towards the phoenix dragon. The moment it hit Rhavna, the room shook from the cry of her pain. Her body began to peel away as if it were nothing more than ash, forging the appearance of a tall Volreyan woman with braided red locks and a snarling expression. Drausmírtus did not stop there, burning away Rhavna's skin until she was nothing but dust and bone, the hatred of her eyes an inferno before they too were gone.

A portal opened behind her, and the shadow of Rhavna fell through, leaving the room in a weakened silence. Cassius had never felt so alive in his undead state.

You killed her so easily, Cassius thought.

The dragon inside him rumbled in amusement. *I am Death. But no, she is not dead. I only delayed her. She will return to Gorvayne, and when she heals from the wounds I inflicted upon her, she will burn the world.*

How do we hope to stop her? Cassius grew tired, the room in front of him swirling in a dizzying state. He was going to pass out soon. Something tugged at his belly, and he realized quickly that it wasn't unconsciousness that threatened to take him; he was being teleported.

Hope is never lost, Cassius, Drausmírtus said as they faded from him, and he was pulled from the room.

Fifty-Two

LINDA

As Linda blinked, the room swayed, and the ball went on as normal around them. The other Misfits stood nearby, each of them looking just as dazed and confused as Linda felt. Cassius wore a cloak now, a long, sweeping black cloak with two silver claws that clasped it shut at his throat, and Linda stared at him curiously. They thought they were dead until Cassius stood, a dragon standing over him as they banished the phoenix dragon away.

At first, Linda thought they'd gone back in time, but no. Everything was how it had been just before they were taken. Music flowed through the air as people laughed and danced, their masked faces flitting in and out of focus.

Rackjack tugged on Rooster's arm, a dwarf once more. "Go-go. We must go-go. Something is not right. Have to flee-scurry before–"

A low rumble in the ground forced everyone to stop dancing. The music paused as the windows of the estate rattled, and Linda watched Helai lock eyes with Zamir, who stood near the entrance to the ballroom.

"Zamir," she cried out, pushing her way through people to speak to him.

"We thought you were dead," Rooster said, clasping Cassius on the shoulder. There was something different about him. The links that chained his illusion together had been reforged and were stronger. Linda no longer smelled the rot of death on his skin, and if they didn't know he was a vampire, they might have mistaken him for merely a man.

"As did I," Cassius admitted grimly.

"Oh, there you are," Itale cried, approaching with Khal and Sode. "Something is horribly wro–" The ground shook violently again, cutting Itale off as the curtains hanging on either side of the windows burst into flames.

The room broke into chaos as the ball guests screamed and pushed into each other, fleeing the flames. Heat soaked the room as it began to fill up with smoke, and Linda's heart pounded as the lines blurred between the present and the past. Instead of a room full of humans, it was greka and krok'ida fighting in a moonlit forest while dark things came out of the trees, burning everything in their paths. Linda was frozen in place as fear and rage overcame them.

A small hand pressed to their forearm brought them back to reality.

"Linda, must go," Intoh said, his eyes wide with fright. "Keep Misfits safe."

Linda grunted as someone rammed into Helai, shoving her to the ground near Linda as she fought her way back to the Misfits with Zamir. Linda nearly lost her in the sea of people attempting to flee, but they reached down and tugged Helai to her feet, shoving anyone that came too close.

Linda's eyes watered as the smoke and fire continued to build. Cassius appeared shaken, his eyes wide and bright; his hair had been liberated from the silk tie that bound it. He and Linda worked in tandem to create a safe pocket between them for the rest of the party, and soon they made their way to the front hall of the estate, where fires coursed through aplenty. Smoke rolled out of the open door as people poured through it, cowering and crying out in terror. Linda watched a woman burst into flames even though she was nowhere near the flames that raged through the estate, and her screams were haunting as they forced themself to look away and rush towards the front door.

"Come! Quickly-fast," Rackjack rasped. "Can sense strong magic here-here." Trepidation soaked the air, and Linda roared in pain as their tail swept through a fire trailing over the vines that lined the side of the estate. Intoh quickly patted it out with a wave of water from the necklace he wore, but the pain smarted, and Linda grumbled in agony. The rose bushes lining the side of the estate roared with flame, their flowers ablaze.

"Help, Linda," Intoh rasped, his eyes rolling with fright. "Cannot run very fast."

Linda conceded, sweeping Intoh up and setting him on their shoulder. The village had been reduced to panicked madness as the estate burned behind them. They nearly lost Rooster in a sea of people rushing to get as far from the fire and chaos as they could, and Rooster shouted at them as he was forced away.

"Meet me at the docks!"

"Stay in front," Linda told Itale, gesturing to the spot in front of them. People seemed to keep a wide pace of Linda, and Itale nodded, steering to run in front of Linda as they hurried across the estate's front grounds. They were on the other side of the fence when the top of the estate exploded, sending chunks of stone flying in every direction. A blast of heat coaxed Linda forward, the dying cries of people filling their ears. Linda glanced behind them as the estate fell to a ruinous state, a vibrant fire still raging as people died on the grounds, the smell of burning flesh pungent in the air.

As they made their way through the trees towards the docks, Helai slowed. "Is everyone uninjured? Cassius—" Her eyes raked over him with uncertainty. "You died."

"No time to talk of that now," Cassius said, pointing to where Rooster waited in the break of trees. "No time to delay at all. We need to reach Rooster and figure out what is happening."

"Helai." Zamir paused, pulling a golden lamp from his belt. It was small; it could easily fit in the palm of Linda's hand, and they stared at it curiously as Zamir hesitantly offered it to Helai. "I know you need this more than I do so you can remove your brand, but I need to return to Alavae."

"What? No—" Helai's brow furrowed. "Then I am going with you. If Massoud is there, I need to find him."

"No, don't go," Linda said sadly. The thought of Helai leaving filled Linda with despair.

"We can talk about this at the docks," Zamir said gently.

Helai hummed but eventually nodded as they ran over to Rooster. Several others rushed through the trees, seeking the docks, but many fled into the woods towards the center of the village. Linda wasn't sure what magic had graced the estate to cause the fires, but it didn't look to be extending past the estate's grounds. Linda was sad to see it burn, though they were glad they'd had Gerta change the ice bear rug into a cloak before the ball. They still wore it now, and even though some of it had been damaged by smoke and flame, it remained relatively unharmed as they hefted it more securely over their shoulders.

"When I fled the estate, I managed to sneak into everyone's rooms and grab armor. The weapons were absent, I'm afraid," Zamir said, gesturing to his bag. Pulling it open, Linda peeked in to note that the bag was far larger on the inside than it was on the outside, and their armor had been tucked away safely inside. It was a relief to see. Linda's heart squeezed painfully when she noted he'd also managed to grab Gloop, Rembrandt's dragon doll.

"Over here," Rooster said, waving them over. His cheeks were dirty, and he walked with a slight limp but seemed otherwise unharmed. "Tripped over a bloody root on the way here, think I've sprained my ankle," he said, hissing as he attempted to put weight on his right foot.

"Let me," Intoh said, weaving his way down Linda to get to Rooster. Sode and Khal spread out as they approached from the estate, their spears gripped tightly in their hands as they made sure no one drew near. Linda was glad to see they lived.

"You've changed," Itale said to Cassius, a peculiar look on his face. "What happened?"

Cassius turned, and Linda noted a dusting of starlight flickering in his irises. "All I recall is being stabbed. I died, but I suppose Death did not want me," Cassius admitted, pressing his fingers to the nape of his neck. He looked to say something else and then decided better of it as a voice called out to them.

"Misfits!"

Linda turned as Khal and Sode crossed their spears, barring Velius from approaching. His hair was down, a cascade of deep red around sharp features as he approached, dressed in plate armor.

"Do not come any closer," Khal hissed, the frill around his neck shooting open in warning. "Will not hesitate."

"Let him pass; he is friend," Intoh said.

Khal and Sode reluctantly drew back their spears, and Velius hurried forward. Beyond the trees at the docks rested the Firebrand, bobbing innocently in the water as if nothing out of the ordinary had just transpired, save for the flurry of people fleeing on their ships.

"What happened?" Velius asked, raising his head to look at the curl of smoke thickening in the sky.

"How did you know to be here?" Helai asked, her voice thick with suspicion. Everyone else looked at Velius with a curious expression except Intoh, who was focused on healing Rooster's ankle.

Velius held his hands up. "I have a doorway set up here. The root that signifies Halvdarc burst into flames this morning, so I sailed for here as quickly as I could. I promise, Misfits, I mean you no harm." His eyes landed on Rackjack, whose teeth chattered in nervous energy as he tilted his head to the side.

"Tantien-filth?" Rackjack asked.

"Rackjack? Is that you? What are you doing here, and why do you look like that?" Velius asked, astonished.

"You know him?" Rooster asked, stepping away from Intoh's magic and ignoring the greka's protest. "Who exactly are you?"

"I–" Velius glanced at something behind Linda, far off in the trees. "It isn't safe to speak here. Come to the Firebrand. We will speak once we're safe."

"Tantien-filth," Rackjack said again as Velius muttered to himself and turned towards the Firebrand, his gaze far off in thought. Linda did not know what was going on, only that they wanted to be as far away from Halvdarc as possible. Some strange magic plagued the air, and the longer Linda was here, the angrier they got. They half-expected their brand to burn, but when they looked down at their leg, they blinked.

The skin on the inside of their thigh was smooth. The brand was gone.

Linda looked up, eager to tell the others, but they'd already reached the docks with Velius. Linda squared their shoulders and followed.

Fifty-Three

HELAI

Helai was too shaken by everything that had just transpired to feel the nauseous pull in her belly the moment she stepped onto the Firebrand. The others were silent, so she remained so as well, even though the presence of Velius filled her with unease. How did he know Rackjack, and why was the rakken calling him Tantien? They spoke to each other in low whispers, too low for Helai to hear. Then Velius led them out onto the deck of his ship as he barked commands to the crew in Eldrasian.

Helai checked her bag to make sure the lamp Zamir had given her was still safely there. The gleam of gold hit the rays of the sun, and Helai's relief was immense despite the twist of her belly.

"Helai." Zamir approached, his fingers twisting anxiously. "If we are to go to Alavae, it would be best to charter a boat from here."

Velius approached before she could reply, gesturing to the door that had once led them to Volendam. Helai had never noticed the roots above the frame that twisted down to touch the doorknob, but one of them was singed and burned, small flecks of red flame etched into the grain.

"I have my heading, but I think it would be wise to seek solace in Volendam for the moment. We can talk there."

"Volendam is still reeling from the siege. Are you sure–" Cassius started, but Velius held up his hand, a small smile gracing his face.

"You will see."

As he pulled the door open, the cold air brushed Helai's skin. She shivered, glancing at Zamir as she followed Rooster through the door. Linda twisted their ring, shifting back into a human, and Sode looked at them with confusion.

"Volendam welcome our kind here. No need to hide," he said, pointing to Linda's ring. "Most port cities kind to us. Bring them a lot of trade."

Linda rumbled in shock before turning to Intoh, speaking quickly to him in Drikotyian. As they argued, Helai looked around the city, shocked to see it still in a manner of disrepair. It did not look like anyone had yet returned to begin rebuilding.

"Not scared," Linda said, twisting their ring to turn back into a krok'ida. "Gonna be me."

"Is that...The Broken Arrow?" Rooster asked, his voice swept with emotion as they moved down the street. Helai swallowed thickly and followed Rooster's gaze, gasping at the sight of The Broken Arrow as it came into view.

The inn was now twice its normal size. The rundown state of the inn was no more, its holes replaced with the finest dwarven stone. The wood frames of the windows and door were of fine eldrasi wood. A dark stain embellished the wood with a sense of elegance, especially among the desolation. A sob curled in Helai's throat for the sign had been rehung.

'The Broken Arrow' was written in swirling gold letters above the inn's sigil: an arrow piercing two mugs of ale clinking together, its tip broken and hanging on by a splinter.

The Misfits' grief was momentarily forgotten as they stumbled inside, much to Felix's and Patrina's shock. The dwarves were nowhere to be seen, and a pinprick of sadness caressed Helai at the absence of Drithan. She'd hoped to see him one last time.

"Misfits?" Felix asked, rushing around the counter. The inn was empty, and Helai threw a quick prayer of gratitude to Dalnor for it as she hurried to Patrina, surprising the bard by tugging her into a hug.

"It's good to see you too," Patrina said, laughing breathlessly as she wrapped her arms around Helai. She wouldn't have admitted to it a month ago, but Helai's relief to see The Broken Arrow and its owners was immense, and she was slow to pull away.

"So this is where you've been holing up?" Zamir said, studying the inn. "I'm impressed, Helai."

"Why didn't I get that warm welcome?" Velius protested, earning laughter from Felix.

"We are glad to see you too," Felix said. "We did not think we would see the Misfits again. Not so soon anyway. It has only been some months since your departure." Months felt like years to Helai, but it was so relieving to see Felix and Patrina that for the moment, she forgot the horrors she'd just witnessed.

"Is that...what I think it is?" Cassius asked, his tone hushed. Helai looked up to see him gesturing behind her.

"'A gift for the Misfits from the dwarves,' Obrand said. They worked some of their magic to make it happen," Felix said as she turned, his voice thick with emotion. "You got your bath house, Cassius."

Cassius drew forward, pushing past Helai to run his fingers over a small sign hitched to the left side of the door. '*Antonia's Bath Hall*' was written in clean letters outlined in red.

"We thought that since it was your idea, it was only right to name the hall after you," Patrina said to Cassius as he pushed open the door and disappeared inside.

"And then we never saw him again," Rooster teased before following Cassius in.

Helai peeked her head through the door. The room was spectacular in design. She'd never been to Hestia before but knew it to be a beautiful country of white marble buildings and gold and red decorum. The bath hall mirrored that, the floors leading up to the main bath of white marble with golden veins. A statue of a mermaid sat upon a rock, pouring water from a vase into the bath, and on the other side of the room were small private baths tucked away behind deep red curtains.

"The dwarves did something to the floors. They're always heated. It's delightful," Patrina said.

"How are you to keep safe from those who would mean to raid this place for its value? The dwarves have truly outdone themselves in their design," Cassius said. His concern wasn't unwarranted. Helai loved this side of town, but she could imagine what kind of skaels someone could get from just a chip off the marble.

"The dwarves took care of that too. Something to do with this rune here," Felix said, pointing to the rune carved into the wall near the door. Helai recognized it as a dwarf rune, and it hummed quietly from where she stood. She didn't know what it did, but she recalled seeing it lining the doors of the dwarf hold in the Spine Mountains.

Cassius looked sadly at the bath and then squared his shoulders. "We have much to discuss. Shall we?" They shuffled out of the bath house, and exhaustion crashed down on Helai's shoulders with a suddenness that took her breath away. Zamir squeezed her shoulder as Intoh took a seat at their booth, and Velius began to pace, his hands clasped behind his back.

Looking around the inn as everyone settled, Helai couldn't help the fear that flickered in her belly. Somehow she knew that the danger they'd been running from since they'd been forced together was only just beginning.

Fifty-Four

ROOSTER

As Rooster slipped into their booth, it felt as if every aching joint in him sighed with relief. His mind continued to reel from everything they'd just witnessed, and by all rights, none of them should have been sitting in Volendam, catching up with old friends.

Rackjack settled down beside him, and Rooster eyed him. His reveal of being a rakken and his familiarity with Velius, whom he called Tantien, was concerning.

"Thanks, Felix," Cassius said as Felix handed him a glass of wine. "Almost dying really makes a man crave what he once took for granted."

"You almost died?" Felix laughed nervously, his eyes brimming with concern. "What happened?"

"Too much to explain," Helai said softly, glancing at Zamir.

"No more brand," Linda said, forcing everyone to quiet. "Don't feel angry."

"You're right," Rooster said, reaching out to touch Rackjack's forearm, which was smooth and free of the brand. "Linda, yours is gone too?"

"Did you use the lamp to free us of it?" Cassius asked, his relief all too clear on his face.

Helai shook her head, setting the small lamp on the table. It pulsed quietly. The power that radiated off it was startling, like it contained something very old and very powerful. Rooster eyed it with curiosity as torchlight gleamed off its golden side.

"The brands were gone before I even thought about making a wish."

Linda, still standing, showed the booth the inside of their leg. It was also smooth with no brand in sight. The absence of it was unexplainable. The corners of Rooster's eyes pricked with emotion, but the shifting of red hair as Velius unfolded his arms and stepped forward reminded Rooster of his anger and frustration.

"You have some explaining to do," Rooster said.

The eldrasi sighed and moved to the table as Felix and Patrina retreated to the bar to give them space, their voices of quiet conversation an ambience as Velius pulled a locket over his neck and set it on the table.

Rooster leaned in, noting with a painful thump of his heart that it was the same locket he'd stolen from the Captain at the Silver Moon Club.

"A locket?" Helai asked, leaning forward to study it.

Velius nodded. "It's my sister's. Her name is Igraine."

Rooster shot up as ringing pierced his ears. Pushing away from the table, he ignored everyone's protests. "Igraine? Who are you?" Rooster's heart thundered as Velius held out a hand in an attempt to calm him.

"My real name is Tantien. Igraine must have sent Rackjack to find you. It is why I know him. My sister disappeared some months ago, and I have been trying to find her ever since."

"Did you know who I was the moment I walked into your forge?"

"I –"

Rooster slammed his fist on the table. "Did you?"

Tantien pursed his lips and stepped back, shaking his head. "I did not. I had my suspicions, but we never had a chance to meet before. I have heard of the infamous Carter Wingman, but my sister and I are not on great speaking terms. When I heard of her disappearance, I knew something was wrong. The only trace I've been able to find of hers is that locket you see here."

"So why didn't you enter the Silver Moon Club yourself if it was so important?" Cassius asked.

Tantien's silence filled the room as Rooster's mind rebelled from everything he'd just heard. Itale, seated at the table next to the Misfits' booth, stared anxiously between everyone, and the greka had spread out to stroll through the long tables in the middle, their guard ever vigilant.

"I was unable to get away from the Firebrand for too long," Tantien explained. "The seas are ripe with dangers, and I knew pirates and Vykra would take advantage of my absence should I let them."

"Where is she?" Rooster asked, his anger a haze that threatened to blind him. "Where is Igraine?"

"Left her on Vitreuse-island," Rackjack protested, his nose twitching nervously. "Should still be there-there."

"I am afraid she has been apprehended," Tantien said sadly, gesturing to the locket. "Her and your crew have been taken by the eldrasi. They're being held at Fraxinus, a prison located off the island of Míradan. I believe a lot of the items from your crew and ship are being flushed into the shadow market, which is how the captain got hold of this locket in the first place."

"We have to go get her," Rooster said, sitting suddenly. His head swam, tilting on its axis, and nausea curled at his belly with an unforgiving grip.

"The prison is nigh impenetrable. I do not know how we can get inside. You are a highly wanted man, Carter."

Rooster blanched. "I'm not ready for you to call me that."

Tantien lowered his head in respect, his hair falling in sheets around his head.

Zamir raised his hand, his mouth parted in contemplation. "I – I believe I know someone who could assist," he said, staring at Helai. "It would require travel into the belly of war though."

"Where?" Intoh asked. "Have things to do. Can't just go on wild chase."

Helai's eyes flickered to Zamir's, then back to the party. "I was supposed to meet my friend Massoud here, in Volendam. Turns out he got stuck in Alavae." Her gaze was uncertain as she looked at Cassius.

"So we are to locate this Massoud?" Rooster asked, waving for her to continue. He didn't like the thought of heading straight into a war-stricken country, but he'd do anything to see Igraine again.

"Massoud's a master illusionist," Helai said. "If anyone can break into a prison such as the one you speak of, it's him. He's posing as a soldier in Alavae. If we can get to him, I have high hopes that he can aid us."

Intoh shook his head. "No more brand connect us. Will stay here."

Linda growled. "Don't be coward. Come with us."

Tantien held up his hands as Intoh opened his mouth to protest. "I have something that might interest you, Intoh. A potion that took me a very long time to obtain. It can add years to one's life if they drink it, and the best part? There are no consequences."

Intoh's eyes flashed. "Potion you say?"

Tantien nodded. "It's yours if you help. Only after my sister's safety is ensured."

Intoh hummed, falling back into his seat. Felix and Patrina cleaned mugs at the counter, pretending not to listen and failing miserably at remaining inconspicuous.

"I do not think I will be much help in war," Itale said nervously, raising his hand hesitantly. His eyes were wide, and Cassius raised his wine towards him.

"Your necromancy will not wait."

"A necromancer?" Tantien's eyes brightened. "I could use a necromancer. I can ferry the Misfits to Alavae if you wish to remain on board with me, Itale. There are matters I must attend to while the Misfits retrieve Massoud. Arrangements to be made when we make our journey to Míradan."

Itale's laughter bubbled anxiously as his gaze darted from Cassius to Tantien. His shoulders slumped and then he shrugged. "I have always wanted to live onboard a boat for a time, so long as it's okay with Sir Cassius. He is to be my teacher, after all."

As the others spoke of plans, Rooster stared at Tantien. Now that he could connect the two, the eldrasi really *did* share similarities with Igraine in Rooster's memories. Their facial structure and hair were the same. "Fraxinus, you say?" he said, interrupting the banter.

Now that he knew where Igraine was, the fight to remain idle was nearly unbearable. His heart ached, desperate for him to go find her. He felt tethered to a string as it tugged him towards her, much like he'd felt when Cassius had been compelled to the armory he'd been searching for, only much smaller. He could ignore the urge if he wanted, but he didn't.

Tantien nodded. "Fraxinus indeed, but if it is to be attempted, I do think we should seek out Helai's friend. It will require a fair bit of luck and even more skill if this is to be pulled off." His shoulders sagged. "I am sorry for not confiding in you earlier. I did not know if I could trust you."

"Velius – er, Tantien," Cassius said, stuttering over the name change. "We are not exactly the most trustworthy of people, so your weariness is just. I apologize for changing the subject." He looked to all of them, his expression grim. "But we should discuss what happened beneath the Welker Estate."

A shudder coursed through the room as the torchlight flickered.

"All I know, you died and phoenix dragon came to life," Intoh said. "Killed Rembrandt and mother, thought we were dead too, then you came back, killed Emir, and sent phoenix dragon away."

"Yes," Helai said as she nodded, her gaze searching Cassius for signs of injury. "What happened to you?"

Cassius was silent for a while, his gaze affixed on his glass of wine. "When I died, I spoke to Drausmírtus." He held up a hand as Tantien moved to speak, his brow furrowed in shock. "All I can remember is that they granted me liberation from my death. They brought me back with a purpose in mind, and I think it is to stop Rhavna from resurrecting the dead dragons." He paused, and Rooster's mind was thick with confusion.

"Who is Drausmírtus?" he asked.

"The god of death," Tantien replied. "Or goddess. Whichever you prefer to perceive them as. Drausmírtus does not let go of what's theirs. How did you evade their judgment?"

Cassius shrugged. "I just know I no longer feel the urge for blood even though I still feel the curse of vampirism in my veins. I am no longer a slave to it, merely someone who coexists with it. Drausmírtus told me it is only a matter of time before Rhavna's strength returns to her, and then she is to bathe the world in fire"

"We cannot let that come to pass," Tantien said.

"Must scamper-run to free Igraine. Sigrun too. She will know what to do-do," Rackjack said, sliding his fingers over the grain of the table.

"Why is that?" Cassius asked.

"Sigrun is from Volreya-north. Rhavna is of her people-kin."

Silence thickened the room as implications fell, a heavy weight on the Misfits' shoulders. There was much to ponder and much to prepare for.

If they were going to find a way to break into Fraxinus and free the people of Rooster's past, they needed to seek out Massoud. Delroy also did not give them much sway in their task to seek out something to put a waking dragon back to sleep. Rooster had a feeling the moment they rescued his crew, their sails would take them to Lyvira.

"To Alavae then?" Rooster finally asked. His heart squeezed painfully. In his mind's eye, Igraine stood aboard a ship, her hair billowing in the wind. Her eyes were sad, too sad, and Rooster reached out for her, his hands catching nothing but air as she disappeared.

Don't worry, Igraine. I am coming.

The rest of the party nodded, their faces dancing in the shadows of torchlight.

"To Alavae."

ACKNOWLEDGEMENTS

I owe a lot of thanks to the tabletop campaign that began this story. Misfits was a way for my friends and I to cope with the world shutting down in 2020. I created Cassius, thinking little of the character due to the tendency for tabletop campaigns to fizzle away. I never dreamed how far things would go. I never expected this campaign to jump-start my career as an author. I never thought I'd thank a character of my own creation for teaching me so many things. Cassius taught me how to be brave, and to hold my ground against the threat of danger, even when that danger for me is way different than it is for him. He taught me how to open myself up to love, and he will forever hold a large place in my heart. I've never had a character quite like him; I don't think I ever will again.

I also owe a lot of thanks to my friends for allowing me the honor of writing their characters. Rooster, Linda, Helai, Intoh, Rackjack, Velius, Itale, Sode, Khal—they would not exist without them. They created them so I could have the chance to run with them, build their stories, seek out their dreams, and expose their fears. I couldn't be more grateful that they trusted me with them. I hope I continue to do them justice.

I endlessly owe my deepest gratitude to my partner in crime, Matlin. Without him keeping me grounded, I would have found myself on the verge of tears more often than not. The process of publishing a book, no matter the fact I'd done it before, is not for the faint of heart. He's been there to juggle ideas when I was stuck on a piece of plot I couldn't seem to translate from campaign to story, he was there when I told myself I wasn't a good writer. You have my entire heart, Matlin. ♥

My heart to everyone who has helped pull this book together—my editor, Miranda, my cover artist, Fran, and my interior illustrations company, Etheric. Without them, I wouldn't have the beauty that is this book.

A big shoutout to Zoë and Katie — being my beta readers for this story was so unbelievably helpful. Even when your commentary just merely just a mess of emotions. Your aid and your joy for the early draft of this story fueled the fires that kept the imposter syndrome at bay.

And once again, thank you to the reader. Thank you for getting this far. You're a Misfit now. You'll always have a place at their side. ♥

WHERE TO NEXT?

If you enjoyed *A Waltz Through Flames*, please consider leaving a review wherever you're most comfortable. If you would like to stay updated with Dugdale's publishing journey, consider following them on Instagram and/or TikTok: @jordandugdaleauthor. The Misfits' journey is far from over; I cannot wait to take you along for their next adventure.

https://www.instagram.com/jordandugdaleauthor/
https://www.tiktok.com/@jordandugdaleauthor